LAWRENCE C. CONNOLLY

VOICES

TALES OF HORROR

Fantasist
Enterprises

WILMINGTON, DELAWARE

Designed by
W. H. Horner Editorial & Design
http://whhorner.com

Published by
Fantasist Enterprises
PO Box 9381
Wilmington, DE 19809
www.FantasistEnt.com
www.FEBooks.net

VOICES: *Tales of Horror*
Trade Paperback First Edition:
ISBN 13: 978-1-934571-04-0
December 2011

Trade Paperback Second Edition:
ISBN 13: 978-1-934571-10-1
July 2018

10 9 8 7 6 5 4 3 2 1

ADVANCED PRAISE FOR
VOICES: TALES OF HORROR

"Connolly is a master of the short story. He writes with an economy that hums with the quiet power of a finely-tuned engine. His stories are artfully constructed and memorable for their smart originality."
—**Tom Monteleone,** editor of the *Borderlands* anthology series

". . . eleven previously published short stories and a pair of originals, all in [Connolly's] trademark style of thoughtful horror."
—*Publishers Weekly*

"Lawrence C. Connolly doesn't just get under your skin, he burrows. His style is deceptively unshowy . . . all the better to jolt you."
—**Stephen Volk,** award-winning screenwriter of *The Awakening* and *Ghostwatch*

"'Shrines' hooked me all the way to the last page. I loved it. It must be amongst the best of Connolly's work. The ideas had me guessing and looking into an abyss that seemed infinite."
—**David Slade,** director of *Hard Candy* and *30 Days of Night*

"Lawrence C. Connolly is a master of the dark fantastic, and *Voices* is a treasure trove of sinister wonders, not to be missed!"
—**Tim Waggoner,** author of *Like Death*

"With his latest collection, Lawrence C Connolly proves yet again, if proof were needed, what a fine, intelligent and above all humane writer he is. These stories—turns creepy, moving and often downright terrifying—are about edges and borderlands, the lost and losing. These are stories about voices, and the clearest voice of all is Connolly's own, and it is a delight to hear it."
—**Simon Kurt Unsworth,** World Fantasy Award-nominated author of *Lost Places* and *Quiet Houses*

ALSO BY LAWRENCE C. CONNOLLY

The Veins Cycle
Veins
Vipers
Vortex

Visions: Short Fantasy & SF

From Ash-Tree Press
This Way to Egress

Some of the stories in *Voices* first appeared as follows:

"Mrs. Halfbooger's Basement." *Rod Serling's Twilight Zone Magazine*, June 1982.

"Moon and the Devil." *The Horror Show*. Summer 1987.

"Traumatic Descent." *Borderlands 3*, ed. Thomas F. Monteleone. Borderlands Press, 1993.

"Smuggling the Dead." *Terminal Fright*. Fall 1996.

"Lesions." *Asylum: The Violent Ward*, ed. Victor Heck. DarkTales, 2002.

"Decanting Oblivion." *The Magazine of Fantasy and Science Fiction*, March 2003.

"Things." *Cemetery Dance* 46.

"Flames." *Shades of Darkness*, ed. Barbara Roden and Christopher Roden. Ash-Tree Press, 2008.

"The Death Lantern." *Gaslight Grotesque: Nightmare Tales of Sherlock Holmes*, ed. J. R. Campbell and Charles Prepolec. Edge Science Fiction, 2009.

"Beneath Between." *The Stories (in) Between*, ed. Greg Schauer, Jeanne B. Benzel, and W. H. Horner. Fantasist Enterprises, 2009.

"Die Angle." *Darkness on the Edge: Tales Inspired by the Songs of Bruce Springsteen*, ed. Harrison Howe. PS Publishing, 2010.

An earlier version of "Siren" originally appeared in *Fear the Abyss* under the title "Human Caverns," ed. Eric Bebee. Post-Mortem Press, 2013.

All other material is original to this collection.

This one is for
Charly Cantor
whose voice, stilled too soon,
is with me still.

CONTENTS

It is a wild adventure we are on. Here, as we are rushing along through the darkness, with the cold from the river seeming to rise up and strike us, with all the mysterious voices of the night around us, it all comes home. We seem to be drifting into unknown places and unknown ways. Into a whole world of dark and dreadful things.

Bram Stoker
Dracula

FOREWORD

I am embarrassed at how late I am to arrive at the Lawrence C. Connolly station. I was blisslessly unaware of this fine writer's work in my beloved horror genre until David Slade, who was preparing his segment of an anthology movie we were putting together, brought me the script to "This Way to Egress," which he wrote with one Lawrence C. Connolly. The title page also said that it was based on Connolly's short story, "Traumatic Descent."

The script, quite faithful to the story, is definitely a traumatic descent, chronicling the deterioration of a mind. It is odd, its movements like that of a sidewinder slithering across desert dunes. It is as slippery as the sanity it is tracking, and is as horrific as it could be, without the usual slashers and demons and corporeal things that go bump in the night.

It wasn't until the film was finished that I had the opportunity to dig into Connolly's other work that you find in this very volume. I was delighted to find that his published work goes back to the eighties, to *Twilight Zone* magazine and other publications that I'd devoured way back when, so I probably had been exposed to his creations without even realizing it.

As I spelunked more deeply into the caverns of Larry's mind, I found much to love. His, like mine—and probably like yours, since you're reading this book—runs dark. I like dark. But I particularly like dark when it's set in such a real, relatable world.

Most good horror stories—indeed, most good *stories*—are personal. Larry's stories feel true, lived in, experienced, and therefore very real. There is a sense of dramatic, purging nostalgia to these tales, something very evident in the work of Ray Bradbury and Stephen King, a kind of wistful quality that renders these stories an almost fable-like quality.

It is said that pain doesn't remain in your psyche as long as joy does, that pain memory is fleeting. The same cannot be said for fear. A good horror story—like the ones in this book—wraps you in fear that settles into your bones, and might even last a lifetime. I've always said that fear is good for you, if you let it be; that it is an exorcism without the priest, therapy without the $150-an-hour bill.

Connolly doesn't feel as much like he is exorcising his fears so much as sharing them with us, with a touch of devilish glee. My favorite theme in the movies, television, and books that I've written and/or directed is something I call "Norman Rockwell goes to hell"; in other words, taking the idealized nostalgia of our memories and throwing a fatal, ugly monkey wrench into the works. Much of what you will find in this book illustrates what I mean perfectly.

Voices is the name of the book, but it should really be singular rather than plural. Lawrence C. Connolly's voice as an author is a singular one, and one that will live in your dreams after you lay the book down and settle into a sleep filled with nightmares.

Mick Garris
Los Angeles, California
June 20, 2018

VOICES

It's dark tonight. The only light comes from a lamp that flickers and dims, guttering like flame when the wind blasts the eaves. Manuscripts dating back to the late 1970s lie piled around me, reams of carbon copies, dry-toner Xeroxes, dot-matrix backups, laser printouts—the artifacts of a writing life that began in the days of the typewriter and progressed through the ages of desktop, laptop, and handheld computing. I've been looking through those stories and notes, recalling the events that inspired them, deciding which ones to include in a book that will be equal parts collection and recollection.

Most of the documents are also on my hard drive, but those are the final versions. Tonight I'm interested in the notes and marginalia as much as the stories themselves. Every story has a backstory, a voice or experience that inspired it. Tonight, we're going to listen to some of those.

Can you hear me? Am I coming through OK? It's a long way from where I am to where you will be, somewhere in my future, holding a book that at the moment is still paper-clipped pages and handwritten notes, but I think we're ready to go. Keep reading. Turn the page. Stay awhile. I can't do this without you.

Tonight, I have stories to share.

THE HAUNTED ATTIC: 1961

The sign on the door was just some ragged sheet of loose leaf featuring a crude pencil and crayon drawing of the Wolfman beating the crap out of Dracula. The text read:

Honted Atic

5 cents

My neighbor TC wasn't much for spelling, but he knew a bit about marketing. This was back in the days when I lived in Levittown, on a street lined with identical houses, little prefab boxes for the incubation of baby boomers. It was a safe place to grow up. It was also pretty dull, and on an August afternoon in 1961, TC and his brother Bill decided to exploit our preteen need for adventure. "We've made a haunted attic," TC told us. "It's scary. I mean . . . *real* scary." He drew out *real*, making it sound like a sentence . . . like it was the only thing he needed to say. Then he took our nickels and told us to head upstairs. There was no need to point the way. The attics in those Levittown homes were all in the same place: up the stairs and to the right. I was first in line, stopping when I reached a second sign, this one showing two skeletons duking it out.

TC pushed in front of me and opened the attic door just enough to slip inside, his blond hair bright against the darkness. Then the door swung shut again, leaving the rest of us alone in the hall with a faint odor of socks and sneakers.

I heard movement inside, the squeak of casters rolling on the plywood floor.

My friend Tommy stood behind me. "What's in there?"

"Something on wheels."

"Like lab equipment?"

"No." This came from Freddy, Tommy's brother. "Where would they get lab equipment?"

"Made it, maybe."

"With what?"

The door opened. A skeleton looked out, or at least a piece of one. It was TC in a plastic mask. But his clothes were the same as before: T-shirt, jeans, sneakers. The eyes were his too, icy blue, staring through the holes. "You!" He pointed at me. "First victim. Enter if you dare."

I stepped closer, getting a peek at what lay inside: piled boxes, sagging insulation, TC's older brother Bill crouching beneath a tarp. A chair with little caster wheels waited beneath the sloping beams. I went in. The door closed. Darkness. A flashlight came on, centered on the chair.

"Sit!"

I did, the casters squeaking.

Then the flashlight went out, and that's when it happened . . . when I learned that what TC had planned for me was something other than were-wolves, vampires, and skeletons. It came on fast, ended quickly, and when it was over I had a whole new appreciation for the art of fear.

Hindsight is tricky, imposing meanings that we seldom realized at the time. Lately, I've been telling people that I learned everything I ever needed to know about horror from my old friend TC. It's a recent revelation, and we'll get to it soon (along with what exactly happened after I sat in that chair), but first a piece of fiction. It features a basement instead of an attic, and an old woman instead of a kid with a skeleton mask, but its roots go all the way back to that hot August afternoon in 1961.

MRS. HALFBOOGER'S BASEMENT

It was early summer. It was early night. And Mrs. Halfbooger hadn't been out of the house in nearly a week. The group of twelve-year-old boys had noticed.

Buckeye was thinking seriously about going home when Max Swanson got the window open. Lanny Rosenberg glanced at Max's puffed cheeks, then up at the window, then back at Max. "Can't you get it open any wider?"

Max stopped straining against the window and peered down at Lanny like he was looking at a maggot. "Maybe you can do better, booger face."

"Maybe I can but don't want to."

"Maybe I can come down there and break your nose." Max was standing on an old 7-Up case that Buckeye had found lying by the creek. Buckeye had picked it up, figuring it was valuable, but Max had taken it from him. Max was one of the bad things that had entered Buckeye's life since he'd been thrown out of parochial school. If it hadn't been for Max, Thomas Edison Middle School might have been heaven. Most of the new friends he'd made there were pretty wimpy. Max was one of the exceptions.

"Sure don't look very wide, Max," Willy Haynek said, standing on his toes to get a look at the open window.

Max gave the window frame another push. "I think it's warped, or something."

"Can you get through?" Lanny asked.

"What do I look like? A rail?"

"What about Sean?" Lanny asked. "I bet Sean could get through."

Max smiled. "Hey, yeah." He looked around. "Hey, Buckeye! What're you doing over there, Buckeye?"

That was another thing Buckeye didn't like about Max. He called him

Buckeye like it was something creepy, and it made him feel like a weirdo every time the fat kid said it. He was beginning to wish that he'd never told anyone at Edison that his old friends had called him *Buckeye.*

Not that it mattered. Max went through life looking for things to pick on, and Buckeye, who'd had an accident with a garden rake a few years back, was an easy mark. It was hard not to be obvious with a left eye that looked like a horse chestnut.

"Hey, Buckeye! You dreaming, or what? Get over here."

"What?"

"You're going inside."

Buckeye looked at the house. The light was bad. The sun had gone down. The round summer moon wasn't up yet. And there wasn't much to see: peeling wood, sagging gutters, and the tight gray space between sash and sill where Max had forced the window open. The house was an old thing, with an eastward tilt that made it look like it could fall over any time. Mrs. Halfbooger was that way too—old and leaning, the stoopingist woman in West Fenton.

The four of them had been watching her for nearly three weeks now, sitting across the creek on a tree-covered hill almost as high as the one Mrs. Halfbooger lived on. They would sit in Lanny's tree fort, drink Orange Crush, and fight over Buckeye's telescope.

There wasn't much to see. Her name was Eva Hofburger. Calling her Halfbooger had started as a joke. No one laughed at the joke anymore, but the name lingered out of habit.

She was fifteen years a widow and all her life lonely. Albert Hofburger had "lived away" for the better part of their marriage. They had no children. And all the boys ever got to see from their across-the-creek tree fort were the comings and goings of an old, empty-eyed woman. Sometimes she would return home carrying packages from Kiddy Mart. Other times she would go out an hour or so before dark and not return until after the boys had gone home. . . .

But these were mysteries too mundane for twelve-year-old boys looking to fill an empty summer. They watched her because the tree fort made it handy. They made her a witch because she was old.

They would watch her driving away, spotted hands perched on the steering wheel of her '47 Buick, and they would scare themselves silly with made-up stories about where she was going—about things she was going to do. They filled their stories with monsters and ghouls and werewolves and bloodsuckers. . . .

But they didn't start getting close to the real horror until one day when Mrs. Halfbooger didn't go out. That had been Tuesday.

They didn't see her Wednesday either.

They saw her on Thursday evening. She came out dressed in neat old-lady clothes and stood by the Buick. She looked sick. Lanny had the telescope, but the other three could tell just as well without it. She put her hand on the hood and stared down the hill, out toward the road that led to Kiddy Mart, out at the setting sun and the hazy glow that was Philadelphia. She stood that way a long time. Then she wiped her eyes and went back inside.

She didn't come out Friday.

Saturday it rained. The tree fort didn't have a roof, so they got together at Willy's and told stories about her.

When she didn't come out Sunday, Max said they ought to see if she was dead. But they didn't.

Nor did they go when she didn't come out Monday.

But when it was Tuesday again—when the long boring afternoon began fading to dusk, they decided to have a look. And a look was all it was supposed to have been until Max got the window open.

Buckeye stared at the window and wondered if being part of this was such a good idea.

"I don't think I'll fit, Max."

"Don't be a creep. You haven't even tried."

"What am I supposed to do if I get in there?"

Max jumped down from the 7-Up case. He was fat—probably the fattest kid Buckeye had ever seen. There were a few older kids at Edison who could get away with calling him *Maximum Swanson* or even *Tiny Tuba*. But the only twelve-year old who'd ever tried it had ended up having to eat a green fly before Max would get off of him. The kid had been Buckeye. And the green fly had been worth it.

"When you get in there," Max said, "you open the front door and let us in."

"What if it won't open?" Buckeye said.

"Don't be stupid. It's just locked—that's all. All you have to do is slide inside and unlock it."

"Maybe he doesn't want to," Willy said. He'd been looking at the house and thinking there might be Dangerous Things inside. Dangerous Things to Willy usually meant animals. It didn't matter what kind. If it was larger than a squirrel, it was a Dangerous Thing.

But Max wasn't taking arguments. His arms were already wrapping around Buckeye. "Naw, he wants to go in there. Don't you, Buckeye?" Max heaved him up and set him on the 7-Up case. Buckeye looked down and saw the red-lettered slogan between his summer-torn sneakers: YOU LIKE IT, IT LIKES YOU.

He looked through the open space below the window. "It smells funny in there."

"C'mon, Buckeye. Try it!"

Buckeye stuck his head through the crack. The room smelled sour, like something going bad.

"What do you see?" Willy asked.

Buckeye looked through the dimness. The room was full of old furniture. A table. Chairs. A sofa with its insides starting to come through. The wallpaper was water-stained—in some places it had crumbled away. Flaking paint hung from the ceiling. The floor was bare, and in it, below the window, was a grill-covered hole that went through to what looked to be a basement.

"Looks spooky," Buckeye said.

"Can you get through?" Max asked.

"I don't know. It's awful tight."

"Like fun!"

Buckeye felt the fat boy's hands close on his ankles, lifting him off the pop case.

"Hey!"

Buckeye slid forward until he dangled from the waist. Something slipped from his shirt pocket. It fell, landed on the floor, stood on edge and tee-tered—a one legged dancer going off balance. And then it fell, sideways, right through the grill-covered hole in the floor.

"My key!"

"What'd he say?" Max asked.

"Monkey!" Willy shrieked, thinking of Dangerous Things.

Max climbed up beside Buckeye, looking through the dirty glass. "There ain't no monkey in there."

Buckeye knew there was no way out of it now. He was going inside. The key was his mother's only one to the front door. She'd given it to him ear-lier that day so he could let himself in while she was up the street having tea with Mrs. Gruber. It was a silly thing, always having to lock the door.

His mother was a little like Willy. Everything scared her—especially things she read in the newspaper. Lately she'd been worrying about Buckeye not being home by eight-thirty each night. It had something to do with the Philadelphia Missing Persons Bureau not being able to locate some kids. Usually Buckeye got in the house at a quarter to nine, and usually he got strapped for it. He wished his mom would stop reading the paper.

And he wished he'd remembered to return the key when she'd gotten back from Mrs. Gruber's.

"I said, 'My key!' It fell through the floor."

She was going to kill him this time. She was going to take the television and pitch his comic books. She was going to put a lock on his bike and make him be an altar boy like wimpy Stevie Steedle. She was going to come down on him the same way she had the morning after he and Timmy Baker broke into Mother of Christ School looking for vampires—only this time it was going to be worse. . . .

He didn't realize he was all the way inside the house until he turned around and saw Max staring at him through the dirty window.

"He got through," Max was saying. "You see that? The little creep went right through!"

Buckeye looked around. The room looked creepier from all the way in, and the sour smell was stronger, like BO and rotten milk.

He got on his knees and looked through the grill on the floor—nothing there. Nothing but darkness. He was going to have to look in the basement.

Max banged on the window. "Hey, Buckeye! How about the door?"

He looked up. All three boys were standing on the pop case now—their faces pressed against the dirty glass. Willy was on one side, his uncombed hair sticking out everywhere. He looked scared. Lanny was on the other side, looking more sure of himself. Max was in the middle. Buckeye thought they looked like Moe, Larry, and Curly.

"C'mon, creepo! The door!"

Buckeye stepped out of the room and moved into a wide hall. There was a light switch. He snapped it. A bulb came on in the high ceiling. Weak, forty-watt light oozed down, spreading over the floor. He could see the wallpaper dimly now. It was a flower design, flowers and children dancing in floor-to-ceiling helices—all but scrubbed away from too many washings. The ceiling was the same as the other room's, cracked and peeling. The floor was the same too, bare and wooden.

He came to the front door, wrapped his hands around the knob and tried turning. It wouldn't budge. He tried pulling. Pulling didn't work either. He kicked it and punched it. No good. It was locked on both sides.

Buckeye went back to the window. "Door won't open."

Max looked mad. Lanny and Willy looked ready to leave.

"Heck!" Max said. "Maybe we should smash the window."

"Isn't that against the law?" Willy asked.

Max didn't answer.

Willy backed away. "I'm going home."

"Hey, wait a minute!" Buckeye leaned out the window. "We gotta find my key."

"How're we gonna do that if you won't let us in?" Max said.

Willy backed up another step. "Let's go home, Max."

Max pretended he didn't hear. "What's it like in there, Buckeye?"

"Just an old house."

"Is the witch in there?"

"I don't see her."

"This isn't even fun," Lanny said. He was now standing where, a short time ago, Buckeye had been standing and thinking about going home. "Come on, Sean. Get out of there. Let's go."

"But my key!"

"Is it that important?" Willy asked.

"My mom'll kill me if I tell her it's lost!"

Max scowled. "You guys are a bunch of queers."

"We'll wait," Lanny said. "A few minutes."

"Hurry," Willy said. "I don't like it here."

"I don't like your face," Max said.

Buckeye pulled his shoulders and head back through the window. He looked once more through the glass, then turned back into the hall, wondering why this stuff always happened to him.

This time he moved deeper into the house, passing a dark second-floor stairway. There was a room at the end of the hall. The weak ceiling light spilled into it. He saw a table, some cabinets, and—dimly at first—heard the sound of water running. He thought of turning back, forgetting the key, taking his chances at home. . . .

The water stopped running. Footsteps moved toward the hall. A little face peeked around the door.

For a gut-stabbing moment, Buckeye was sure he was going to pee his pants. Then the initial fear vanished, and, as the aftershocks echoed through him, he realized he was looking at a little girl.

They looked at each other for a long moment. Buckeye expected her to call the old woman. But she didn't. She only stood there, and finally she asked, "Are you new?"

"Huh?"

"What happened to your eye?"

Her hair was dark. She was pretty. "I had a fight with a vulture," he said. It was the usual story he used to impress people. "I had to break its neck."

"Oh." She held a glass of water. She drank some and then poured the rest out, slowly, making a puddle on the floor. There was no one around to stop her. She kept pouring till the glass was empty. "I heard you moving around." She tapped her foot against the puddle. "I thought maybe you were Billy or Paul. But I don't know you."

"I just got here."

"Did you come with her?"

"I came with Max."

"Max Palmer?" she asked.

"Uh-uh. Max Swanson."

"I don't know him either."

"I—I'm really not supposed to be here," he said. "I lost my mom's key. I think it fell into your basement."

She looked confused.

"It was Max's idea," he said. "I wouldn't even be here except he couldn't fit through the window."

She kept staring.

"Can you show me how to get to the basement?"

"You don't know?"

"No."

"Oh my."

Laughter rolled from the stairs.

Four boys came tumbling down, three riding pillows, one on the banister. They got to the bottom and started pelting one another with the pillows.

They stopped when they saw Buckeye.

"What happened to your eye?"

"A vulture," the girl said.

There were more questions, almost identical to the girl's.

One of the boys took out a crayon and started drawing on the wall.

Buckeye watched. The crayon made a big face with a long nose, squinty eyes, glasses—it was the old woman.

"Won't you get in trouble?" Buckeye asked.

The face had big lips and a long tongue. The tongue stuck straight out, catching snot from the running nose. "Trouble?" the artist said. "What's she going to do to us?"

"You ought to go upstairs," another said. "She's still in bed. Dying maybe."

"Is she your grandmother?"

"Naw. She'd just like to be. Silly old bag. Did you really come through the window?"

"Yeah."

"Then for sure you have to go up there. You'll scare the daylights out of her, I bet. Get up real close and look at her with your eye. Can you see through it?"

"No."

"Then just pretend. She hasn't given a good yell all day."

Buckeye looked at the stairs.

"Go on."

There was more laughter upstairs. Girls and boys.

"I've really got to get my key."

"I'll get it for you," the girl said. "You go up."

"She won't be mad?" Buckeye asked. "I mean, I sort of broke in."

The boy with the crayon laughed. "But that's the idea," he said. "The idea is to get her mad. The old creep."

Buckeye looked up the stairs. The boys got behind him and started pushing. And before he knew it, he was starting up.

The stairs were narrow and full of the same smells he'd noticed when first coming into the house. He turned on another light. Drawings covered the stairway walls. He moved past them, reaching the seond floor just as another band of kids burst through a door at the hall's end. They plowed into him, grabbing the banister, making screeching-tire sounds as they turned, starting down. One of the kids looked at him and stopped. "Oh, we got her good this time. Boy, did we ever!"

And then they were gone, tumbling down, spilling into the first floor, laughing, screaming, yelling.

Buckeye looked at the open door down the hall and turned on another light.

There was writing on the wall—large letters in black crayon: HOME OF THE CAVE HOG.

He moved toward it, set his hand on the door, and peeked inside. Mrs. Halfbooger lay in bed, looking old and sick. There was a mound of dirt sitting on top of her, spilling over the bed and onto the floor. They'd gotten her good, all right.

He eased into the room, stepping softly, coming alongside the bed. She looked even older up close, almost like a skeleton. It hardly seemed there was a body under the blankets, under the dirt. She opened her eyes and saw him. "Which one are you?"

He stepped back.

"I didn't bring you here," she said.

"No." He looked at her, frightened at how her faded skin pulled across her chin and cheeks, facial bones nearly sharp enough to break through. He swallowed, finding his voice. "They put dirt on you."

She looked down, wincing. It was as though she were seeing the dark mound for the first time. Her head trembled and fell back again, barely pressing a dent in the pillow. "From the basement. They've made a mess of my basement, you know?" She breathed deep, or tried to. Her face buckled, showing an empty mouth, dark gums. "They spite me. All I want is to love them, and they spite me."

"Are you their aunt, or something?"

"No. I just brought them here. All I wanted . . . all that I. . . . What did you say your name was?"

"Sean."

"That's a nice name . . . nice . . . nice . . . I brought them things, you know? I would buy them things and go driving. I'd bring things home and wrap them up nice . . . and I'd go driving . . . and sometimes I'd see a boy or a girl playing alone, and I'd go talk to them. I know all about being alone, you know? All about it. I'd tell them I had presents and they'd come . . . to the car. And we'd unwrap things and sing and drive away. . . . Nobody ever suspects an old woman. I'd walk away with them . . . I'd drive away with them . . . and nobody ever suspected that . . . that. . . . Did you tell me your name?"

"Sean."

"Yes. That's right. I didn't bring you here, did I?"

"I came through the window."

"I should buy you something too, Sean. When I get better we'll drive down to Kiddy Mart and get you . . . get you . . . whatever . . . anything you want. We'll wrap it up too, so you can open it . . . like Christmas or a birthday. . . . When I'm better. When the headaches stop. Oh my, but I do get the headaches. Like battering rams."

"You don't have to buy me things."

There was a crazy look on her face—a spastic, thin-lipped scowl. "I'd be so nice to them and they get like this. They say they don't want to stay and I have to . . . make them . . . and they get like this. You should see my basement. Oh my . . . I try so hard and they get like this."

"Want me to push off some of this dirt?"

"Dirt?"

"They put dirt on your bed. Remember?"

She looked up again. "Oh, dear me. I thought that was yesterday . . . or. . . . Isn't it something how it's all gotten outside my head like this? Push it off for me? Oh yes."

He leaned over and started shoving heaped clay onto the floor. It thumped on the wooden boards.

"You're different, aren't you?" she said. "I won't have to make you stay."

"Stay?"

"With me. Like a family."

"Never go home?"

"This can be your home."

There was an awful look in her face. Buckeye didn't like it. "I could come visit. It's just that right now I've got to leave and—"

"No!" Her head rose off the pillow. Her yellow eyes turned ugly—like Old Yeller's right before they shot him.

And suddenly he remembered the key and the three friends waiting outside.

"I gotta go."

He turned and ran toward the stairs, stopping once to see if she was following. She wasn't. Her head had fallen back again. Her eyes had closed. But he was scared now. The woman was nuts.

He ran down the stairs, looking for the other kids, looking for the girl who'd promised to find the key. But they weren't in the hall. They weren't in the kitchen, either.

"Hey!" he shouted.

No answer. Only his own echo in the lonely house.

There was an open door by the stove—a door with steps leading down. They'd gone to the basement. He leaned inside the door and fumbled for the light. There was no switch on the wall. He looked around. Above his head a dirty string dangled from a bare bulb. He reached high and pulled it. The light came on. And below him, at the bottom of the stairs, was another string—another bare bulb.

He moved down. "Hey, you guys. You down here? What're you doing in the dark?" He pulled the second string. The second light came on, and at first he thought the basement was empty.

Then he saw them. All in rows. Ten neat little mounds rising out of the basement floor.

And on one of them was the key.

He walked toward it, head spinning. *You should see my basement. I try so hard and they get like this.*

He fell, dropping to grass-stained knees. What kind of crazy woman was she?

His hand shot toward the key, sinking past it, clawing at the soft mound of dirt. *They say they don't want to stay and I have to make them.*

And then he saw.

And then he was up, running, stumbling, falling up the stairs, through the hall. There were no drawings on the wall. No kids in the kitchen.

He tripped and skidded into the dark living room. The moon was up, glowing thinly through the trees, through the window.

The window looked like the other side of the world.

He pulled himself up and ran. Scared. Thinking of the woman. Thinking of her coming down the stairs. Thinking of her grabbing him as he squeezed through the window, holding him with cold dead fingers, pulling him, dragging him to the basement. *Oh, God, please, this is Buckeye calling! Get me out of here and I'll be Pope . . . anything you want . . . just get me out of here!*

He was halfway through, struggling, pulling, praying a blue streak that he wouldn't get stuck. And then he was falling, tumbling. The ground raced up. He hit and rolled, losing his wind, but scrambling up anyway—scrambling to his feet and running down the hill.

The creek was cold. He splashed through the deep part, forgetting the stones.

They hadn't waited. None of them. Not even Max—big-talking Max who wasn't afraid of anything. They had all gone home. Or maybe they had been back there hiding, waiting for him to come through the window so they could jump out at him. Maybe they were still back there, wondering what had happened. . . .

It didn't matter. Nothing mattered. There was only running. There was only getting away from the house.

He ran past Lanny's tree fort and then down the hill to the highway and then across the field to home. His stomach hurt. His chest hurt. His clothes were wet from the creek and there were splinters in his hand from falling in the house.

But he didn't stop. He kept seeing the little face in the shallow grave. The little eyes that hadn't closed. The little nose. The dark hair. She wasn't so pretty after lying in the dirt all that time.

And then he was on the street. He was turning the bend, climbing the walk. Home. The door. He fell against the screen, forgetting the key, pounding, kicking. . . .

The television was on inside. Laughter. A family show. Happy people. Happy endings.

His mother moved toward the door. "You've done it this time, Sean. It's after nine! Don't you know there's crazy people out?"

But he didn't hear. There was only the little girl looking at him from the dirt halo. There was only the sound of his own screams.

MONTE

I've never run from a basement full of graves, but I've run from an attic, all right. And just like Buckeye, when I ran, I ran alone.

My friends Tommy, Freddy, and the others were already gone by the time I broke through into TC's second-floor hall. Good thing for them. Too late for me.

See, as good as they were at building anticipation, TC and Bill really sucked when it came to delivering an artful payoff. They could have assaulted me with fake blood, a few decapitated dolls, maybe even a sound-effects record playing rattling chains and screaming ghosts. But no–they just cut the crap and went for the real thing.

"Sit," TC said, voice muffled through the plastic mask.

So I sat, and just when the show should have started, Bill grabbed the chair, pulled it out from under me, and threw it back against the wall. I hit the floor, and then they were on me, hammering me with pillows . . . or maybe it was just pillowcases with stuff inside, things that TC and Bill thought wouldn't hurt too much, things like clothes and socks. Yeah, socks! I could smell them. That ever-present odor of old socks in TC's house: *Wham! Wham! Wham-Bam-Bam!*

I screamed, and that must have given the other kids in line a pretty good sense of what was going on, that and the banging chair and thudding pillowcases.

Even as it was happening, part of me was amazed at the simplistic approach to making something *real* scary. Who needed monsters when you could induce screams just by pummeling the crap out of someone?

I fought back, kicking and swinging, sometimes connecting, and thinking that at any moment my friends in the hall would open the door and come to my rescue.

Yeah, right!

I'd like to think that my friends outside would have come to my aid if TC hadn't latched the door, but more likely the racket convinced them that the best thing to do was forget the haunted attic and flee into the boring normalcy outside.

I scrambled for the door just as Buckeye would one day scramble for the window of Mrs. Halfbooger's house. I found the improvised latch, pulled it back, and ran for my life—into the hall, down the stairs, back to the safety of my house next door.

Yeah! That's what happened. Honest! Would I make this up? I still remember my dad's reaction when I told him. "You what? Paid a nickel to get beat up?"

So here's the thing, the lesson, the takeaway. Horror is relatively easy to inflict. Evoking it, however, is another matter.

I wrote "Mrs. Halfbooger's Basement" back in the spring of 1980. At first, like Buckeye, I had no idea what I would find inside the old woman's house. Writing the first dozen pages was fun. Like TC with his hand-drawn monsters, *real*-scary promises, and skeleton mask, I enjoyed building the tension, creating expectations, and making a promise that the payoff, when it came, would do justice to the setup. But at some point I had to reveal what was hiding in the old woman's basement, and doing that took time—not in the delivery, but in the staging, drafting, and revision. I must have reworked those last few pages 20 or 30 times during the course of a week: writing, reading aloud, sharing with friends, getting feedback. Doing it right took effort, but that effort paid off.

"Mrs. Halfbooger's Basement" was my second attempt at writing horror. I had sold the first to *Amazing Stories*, one of the lowest-paying markets at the time, but Mrs. Halfbooger went to *Rod Serling's Twilight Zone Magazine*, whose pay rates and circulation were second only to *Omni*. Within a year of its first publication in June 1982, the story was picked up again by Karl Edward Wagner for *Year's Best Horror*. Clearly, my 5-cent tuition to the TC and Bill School of Horror had been a good investment.

Now, let's consider a story I got for free.

My brother used to have an apartment in New York's Chelsea Hotel, the same place where Arthur C. Clarke wrote *2001: A Space Odyssey*, Allan Ginsberg came and went, and Sid Vicious and Nancy Spungen lived and died. The apartment was a one-room cubicle with a closet-sized bath and kitchen. The walls and a portion of the only window had been painted white, and it was there that my brother, a journeyman actor, lived while attending auditions and cattle calls in the city that never sleeps.

I used to stay with him while visiting editors and publishers, and in between those meetings he and I used to wheel around Manhattan on his Yamaha 450. It was on one such day that we happened on a crowded corner, people standing with their backs to the street, transfixed on something beside a graffiti-covered wall.

My brother steered toward it. "You'll want to see this."

We parked the bike and pushed through the crowd until we saw a man standing behind a couple of boxes, one on its narrow end, the other resting atop it to form an improvised table. The flat top was the performance space. On it were three playing cards, each creased longways. Facedown, they resembled the sloped roofs of Levittown houses.

The man behind the table was tall and slim, with sinewy arms ending in the longest fingers I'd ever seen. He spoke as he moved the cards, turning them one at a time, revealing their faces. "Here's a black. Here's another. Watch for red . . . *undercover*!"

He had his voice pitched somewhere between song and chant, spieling with a rap delivery that in 1983 was still a few years from hitting the mainstream.

The effect was mesmerizing.

A woman put some money on the box and pointed to a card.

"Red, red—what my lady said." He flipped the card, revealing the ace of hearts.

The woman had won.

"Pretty face finds an ace." He moved the cards faster, but it was easy to keep track: red in the middle, then on the left, then back in the middle. . . .

A man dropped a five on the table, pointed to the middle card.

But this time the red wasn't where it seemed. The middle card, when flipped, was a ten of clubs.

The money vanished. "Try again. Win instead. Double up! Pick the red." The player's hands moved slowly now.

"The woman's working with him," my brother whispered. "She wins. Everyone loses. Let's go."

But I stayed, transfixed until the man—getting a signal from a lookout— grabbed his cards and bolted, vanishing into the shadows, making off with his winnings just a few seconds ahead of the cops.

He had his cash.

And I had him.

Someday, I was going to put that guy in a story.

MOON AND THE DEVIL

I guess this story more or less starts at Gil Oliver's Doghouse, known as the G.O.D., also known as The Dog. I went to work there shortly after I left Milton, Pennsylvania, which was shortly before I realized that the opportunities for a nineteen-year-old nobody don't necessarily increase with city size. I never knew what I wanted to be. I only knew that I wasn't being it in Milton. So I moved to Pittsburgh. And when my money ran out I went to work grilling devil dogs. It wasn't a bad job, and I might be there today if Gil O. hadn't caught me emptying the cash register.

Then there was the lottery. I hit it for thirteen hundred bucks during my second week of unemployment, and for the first time in my life I had things. I bought a rusty Ford with a good stereo, and for days I just cruised, speeding around with the sound on, going nowhere, watching the road unwind while classic rock raced after me from backseat speakers.

Then I lost everything to a man named Moon and a street-corner game called monte.

That's when the trouble started.

Moon stuffed the last of my money into his pocket. He looked at me and grinned. People were watching. I felt like an idiot.

"Try again?" Moon's hands moved to the three face-down cards sitting on the flat edge of an upended box. He started moving the cards, sliding them around, mixing them with deceptive slowness. "Once more, eh? Win big this time, I bet." There was something funny about his voice. He didn't have an accent, but he didn't sound Pittsburgh, either. And his skin wasn't your usual black. It was deeper, like wet asphalt in a dark alley, like the empty patches of sky when there's nothing up there but stars. "Go for it, kid!

Can't stop now. Luck's gotta change."

I watched him move the cards. There were three of them, like I said. Two were black, spades or clubs—I don't remember. The other was red, a Jack of Diamonds. I remember that. All I had to do was keep my eye on the red one and point to it when he stopped shuffling. Of course, they were facedown. But even then it should have been easy.

But it wasn't.

"There's a trick to this, isn't there?" I said.

"Trick?" Moon kept sliding the card, moving so fast that it almost looked like he had three hands going instead of two. "No trick. Game is all. Easy odds. One out of three."

He was lying. He had to be. But I believed him. It didn't matter that I knew the monte game was a hustle and that Moon was a con man and that if I bet one more dollar I would lose it as certain as I'd already lost all those other dollars. None of that mattered. And if Moon would've taken the fuzz in my pockets, I would've emptied them completely and lost it all. I can't explain it. It's just the way it was. Moon was convincing as hell.

"I'm broke," I said.

There was a moment's silence, an uneasy second or two in which the crowd that had built up around us began shifting and breaking apart—an awkward silence that ended after the last onlooker left and Moon reached into his pocket and pulled out the wad of bills that had once been mine. He snapped a twenty off the top, dragging it with his thumb and cracking it flat between his fingers. Then he handed it to me.

"What's this for?" I asked.

"First commission," he said. "In advance." He stuffed the wad back into his pocket and looked around at the now-quiet corner. He grinned, and for a moment his mouth looked too large for his face. "Never seen anything like that," he said. "A crowd that big. And it was because of you."

He kept talking while he picked up his cards and makeshift table, and he told me his plans while we cut through a trash-lined alley in the blue-gray twilight. He told me that getting a crowd interested was half the game. Then he said that getting them to bet was the other half, and people were sure to bet if they saw a guy like me (who was white) winning off a guy like him (who, like I said, was black). Me winning would make the hustle look honest, and making it look that way was the only dishonest thing we ever did until Moon brought home the Devil.

* * *

I was sitting by the window when Moon walked into the alley that led to our apartment. It was late, but I could see him easily as he passed out of the city lights and into the brick-lined shadows. And I saw the dog, too. It was all wrapped up in Moon's arms with paws dangling and tongue hanging out. I watched him walk down the alley and disappear under the mossy awning that overhung the stairs leading to the second floor. A few minutes later, the apartment door swung open and in walked Moon, still carrying the dog.

"Here!" Moon leaned toward me. "Take him!" And he plopped the dog into my arms and stumbled toward the bathroom down the hall.

The dog looked at me. There was blood on its fur, but it wasn't bleeding. I kicked the door. It banged shut, but the dog didn't flinch. It just sort of hung there, a deadweight in my arms. I turned toward the hall and a trail of blood that led into the bathroom. "Hey, Moon! You all right?"

Water splattered into the bathroom sink, rushing out from banging pipes, giving Moon an excuse not to hear me.

I moved toward the open door.

"Moon!"

"What?"

"Did this dog bite you?"

"Ain't no dog."

Moon had his sleeve rolled to his elbow, and as he raised his wrist and hand from the sink, I saw that something (the dog, from the looks of it) had put a gash in his lower arm. It was a jagged tear, so deep I could see muscles working against the bone. I considered telling him to go to a hospital, but telling Moon to do something was never a good idea. Besides, there were things that I wanted to know.

"What do you mean it's not a dog?"

"Just what I said." He held his hand under the spigot. Blood and water spattered the basin. He winced. "Ain't no dog." His voice tightened. "It's the Devil."

I looked at the dog.

The dog looked up at me, keeping its head level and raising its eyes, the way dogs do when they're not quite sure about you. Then it opened its mouth and ran its tongue across its muzzle, licking Moon's blood from its whiskers.

"Sure looks like a dog," I said.

"That's the idea."

"Looks like a big terrier."

"Pit bull," Moon said.

"What's a pit bull?"

Moon looked up from his wrist and fixed me with a gaze that seemed to say it was a shame I was so ignorant. Then he pulled a dirty towel from the rack and wrapped it around his hand, wrist, and arm. Then he stepped into the hall, heading toward the living room.

I followed, stumbling a little. The dog was getting heavy.

"We're going to be rich, Salty." He always called me Salty. "We're going to be stinking rich."

"How?"

Moon stepped into the kitchen and came back with a quart of wine. Then he sat on the couch and took a drink right from the jug. "Man!" He wiped his mouth on the towel that he had wrapped around his arm, looking at me as he set the jug on the floor. "Better put the Devil down, Salty. I don't think he likes being carried around the apartment."

"Huh?"

"Put him down."

"I thought you wanted me to hold him."

"Did I *say* I wanted you to hold him?"

"Yeah! You said—"

"I said to *take* him. I didn't say anything about *holding* him. Put him down, Salty. No point in him hating us both."

So I did what Moon said. I set the Devil down. I plopped him on his dangling legs, and then I backed away to see what he'd do. But he didn't do anything. He just stood there like I'd nailed his paws to the floor.

"Don't let him worry you." Moon leaned forward. "He'll behave." He pointed at something on the Devil's neck. It was a gold coin, dangling from a short strip of braided leather, swinging and flickering like a tethered flame. "That coin," Moon said. "That's what you call a talisman. And as long as it's around his neck, he's mine. And as long as he's mine, he's got to do what I say. He doesn't have to like it, but he's got to *do* it—no matter what it is."

I moved forward, ready to back away if the Devil decided to get frisky. But he didn't. He was as quiet on his feet as he'd been in my arms. I touched the coin, lifting it slightly, moving it out of the glare of the lamp. The Devil didn't move. He only watched, staring at me while I studied the coin and the bossed image of a horned animal with chained hooves. A silver rivet driven through one of those hooves held the coin to the collar. There were letters on the flipside, but they didn't spell any words I knew. I let the talisman drop back against the Devil's neck and turned to Moon. "How come the Devil looks like a dog?"

Moon shrugged. "He's got to look like something."

"But why a dog?"

"Because it's not obvious. Think about it. When the Devil comes to Earth, the last thing he wants to do is be obvious. He looks like a dog so people like you won't recognize him."

"And how do people like *you* recognize him?"

Moon just grinned, letting me know that recognizing the Devil was like moving monte cards. I didn't have to understand to be in on it.

I backed away from the Devil, weighing the things I knew against the things I didn't. Something troubled me. I looked at Moon and asked: "What happens if that collar comes off?"

"Depends," Moon said.

"On?"

"On how mad he is when it comes off."

That wasn't what I wanted to hear, and I guess it showed because Moon reached forward and patted my shoulder. "Don't worry about it," he said. "Look at me. I'm not worried. And if that talisman comes off, I'll be in the fryer a lot deeper than you."

That wasn't much consolation, and Moon knew it. So he changed the subject. He sat back and started telling me about pit bulls and dog fights and a whole subculture that I had never known existed.

And I listened.

I always listened when Moon talked. And I always believed what he said. And I spent that night listening and believing that the Devil was going to make us rich.

And he did make us rich—for a while.

Moon spent the next few days talking to people, and by that Friday we had the Devil scheduled in a fight somewhere in the city's East End. Moon wasn't exactly sure where that somewhere was. He had directions, but all they did was get us lost, driving in circles through brick-walled alleys with the Devil sitting bone still in the backseat. I was beginning to think that the fights would be over before we found them when Moon suddenly stopped the car.

"What're you doing?" I looked around at sooty warehouse walls, overflowing dumpsters, and oily puddles that stretched away toward a dim intersection. "Where are we, Moon?"

He motioned for me to be quiet, and then he shut off the engine and leaned out the window. "Hear that?" he said.

I didn't hear anything.

He slid back into his seat and started the car. "It's that way." He pointed left. Then he hit the gas, steering through the intersection and into an alley that I could have sworn we'd been down before. But I guess I was wrong because this time it led us straight into the damnedest thing I'd ever seen.

The alley opened into a wide lot, and in the middle of that lot was a circle of cars. The cars were running, and centered in their headlights were two fighting dogs. The air reeked of car exhaust and blood—a sharp smell, like pennies when you rub them together. I never got used to that stink. The Devil fought twelve times. And he won twelve times. And each time that copper stink hit me like I was breathing it for the first time. But that smell wasn't the worst of it. The worst had to be the way the Devil always worked over the losing dogs after they were dead . . . and the way he licked his chops as Moon dragged him to the sidelines . . . and the way he looked at us when we loaded him back into the car. Sometimes his eyes caught the dome light before we shut the door, and when they did it was almost like they had fires burning deep inside. *I got time*, the eyes said. *You don't, but I do. I got all the time there is.*

This story ends with good news and bad news, and the good news is that I didn't have to watch the Devil fight more than twelve times. But let me tell you the bad news. Let me tell you about the Devil's last fight.

The night was hot, the dogs were irritable, and the collar on the Devil's neck was coming loose. You can't tie something with leather and expect it to stay, especially not if you're going to have dogs sinking their teeth into it three or four times a week. I saw it was coming loose as I led the Devil toward the ring of rumbling cars.

I ran my fingers over the weak spot, a place where some of the braids had been bitten clean through. The Devil just sat there, not panting or barking like the other dogs. His ears cocked back as I talked to Moon. "I need to fix this," I said.

"You got the spare leather?"

"No."

Moon didn't say anything.

"Maybe we should leave," I said.

"Yeah, right," Moon said, his voice making it clear that he had already bet everything on the Devil.

I tried thinking of a plan, but already the referee was standing in the headlights, swinging his police whistle on the end of a chain, glaring at me over the end of a glowing cigar.

I heard Moon shifting behind me, boots scraping the pavement as he backed away. "You'd better get the Devil out there," he said. "These guys would love to call a forfeit on us."

A quick glance at the ref convinced me that Moon was right.

"Go on, Salty. Do it!"

The other dog was already out there, standing with his tail toward the center of the ring. That's the way the fights always started, with the owners backing their animals into the ring and keeping them from turning until the ref blew his whistle.

I backed the Devil into the lights, trying to look cool while everyone looked down at me from the hoods and bumpers of those parked cars.

I closed my eyes and waited for the whistle. When it came, I released the collar and prayed.

The Devil spun and raced into the ring. The dog did the same. Then they ran, straight toward one another, high-beam headlights dancing on their fur like moonlight on black water. And for a moment there was no sound but the clackety-clackety-clackety scratch of claws on pavement. And then the animals collided.

Whooompf!

You could hear the air go out of them as they slammed together. Then came the deep gearing-down growl of the fight. The dog opened its jaws, teeth flashing toward the Devil's neck. But the Devil was faster, clamping the dog behind the ears, biting deep, and slamming it to the pavement.

I wanted to look away. I hated to see the Devil work over a downed dog, but I had to watch. I wanted to know the moment it was over. The dying dog struggled, pushing with its paws, clawing the Devil's neck, snagging the collar. . . .

Then it was over.

A tremor went through the Devil's jaws as it closed its bite. I heard the snap of neck bones. Then the Devil backed away. And then he stood up, rearing back, hind legs straightening, feet splaying out against the ground.

And beside one of those feet, looking like a braided worm against the pavement, lay the broken collar with its facedown talisman.

I saw all these things with a strange calm that told me it was too late to change anything, but that didn't stop Moon from running into the lights, slipping on blood, scrambling to pick up the talisman so he could wrap it back around the Devil's neck.

But it was already too late.

The headlights were gone.

And the Devil was finished being a dog.

Welcome to hell.

I don't know what the Devil's got planned for you, but I wouldn't worry too much about it. You'll get by as long as you don't get noticed. That's where I went wrong. I got noticed. I got noticed real good.

I don't mind being turned into a dog. What I hate are the fights. There'll probably be one soon, so you'll get to see firsthand what I've been talking about. You shouldn't have any trouble recognizing me. I'll be the dog that wins. I win every time. I win so much it makes me sick.

Don't say it. I know what you're thinking. You're thinking that winning's got to be better than losing, and I guess it is. But wait until you see how I rip open those other dogs. I can't stand that. I can't control myself when I'm doing it, but wait until you see the mess. You'll understand.

And there's something else, too. There's something about those dogs that I keep ripping apart. Something that bothers me. I've been doing a lot of thinking lately, and I'm beginning to understand.

I think I've been killing the same dog over and over.

And I think I know that dog.

I think it's Moon.

MUSIC, DREAMS, AND TRAUMA

From the outset of "Moon and the Devil," the reader knows that the narrator is telling the story in the first person, but only in the dénouement does it become clear that the reader/listener is also a presence in the story, taking part in a welcome-to-hell orientation. Thus, Salty is a kind of scop—a storyteller.

I have long been interested in oral storytelling, and recently I've been exploring the form in a project called The 21ˢᵗ Century Scop—a series of story presentations designed to be more than book readings. You see, those early scops never came to town carrying books. The books were in their heads, the stories recited from memory. No books needed. But in many cases, what each did carry was an instrument to provide musical accompaniment to the performance. Those early storytellers knew that delivering a story was more than just reciting words, and I think a rediscovery of that tradition is long overdue.

I got my first sense of the power that music can lend to a live reading way back in the spring of 1968, when my high school English teacher talked me into attending a performance by Lawrence Ferlinghetti.

For an hour the performance was just the poet and his voice, but then, for his final piece, he produced a tape player, a clunky thing with a row of big black buttons and a single six-inch speaker. He adjusted the podium microphone so that it hung midway between his face and the machine, and then—in the tradition of the Anglo-Saxon scop—he read "Moscow in the Wilderness, Segovia in the Snow" while guitar music played from the tiny speaker.

In the years that followed, I heard others attempting their own fusions of music and spoken words, most notably Patti Smith, who gave readings accompanied by guitarist Lenny Kaye in New York in the early '70s; and four-time Bram Stoker Award winner Michael A. Arnzen, who in 2007 released *AudioVile*, a CD featuring some of his stories read to original music. But live meldings of music and spoken words are hardly the norm, even though modern technology makes it easier than ever to bring quality sound to a reading. Indeed, full multi-media accompaniment—laptop, PA, projector, and screen—can fit easily into the trunk of a Cobalt.

Part of my interest in 21st-century scopping is academic. I'm the product of a fairly traditional graduate program that focused on Anglo-Saxon, Medieval, and Renaissance literature (literature written primarily for the ear), and I've been playing, composing, and performing music most of my life.

In 2008, as Fantasist Enterprises was preparing the release of my novel *Veins*, I began working on a studio CD of music inspired by the book. Part of the impetus for the project was a concept album that the singer-songwriter Poe had produced as a companion piece to Mark Z. Danielewski's novel *House of Leaves*. But also in the back of my mind was that 1968 performance by Lawrence Ferlinghetti. If all went well, I figured the new music might provide accompaniment for live readings.

The resulting CD, *Veins: The Soundtrack*, was released in 2009, and that summer I took the CD and book on the road, giving multimedia readings in six states, sometimes to intimate gatherings in bookstores and libraries, other times in the auditoriums of schools and convention centers. At each event, I was able to gain the attention of potential readers much more effectively than I could have by sitting at a table in the corner of a superstore.

"Moon and the Devil" was accepted right out of the gate by *FTL Magazine*, a proposed large-circulation publication underwritten by New York's West End Games—the company that would go on to produce RPGs based on such high-profile properties as *Star Wars*, *Indiana Jones*, and *Men in Black*. But only a few months after purchasing "Moon," the magazine lost its publication deal, and the story was mine to sell again.

FTL's pay rates had been similar to those of *Twilight Zone*, and I figured I might double my money by sending the story to Ted Klein. But Ted, who described himself as a "fanatical animal lover," had been actively speaking out about dogfighting in *Esquire* and numerous letters to Congressmen, and although he acknowledged that the story didn't condone mistreatment of animals, he nonetheless felt he had to give "Moon" a pass. We talked about this and other things over a long lunch at Costello's Restaurant in New York City where James Thurber had covered the walls with doodles and drawings. A cartoon dog seemed to be looking over Ted's shoulder, staring at me through the entire meal. I didn't bother putting up an argument in the story's defense. I figured I was outnumbered.

The story went instead to David B. Silva's *The Horror Show*, appearing in the Spring 1987 issue.

"Moon and the Devil" and "Mrs. Halfbooger's Basement" are fairly conventional horror stories. Tropes such as devils and haunted houses are a lot of fun to write about, but it seems to me that each also provided a sense of familiarity that might actually work against a horror story.

All right, the reader says. *I know what this is. It's a ghost . . . a zombie . . . a vampire. I know the rules.*

And what's the point in that? Where's the strangeness in convention?

Over the years, writers attempting to create something new have looked to their dreams for inspiration. Mary Shelley's *Frankenstein*, Samuel Taylor Coleridge's *Rime of the Ancient Mariner*, and Horace Walpole's *Castle of Otranto* all originated as dreams, and although you might take issue with the merits of Walpole's book, it nevertheless launched a literary genre.

The next story, "Traumatic Descent," began as a nightmare. There was no plot to the dream. No sequence of events. There was simply a place, gray and oddly out of plumb—like something from an old German expressionist film: *The Cabinet of Dr. Caligari, Der Golem, Nosferatu*. The place had a single window, a pane of translucent glass as gray as everything else in the room. Now in this dream, which lasted only a moment, I watched a woman move through the gray room and toward that window. I watched her set a hand on the glass, pushing it back to reveal another, smaller space. This second space had a desk, a filing cabinet, and a piece of shadow that seemed to belong to a person standing around a blind corner. Except that the little office had no blind corners. The entire room was in view through that open window.

But it isn't, I thought, still dreaming. *There are things she isn't seeing. But she'll see them soon. She'll see them because the room is changing. In a minute it will not even be a room. In an hour it will be the most frightening place imaginable. When that happens, she will see the shadow's source . . . and the source will drive her mad.*

I was frightened now.

I backed away from her, turned, and looked for an exit. I didn't see one, but I knew there was a way out. It was there for me if not for her. It was the gate of dreams. If I wanted out, all I had to do was wake up. But once I did that, the gate of dreams would cease to exist, and the woman would be trapped forever.

I woke terrified. But it was a good terror. Lying there, staring at the darkened ceiling, I knew I was on to something.

"Traumatic Descent" appeared in *Borderlands 3*, where it caught the attention of David Slade, who at the time was making some jaw-dropping music videos for MTV. One of them, Stone Temple Pilot's *Sour Girl*, is a four-minute nightmare in which plush bunnies become leering homunculi.

In the summer of 2000, David shared a copy of *Borderlands 3* with his longtime friend Charly Cantor, who had just finished his second film, an edgy riff on vampirism titled *Blood*.

The two decided that "Traumatic Descent" would make a good film project, and Charly contacted me to inquire about a film option. We struck a deal, Charly came to the States to begin collaborating on the script, then invited me to London to meet David and the producers. Before long, Charly had a script titled *This Way to Egress*, and David was relocating to Hollywood to make the film with American backing. For a while, the project seemed to be on track, but then Charly passed away in 2002. Things lost momentum after that. Charly's script has yet to be filmed.

Two years ago, when Ash-Tree Press expressed interest in bringing out a limited edition of my stories, I asked David if he would mind if I used the *Egress* title for the book. I was looking for a way to bring my collaboration with Charly to closure, and putting that title out in the world in a beautiful limited edition seemed like a good way to do it. And so, eight years after Charly's death, I found myself back in England, this time attending World Horror in Brighton and taking part in Ash-Tree's launch of the book titled *This Way to Egress*.

The story appears here under its original title.

TRAUMATIC DESCENT

At last the receptionist returned.

"Excuse me," Helen said.

The receptionist began clearing her desk.

Helen crossed the room. "Excuse me!"

The receptionist was one of those big women with brutally masculine features. She turned slowly and stared through the rectangle of sliding glass that separated the reception office from the waiting room.

Helen stared back, trying not to flinch at the woman's sloping forehead and receding jaw. "My appointment was for 3:00," she said.

The receptionist forced a wrinkled smile. "Sorry. Dr. Salvador's running late."

Helen wanted to protest, but instead she returned to the couch.

Eric looked up from a coverless comic book. "What'd she say, Mom?"

"A few more minutes."

"Yeah sure! She told you that an hour ago."

"Yeah," Chris said. "An *hour* ago!"

Helen reclaimed her place between them. It was nearly 5:00.

"I'm *starving!*" Chris said.

"Just a few more minutes." She looked across the waiting room, toward the reception office behind the sliding-glass, and tried believing that the woman had gone to tell Salvador that he had one more patient waiting. She hoped to hear the far-off rumble of Salvador's voice. ("Yes. Send her in.") But all she heard was a muffled click, and with it one of the lights in the reception office winked out.

"Looks like they forgot about you," Eric said.

"Don't be silly, honey. I just talked to the woman. She said a few more minutes."

"Yeah sure!"

Helen looked at the boy. In a way, his childish belligerence reassured her. It was familiar behavior, and familiar things were so much easier to deal with. "You shouldn't talk back, Eric."

"All I said was 'Yeah sure!'"

"You shouldn't say it. It's disrespectful."

"Yeah sure!"

A shadow moved beyond the sliding glass. Helen got up and returned to the window, this time pushing it back. She leaned inside.

The receptionist, now squatting by a file cabinet, turned and looked at her.

"I hate to be a pest. But my children—"

"Try being patient!" The receptionist turned and opened the bottom drawer of the file cabinet. She reached inside and pulled out a pair of large sneakers. Then she removed her dress shoes and placed them in the drawer where the sneakers had been. She had incredibly large feet: flat as skillets and nearly as broad; she raised the left one, turned its leathery sole to the window, and pulled on one of the running shoes.

Helen cleared her throat.

The receptionist turned from a half-tied shoelace. "What is it now?"

"I was just thinking that maybe . . . if this is a busy time—"

"It's not. You're the only one here." She grabbed the lace of her second shoe, yanking it taut. "Besides, the appointment book's already closed. I can't cross you off now." She knotted the lace, stood up, and took her coat from a hook in the corner. Her arms hissed into the sleeves as she turned her back to Helen. "We did you a favor by squeezing you in. You did say it was an emergency, didn't you?"

"Yes."

"Then why would you cancel the appointment?"

"Sorry." Helen turned away, crossed the room, and sat down.

"Mom," Chris said. "I gotta take a shit!"

"Don't use that word."

"I gotta poop."

"I'll take him," Eric said.

"No! No one goes anywhere without me."

"Not even to the men's room?"

"Not even." The waiting room had seemed almost normal two hours ago, but now things were changing again: chairs clenching in on themselves, end tables hunching low, and the magazines. . . .

(A voice in her head said: "Look at the magazines!")

She trembled as she looked into the grinning face on a nearby cover of *GQ*. She pressed her hands between her knees, steadying herself. "I don't want you kids leaving me alone in this office."

"Why?" Eric said.

"I don't like the looks of it."

Eric looked around. "Yeah sure!"

She was beginning to accept that Eric and Chris didn't see what was happening to the world.

("But you see it, don't you, Helen?")

Yes, she saw it, and where did that leave her?

("In a psychiatrist's office, right where you belong.")

"But I'm not crazy," she whispered.

("No? Then why don't your kids see it? Why don't they see what's happening to the faces on the magazines?")

Helen glanced again at the coffee table. Preppy men in polo sweaters, faces buckling, growing uglier before her eyes. She clenched her fists, knowing that soon the world would be as terrible as it had been yesterday morning, as hideous as when she opened her eyes after a night of fitful sleep to find herself tangled in foul-smelling sheets in a strangely empty bedroom. She had tried running then—running from the stinking bed, from the hollow room, from the cavernous house—and she might still be running if the children hadn't caught up with her, brought her back home, and dressed her in ill-fitting clothes from the musty closets. It was strange to think how helpful the children had been.

She squeezed Chris's hand.

Across the room, a door clicked open. The receptionist leaned into the waiting room. "The doctor will see you now."

Helen turned to Eric, touched his face, his well-formed jaw.

"Cut it out, Ma!" He pulled away.

Helen stood. Her purse lay on the floor. She picked it up and felt the weight of her deadly *ticket out* shifting against the loose change and wadded tissues that lined its bottom. Funny, she'd almost forgotten the thing was in there.

"Please hurry," the receptionist said.

The purse weighed against her shoulder as she crossed the room and entered a short hall.

The receptionist pointed toward a door. "He's waiting."

Helen walked down the hall and entered the office.

The doctor sat writing at a desk, his back to a door of translucent glass. Beyond the door, shadows moved through a dim hall. Helen supposed they were the shapes of office workers—healthy, normal-looking people rushing to catch elevators and busses. She tried not noticing how hunched the shadows were, or how their shoulders rolled with the weight of elephantine arms.

"Sit down," Salvador said.

Helen moved to a chair. It looked comfortable, but the moment she touched the cushions she knew the dimensions were wrong. She tried settling in; the chair wouldn't yield.

Salvador looked up from his pen.

Helen held his gaze, relieved by the sight of his well-defined chin, strong brow, slender nose.

"When you called," he said, "you mentioned something about being afraid."

"Yes."

"Why are you afraid?"

"Things keep changing."

"Changing how?"

"Getting different."

"Different how?"

She bit her lips, looked away.

"When did you first notice these changes?"

"Yesterday morning. Things were bad yesterday morning. Then they got better. Now they're getting worse again."

Salvador picked up his pen and wrote something. When the pen stopped moving, he asked: "Have you mentioned this to your husband?"

"I . . . don't have a husband."

Salvador wrote.

"I mean," Helen said, "I *had* a husband, but he left two days ago and—" She looked at the floor. "My husband has nothing to do with the problem."

Salvador leaned forward. He removed his glasses, folding them neatly. He waited for her to look at him. Then he said: "Do the people around you seem to be changing?"

She swallowed.

"Answer my question. Are the people around you turning ugly?"

"Yes."

"You hesitate. Aren't you sure?"

"No. I'm sure. But how do you know? Do you see it too?"

"Tell me about your children. Have you noticed similar deformities in them?"

"Oh no! Not my children! They look as normal as I do. As normal as . . . as normal as you. They brought me here, you know?"

"How old are they?"

"Six and ten."

"And they brought you here?"

"Yes. There've been moments during the past two days when they've seemed very mature."

"Mature?"

"Yes. This morning, after I found—" She glanced at her purse.

"Go on."

"It was Eric who found your number in the book. He made me call."

"And this sudden maturity is the only change you've noticed in them?"

"Yes. But it doesn't last. Usually they act like kids."

He picked up his pen, wrote something, then looked at her. "What about everyone else—people other than you, me, your children? Is everyone else strangely deformed?"

"Yes."

"Has this changing accelerated since 4:00?"

"Yes."

Salvador wrote, pen whispering against the paper. Then he looked up again, not at her this time, but *into* her, peering deep. "Do you consider yourself suicidal?"

The intercom buzzed.

Salvador turned. "What is it?"

"Your colleagues are waiting."

"Thank you." To Helen, he said: "I have a meeting with some field workers, but I want to see you again tomorrow."

"Tomorrow?"

"We open at 9:00, but I want you back here at 8:30."

"But—"

"Tomorrow." He stood, compelling her to do the same. "Eight-thirty."

"But there's something else you should know."

He led her to the door.

"You asked if I considered myself—"

"We can discuss that tomorrow."

"Why won't you help me *now*?"

He pushed her into the hall.

"Tell me," she said. "If I'm crazy, just tell me. It would make things so much easier if someone would just—"

The door snicked shut.

Misshapen chairs crouched in the darkened waiting room. Only the hum of ductwork broke the silence.

"Eric?"

No answer.

"Eric! Chris, honey!" She found a switch, turned on the lights.

The children were gone.

Outside, in the main hallway, a bell rang.

She ran for the door.

"Eric!"

She hurried into the hall. Fifty feet away, a coat-draped figure moved toward an elevator. Helen recognized the coat.

"Hey! Wait a minute, please!"

The thing stepped into the elevator, door closing behind it.

"Wait! *Please!*"

A glove reached out, caught the door, pushed it back. The receptionist, even uglier than before, leaned into the hall.

"Going down?" Its sloping forehead ended in a matted brow. Its chin was gone. Its face came to an impossible point. It spoke with a heavy grunt that distorted the words nearly beyond recognition. *G'an dahn?*

"Where are my children?"

"What children?" *Watt chill'n?*

"My children!"

"Sorry, honey. I didn't see any children." *Soree,'onny. A'dn't s' any chill'n.* The receptionist pulled its glove from the rubber bumper.

"Wait!"

The door closed. The car descended. Elevator cables clicked and hissed, and, like all powerful things in the world, the sound was disturbingly masculine. And it spoke to her. "Purse . . . purse . . . purse!" The sound low and deep—like Eric's voice. *Big* Eric. Eric, Sr. She shook her head, trying to dislodge it. And then, from farther down the hall, she heard the whoosh of a flushing commode.

* * *

She ran toward the men's room.

"Chris!"

Another flush, then another.

"Eric!"

She rounded a bend. The men's room door came into view. The kids were in there, both of them, being bad, flushing the toilets one after another.

Ka-WOOOSH!

Ka-WOOOSH!

Ka-WOOOSH!

"Eric! Chris! Stop that!"

She opened the door and stepped into the stink of urine and disinfectant. The flushing continued from beyond a row of gray stalls. She stepped closer. A shadow appeared, short and bloated, sliding like a flattened toad across the wall. Then, in a mirror, she saw its face: no teeth, cheeks, or chin. Its nose rose out of its upper lip. Its eyes, like blisters, stared from either side of its flattened forehead. A tuft of green hair grew on a hump in its brow.

"Looking for someone?" *Oookin'er umm-un?*

"My children."

"Children?" *Chill'n?*

She grew bolder, walking forward until she stood a few feet from the toady man. "I'm looking for my children!"

It shook its head.

For the first time she noticed its clothes: bib overalls with an oval name tag. The thing was a janitor. Its name was Ron.

"Were they in here?" she asked.

Ron scratched thoughtfully at his crotch. Then he shook his head and turned away.

"Will you help me find them?"

Ron pulled a rag from his pocket.

"I'm asking you a question!"

No answer.

"Why are you ignoring me?"

Ka-WOOOSH!

Helen shifted her purse to her right shoulder, and once again she felt the awful weight of her *ticket out.*

("Use it!")

Helen reached inside the purse and pulled out the gun.

* * *

Like the receding jaws and sloping foreheads, the gun was not part of her normal reality. This morning she had discovered it lying on the bed beside her. Beneath it she had found a note telling her how to release the safety and cock the chamber. The note had referred to the gun as her *ticket out*, and it assured her that it was loaded with a single, hollow-point bullet—the kind that would enter small and exit large. All she had to do was put the gun in her mouth and pull the trigger; after that, the madness couldn't touch her.

("Ticket out!")

Helen released the safety. She racked the slide and chambered the round. Then she raised the gun, aiming at the back of Ron-the-janitor's head.

The man-thing turned, saw the gun, waved her away with the dripping rag: "Get out of here!" *G'outa ear!*

Helen fingered the trigger.

The thing turned, giving Helen its humped back as it went back to scooping crud.

"Hey!" Helen yelled. "Look at me!"

Ka-WOOOSH!

"Damn you! I've got a gun! LOOK AT ME!"

The thing moved to another urinal.

("It doesn't care about you.")

The gun grew heavy. Her hand trembled. Her arm dropped to her side. The weight of her own insignificance sent her running from the room.

The hall had changed: walls closer together, ceiling suspended low above an ashen floor. The elevator was gone. In its place stood a steel door and a sign reading:

THIS WAY TO EGRESS

Helen slumped against the wall. "When's it going to stop?"

("When you use the ticket," said the man in her head.)

"I need it to start making sense! Please, God—make it make sense!"

("Kill yourself!")

She slammed her head against the wall. Pain flashed behind her eyes . . . .

And then, from down the hall—muffled through the translucent glass of an office door—a voice said: "Yeah sure!"

She held her breath, cocked her head, listened.

Another voice spoke, younger—Chris's voice! She tried making out words, but all she heard was: "Psychosis."

It was happening again, her six-year-old talking like an adult.

("And he's talking about *you*!")

Helen shook her head, trying to dislodge the inner voice. Her brain shifted, thudding inside her skull. She shook harder. Light flashed behind her eyes. The inner voice gave way to thudding pain.

Another voice spoke, deeper, more forceful. "Do you think she'll do it?" It was Dr. Salvador.

She moved closer.

"Yes," Eric said. "We haven't left her much choice."

"I think so too," Chris said. "I only wish we'd given her poison instead of a gun."

"She won't take poison. She needs to do something aggressive."

"How many bullets are in the gun?" Salvador asked.

"One," Eric said. "That's all she'll need. Provided she doesn't miss."

"And provided she uses it on herself."

She stood beside the door, holding her breath, listening, waiting. Please, she thought, *please* let me hear them say what's wrong with me.

"In a way," Chris said, "I feel sorry for her. It's not her fault she descended."

"It's no one's fault," Salvador said. "Descent from the higher realities is neither fair nor unfair. It's a fact. It happens. It's up to us to deal with it, not to pass judgment on it."

"Do you think it was her husband deserting her that caused it?"

"That's possible. Have you read Dr. Pico's study on Traumatic Descent?"

"No."

"Do so. If you're going to make field work a career, you'd be wise to keep up on the literature."

A moment's silence, and then Chris said: "I just keep thinking that it'd be so much better if we could elevate her back to her own reality."

"Yeah sure! How're we going to do that when we don't even know *which* higher reality she came from?"

"We might be able to figure it out," Chris said. "We know she had a family. We know she had two boys, Eric and Chris. We know she loved them."

"We don't *know* that."

"We can infer it. Haven't you seen how she looks at us? It's not the way she looks at other things. When she looks at us, she's seeing the children she left behind."

"She told me about that when we talked," Salvador said. "She also told me that *I* looked normal. I also believe that she only heard half of what I said to her. She's having auditory as well as visual hallucinations."

She slammed her head against the wall. Sparks erupted behind her eyes, but somehow she remained standing, holding her ground while Chris asked: "Are we sure suicide's the only solution?"

"It's the only *practical* one," Salvador said. "There's a slight chance—a *theoretical* chance—that she could return to her own world, but that would require a resilience she doesn't have."

"So we have to kill her?"

"No. She has to kill herself. We're physicians, not murderers."

Another awkward silence, and then Chris said: "Where is she now?"

"Outside," Salvador said. "In the hall. Listening."

"You're kidding."

"Open the door. See for yourself."

Helen froze.

Inside the office, heavy feet shuffled against the floor. She wanted to run, but she could only brace herself against the wall while Salvador said: "I'm sure I heard her moving out there." His voice changed as he spoke. *I'm sure I'erd'r mooen'a'der.*

Helen raised the gun, holding it high while she reached for the door. Was it locked? She turned the knob. The latch clicked. The door opened into a distorted room, furniture crouching beneath a low ceiling, three bug-eyed toads staring right at her.

She raised the gun. When she squinted, two of the toads looked almost like Eric and Chris. The third had to be Salvador. She aimed and fired.

BLAMMMM!

Flame shot from the barrel. Her hand jerked. A third nostril opened in Salvador's nose. His skull exploded. Sludge slammed the wall. The body struck the floor.

"Oh shit!"

She spun around. "Who said that?"

Chris looked away.

"Chris!"

Chris glanced at the smoking gun.

"I warned you, Chris. I warned you about that kind of talk."

Chris looked at Eric. He seemed to say: *What now?*

She crossed the room, took Chris's hand. It felt warm and soft in her closing fist. "Come on."

"Where're we going?"

"Home!"

She pulled Chris toward the door.

Eric followed.

They descended the stairs to a filthy street of sooty buildings. Toad-like men paused and shied away from the gun in her hand. A bloody sun lay low upon the city's domes. Ashen moons rose in the west.

("You're totally mad. It's all insanity. The only thing real is your madness.")

When she squinted, the rusty, iron sidewalk looked almost like the road to home.

ILLEGAL ART

In the winter of 1990, seventeen months before the fall of the Iron Curtain, I traveled to Russia to take part in an arts exchange with a school in Leningrad, and I remember thinking—as the Aeroflat jet made its steep descent toward Pulkovo Airport—that I was out of my mind.

By touchdown, I'd been awake for the better part of a day, having left Pittsburgh in the afternoon on March 19 and then flying through the night to land in Helsinki early the following morning. The stopover was nine hours, plenty of time for a whirlwind tour, but no time for sleeping.

There is a point beyond exhaustion when a new kind of consciousness kicks in, a surreal state that is part reflex, part waking dream. You can imagine what such a frame of mind did to my first impressions of Soviet Russia.

I remember my hosts taking me to a dinner at a restaurant specializing in suckling pig, little oinkers on silver trays, cranberry eyes seeming to stare at me while I stared at them.

Someone asked me to carve, which conjured memories of my days as an undergrad, failing my bio-lab dissections of pickled frogs and fetal pigs. I tried refusing the knife, hoping she would understand. I had learned some Russian in preparation for the trip, but things like *Hello. I'm from America. This is a beautiful city. Where is the toilet?* weren't going to get me out of this one. In English, I said: "I really think you should do the honors."

"*Da!*" She nodded, gesturing first to the knife in my hand, then to the pig. "*Da! Da! Da!*"

What could I do? I carved, I ate, I asked for the toilet, and as the night wound down I noticed two things standing out among the blur.

One was a man picking through the carvings, collecting bones in a napkin. My host explained that he was taking the bones to make soup and art—in that order. I nodded, thinking that maybe I'd understood. I'd heard that artists in Soviet Russia had to be licensed to purchase supplies, exhibit in galleries, and sell their work through official channels. Unlicensed artists relied on what they could buy illegally or scavenge on their own. Their works were sold on the black market and sometimes smuggled to the States to fetch exorbitant prices at galleries. So what was I seeing here? Was this bone collector an unlicensed artist? Did he make sculptures from leftovers? Or had I misunderstood my host entirely?

The second thing I noticed came as we were leaving. A man stood in the shadows outside, eyeing me as I crossed the sidewalk. He held a large sample case, which might have contained black market merchandise. I'd heard about this too, having been warned to watch for people who followed American and European visitors in hopes of selling them souvenirs and designer knockoffs.

I noticed these things in a kind of dream state, barely thinking about them, concerned with little more than staying awake long enough to make it back to the hotel. Alas, when I got to the room, I found my roommate—another exchange artist—already asleep, snoring in the style of someone trained in dramatic oratory, from the diaphragm.

rrrrRRRRRR! rrrrRRRRRR!

I found my bed in the dark and dropped face down on the covers, too tired to undress, convinced that the snoring wouldn't keep me up. A few more minutes and I wouldn't even hear it.

But that didn't happen.

rrrrRRRRRR! rrrrRRRRRR!

I gave up and left the room, thinking I'd fare better in the hotel lobby.

And that, as my old friend TC would say, is when things got *real* scary.

The hotel was a high-rise with block-long corridors that zigzagged through a series of dog-leg bends, and I was rounding one of these when I found my way blocked by two men. They were smoking, leaning against the wall. One had Cyrillic letters tattooed on his fingers, aligned in a way that recalled Robert Mitchum's hands in *Night of the Hunter*. (You remember that guy? *HATE* inked on one fist, *LOVE* on the other.) He wore a striped T-shirt, or maybe it was a short-sleeve sweater. He was big—wrestler big—big enough to make me consider turning around and going back the way I had come.

Right, I thought. *That'll look suspicious.*

So I kept going, avoiding eye contact until he stepped away from the wall—swinging like a refrigerator door, blocking my path.

The other guy came up behind him, holding a briefcase across one arm as if delivering a pizza. The latches snapped, the lid opened. I didn't look. I was too busy staring at the big guy.

"*Hello,*" I said, speaking Russian. "*I'm from America.*"

"OK!" He smiled. Big teeth, one missing on the side, a gold beacon in front. "You want gifts? Good stuff!"

So that was it. He and his briefcase buddy were black marketeers. But here? In the hotel at 2:00 AM?

"No thanks." I tried waving him off. "*Nyet spasiba.*"

"Rolex?" He picked a watch out of the briefcase and put it on his wrist to show me how nice it looked on. "Twenty dollars."

"*Nyet spasiba.* I have a watch." I tried moving past him.

He sidestepped. "Cigarettes?" He showed me a pack. "Marlboro. Good stuff!"

"I don't smoke."

"*Da!* OK. American!" He picked up something else. "Maybe this, eh?"

I did a double take. What was it?

"Good stuff! Twenty bucks!"

It was a black cube, two inches square, polished to a mirror finish. I saw myself staring back from the top. My eyes were red, bloodshot cranberries.

"Ten bucks," he said. "A deal. Take it home."

"What is it?"

"Lacquer box. Handmade. Illegal."

"Illegal?"

"Dissident," he said. "Nonconformist! Sell it for a hundred bucks in USA."

I didn't think so. I might be able to turn a profit on an unlicensed painting . . . possibly a statue made from pig bones. But this thing was just a box. "No thanks."

"Touch it, OK." The cube seemed to change as he handed it to me, momentarily becoming a piece of negative space—like those optical illusions that seem to rise toward you one moment, then fall away from you the next. The box did the same thing. First it looked solid, then it became a cube-shaped hole in the man's palm. "Here!" He pressed it into my hand. "See?"

I felt the box's hard-edges, but little else. The thing had no perceptible weight. It was like holding a cube of solid nothing.

"Open it," he said.

I did, the lid sliding off with a hiss of displacing air. The inside was painted red, polished to the same mirror finish as the black exterior, and looking somehow deeper than the box itself.

"Ten dollars."

Buying it seemed like the easiest way to get past him. So I took out my wallet, wondering as I did if they might just jump me and take it all. But the big guy was all business. He took my money, gave me the box, and let me pass.

The encounter had worn me out, but not so much that I headed straight back to my room. There was no way I wanted these guys camping outside my door. So I pushed on, around another bend in the hall and into a stair-well that took me one flight down. Then I doubled back, returning to my room and the drone of snoring. But this time I was out as soon as I hit the mattress, sleeping until my roommate woke me in a rushed panic.

The alarm hadn't gone off. We were late for a meeting.

Fortunately, I was still dressed.

I don't know what became of that lacquer box.

My roommate, who helped me search for it the next day, insisted that I had dreamed the incident with the black marketeers. But I think it's easier believing that I simply misplaced the box in the ensuing rush of meetings and events. It was certainly small enough to fall behind something. Or per-haps it had gone into illusion mode, folding into itself to vanish in plain sight. In any event, I picked up a replacement in a store on Nevsky Prospket a couple weeks later.

Upon returning to the States, I discovered that a gallery near my home—a place that I had not known about before travelling to Russia—was one of the foremost importers of illegal Soviet art. Coincidence? I paid them a vis-it, toured their collection, then went home and started work on "Smuggling the Dead."

SMUGGLING THE DEAD

I stood beneath a flickering light in a concrete stairwell while Sergey felt his way through a dark recess beneath the steps. I heard a crackling—like crumpling paper or sputtering flame—and then Sergey stepped back into the light with a bottle of Stolichnaya and a narrow box wrapped in crisp, red paper.

"Is that stuff ours?" I asked.

"Yes," Sergey said. "Dolorous Vady arranged for them."

"What are they for?"

"For Dante." He handed the gift-wrapped package to me. "It would be rude to visit him without a gift."

"What's the vodka for?"

"For toasting," Sergey said. "For courage. It's not every night a man takes possession of the dead."

Sergey was an ugly Russian with sharp features, close-set eyes, and an aquiline nose that looked as if it could punch holes in metal. He held his lips in a sphincter-like pucker. His most expressive emotion was disgust, which he showed by thrusting his cleft chin forward in a closed-mouth *hummph!*

"Come on," he said. "But be careful." He pointed toward my feet as we started our climb. The edge of one of the steps had broken away, exposing a wire skeleton of reinforcing iron. "Soviet concrete—*hummph!*"

I climbed the stairs, watching my feet as my shadow waxed and waned beneath the stairwell lights. I kept my hand on the inner rail and thought about the money. For my services as an underground courier, Dolorous Vady was paying me $2,000—more than I cleared in a month as a middle school art teacher in the States.

"The job is easy," she had told me as we sat in the linen-paneled drawing room of her mansion in Laurel Heights. "I'd do it myself if I could."

"Why can't you?" I asked.

"I've been told to stay out of Russia."

"By whom?"

"Powerful people," she said. "I got into trouble on my last trip. Illegal transactions are tolerated as long as they're discreet. Last month I got sloppy."

"This thing you want me to do. Is it illegal?"

"Yes. But it's safe. Trust me, Nicky. It'll be the easiest money you've ever earned."

I believed her then. Sitting in her linen-paneled room, I felt sure that Dolorous would never do anything to put me in danger. But her reassuring words seemed far away as I climbed that bleak stairway in Leningrad. The city was still called Leningrad then, and the country was still the Soviet Union. So much has changed.

The stairs ended at the sixth floor where Sergey and I entered a hall that stretched past a succession of wooden doors. Somewhere, a violin played softly, like measured weeping. I heard muted voices, the muffled crackle of radios, the distant bang of dishes, and—from far off—the almost subliminal wail of a child.

Stenciled numbers identified the apartments. Finding the number he wanted, Sergey stopped and unlocked the door. Inside, where I expected to find a gallery of illegal Soviet art, I saw only threadbare furniture in a narrow room.

"This is Dante's apartment," Sergey said. "He never uses it."

Sergey crossed the room, leading me to a closet door. "This is where Dante lives." He shoved a key into a large, crudely installed lock.

"He lives in a closet?" I said. "You're not serious."

"*Hummph!* I am always serious." The lock groaned as Sergey turned the key. "Dante put this bolt in a few days ago. He thinks people are trying to kill him. He is paranoid." Sergey opened the door. The closet was empty except for a wooden ladder that ascended through a rectangular hole in the ceiling.

A voice called down: "*Pri`viet?*"

Sergey called back. "*Kak de`la*, Dante!" Then, in English, he added: "Dolorous Vady's American is with me. We're coming up."

We climbed the ladder—straight up into the Soviet underground.

* * *

Once, in my twenties, before I exchanged my dreams of becoming an artist for the reality of being a middle school art teacher, I maxed out my credit cards and invested in a cinder-block building in a dying, western Pennsylvania steel town.

The venture was called the Underground Loft. My fellow investors and I planned to rent space on the upper floor to struggling artists. On the first floor, we would hold exhibits. But six months after opening, buried in unpaid bills and unsold paintings, we realized that few people gave a damn about the work of underground artists from Pennsylvania. One of my partners, Harvey Younger—a pragmatic kid who had studied business administration while majoring in art—suggested we get a bank loan and use the space to open a printing business. I didn't want to be a printer. I was an artist. I decided to sell out to Harvey for thirty cents on the dollar rather than sell out my dreams. I took my losses and went into teaching—a temporary compromise, I told myself.

Ten years later, still compromising, I got a call from Dolorous Vady. I recognized her name. I had taught her son—a surly kid who called art class *fart* class and who eventually went on to study law at Harvard. Dolorous was also one of the school's trustees and a supporter of the arts. People said she ran a private gallery—a by-appointment-only place that catered to *serious* buyers.

"Do you have plans for spring break?" she asked.

"No big plans," I said. "I'll do some painting and—"

"Do you have a passport?"

"Why? What's this about?" The seventh-period bell had just sounded, and the art room was filling with eighth graders—careening vessels of hormones who would tear the place apart if left unsupervised.

"I've got an opportunity for you," Dolorous said. "Can you come see me this afternoon?"

That's when it started. That's when my life took the U-turn that sent me soaring back into contact with the world of struggling artists. Only this time the struggle was half a world away from the imagined angst of my middle-class life. This time the struggle was real.

Dante wore battered shoes, patched with duct tape and spattered with paint. They stepped toward me as I climbed through the gallery's trapdoor. Above the shoes were baggy pants and a slim torso draped in a bulky sweatshirt. The face above the sweatshirt was lean and pale—angular as cut quartz, smooth as polished marble. He took my hand and guided me onto a sheet of plywood that lay atop the beams. The air reeked of paint and solvent. I handed him my red-wrapped package.

"What's this?" he asked.

Before I could answer, Sergey entered behind me, cracking the seal on the bottle of Stolichnaya. "We both brought gifts." He handed the open bottle to Dante.

"Two gifts!" Dante took the bottle and set the wrapped package on a paint-spattered table. "I'm a rich man!" He took a swig and passed the open bottle to me.

I drank, not wanting to be rude. The vodka burned my gut as I passed the bottle to Sergey.

"Welcome to my gallery." A vodka flush rose in Dante's cheeks as he spread his arms at the vast, triangular space behind him. We were in an attic, beneath a ceiling of angled beams. Unframed paintings were everywhere, pinned to the ceiling, leaning on easels, even lying on the plywood floor. And there were statues too: welded metal, molded clay, carved stone, and a few that looked as if they had been made from dried garbage. One of them resembled a grimacing face, a rusty hammer embedded in its forehead, a sickle dangled from its jaw.

"You like it?" Dante said.

"It's interesting."

"*Da!*" He laughed. "Interesting!"

Sergey took a second swig before passing the bottle back to Dante.

Dante drank, the flush in his cheeks deepening. "Too bad you have not come here to drink and talk. I could show you some new works. Very *interesting* works. See—" He tilted the bottle toward an unfinished painting beneath a darkened skylight. "We are a studio as well as a gallery." He passed the bottle to me. "Did Dolorous Vady tell you that?"

"Yes."

"She is an *interesting* lady, da?"

"Yes. Very interesting." I drank again, my thoughts drifting to the previous afternoon—back to the art-covered walls and coffered ceilings of Dolorous Vady's estate in Laurel Heights.

"Everything you see on these walls had to be smuggled out of Russia," Dolorous said. "It's a noble cause, Nicky. Without my help, these works would have been lost forever. As it is, we're only looking at the tip of the iceberg."

Dolorous and I stood in the center of her mansion's east wing—a great hall that had once been a ballroom and which was now a climate-controlled warehouse containing the works of over a thousand unlicensed Soviet artists.

"The tip of the iceberg," she said again, pivoting to stand between me and a bust of Lenin made of nails and rodent bones. "And the iceberg is melting. Even as we stand here, the works of dissident artists are being lost or destroyed. It's up to people like us to save what we can."

"So you want me to smuggle art for you?"

"No. Not for me. For them." She tilted her head in an understated gesture that took in the entire room. "For the illegal artists, Nicky. We do it for them."

"And for money?"

She smiled, honoring me with a glimpse of her perfect teeth. At fifty-four, she had a way that was at once seductive and motherly. She shook her head and whispered, "No, Nicky. This time it won't be for money. *You'll* be paid, but I won't earn a cent." She took my arm. "This time I really am doing it for the artists—a generation of illegal artists, Nicky. You and I are going to set them free."

"What *exactly* do you want me to smuggle out of Russia, Dolorous?"

She leaned toward me. In a throaty whisper, she said, "Souls, Nicky. Human souls. Over four hundred human souls."

"I'm a dead man," Dante said, taking the bottle from Sergey. "Until now the state has tolerated my dealings with Dolorous Vady. But a few days ago I did something they will not forgive." He drank and passed the bottle to me.

I glanced at the gallery's skylight. Beyond the glass, clouds churned in an inky sky. Wind rattled the eaves. In spite of the burning vodka, I felt cold. I passed the bottle to Sergey. "Sorry," I said. "I can't drink this."

Sergey snorted. He grabbed the bottle and took a deep swig to show me how it was done.

To me, Dante said, "Let me give you what you came for." He reached under the collar of his sweatshirt and drew out a leather necklace.

"You've been wearing it?" Sergey said. He sounded edgy.

"I like keeping it where I know it's safe."

A canvas pouch dangled from the end of the leather strap.

"You might have bumped it," Sergey said. "It might have shattered!"

"A bump wouldn't shatter it. Trust me—around the neck is the safest place." He opened the pouch, reached inside, and removed what looked at first to be a fistful of darkness.

Dolorous led me into a room that had once been a library. Shelves of lacquer boxes lined the walls. She took one down and handed it to me. Its sides were a deep, translucent black. On its lid, carefully inlaid with silver and gold, was a Russian Orthodox cross. The box felt incredibly light.

"It's made of paper," Dolorous said. "The artist takes paper sheets and covers them with lacquer. Then he sets them in a damp place to dry."

"You mean a *dry* place to dry?"

"No." Dolorous smiled. She was teaching the teacher who had given her son's eighth-grade project a C-. "Lacquer hardens best in adverse conditions. And it hardens slowly, remaining pliable while the artist molds it."

I looked carefully at the box's rounded contours.

"Once it hardens," Dolorous said, "it can never be reshaped. Try to reform it, it will shatter."

"All right." I squeezed it gently, testing it, feeling its strength. "But what do lacquer boxes have to do with human souls?"

Dante slipped the box back into the leather pouch. He pulled the pouch's mouth taut and slipped the leather cord around my neck. "A heavy load," he said, forcing a grin as he let the nearly weightless pouch fall to my chest. "Can your American shoulders bear the weight of so many Russians?" His eyes grew glassy. He wiped them with a paint-streaked hand. "I would make you stay if I could. They will not kill me while you are here."

"*Hummph!* You're paranoid."

"No. I know the signs. I have been seeing them ever since the KGB questioned Dolorous Vady."

"*Nichevo!*" Sergey said. (I could tell by his tone that the word meant *screw it—it doesn't matter!*) "They only questioned her. Then they let her go. So what?"

"But they will not let *me* go."

"*Hummph!*" Sergey handed the vodka bottle to Dante and headed toward the trapdoor. "You're just a paranoid artist with a head full of vodka." He turned to me as he lowered himself onto the ladder. "Come on, American. Your adventure's almost over."

But Dante grabbed my shoulder. "One moment." He reached into his mane of disheveled hair, looped his finger around a tight curl, and pulled.

Roots snapped. "You gave me a present, now I'll make one for you." He twisted the hair into a ring around my finger. "Gypsy art," he said. "It means my spirit goes with you."

I wanted to ask for an explanation, but Sergey was already at the foot of the ladder and calling for me to follow.

"Better go," Dante said. "If they kill me tonight, at least I'll know the souls are free."

Dolorous and I sat in a darkened room watching black-and-white images scratch across a monitor. The video was silent. Emaciated prisoners trudged between wooden barracks and a barbed-wire fence while Dolorous narrated.

"Toward the end of the 1930s, Stalin established death camps for people who didn't fit the Soviet mold."

The image on the screen cut to the inside of a dark, narrow room. The camera closed on a design that had been cut into a wall beside a splintery bunk. The design was graceful, a swirling curve that spiraled like the eye of a tornado.

"Some of the prisoners were artists."

Another abrupt cut: guards in greatcoats dragged a skeleton through deep snow. The skeleton was alive, struggling as the guards forced it to kneel beside a snow-covered stump.

"The act of defacing Soviet property was punished severely. Unfortunately, everything was Soviet property, and only official artists were allowed to shape it, carve it, or paint on it. An unlicensed artist's work—even the simplest mark or design—was, by definition, a form of defacement."

One of the guards tied the living skeleton to the snow-covered stump while another picked up an ax.

"I'll skip this part," Dolorous said. "There's something else I want you to see." The arm of her chair was fitted with a track ball. She clicked the control, and the skeleton vanished behind a multicolored menu.

"Where did you get this stuff?" I asked.

"From friends in the Soviet Union, people who care about the plight of illegal artists."

"But who shot the film?"

"Soviet guards. Like Hitler, Stalin reviewed footage from his death camps. Films such as these are still on file in the Soviet archives in Moscow."

"How were your friends able to get them?"

"Money," she said. "In Russia, everything has a price." She clicked the ball. The screen filled with a new image, a man knee-deep in brown water. Shelves rose around him. Stacked canvases covered the shelves. "This footage is only a few weeks old, Nicky. It was shot in the flooded archives of the largest art museum in the Soviet Union."

"The Hermitage?"

"Yes. The museum has been sinking for years. Engineers have been working to save it, but it's a losing battle."

Stacked canvases sat within inches of the rising water.

"Archivists have been removing tons of uncatalogued art." She fingered the track ball. "A few days ago, while working in the flooded archives, one of my suppliers happened upon something that heretofore had been known only in legend." The screen filled with the image of a cube with rounded corners. The cube's surface was a deep, translucent black. Suspended in the translucence was what looked to be a swirling constellation of ivory stars.

"I received this image yesterday. The artifact is a lacquer box—a seven-centimeter cube fashioned from the blood, skin, and bone of over four hundred illegal artists who died at the Kolargon concentration camp during Stalin's Holocaust."

"Blood, skin, and bone?"

"Illegal artists are adept at working with whatever materials they can find. In the case of this box, blood was mixed with lacquer, and the mixture blackened as it was brushed across the flayed skins that formed the foundation of the box. Those flecks of white suspended in the lacquer are splinters of bone." She gave me time to study the image before she added, "It's a box of fragments, Nicky. The legends call it the *box of souls*." She clicked the tracking ball. The screen went dark. The lights came on. She turned to me, looking serious. "I may be a romantic, but the legend fascinates me."

"And now you want to own the box?"

"No," she said. "I want to destroy it."

"Excuse me?"

"I want you to go to Leningrad, take possession of the box, and bring it to me in Helsinki. I'll meet you at the airport. I have a cottage on the Baltic; we'll go there and destroy the box. We'll shatter it and bury the pieces in the free earth of Finland."

"I don't understand."

"The souls have been suspended in the lacquer for sixty years, waiting for someone to carry them to freedom, waiting to find rest outside the Soviet Union."

I sat back and pushed a hand through my hair. "You really believe this?"

Her expression softened. She looked down at her hands, shook her head. "No, but the legend means a lot to the Russian people—especially to the illegal artists who consider the story of the box part of their underground heritage. I'm doing this for them, Nicky. But I need an American messenger."

"But I've never been to Leningrad. I don't speak Russian. I won't know the first thing about—"

"You'll have a guide. Sergey Kafyrov. He's been one of my principal contacts for years. He'll meet you in Helsinki."

"Wait a minute," I said. "If your man can get to Helsinki, why do you need me?"

"The courier has to be an American—preferably someone with no prior involvement in my operations. Someone like you, Nicky."

Belching soot, Sergey's car sputtered from the shadows of the gray building that housed Dante's apartment and closet gallery. Sergey spun the wheel, pulling us into a U-turn that straightened into a dash down Zanevskiy Prospekt.

"We're late," he said.

Thunder crackled in the night. I sensed a distant flash. Looking skyward from the car's side window, I saw a shower of flaming rain.

I turned to Sergey. His eyes remained fixed on the road as we sped away. I looked back toward the building. The concrete walls receded behind us. I lowered my window for a better view.

"Hey!" Sergey said. "Roll that up!"

I pushed my head into the icy wind. Looking skyward, I saw flames shooting from the shattered skylight of Dante's loft.

"Dante's in trouble!" I said. "There's a fire!"

A monstrous truck pulled alongside us, blocking my view.

"*Nichevo!*" Sergey slowed to make a turn onto Nevsky Prospekt.

The truck passed us. On its trailer a tangle of mud-caked machinery swayed in a skein of tethering ropes. Through the web of hemp I saw something sail into the night from Dante's flaming skylight. It hung for a moment on a ledge of air, then tumbled to the street below. It was a canvas. Another followed. Then another. Dante was tossing canvases from the gallery, trying to save them from the flames.

Sergey grabbed me, pulling me back into the car while one last flaming bundle flew from the skylight. I glimpsed it for a moment, then, with a thud, I was back in my seat.

"Idiot!" Sergey said. "Do you think that watching makes a difference?" He gunned the engine, changing lanes as we picked up speed.

Sirens wailed in the distance. I looked back and caught my last glimpse of the burning studio as it passed behind the buildings of Nevsky Prospekt. The illegal art had stopped falling, and I realized that the last flaming bundle had been Dante.

"Close the window!" Sergey said.

I worked the crank, my reflected face glaring at me from the rising glass.

"*Nichevo!* You cannot help the dead. Worry about the living."

But it hadn't been concern for the living that had brought me to Leningrad. I sat back, pressed a hand to the front of my coat, and felt the corners of the lacquered dead resting atop my racing heart.

We flew to Finland where a silver Mercedes met us on the lower level of the Helsinki terminal. Dolorous sat inside, looking sleek and warm in the wool of a gray Armani suit. Her eyes asked the silent question as I slid in beside her. I took the leather cord from my neck and gave her the pouch. She looked inside while Sergey climbed into the front beside the driver. She examined the box, tucked it back into its leather pocket, and turned to me. "You look exhausted."

The driver started the engine. The Mercedes soared out of the terminal and into a wall of falling snow.

"It's an hour to my cottage, Nicky. You should try getting some sleep." She squeezed my hand. "Your seat's adjustable. Tilt it back. Get comfortable."

I glanced at the controls on the armrest.

"Go on, Nicky. You've earned it."

I wanted to talk to her about what had happened, but I did as she said. Dante's ring twitched on my finger as I worked the controls. The seat tilted with a drowsy whir. I sat back.

Exhausted, I drifted into fitful sleep.

I dreamed that I stood in darkness, surrounded by glossy black walls. Overhead, stars swirled in strange constellations. Somewhere among the stars, Dante's voice whispered: "Your friends killed me."

I turned, hunting the source of the voice. But I was alone, encased in darkness.

"In a few minutes," the darkness said, "they will try killing you."

I flinched. The dream faded. I heard the rumble of the car, felt the contours of my tilted seat. . . .

"No," the darkness said. "Don't wake up. Stay with me. Listen."

The car's rumble receded.

Darkness thickened.

"There isn't much time," the voice said. "A man is waiting along the highway. He wants to arrest you for fire bombing an apartment on Zanevskiy Prospekt."

My pulse quickened.

"You will have an accident while in the man's custody, and that will be the end of it. The KGB will have its arsonist . . . and Dolorous Vady will have a beautiful box of souls that the KGB will believe was destroyed in the firebombed gallery."

I tried protesting, but my jaw felt tight and far away. I heard Dolorous speaking Russian. I felt the car slowing down.

"Dolorous Vady has no intention of freeing the souls," the voice said. "She wants the box. She wants to *own* it. It's up to you to free the souls."

I heard the crunch of roadside gravel.

"Stay asleep!" the voice said. "There's one more thing!"

I heard the click of the Mercedes' transmission sliding into park. I felt a rush of cold air as Sergey's door opened. I heard the passing whoosh of highway traffic.

"The driver has parked on a narrow shoulder, but the snow is deep. He is too close to the road, and the pavement is icy. These things will provide you with one chance to get away."

I heard someone moving outside the car.

"When the chance comes, run into the woods. When you are alone, dig a hole and shatter the box."

I heard the click of an unlatching door.

"Bury the box quickly after breaking the lacquer. Bury it and run. If you don't—"

The door beside me swung open. Cold wind rushed in. I woke to a puffy face with angry lips and dark eyes. Behind the face, a snowstorm churned. The man jabbed a Makarov at my chest. "Get out," he said.

I glanced at Dolorous.

She stared straight ahead, as if I wasn't there. Beside her, churning snow flickered with the rise and fall of speeding headlights, the Mercedes shuddering in the wake of each passing car. And there was another sound: distant, growing louder, coming on fast: the thunder of a downshifting diesel.

The man with the Makarov leaned toward me. "I said get out!"

The diesel raced nearer, swerving as it filled the Mercedes' rear window with snowy light. I heard the crash of locking brakes, the scream of skidding tires. The gunman turned, staring at the light, eyes wide as the squeal rose to an ear-splitting shriek.

And then suddenly everything was racing.

The door slammed. I flew from the seat, tumbling with Dolorous, banging against her as the car pitched onto its roof and skidded down the bank beside the highway.

Then there was silence—a strange, muffled hush. Above me, safety belts dangled from the seats. To my right, snow drifted in from a shattered window.

Dolorous crawled toward the door. I sat up, blocking her way. She growled—no words, only a feral snarl that became a scream as I snatched the pouch from her hand. She lunged at me. I rolled, scrambled through the window and into the snow that glowed with light from the stalled diesel.

Sergey and the gunman raced toward me, snow fanning about their legs, breath steaming as they yelled at me to stop. But I was already running out of the light, careening away from the edge of the highway, and plowing toward a dark forest of snow-covered birches and pines.

From the car, Dolorous yelled, *"He has the box!"*

I ran, kicking through the snow, expecting to hear the blast of the Makarov. But no shots came. Glancing back, I saw cars jammed together in a chain-reaction accident. My pursuers wouldn't kill me with all those people watching. I would be safe until I reached the woods.

The ground fell away, sloping down. I looped the strip of leather around my neck as the woods swallowed me. Buried twigs clawed at my shoes, snapping beneath the snow. I looked back. Sergey and the gunman were closing fast, the highway little more than a glow between the trees. . . .

The gun fired. I saw the flash reflected on the falling snow, heard the muffled pop of the suppressed muzzle, and felt the thump of the bullet hitting the ground close to my feet. The gunman was aiming low, shooting at my legs to avoid hitting the box.

I glanced back.

They were right behind me. The gun flashed again. Pain stabbed my leg. Something snapped, and I went down, falling forward to slam a fallen tree. Things broke inside me. I gasped, rolling onto my back, and against the frozen trunk. My ribs creaked. Blood bubbled from my leg. . . .

A foot away, the dark bore of the Makarov stared me in the face.

Sergey stepped forward, reached down, grabbed the pouch from my neck. "We'll kill you here." He backed away. "OK with you, *sooka*?"

The gunman pressed the pistol to my face. The metal was still warm. I closed my eyes and wondered if I would hear the bullet. . . .

But all I heard was a muted, almost dumfounded "*Hummph!*"

The pistol left my face. I opened my eyes. Sergey frowned as he kneaded the pouch with a gloved hand.

"*Prasteete?*" the gunman said.

"It's broken!" Sergey glared at me. "You son of a bitch!" He tugged open the pouch. He looked inside. "It's in pieces!"

And then it happened.

A glow billowed from the mouth of the pouch. Something shot upward, a fine mist like a flurry of ice climbing into the air above Sergey's head. It coalesced, gathering into a luminous cloud, and then, like a jet of steam, it shot toward the gunman.

The man had no time to react. The dust hit him in the face, knocking him backward onto the frozen ground. The gun discharged, bolts of white flame shooting from the barrel in a rapid *pop! pop! pop! pop! pop!* that echoed from the trees. The gunman screamed. The dust enveloped him. He writhed, kicking with arms and legs that spurted blood as the dust tore him to pieces. . . .

Then, when it had finished, it spiraled back into the air.

Sergey dropped the pouch and ran, looking back only once as the dust shot forward to strike him between his eyes. He struggled as he fell. He had seen what the stuff could do to a man, and he thrashed across the ground, trying to slap it away. And he kept slapping even after his hands became hooks of serrated bone. The ground ran black with blood before Sergey's screams dwindled to a gurgling mew. . . .

When the dust rose again, Sergey no longer looked human. He had been reshaped, fashioned into a mass of bone and sinew that resembled one of the garbage sculptures in Dante's studio. I glanced at it, then looked away, turning my gaze to the cloud that was once again gathering in the air. It spun slowly, thickening along its axis, resuming the form it had held while imprisoned in the lacquer. It seemed to be bracing for another attack, spinning faster while the things that had been Sergey and the gunman tried righting themselves on the crusty ground. And then, a voice called from the distance: "Sergey! Vitaly!"

A silhouette stumbled through the trees. Gray wool billowed in the wind as Dolorous paused in the clearing and looked down at the grotesque tableau.

She stepped backward, glaring at me. "You broke it!"

The dust gathered into a glowing sphere.

"Do you realize what you've done? Do you re—"

The dust shot forward, catching Dolorous in the side of the face as she turned to run. She shrieked, the sound constricting into a bleating rasp as the dust reshaped her lips, cheeks, teeth, and jaw. Her legs and pelvis swelled into a pedestal of cartilage and bone. Her arms became sinewy spires. Her Armani suit flapped like a bloody flag. . . .

The glowing cloud rose again, hovered a moment over its third creation, and then it shot toward me, splitting into five needle-fine prongs. One of the prongs slammed my forehead, nearly knocking me unconscious as my head jerked back against the trunk. Two others struck my hands. The last two entered my chest.

I screamed.

Eventually, my screams brought the paramedics from the side of the highway.

The Soviet Union collapsed five months later. Corrupted Communism became corrupted capitalism, and the heavy hand of the KGB gave way to the strong arm of organized crime. The borders opened. Artists swarmed to the West where they sought to cash in on the free world's hunger for illegal Soviet art. But the art, now that it was neither *Soviet* nor *illegal*, lost its allure. Russian artists found work as cab drivers. Russian art found work as vodka ads.

Until a year ago, I had been certain that Dolorous, Sergey, and the gunman had died after the horrified Helsinki paramedics carted them away. I dared not believe that things so contorted and misshapen could go on living. But then I saw a headline in a supermarket tabloid.

LIVING ABSTRACTS
IN RUSSIAN GALLERY

Their photos were on page 28.

I don't understand the mechanics that caused Dolorous to end up on display in St. Petersburg. Perhaps she was stolen and sold on the black market. Dolorous Vady's estate is now in the hands of her son—a young man who has no interest in Soviet *fart* work. Sotheby's auctioned the entire collection in the spring of 1992, and though the works did not bring in nearly as much as they would have before the collapse of '91, the revenues from the sale were more than enough to launch Charles Vady, Esq., into very early retirement.

As for me, I have taken a loft in a dying steel town. I've gone back to being an artist, but the art that my hands create isn't entirely my own.

On a window beside my cot hang the X-rays that I had taken after I returned from Helsinki. The images, which mystified the doctors, show knobby growths on the bones of my chest and hands. The X-rays of my head show splinters embedded in the front of my brain. The splinters curve like a constellation of dust.

The souls are with me, buried deep, and free at last.

DANTE'S CITY

"Smuggling the Dead" was originally a much longer work, and reading it again I see that it moves perhaps too quickly through its final act. Nevertheless, I was having trouble selling it at its original length—too long for most magazines, too short for a standalone novel. When *F&SF* passed on it in the summer of '95, I figured I had no choice but to trim it, condense the actions, speed up the plot.

The scene in which Dolorous Vady gives Nick a crash course in the history of dissident art still seems to do a serviceable job of filling in the backstory. As I recall, that scene originally included some needless explanations about how the old films had been burned onto a series of CDs, smuggled to the States, and transferred to a computer hard drive. At the time I was afraid that readers wouldn't accept Dolorous Vady's display of randomly accessible footage. Today, of course, everything she shows Nick is probably available on the Internet.

Another element of the story that got cut down significantly in the final version was the character Dante, the underground artist who serves as caretaker for the box before passing it over to Nick. I actually did meet an artist named Dante in Leningrad, a tall, dour man with an aquiline nose whose profile called to mind Gustave Doré's depictions of another illegal artist, the Florentine Dante Alighieri, author of *The Inferno*. More about him in a moment.

On balance, I believe that the cuts I made to the manuscript resulted in a stronger story. But I have no way of knowing for sure, since I can't find the original manuscript either amid the old laser printouts that I have spread across my desk or in the folders of my current hard drive. All I have is the abridged version that appeared in the final issue of *Terminal Fright Magazine* in the winter of 1996.

Although I usually make a point of keeping all versions of a story, it seems that the extended cut of "Smuggling the Dead" has gone the way of the lacquer box that inspired it.

Now, a few words about Dante Alighieri, the outlaw artist who invented the horror novel.

Yes, seriously. Don't believe me? Go read his *Inferno*. It's all there. The dark terrors, terrible beasts, demons, a nightmarish descent that concludes with one of the most harrowing and inventive escapes in literature. Yes, it's written in rhymed verse (although the English translations of John Ciardi and Robert Pinsky make that less intrusive), and the action does tend toward the episodic. Nevertheless, it's hard to find something being done in modern horror that wasn't anticipated by Dante.

Clearly, I'm a fan, and it was my interest in his life and work that drew me to Florence in the summer of 1998.

I rented an apartment on Via San Zenobi and spent my days getting to know the terrain, taking excursions into the Tuscan countryside, visiting places that Dante wrote about while in exile. At night, I wrote in the apartment's small kitchen while my family slept in the adjoining rooms and the city hummed beyond the wide unscreened windows.

Much of my writing recorded impressions of things seen while exploring Florence and Tuscany, but one night found me making notes on a story inspired in equal parts by the labyrinthine architecture of Florence and Dante's concept of symbolic retribution: as they sin, so shall they suffer.

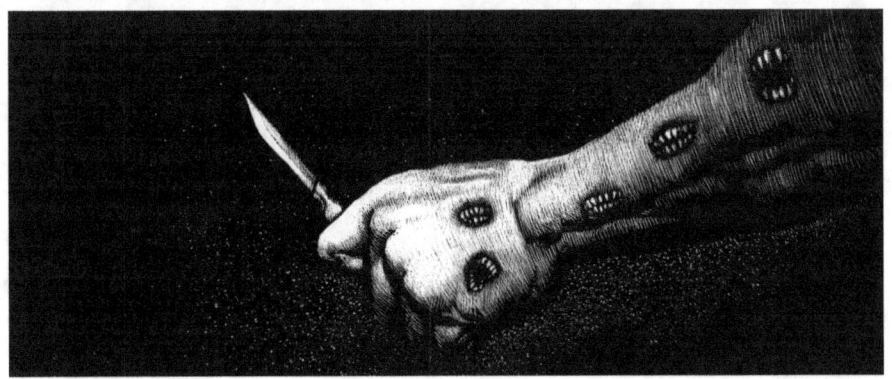

LESIONS

Todd studied her, gauging the size of her head, breasts, and hands, imagining how they would look arranged in a crystal bowl.

She sat across from him. "So tell me," she said. "How long have you had the condition?" Her English was excellent, as easy as her manner.

"The rash started a few weeks ago." Todd gestured to the front of his shirt. "Then came the blisters. Then—" He shrugged. "I can't describe what I've got now. Maybe I should just show you." He leaned forward, letting his shirt sag away from his skin before touching the buttons.

She noticed his fingers. "Those cuts," she said, "are they—?"

"Yes." He worked the buttons slowly. "From touching the—*condition*." He removed the shirt to reveal his ravaged chest, shoulders, and arms.

Her expression remained fixed. "Have you shown this to anyone else?"

"No." He let the shirt fall across the back of his chair. "I've been afraid to." She leaned closer.

"I tried doing some self-diagnoses after the rash erupted," he said. "I read books, surfed the net, visited chatrooms. But I couldn't find anything. I was afraid I was some kind of patient zero."

"Patient *zero*?" Her Tuscan vowels gave the phrase an exotic inflection.

"The first person with a new condition. You know, like the first AIDS patient?"

"I see." She turned to a line of instruments on a porcelain tray. "Your condition is not AIDS." She selected a probe—a steel shaft with a tapered end. "And you are not a patient zero." Her wheeled stool whispered as she rolled in front of him.

"So you've seen this condition before?" he asked.

"Similar conditions."

He sat back. "Thank God!"

"Yes. Thank Him. He led you to me." A crucifix dangled from her neck.

"Actually, it was the Internet," he said. "Your clinic came up in a discussion on Kaposi's sarcoma."

"*Clinic?* The people in the discussion called this a *clinic?*"

"Yes."

"And me? What did they call me? *Doctor* or *Sister?*"

"Sister."

She looked pleased. "People sometimes get that wrong too."

He could see why. She carried herself more like a physician than a nun.

She lowered the probe toward his shoulder. "It is a long journey from the States."

"I felt compelled to come."

"It was the hand of God." She tapped the probe against one of the lesions. The flesh quivered. She sat back and took a pair of half-lens glasses from her pocket. "I need you to move just a little." She leaned toward a wedge of sunlight from the backdoor window. "This way." The light caught the ringlets of her hair. "This is better." She tapped the lesion. Its sides dilated like lips.

"They seem almost alive," he said.

She lowered the probe. The lesion closed.

Todd heard the click of tiny teeth.

She wiggled the probe, pulled it free. "Do they itch?"

"Yes. And burn. Like fire sometimes. I've tried salt baths and sprays. Nothing works."

Her stool squeaked as she inspected his chest. She smelled of flowers—fruity hyacinth, spicy dianthus, elusive orchid. He imagined how she would smell if cut and dried—a potpourri of skin and hair.

"We've been caring for a man from England." She probed a fleshy knot on his chest. "Our subjects come from all over the world, you see." The knot quivered like a fetal hand. "From *all* over the world. If people need us, they find us. One way or another, they get here in time."

In time—he liked the sound of that.

She returned the probe to the porcelain tray, setting it alongside scalpels, scissors, clamps, tongs—smaller versions of the dissecting tools that he kept in his own studio back home. "The Englishman came to us with a condition on his neck, growths like hands." She raised hers to illustrate, pushing her thumbs into the hollow of her neck, wrapping her fingers around the base of her jaw. "He thought he had goiters."

"Did he?"

"No. He had something else—a terrible secret." She took her hands from her throat. "He had strangled his wife, you see." Her eyes narrowed as she took the half-lens glasses from her nose. "He strangled his wife, and his skin betrayed him." She slipped the glasses into her pocket. "I need to begin some tests." She stood. "I'll be right back." She left, passing into an adjacent room, becoming a shadow on a wall as she reached for a telephone. A moment's silence followed. Then she spoke, voice low, muted by a cupped hand.

He was reaching for his shirt when he heard what sounded like: "*Polizia.*"

He dipped his arms into the sleeves and backed toward the door beside the tray of instruments. Scalpels glinted in the sun, bright against the porcelain. He took one, cupped it in his hand, and looked out the window at a stone path winding through a garden courtyard. It was not the way he had come, but it might serve as an exit. Should he leave? There was no way she could know about him, who he was, what he was running from. His crimes were known, but not his identity. And yet she was calling the police.

He slipped out the back door and into the garden, maintaining his calm until a voice shouted after him. He didn't understand the words, but the meaning was clear. *Stop! Hey! Stop!* Another voice joined in. Then another, shouting louder as he took a right around the garden wall. The path ended there, became a stairway. The voices reverberated behind him, louder but no nearer. He took the stairs, descending to a stretch of pavement that veered beneath a granite arch. A splash of yellow illuminated the stone. *Sunlight*, he thought. *An exit to the street.*

The voices faded as he hurried through the arch, past a high window (the source of the sunlight) and into a corridor dotted with incandescent bulbs. More stairs waited in the distance, rising back toward street level. He hurried toward them, ascending into a hall lined with padlocked doors.

His lesions stirred, quickening as they always did when he broke a sweat. He balled his fists, resisted the urge to scratch, and continued on until he came to a perpendicular corridor. Street sounds echoed from the right: horns, voices, mopeds. The sounds seemed to come from just beyond the wall, and here he paused, leaned against the stones, held his breath, listened. The city was there, inches away. All he had to do was find an exit.

The sounds faded as he reached another intersection, padlocked doors stretching away in both directions. Voices called out, muffled by shuttered portals. He couldn't discern the words, but the emotions were clear: fear, remorse, desperation. . . .

His shirt clung to his skin, exciting the lesions, making them writhe as he hurried on, gripping his stolen scalpel. When a quieter corridor opened to his right, he took it, advancing until he realized he was being watched.

A shutter had been pulled back from one of the portals. A pair of eyes looked out.

Todd stared back. "You speak English?" He stepped closer. "Can you tell me how to get outside?"

"Outside?" The accent was East-London. "There's no outside. Not no more." A gasp for breath, and then: "Not for us." The eyes backed away, slipping from view, retreating into the cell, revealing the shadow of a crooked neck and a pair of strangling hands.

His skin betrayed him.

The silhouette vanished, slumping along a wall, merging into a dark corner of the cell.

Our subjects come from all over the world.

Todd backed away.

One way or another, they get here in time.

The corridor forked again. He turned right, wending through more passageways—some silent, some ringing with shouts and moans. Each door had a portal, all sealed. Only the strangler's shutter had been open, as if someone had known Todd would go that way, as if someone had wanted him to see the man with the Judas skin.

He kept turning right. Sooner or later, the turns would lead to an exit. The building couldn't stretch much farther. He had gotten a good look at the town during his ride from the airport. It was an old city, crosshatched with narrow streets and small buildings—not one of which had seemed large enough to contain this maze of corridors. But what if the maze ran through basements, beneath streets, between buildings? What if the corridors had grown with the city, expanding as more space was needed?

If people need us, they find us.

Someone moved behind him. A latch clicked. Hinges creaked. "The first test is positive."

He turned.

She stood in the hall, her ringlets glowing in the haze of a dangling bulb. Beside her, light seeped from an open cell.

"You look tired," she said.

His legs trembled, ready to buckle—as if her words had given him permission to accept his exhaustion.

"There's a cot." She gestured into the cell. "And water." She stepped away from the door. "A penitent will bring you bread and oranges in the morning."

He raised his hand. The scalpel flashed.

She held her ground.

"I could kill you."

She shook her head. "No. Out there, maybe." She indicated the world beyond the walls. "Not here."

"I can!" But he didn't.

"You're here because you need to be," she said. "It's the hand of God."

He looked into the cell. And then he was no longer just looking, he was walking, entering the chamber.

She followed.

He opened his fist, dropped the blade.

Indigo sky glowed beyond a small window. A narrow breeze curled in. He smelled hyacinth, dianthus, something elusive. . . .

She moved behind him.

He turned to see her holding the door. His lesions twitched, rippling against his shirt. "Can you help me?"

She slipped a padlock from her pocket.

"Is there a cure?"

"Yes." She palmed the latch. "But not in this life." She pulled the door, closing it with the thud of wood kissing stone. The shutter hissed, her face framed within the portal. "The asylum is only a holding place, a corporeal warehouse. You'll stay until your spirit moves on." She closed the shutter. The padlock clicked. Her footsteps whispered in the stone hall, fading away.

He called to her. His voice echoed, first from the walls of his cell, then reverberating from all directions as other inmates took up the call. He pulled himself up on the outside window. There was no glass, only a stone-rimmed patch of sky bisected by a single bar. Outside, angry voices raged in the fading light, echoing like the ones he had heard while running from the examination room. And now, looking at the path below, he could almost see himself racing between the flowers, hurrying toward a flight of descending stairs.

"Hey! Stop!" Todd added his voice to the yelling chorus. "Go back! Don't go down there!"

Too late. He had gone there. Now he was here. He released the bar, collapsed onto the floor. His lesions writhed, biting his shirt, ripping the cotton. The scalpel lay beside him, resting where it had landed after falling from his hand. He picked it up, sat back, and tore the shirt open. The lesions snapped at his fingers, drawing blood. He ignored the pain, flung the shirt to the floor, and studied the riot of mouths and fingers that had sprouted from his skin. A delicate hand protruded from his breast. Its painted nails resembled those of one of the hands he had kept in a cut-glass vase in his living room. Each weekend he had gathered new hands, and each Monday he arranged a bouquet—keeping it through the week until the fingers withered and the nails dropped like petals. Then he gathered again. Those had been happy days—the simple days before he had advanced to more elaborate arrangements of still-life lips and eyes. . . .

Looking at the lesions in the half-light of his cell, he realized he could have those days again. They were his for the cutting.

The lesion quivered as he pressed the scalpel to his chest. Blood ran in rills along his skin, dripped down, formed stars against floor.

The tiny hand stopped twitching as he cut it free. He placed it on the ledge beneath the barred window. Blood seeped from its stem, glistening in the sunset. He studied his skin. There were enough lesions for a dozen miniature arrangements, and more were sprouting—an inexhaustible supply.

He sat on the floor and went to work.

Tomorrow, when the penitent brought his food, he would ask for a vase and a small square of white linen.

BEANS

When I was in junior high, my family moved to western Pennsylvania, trading one prefabricated community for another. My new school was into fundraisers, and for one of these I was given a sales kit and sent out into the neighborhood to peddle magazines. It wasn't just me, of course. It was all the students. And some of those kids really racked up the sales, bringing in tons of dough for the school district and earning a few bonus prizes for themselves.

Not that the bonuses were anything special.

For starters, each kid who sold a magazine got to write his or her name on a paper banana and hang it with all the other paper bananas on a display board. Why bananas? Because selling magazines made you part of the bunch. Get it?

The next incentive beyond a banana was a Hershey Bar that just might have a five-dollar bill folded between its outer and inner wrappers. The teachers never told us the odds of getting one of those fivers, but I never knew any kids who got one. For the most part, we were working for paper bananas and Hershey Bars. But it was enough to get me motivated . . . at least enough to knock on a few doors and get my first taste of wholesale rejection. Great training for the writing life.

But the most meaningful thing I got out of trying to sell those magazines was something I discovered while reading through the hundreds of titles on the sales kit's order form. There, amid the likes of *Life, Look, Popular Mechanics*, and *Redbook* was something called *The Magazine of Fantasy & Science Fiction*.

A subscription was five bucks. I asked my mom for the money, and the next day my name was on a banana.

Famous at last.

* * *

My first issue of *F&SF* was dated January 1967, and it contained a story about some guy going around knocking on doors, selling books, and meeting with wholesale rejection. Well, that was something I knew about. But within a few pages the story started getting strange—*real* strange, as TC might say. I'd never seen anything like it. The setting was ordinary enough, but the premise was weird as hell.

The story was "Bait" by Bob Leman. It was his first published sale, and I will tell you no more about it other than that you can find it in a collection titled *Feasters in the Lake and Other Stories*. Seek it out. It'll change your life.

A decade passed before *F&SF* ran another Leman story, and after that his fiction began appearing regularly. When an issue arrived with his name on the cover, I dropped everything and started reading. His stuff was that good.

Then, in the early '80s, about the time my own fiction started making it into print, I learned that Bob Leman lived in Pittsburgh's South Hills, across the river from my apartment in the city's East End.

It was my good friend John Dechancie who finally talked me into giving Bob a call, and pretty soon John and I were regulars in the Leman living room, spending long afternoons trading stories.

In time Bob became both my mentor and toughest critic. Looking back, I find myself recalling what Gene Wolfe wrote about Damon Knight, a debt of gratitude expressed in the dedication to the book *The Fifth Head of Cerberus*:

> To Damon Knight
> who in one well-remembered
> June evening in 1966 grew me from a bean.

Bob's influence on me was every bit as transformational, only in my case it took a lot more than a single night in June.

I recall an expression that Bob liked to use, a sly bit of grammar-bending praise that he more often directed to John than to me. "You know, John," he would say. "You write *good*." He always said it with a smile. No need for formality. Just friends talking. Bob was one of the strictest grammarians I knew, but when he paid a compliment, it came without formality.

I remember sending Bob a story I'd written that was different from nearly everything else I'd done. It was titled "Prime Time!" I gave him a day to read it, then dropped by in hopes of getting his reaction. Now, whenever he had just read something of mine, he would never open the conversation by telling me what he thought of it . . . or even mentioning that he had read it. So for a while we chatted. And I waited, trying not to seem anxious. Then he raised an eyebrow, looking as if something had just occurred to him. "Oh." He grinned. "I read that new one." He nodded, looking right at me. "You know," he said. "You write good."

"Prime Time!" became my first sale to *F&SF*, and you can read it, along with some additional novelettes that first appeared in that same magazine, in *Visions*, this book's companion collection. Of all the stories that I was able to share with Bob before his death in 2006, the one that he praised the most was the novelette that I'm including here.

Like many of Bob's own stories, it straddles the genre of horror and sf, and I share it now with a tip of the hat to my master, the storyteller I first met in the pages of *F&SF* when I was barely 15, the teacher who helped me find my voice . . . and raised me from a bean.

DECANTING OBLIVION

She saw them racing toward her as she pedaled south on Smithfield. Shirtless, gaunt, and oozing blood from wounded chests, they cut across her path in eerie silence—a flood of emaciated figures running through the empty Friday-evening streets of Pittsburgh.

One of them paused, sizing her up as the others blurred behind him. He sneered, revealing notched teeth in blackened gums. He seemed about to speak, but instead he turned, showing her the back of his head as he rejoined the stream of pumping legs and slapping feet.

Something protruded from the base of his skull.

She reached for her transmitter, pressed the talk button, and spoke into her headset. "Nix to dispatch."

Nix was short for Double Nickels. Her other nicknames were Speed Limit and Speed. All but the last referred to her courier number: 55. Her real name, Gati Doolin, seemed to be part of another life.

The runners kept coming, churning past her like a river of dark flesh, darker wounds, and pitch-black eyes.

"Nix to dispatch! Talk to me, Bryan!"

Bryan owned Hilltop Couriers, which he operated out of a renovated Mt. Washington home. He employed a staff of dispatchers during peak shifts. After hours, he ran things on his own.

"Dispatch. Go ahead, Nix."

"Go to your window, Bryan. Look toward Smithfield."

Bryan's home sat on a bluff across the dark waters of the Monongahela. His office windows offered a panoramic view of the 800-acre patch of land that formed the western edge of the city—the triangular-shaped downtown known as the Golden Triangle.

"What's going on, Nix?"

The people kept running, funneling into the tight confines of Hobbs Way.

"Just look, Bryan!"

She heard him getting up, breathing angrily into his headset as he crossed the room and panned his tripod-mounted binoculars. "What am I looking for, Nix?"

The runners lost definition as they spilled between the walls, fading to pulsing shadows, becoming black waves in a pocket of night. Another beat, and they were gone.

"You missed it, Bryan. There were all these people."

"People I can see anytime."

"No. Not like these. They came out of nowhere. And they looked like—"

She realized what he must be thinking.

"You feeling OK, Nix?"

"Yeah."

"You clean?"

"You know I am."

"Just checking. You'd tell me, wouldn't you? If you were sliding back—"

That's when it hit. Silent thunder—a rumble that registered in Nix's flesh but not her ears. Hairs bristled on her forearms. Prickles rose along her neck. In her bones, she felt the dissipating roar of something beyond sound. . . .

She knew the sensation. She had felt it before, had even researched it in that other life that she had been forced to put on hold. But why was she feeling it here?

Nix braced herself as the tremors left her bones. A moment's calm, and then the rumble came again. This time she was sure. The waves were coming from Hobbs Way.

"Nix? You all right?" Bryan couldn't feel the concussions. His hilltop home put him well out of range. She considered what he must be thinking, looking down at her as she quaked silently against her handlebars. "Talk to me, Nix."

The wave passed. She straightened up, cocked her foot against the pedal, and kicked off toward the source of the silent thunder. "Gotta check on something."

Sirens wailed behind her, racing in from the east.

"Check what, Nix?" His voice filled with static as she slipped into the high-walled alley. No colors here, only the variegated grays of dusty asphalt and dusky shadows.

The emaciated figures stood in the thickening gloom, pressing together in the alley's center: bodies meshing like clouds, limbs entwining like mist. And it was then, as she reached for the switch on her helmet light, that the silent roar came again. And this time, Nix found herself at ground zero.

Her reflection hovered against the transparent side of a one-way window. She looked exhausted. Eyes like piss holes. Mouth a lipless line. Still, she looked better than the test subjects beyond the glass.

There were twelve of them: a half-dozen grad students, five laid-off flight attendants, and an out-of-work bank teller. Each would earn $300 for completing four days of testing. Between tests they could eat, watch DVDs, play cards, and take cold showers. What they could not do was sleep.

At the moment they were building Lego cars—four-wheeled rectangles that took five seconds to assemble. Each subject sat at a small table with two shoeboxes. The job involved taking a rectangular body from one box and wheels from the other. Four snaps and the finished car went into a pile beside the table. It was easy work, even for people whose minds were fried from exhaustion.

Gati turned from the window, checking the digital graphics on her computer screens. The subjects all wore MEG caps that provided enhanced magnetoencephalographic images of their sleep-deprived brains. At the moment, the brains showed only light activity in their prefrontal cortices. Gati recognized the condition: Automatic Behavior Syndrome, the state when exhaustion knocks consciousness off-line, leaving the body to run on muscle memory and reflex. Gati had more than a professional relationship with the condition. During the last few months, she and ABS had become inseparable, bound fast by the demands of her daytime studies and nightlong research.

She checked the clock. 4:28 a.m. The core team wouldn't arrive until 9:00. She was on her own until then. Just herself, the subjects, ABS, and her new associates—Bennie and Meth—stimulants that she truly believed she could handle. After all, if a psychology major couldn't manage a little substance abuse, who could?

A groan pulled her back to the moment. She looked up to see one of the subjects, former bank teller Sara Woo, staring at the glass, making one-way eye contact from the mirror side of the window. Gati touched the intercom. "You all right, Sara? Need a break?"

Sara stared unresponsively. And then it hit, a silent rumble that moved through Gati like a vibrating wave.

She gripped the console as the test subjects fell against their workstations.

They looked dazed, more confused than frightened.

"Everyone OK?" Gati stood. "Stay in your seats. I'm coming out."

They just stared, gazing blankly at their reflections as Gati crossed to the booth's door. She reached for the knob, but it slipped from her fingers as another blast threw her back into the tiny room. She tried catching the chair. The backrest swiveled. She went down, falling toward the video monitors, glimpsing screens where bursts of MEG light ignited like fire across digitized cortices. The fire spread as it blurred out of her field of view. A shaved second later, she was on the floor.

Only it wasn't a floor. It was pavement. Grit shifted beneath her hands. She opened her eyes. Above her, walls tapered toward a darkening sky. Close to her ear, something hummed—a soft whirring, like a repeating whisper of wind. She turned toward it.

A few feet away, her bike lay on its side, rear wheel spinning in the air.

She remembered her test subjects: the grad students, the flight attendants, and bank teller. But that had been months ago. This time it had been emaciated runners in a narrow street. The fresher memory drifted before her as she stared into the darkness. She could still see the runners. It was as if their images had been burned onto her retinas, flashing back at her as she blinked. It made no sense, but there it was. She saw them again as they had been when the silent blast threw her from her bike. And that was the part that made no sense. She blinked, watching again, seeing without comprehending: the runners had exploded.

To her left, something stirred: gritty footsteps approaching from Smithfield. She pulled herself up, looking toward the sound as a pair of flashlight beams converged on her face. Behind the beams, twin silhouettes stood backlit by a flashing cruiser. One of the silhouettes spoke. "You hurt?"

She tried rising to her feet.

A second voice spoke, softer than the first. "Take it easy."

Nix shielded her eyes. Two Pittsburgh cops coalesced between the beams. One officer was a man, the other a woman. Both were white.

"I'm OK." She stood.

The male officer asked, "What happened?"

She considered what he saw when he looked at her: a dark-skinned woman in dirty spandex, dreadlocked hair, and fingerless gloves—a suicide bomber from central casting.

Again, he asked, "What happened here?"

"Not sure." She felt it wise to avoid the whole truth. Mention of a silently exploding mob would only complicate things. In a world preoccupied with terrorist strikes, it was best to keep things simple. "I was just riding. Then I was on the ground."

"There've been reports of explosions. Hear anything?"

"No." That much was true.

"Can I see some identification?"

She dug in her wallet, hunting for her courier ID, but coming out instead with her expired card from the University of Pittsburgh.

The cop put his flashlight on it, pronouncing her name as if it were a nervous sigh: "Gati." He turned the light back onto her face. "What kind of name's Gati?"

"Indian." She looked right at the light, refusing to squint.

"What kind of Indian?"

"Indian Indian."

"You from India?"

"No. Pleasant Hills. My mother's parents were from Bombay."

"So that makes you what?"

"American." She didn't have time for this. She turned to the female officer. "Can I go?"

The male officer lowered his flashlight, looking again at the ID. "You a student?"

"Was."

"Now you're a courier."

"Yeah." It hurt to hear the struggle reduced to such simple terms. "Now I'm a courier."

"I need to see that courier ID," the officer said.

She looked again, digging through the crap that had accumulated in her tiny wallet: bankcard receipts, maxed-out Visa, Social Security card. . . . "Here it is." She pulled it out.

The officer studied it. "What were you doing in this alley?"

"Cutting through."

Her headset crackled, short-band hiss giving way to Bryan's voice: "Nix! Location!"

To the cops, Nix said, "Excuse me. Gotta check in." She hit the stud on her transmitter. "Nix here. Hobbs Way."

"Damnit, Nix! What's going on down there?"

The male officer said, "That Bryan Cole?"

Nix nodded.

The officer's face lost its edge. He returned her ID. "Tell him you're heading back."

She pressed her talk stud. "I'm heading back, Bryan. Police escort."

"What's going on, Nix?"

"Couldn't tell you."

"You gotta know something. Downtown's been filling with cops since you ducked into that alley."

"Like I said, Bryan, I don't know anything." She raised her bike from the pavement and followed the cops.

"Listen, Nix. I just got a call from a driver. He's got a package going downtown, but the cops won't let him cross the bridge. He wants to know if we can make the delivery."

She tugged the jack from the transmitter as she stepped toward the red-blue glare of Smithfield Street. Bryan hated when she disconnected the headset, but she had enough going on in her brain without his voice adding to the commotion.

"We're sealing off downtown," the female officer said. "Everything west of Smithfield."

They stepped out into the strobing lights. Two vans had pulled across the entrance to the Smithfield Street Bridge. Other vehicles blocked the major intersections between Fort Pitt Boulevard and Liberty Avenue.

The female officer said, "Bomb squad's on its way. No one's found any damage, but we're not taking chances. We're asking people to leave the area or stay indoors."

Nix cocked her foot against a raised pedal. "For how long?"

The female officer tensed, her pale skin changing colors in the flashing light. "Till someone figures out what's going on."

Gati stood in the back of the booth while the core team studied the playbacks. On the video screen, test subjects gripped their workstations, holding tight as if the floor were shifting beneath them.

Above the video screens, MEG displays showed a dozen brains glowing with hyperactive yellows and reds.

Dr. Qualin turned, looking at Gati. "Can you remember anything else . . . anything that isn't on the tapes?"

"Just what I said. Two tremors. One mild. One strong enough to knock me down."

Qualin looked skeptical. He turned back to the monitors. "Let's rewind to where Gati asks Sara if there's something wrong." He spoke softly, without accusation, but Gati sensed his suspicion. Something had triggered the group reaction. Qualin seemed to think it was something she had done.

Gati turned, left the booth, and slipped into the lavatory that the test subjects had used as their wash room. The subjects were gone now, sleeping like corpses in the recovery area. Gati envied them.

Three sinks stood against a mirrored wall. She walked to the center basin and wrenched the handles. Water flowed from the spigot. She leaned forward, thrusting her hands into the stream. The cold felt good. She splashed her face, holding her eyes open as the water broke across them. She had a class in less than an hour, and already she was crashing.

She leaned forward, looking at her piss-hole eyes while the door opened behind her. A concerned face looked in. It was Ellen Slater, her academic adviser, Qualin's research partner. "All right, girl?"

Gati tugged a handful of towels from the dispenser. "Nothing a week of sleep won't cure." She wiped her face.

Ellen moved closer. "Just so you know, Dr. Qualin's not pissed at you. It's the grant. He's having problems."

"Last month you said it was certain to be renewed."

"That was last month. It's a new world, Gati. We all need to be thinking military research. That's where the money's going, armed forces and homeland security."

The water in the sink grew warmer. Mist rose, fogging the mirror, softening Ellen's reflection as she leaned close. "You look exhausted, girl."

Gati shrugged. Exhaustion didn't matter. "Those tremors were real, Ellen." She turned off the water. "I didn't fall because I was tired. Something knocked me down."

Ellen gave Gati's shoulder a reassuring squeeze before backing away. "Go home, Gati. Get some sleep. Check your e-mail."

"My e-mail?"

"I'll send you something."

"Something like what?"

"Something that can wait till you're rested." She opened the door. "We'll talk tomorrow." And then she was gone, leaving Gati leaning against the basin, torn between work and the sleep that threatened to swallow her whole.

She turned the water back on, just the cold this time. Her class started at 10:00. She reached into her pocket. The pills were there.

She cupped a hand under the spigot.

Nix found Bryan by an office window, looking at the downtown streets through high-powered binoculars. "You unplugged your headset." He spoke without turning. "I hate when you do that."

"Sorry. I had enough to deal with."

"And now you got more."

"Meaning?"

"That package." He pointed without turning. "It's on the desk."

"I didn't say I'd deliver it, Bryan."

"You didn't say you wouldn't. The driver needed an answer. I told him you'd do it."

"The bridges are closed, Bryan."

"Which is why it has to be you making the delivery."

Nix crossed the room, knees still warm from muscle burn, shoulders aching from the uphill climb out of the city. Usually she hitched rides by grabbing the fenders of outbound cars, but tonight the traffic had been light, made up of vehicles being turned away at the bridge barricade. All had raced by at full throttle, too fast to catch.

At least the muscle burn felt good. It was healthy pain, more bearable than the ache that lingered from hitting the pavement in Hobbs Way. Her shoulder spasmed as she crossed to the desk and picked up the package: cylindrical, fifteen inches tall, six inches around, wrapped in insulated Tyvek. It felt heavy and cold.

"The driver said he'd make it worth your while, Nix."

"How much does he think my while is worth?"

He told her.

She stuffed the package into her bag. Then she rounded his desk to stand beside him at the window. Across the river, intersections flashed with the lights of idling cruisers. Between the intersections, empty streets angled toward the city's western edge.

Bryan tapped the glass. "TV says the tremors were all west of Smithfield. Lots of people felt them. No one saw a thing."

Nix flexed her shoulders, reserving comment.

"And there's no damage." Bryan turned from the window. "This doctor on Channel 4 thinks it's group hysteria, but the cops aren't taking any chances." His face caught the glow from his desk lamp as he leaned back against the glass. Spider veins lined his cheeks and nose. Dark circles rimmed his eyes. He looked tired. "I wouldn't ask you to do this if I thought there was—" He broke eye contact. "If I thought there was some kind of incident going on."

She tightened her straps. Even through the layers of nylon and spandex, the package felt cold against her shoulders. "So where's this package going?"

"Riverfront Hotel."

"Doesn't get much more *downtown* than that. What's the room number?"

"No room."

"The suite, then."

"No suite. The client's renting the twenty-second floor. The night manager will take you up."

"What kind of man rents an entire floor?"

"A rich man." Bryan walked with her to the office door. "His name's Summit. First initial A. Middle initial J."

"A. J. Summit." The name rang of self-importance. It also seemed faintly familiar: not a name that she knew, but the echo of one.

"Been living at the Riverfront for two weeks. I hear he had the space remodeled to some weird specifications."

"How weird?"

"Didn't hear that. Just heard weird."

"Remodeled an entire floor?"

"Like I said, he's rich."

She glanced back at Bryan's office windows, toward the glowing hotel that stood on the city's western edge. The windows of the top floor were all dark. She asked, "Did you inspect the package? If I get stopped, I'll be in enough trouble for just being in the city. I don't want to get busted for carrying contraband."

"It's nothing illegal, Nix."

She knew better than to question him further. Bryan lived by the dictum that a courier's concerns ended with *where* and *when*. Everything else was between management and client.

Bryan said, "The driver's already covered the delivery charges. Mr. Summit will pay you the rest in cash if you reach him by 9:00."

She checked her watch: 8:20. "Forty minutes to enter and cross a curfewed city?"

"You can do it."

"You want me to ride Hot Metal, don't you? I nearly killed myself last time."

"I'm not telling you how to get there." He turned back toward the window. "The package is due at the Riverfront by 9:00. The extra cash and how you collect it are your business."

Ellen's e-mail came with a single line and a 4.86 MB attachment. The line read: "There might be a thesis here." The attachment was titled "Alpha Tremors."

Gati started the download and then climbed into a hot shower. The water didn't calm her. She had reached the plateau of dull anxiety—a terrible state that stretched between chemical high and physical crash. She wished now that she had taken Ellen's advice about skipping the day's lectures.

She left the shower and returned to her computer. The attached document turned out to be a series of magazine and newspaper articles. Most of the datelines were from Malaysia, Indonesia, Pakistan, China, India. All of the articles were about sweatshops.

A picture scrolled into view. She took her finger from the arrow key, reading the headline above the digitized photo: "Work Continues as Workers Shake."

The photo showed a cavernous room packed with hunched children and ancient sewing machines. Cables dangled from a low ceiling. Bolts of fabric leaned against windowless walls. One of the workers grinned, revealing notched teeth that looked as if they were used for cutting thread. The caption read: *Sweatshop workers brace against phantom tremors in Bhiwandi, India.* She clicked a hyperlink, accessing an additional note:

Tremors may originate in a nearby factory. Bhiwandi is the suspected home to at least one non-sleep shop.

What the hell was a "non-sleep shop"?

She scrolled on, skimming text, pausing at photos. Many of the articles were from human rights publications. Most were in English. A few were in Hindi. Others were in languages she couldn't read, but these were partially translated in hyperlinks. She paused to reread one of them:

The tremors are not earthquake related. Although reports in India were attributed to movement in the Kachchh Fault, what can we make of similar phenomena in non-seismic zones such as Malaysia?

She kept scrolling, reading with waning comprehension until the string of documents ended with a grainy, underexposed photograph. The image showed workers hunched over massive machines. One of the workers had his back to the camera. Something protruded from the base of his skull. The caption was in Chinese. She clicked the hyperlink translation:

> Photo purportedly taken in a non-sleep shop in the garment district of Zhongshan, China.

Bryan's home vanished in her rearview as she steered onto a sloping side street. Her return trip would avoid the main arteries that led up the side of Mt. Washington. Instead, she would stick to neighborhood streets and alleys that had been paved before city codes limited angles of descent.

Hurtling down a thirty percent slope, past houses that all had first- and second-floor doors, she caught a glimpse of the south-shore valley and the old J&L Bridge. The span, once used for hauling hot metal, had been partially dismantled. Now it was little more than I-beams atop a corroded truss. She had ridden it before, but she'd been high on crystal meth. Could she ride it again, stone sober, powered by endorphins? She'd know soon enough.

The hillside alleys leveled toward the Southside. She headed northeast, through the bright lights of Carson Street, angling into the narrow lanes that had once been home to Europe's hungry and poor—exploited workers who had labored twelve-hour shifts at ten cents an hour. Her paternal grandfather, a blind Irishman who'd lost one leg to the mill and the other to diabetes, had told her stories passed down from his father—epic nightmares of life in a lidless hell.

She cut down a cobble lane, past row houses with doors that opened directly into the street. Seconds later she emerged along the northern edge of a dismantled foundry—the ghost of a mill that had once stretched for 276 acres along both sides of the Monongahela. She veered left, toward a chain-link fence and a ragged hole large enough to accommodate a bike. She hunkered down and coasted through. Up ahead, the sooty walls of the old mill blocked her view of the river. Just as well. She didn't want to see the I-beams until she was on them. See them too soon and she might turn back. . . .

Bryan's voice crackled in her headset. "See you, Nix. Looking good."

She kept pedaling, heading toward a gap in a boarded doorway. Through the opening—beyond a stretch of industrial darkness—another door opened toward a band of river lights.

"You're making good time, Nix. Keep this up, you'll be there before—" The headset filled with static as she entered the gutted mill. She knew the shortcut. She'd taken it before, but tonight there was something wrong with the darkness.

Beyond the glow of her headlamp, clotting shadows became bowed shoulders and withered hands. Shapes coalesced, forming rows of chugging machines, stretching deep in all directions, surrounding her with specters of industrial slavery. But these were not the enslaved immigrants of Pittsburgh industry. These ghosts were not making steel. . . .

Pulsing needles thundered in the thinning darkness. She saw ancient sewing machines and workers in sandals and loose-fitting pants. And behind each bent figure, dangling from a hook on a metal pole, a bag of milky fluid dripped into a transparent tube.

She found herself focusing on an androgynous figure with bare breasts and close-cropped hair. It was a tiny man, bent and wasted. The feeding tube slipped over his shoulder and into a crusted shunt beneath a protruding clavicle. He was being fed intravenously.

On his head, he wore an elastic band that sagged behind his ears. And as he turned to drop a finished sleeve into a bag, Nix saw a second shunt protruding from the base of his skull. Cradled in elastic and Velcro, this implant was larger and heavier than the one in his chest. Vapor condensed on its metal shell. A steel nipple extended from its base, connecting to a tube that ran into a pump box beside his chair. From the box, a second tube extended back to the base of the worker's skull.

She saw all of these things in an instant, absorbing them in a glance that ended when she noticed a calibrated panel in the pump box's side. Behind the panel, fluid collected in a graduated cylinder. It held her gaze. She couldn't look away. She felt herself falling. . . .

WHAM!

She flew through an open doorway and hurled toward a line of river lights. The wind felt unreal against her face. Where was she?

She skidded on weedy gravel. Dust climbed around her shoes as she stopped and looked back. Inside the foundry, shadows fell from concrete pillars, crisscrossing beams, and dangling cables. The sweatshop had evaporated back into empty darkness. No emaciated workers. No drumming needles. No dripping tubes.

"Nix! Something wrong?"

Bryan's voice brought her back. She reached for her transmitter. "Taking a breather." She had no desire to share the hallucination. "Everything's fine." Her therapists had warned her about flashbacks. Was that what she had just ridden through? A flashback? The belated effect of having spent too many amphetamine nights staring at photos of block-long sweatshops and researching the stats of enslaved lives?

"Clock's ticking, Nix."

She reoriented herself, feeling the wind on her face, the rubber grips against her palms, the dirt beneath her shoes. No time to puzzle over the ghosts of past addictions. No time for anything but riding. "Right!" She turned her bike and pushed off, steering onto the riprap at the base of the Hot Metal tracks. Then, with pedal-strapped shoes and bar-gripping hands, she pulled up on the bike, bunny hopped over a discarded rail, and landed on the back of an I-beam.

"I see you, Nix. Looking good."

Coasting, holding the handle steady with one hand, she reached for the transmitter and disengaged the headset. She did not need Bryan distracting her. This ride was between her and the bridge. . . .

She remembered the last time she had ridden the span. It had been the middle of a sleepless week, forty hours after disillusionment over her thesis had forced her out of school, five days before drug abuse had landed her in rehab. On that night there had been enough crystal meth in her veins to power a small borough, and Bryan's office had been full of couriers—all watching in amazement as she rode the beam.

But now she rode on cool nerves, following her helmet beam as it raced along the elevated strip of iron. The trick was to concentrate on moving ahead—not worrying about where she was, but concentrating on where she would be. The ride was easier without drugs. Clear vision kept her focused on the light. Controlled effort propelled her forward.

As the span ended, she braked and pivoted onto an eroded slope that angled along the bridge abutment. Her body flowed with the maneuvering bike—in balance, in control.

Ellen gave her the news over coffee in a Forbes Avenue Starbucks. It was official. The grant would not be renewed. "Your stipend runs through December, Gati. You can use the time to start your thesis."

"A thesis on alpha blasts?"

"Maybe. But don't call them alpha blasts. That wouldn't go over."

"What do I call them?"

"Nothing yet. But you and the test subjects felt something. You've got access to their exit interviews, the videos, the MEG scans. And there's your personal impressions. Something happened, and you felt it. If you can document it, you might encourage further inquiry."

"Into?"

Ellen grew serious. "Those documents I sent you were collected by a technician who spent eleven months doing peptide research in a Hong Kong lab. She left when she realized the implications of what she was doing."

"What was she doing?"

"Developing a process to inhibit sleep."

"Sounds like a noble cause."

"Until you consider the application."

Gati remembered the blurred photo from Zhongshan, China. "Non-sleep sweatshops?"

Ellen nodded. "Labor is a shop's least efficient component. Machines don't tire. Factories and warehouses don't close. Only people need time off to recharge."

"You think that's a good thing, biological downtime?"

"It's a natural thing."

"So is hunting and gathering, but who does that?" Gati eased back from the table, turning toward the stream of morning traffic beyond the café windows. Her bike sat by the door, waiting to carry her to a morning interview at a place called Hilltop Couriers. If she got the job, there was a chance she could afford to stay in school once her stipend ran out. "Funny thing," she said, staring into the angled light. "I used to ride for fun. Cross-country. BMX. No time for that now." She looked back at Ellen. "Now everything's work."

"Shouldn't be that way."

"But it is." She studied Ellen's face, trying to read between the gentle lines. The woman had mastered the aspect of a clinical psychologist, but beneath the detachment Gati detected a stratum of guarded caution.

"Listen, Gati. What if lack of sleep posed a danger, not just to the people who didn't sleep, but to the people around them as well?"

"That's nothing new. ABS causes—"

"I'm not talking about sleeping drivers." Ellen leaned forward. "What if the tremors you felt in the lab were only weak versions of a more disruptive phenomenon?"

"Disruptive where? Egypt? Malaysia? Who's going to care about that? You said it yourself, Ellen. The world's changed. No one cares about workers' rights, and alpha blasts aren't exactly the third-world disturbances that are making news these days."

"If the proof existed, people might listen."

"Maybe. But would they be the right people?"

"Who are the right people, Gati?"

"The people in a position to affect change. Shop owners, for example. What do they care about tremors if they've got a maximized workforce? And the workers, what about them? More job time means more income. They're not going to give that up. I know I wouldn't."

Ellen didn't answer right away. For a moment she sat, digesting the words, looking thoughtful. Her days of wild hypotheses and reckless investigation were behind her. She could not afford to investigate alpha blasts and non-sleep sweatshops even if she wanted to. And despite the forced calm of her face, her eyes made it clear that she wanted to. At last, she said. "It's a thesis topic, Gati. You could do worse."

"I'll think it over."

"Do."

Gati started to stand, pausing when Ellen seemed ready to say something more. But the moment passed in silence, with only a soft change in the woman's expression. It was a subtle change, but Gati caught it. And with it she glimpsed the truth beneath the surface. Intuitively, Gati realized that the Hong Kong technician had not been one of Ellen's associates. "All right," Gati said. "I'll think it over. I'll let you know."

The technician had been Ellen.

The wharf stretched beneath rusting trestles, following the curve of the river toward a pedestrian tunnel that had long ago become home to a tribe of hardcore urchins and transient runaways. They all knew Nix, and usually they let her pass without comment. Tonight, however, they were gone—either routed by cops, or (more likely) watching from the city's shadows while the police puzzled over phantom tremors. Their cardboard beds and trash-bagged possessions flashed in her headlamp's glow as she pedaled on.

Up ahead, a red-and-blue haze spilled across the tunnel's end. The police were out there, positioned on Commonwealth Place. But even if they looked toward the tunnel when she emerged, what would they see? A blur of shadow? A silent streak vanishing into the dark expanse of Point State Park?

If they called to her, she would keep moving. If they gave chase, she would lose them on secret trails that diverged from the paved walkways. And if they caught her, she would be no worse off than if she hid in the tunnel and waited for a better plan. She had eight minutes to get to A. J. Summit. She had to keep moving.

Pedaling furiously, she left the tunnel, traversed a twenty-foot courtyard, and crashed through a line of broken shrubs. She shifted to a power gear, jumped a ditch of muddy runoff, and coasted up a wedge of gritty earth.

Another wall of shrubs blocked her path. She braced, stayed the course, and crashed through onto a sloping berm. Almost there. The hotel's west face loomed before her.

Ellen looked up as Nix blew into her office.

"I've got like five minutes." Nix threw her helmet on the floor and slumped into a chair. "What did you think?" The tiny office filled with a soft metronomic tapping—muffled beats like pulsing pistons. "Did you get my first draft. Did you read it?"

Ellen turned from her computer screen. "Yes." She looked concerned. "I read it."

"And?"

"Honestly?"

Nix sat forward. "Christ!" The tapping grew louder. "You didn't like it?"

"It's not the draft." Ellen set her glasses on the desk. "The draft is promising. Some good analysis of the MEG data. Nice handling of the exit interviews. . . ."

"So what's the problem?"

"Honestly?"

"Yeah." Nix glanced at her watch. "I've got like four minutes. Hit me."

"All right, Gati." Ellen paused. For a moment, she too seemed to be listening to the phantom tapping. "No bullshit, Gati. I'll give it to you straight. You look like hell."

"Me?"

"What do you weigh? Ninety pounds?"

"Ninety six."

"That's what, ten-percent underweight?"

"I'm small boned."

"You're five-eight, Gati. And you're losing muscle."

"I'm riding full time. How can I be—?"

"Still taking amphetamines?"

The tapping grew louder, filling the room.

"I thought we were going to talk about my thesis."

"We did, Gati. It's a good start, but you'll never finish it if you keep wearing yourself down."

Nix looked at her watch.

"What's going on, Gati? Where do you have to be that's so important?"

"Work."

"Your shift's over."

"First one's over. I'm doing a second. Just for today, to cover the rent." She picked up her helmet. "E-mail me? Tell me what I need to do—with the thesis, I mean. Just the thesis. Tell me. I'll do it." She stood. The thumping stopped. She looked down. The sound had been coming from her feet: Automatic Behavior Syndrome. She had left the bike outside, but her feet had kept on riding.

She steered toward the hotel's service entrance where she locked her bike in the shadow of a dumpster. Then she rounded the building's southwest corner and stepped out into the blazing headlights of three idling busses. People climbed aboard, looking tired and anxious as bellhops loaded their bags. What did this mean? Was the hotel being evacuated?

She pushed through the crowd and into the lobby.

At the main desk, the night manager spoke into a telephone, the receiver wedged between his ear and shoulder. He sorted receipts as he worked the phone: two tasks at once, the bane of frontline management.

The clock behind him gave a muffled tick: 8:55.

She stepped toward the desk. "Hey!" She slapped the counter with her gloved palm. "Hilltop Couriers."

He looked up. His eyes had the same red-rimmed glare that she often saw in Bryan's. To the phone, he said, "One moment." Then, to Nix: "Excuse me?"

She unstrapped her pack. "From Hilltop Couriers." The pack thumped the desk. "Delivery for Mr. Summit."

His brow buckled. "Delivery?"

"For A. J. Summit." She glanced toward the busses. "He still here? My dispatcher said you'd show me up."

Again, to the phone: "Right back." He stabbed the hold button and dropped the receiver. "Sorry." He brushed a hand against his high forehead, straightening the memory of a forelock. "Can't take you up, but I can show you the way." He turned and took a set of keys from the wall behind him. "Follow me." He swung the keys around his thumb, catching them in his palm. "I thought downtown was closed to incoming traffic." He looked back at her as he walked. "It been reopened?"

"No." Her tone let him know that she didn't want to go into it.

He walked on, leading her to a service elevator where he pushed a key into a battered panel. Then he opened the grate. "It's the only way to get to twenty-two. Other than the stairs, of course. And you wouldn't want to take them." She stepped inside as he pulled the key from the panel. "The regular elevators will bring you back down. They just don't carry passengers up there. You know. For privacy." He closed the grate. "I'd take you up, but I can't leave my post. We're moving some guests uptown, out of the curfew area. Right now it's voluntary, but the cops say everyone's got to go if those rumbles start again." He swung the keys. "You might mention that to Mr. Summit. He won't like being moved, but if the cops insist—"

"I'll tell him." She looked at the rows of buttons on the elevator wall. "This like a normal elevator? I just hit the button for twenty-two?"

"That's it."

She hit the button.

The elevator lurched and started to move.

Subj: Your Thesis
Date: 1/17/02
From: Dr. Ellen Slater <eslater>
To: Gati Doolin <nix55>

Gati:

Attached document contains my comments. As I said, you've produced a good first draft, a respectable start, but I'm concerned about your lack of support for the existence of non-sleep sweatshops. More problematic, your so-called "dream solution" (top management becoming concerned with the health and well-being of low-level workers) is unrealistic. You said it yourself a few months ago. Those who can affect change need a compelling reason to listen. Without one, I'm afraid the concluding argument breaks down. A thesis is no place for "dream solutions."

* * *

She tried reconnecting her headset as the clattering cables pulled her upward, but to her surprise the jack was still in the transmitter. A broken wire dangled from its end. She had evidently snapped it while riding the bridge, broken it when all she'd meant to do was pull the plug. Bryan was going to be pissed.

She removed her helmet, then the headset. The latter was merely an ear-plug and a pinhead mic, held in place with a Velcro band. She wrapped the broken wire around the Velcro and dropped the unit into her helmet.

The floors scrolled by, rolling like an image on a badly tuned monitor: a succession of door-lined halls, then a utility floor of steel beams and humming compressors, then more floors of rooms until the car emerged into a foyer smelling of fresh paint and plaster.

Nix pressed the button to send the car back down. Then she stepped out, advancing toward a wood-veneer door.

Near the ceiling, a camera glared with an LED eye. To its left, a voice buzzed from a half-inch speaker. "You're the courier?"

"Yes."

The elevator clattered behind her, slipping away on groaning pulleys. It was then that she realized something was missing from the foyer. The night manager had told her to use one of the regular elevators when she wanted to leave. But there were no such elevators here. There was only the service elevator's grate-covered shaft, the wood-veneer door, the camera, the speaker, and the buzzing voice: "You have my package?"

"Yes."

The door clicked, disengaging from its frame.

She pushed inward. Squinting as intense light spilled from the room.

Again, the voice spoke, coming to her first through the speaker, and then, a quarter second later, from somewhere deep within the light: "Hurry." *Hurry*.

The entire level had been gutted, walls and fixtures carted away until all that remained was an orchard of widely spaced pipes and beams—all illuminated by a powerful glow.

Across the space, dwarfed by distance, a man leaned before a fluorescent wall. He seemed strangely deformed: shapeless body, diminutive head, reed-like hands. Beside him, stretching across a raised iridescent plane, stood a line of puzzling objects: a rhombic rectangle, a suspended teardrop, and an empty fishbowl balanced atop a glass pedestal. The tableau resembled something from a Richard Powers painting—futuristic images from the mid-twentieth century.

Nix stepped onto the raised floor, a grid of Plexiglas panels illuminated from below. The ceiling was much the same. And so were the walls: rows of fluorescent tubes behind translucent sheets. All the windows had been covered, blocking out the night, holding in the glare. "You A. J. Summit?"

"I am."

The room extended for nearly a city block—400 feet of glowing void.

She moved forward, advancing between exposed pipes and beams. Deprived of their shadows, they resembled paper cutouts—two-dimensional artifacts against a blinding backdrop.

Mr. Summit condensed from the glow as she moved toward him. She saw that his misshapen shoulders were actually the lumpy folds of an oversized saffron robe. His head, shaved from crown to chin, held a face that was at once agitated and exhausted. Like the pipes and beams, his robe-draped body cast no shadow—nor did the few necessities that stood behind him: cot, footlocker, and a sink and commode that grew like porcelain tubers from exposed pipes. Forty feet beyond the fixtures, white walls formed a floor-to-ceiling partition large enough to hold a stairwell and a bank of elevators.

Summit stepped forward, gesturing toward her bag. "Is that my package?" He spoke with the guarded precision of one who had mastered English as a second language.

She tugged the zipper and removed the cylinder. "And I was told you'd have something for me."

"It is there." He pointed to the iridescent plane that stretched beside him. She saw now that it was a transparent table. Along the top, the three mysterious objects proved to be a wafer-thin computer screen, a crystal decanter, and a brandy snifter. And there was a fourth object—an envelope with an open flap.

"The envelope is yours." He reached toward her. "And that cylinder is mine." His fingers brushed hers as he took the package. His hands felt cold, wet. They trembled. She knew the symptoms. Junkie hands.

She put her helmet on the table and picked up the envelope. She looked inside. The first bill was a hundred. So was the one under it. She ran her thumb along the edges. Ten bills. "There's a thousand dollars here."

"Yes." He drew a knife from the pocket of his robe. "Is that a problem?"

"It's more than I expected."

"Then you will stay." It wasn't a question.

"Stay?"

"To help." He ran his knife along the package. Mist rose from the incision. He peeled back the lid, looked inside, then placed the package on the desk.

His hands trembled. "You must help me." He pushed it toward her, the top now cut away. Something shone within. "I am not able to do it." He raised his hands—withered, trembling. "Take it out for me. Please."

She folded the thousand-dollar envelope and slipped it into her bag. Then she stepped forward, reached into the package, and lifted out a stainless-steel cylinder. Moisture beaded on its sides, collecting around her fingers as she set it on the table.

"Dispose of that, please." He pointed to the empty package. "I do not like clutter."

She crumpled the insulated Tyvek and stuffed it into her bag.

"And now this." He turned to the stainless-steel cylinder. "Open it, please." He slipped into a padded chair, settling into the groan of pneumatic supports.

She gripped the stainless-steel lid, twisting till it came loose in a jet of dark mist.

"And pour it, please." He pushed a trembling hand toward the crystal decanter. "You must pour it into here. It needs to warm before I can drink it."

She set the lid on the table. A corona of mist formed at its base, spreading in white rays across the Lucite.

"But carefully, please. It mustn't be agitated once it is open."

A black stream slipped from the cylinder as she tilted it toward the decanter. The stream fell silently, fanning as it struck the crystal bottom.

"I usually have my attendant pour it. He took my car to the airport to pick up the package. When he tried to return, the police would not let him into the city."

She barely heard him. Her attention was on the decanter and the black thread that poured through its cut-glass sides. One moment it resembled liquid. Then it looked like falling sand—fine as onyx dust. But mostly it looked like nothing, a void, a gap in the physical world. She felt herself falling, as if the negative space within the crystal were compounding her exhaustion.

"Careful! You're spilling it!"

She straightened up as a teaspoon of spilled blackness turned to vapor on the Lucite. "Sorry." The cylinder gave a hollow thump as she returned it to the table. "I'll wipe it up."

"No. Let it go. It evaporates quickly." He pointed to the snifter while the spill vanished into mist. "Pour some into there."

She raised the decanter, held it to the glass, and poured three fingers of icy void. Vapor rose, filling the snifter.

"Bring it to me."

The front of his monitor came into view as she rounded the desk. A pinhead microphone and crystal speaker lay embedded in the plastic frame. Below them, a flat screen glowed with colors undimmed by the surrounding glare. Upon its surface, images stood stacked like comic-book panels. One frame held a grid of touch-activated icons. Another showed the empty foyer that she had passed through moments before. Each of the others displayed rectangles crammed with emaciated workers. Fitted with shunts, feeding tubes, and catheters, each figure recalled the specters she had glimpsed in the Southside foundry.

"Those people?" She looked closer. At the base of each shaved head, an implant lay cradled in a nest of Velcroed elastic. "Are they working for you?"

He didn't answer.

She studied him through the glare. His features looked faintly Indian. She considered his name: A. J. Summit. She had known many Indians who'd adjusted their names, modifying pronunciation and spelling to appeal to western ears and eyes. Sandhya became Sandy. Samir became Sam. Neelish became Neil. Those with names like Gati had to be more creative, but the practice was common enough to make her doubt the authenticity of a name like A. J. Summit. What if the initials weren't initials? Not *A. J.*, but *Ajay*. And what of the last name? Lose an *m* and you had *Sumit*. She knew that name. Ajay Sumit. She had seen it while researching fabrication plants in western India. . . .

She asked the question again. "These people . . . are they working in your factories?"

He pressed the snifter to his chest, steadying his hands as they warmed the drink. "They must look ghastly to you—all those tubes. But the procedure is actually a good thing, part of an adjustment that allows each worker to triple his income." He pressed his nose to the vapor that gathered in the snifter's bowl. He inhaled, drawing the mist into his nostrils.

She watched him, realizing that she was standing before the Holy Grail of her abandoned thesis. Ajay Sumit, the shadowy presence behind a propagation of non-sleep sweatshops.

Her heart knotted. "Those IV tubes." She winced, feeling the anxious exhaustion from halfway around the world. "You're giving these people drugs to keep them awake."

"No. Not giving. Removing. Those tubes are extracting peptides. Endogenous narcotics. The chemicals of natural sleep. They can be separated from the blood and spinal fluid. Someday, we hope to market them—make them available to people who can afford to savor the luxury of organic oblivion." Again, he put his face to the snifter, but this time he didn't inhale the vapor. This time he pressed his lips to the rim, leaned back, downed the liquid. Then he lowered the glass, lips trembling. "Our chemists haven't perfected the liqueur. There are problems. They've advised me not to drink it, but it's the only way I can sleep." He pushed the snifter into her hand. "More, please."

She returned the snifter to the table. "I want no part of this."

"I've paid you."

"Some things don't have a price."

"Everything has a price!" He gripped the sides of his chair, composing himself. "The workers have agreed to the procedure. They embrace it. They stay on for days . . . weeks at a time."

"I imagine you have quite a waiting list, workers standing in line, ready to snatch any vacancy."

"Yes. It's a terrific windfall."

"For whom?"

"Everyone. Management gets a maximized workforce. Labor gets a living wage."

"And sleep becomes a value-added byproduct?"

"No. Not yet. It's still in development. I shouldn't have started drinking it. Now I can't stop."

"Can't or won't?"

"I can't expect you to understand."

"Try me."

His mouth quivered, poised between continuing his story and commanding her to refill the snifter.

"You might be surprised how much I can understand," she said. "I might even be able to help you."

"You can help me by pouring the drink."

"That's not the help you need."

"There's no other help. No other escape." He turned toward the screen. "They've been chasing me for months. Mumbai, Hong Kong, London— wherever I hide, they come. I thought that watching them might provide hints of when they were coming, but they just keep working—on and on, with no warning until I feel their thunder. That's when I know I have to run. But no more. I'm through running. This time I stay where I am." He looked at the empty snifter. "Tonight I'll hide in their sleep, their deep sleep—beyond reality, beyond dreams."

She looked at the screen. "How can they come for you if they're working?"

"It isn't their bodies that come. It's something else—gathering shadows . . . booming darkness."

"And what will these shadows do when they find you sleeping?"

"I don't know. I don't want to know. If I'm sleeping, I won't know." He reached for the decanter. "Please. Help me. I'll pay you more if you want. Name your price, just pour it before—"

Nix's bones quivered with a welling tremor that seemed to spill from somewhere beyond the giant room. Floor and ceiling panels remained fixed within their frames. Decanter and snifter stood as before, unmoved atop the Lucite table. Yet Nix felt the tremors.

"They're here!" He turned to Nix. "They've found me." The pits of his eyes were impossibly black, like the stuff in the decanter: a total void, the absence of color, the negation of the physical world.

The rumble came again. Nix steadied herself on the table and turned toward the door that led to the service elevator. "It's coming closer."

He grinned, a forced twisting of the lips. "I suspect it's been causing confusion in the city. Explosions without fire, without smoke. The police should consider themselves lucky, don't you think? How lucky for them that they don't see what we see?"

"What we see?"

"You've seen the gathering shadows. I can tell. They've left their stain in your eyes."

It came once more: the tingling crackle, the quivering roar. And now she realized the reason for the vast, glowing room. For a man who fears an invasion of shadows, light is a tireless sentry. He had ripped out the walls, giving himself clear view of a shadowless domain. Darkness would not surprise him here.

He leaned against the Lucite, reaching toward the decanter. Perhaps he had resigned himself to pouring it on his own. Or maybe he intended to guzzle it unwarmed straight from the crystal. Either way, she had to stop him. She stepped forward, picked up the decanter, and backed away.

"Please." His hands closed on empty air. "Pour it for me. I'll pay you anything you want. I'll—" His eyes focused on something behind her.

She turned.

Across the room, a thread of darkness condensed in the glowing air, fanned out, and expanded into advancing waves.

"What is it?" she asked.

"The shadows of their dreams." He glanced at the monitor. "I took their sleep. I left their dreams."

Misty tendrils coalesced into human forms. Gaunt and emaciated, they pushed forward—shrouding the light as they spilled over the glowing panels.

He looked at the monitor, peering into the stacked frames. "See! No change! They just keep working. On and on."

In the center of the room, the advancing forms solidified until they resembled the racing bodies that she had followed into Hobbs Way. They crossed the room, approaching the Lucite table. Ajay Sumit sat rigid as they flowed around him. He gripped his chair with trembling hands, afraid to move, unable to speak.

Nix scanned the dark faces, gnarled hands, bleeding shunts—the dream images of people trapped in a waking nightmare. As one, they raised their withered arms. Empty hands clenched and opened, clenched and opened. She felt the heavy coldness in her own hands, and she realized what she had to do. She stepped toward them.

Sumit coughed. "What are you doing?"

She held out the decanter, offering it to a child with vacant eyes.

The springs of Sumit's chair gasped as he leaped to his feet, reaching out—but he was too late. The child's hands were already reaching for the crystal . . . and Nix was already letting go.

"No!"

What happened next was something she should have expected. The child's hands were no more substantial than mist. The decanter slipped through them, tumbled, and shattered against the floor.

Sumit grabbed Nix's shoulder. She pulled free, stepping back as the liqueur spread across the panels, forming a blackened starburst that sputtered and foamed. And then, as the spill evaporated, the ghostly shapes changed one last time. Sumit covered his eyes, but Nix kept staring, watching the skeletal arms become streamers. Faces angled into geometric rays. Chaos became symmetry. Colors bloomed. For a moment, the transformed figures fused with the evaporating liqueur. The air filled with rings and ovals and braided swirls—a mandala condensing out of mist and shadow. And then, with an alpha blast that rang deep in Nix's soul, the beauty exploded into streamers of light.

* * *

"They weren't coming for you." She stared at the shattered crystal. "They only wanted to make you give back what you'd taken."

Pneumatic supports sighed as Sumit collapsed into his chair. "God!" He spoke it more as a prayer than a curse: soft, breathy, full of awe. She turned to find him staring at the monitor. "And still they work," he whispered.

Footsteps approached, muffled, coming closer, rising through the partitioned stairwell until the door flew open and firefighters stormed into the room. They hurried toward Sumit and Nix. "Everyone out!" Their boots squeaked on the Lucite panels.

Sumit touched the screen. The display went dark. He lifted the monitor, folding the base so that it became a protective cover. His hands no longer trembled. Now his movements appeared sluggish—almost drugged—as if the single drink had begun taking effect. Nevertheless, his eyes flashed as he turned to Nix. "Tell no one," he whispered, tucking the closed monitor beneath his arm. "I'll pay you."

So that was it. He wouldn't stop here. He would continue as before—exploiting the workers, robbing their sleep, and, when necessary, appeasing their errant dreams with spilled liqueur. And now, to keep things neat, he intended to buy her silence, as if her integrity had a price.

"I'll contact you," he said. "Through the courier office. I'll make it worth your—"

"Now people!" Two firefighters grabbed Sumit's arm, leading him toward the stairs.

Another took hold of Nix. "You a courier?"

"Yes." She grabbed her helmet as he pulled her toward the door.

"You delivered something?"

She looked at Sumit and said, "I'm sorry." Then, to the firefighter: "It was a package. He asked me to open it. There was a decanter inside, but I jumped when I felt the tremor. I dropped it. It shattered." Again, she glanced at Sumit. "I'm sorry. It must have been very expensive."

He smiled as if he forgave her, but she saw his expression for what it was—a conspirator's grin. She had taken his offer. Like everything else in his world, her silence could be bought.

They wouldn't let her retrieve her bike. Instead, they whisked her through the lobby and onto a bus full of frazzled guests. Airbrakes sighed. The bus lurched forward, only to stop again as a black limousine cut across its path.

She sensed that Ajay Sumit was inside that sleek black car, riding alone, perhaps asleep in the folds of his saffron robe, temporarily safe within private darkness. . . .

She had once spoken to Ellen about the futility of railing against nonsleep sweatshops, an assessment that Ellen had echoed when Nix had tried ending her thesis with a carelessly thin "dream solution." Change could never be affected unless the people in power had an incentive to listen.

But now someone in power could be given that incentive. Ajay Sumit, temporarily safe in his stolen sleep, would awake to find that the price of Nix's silence was the adoption of her dream.

REVISION

Decanting Oblivion" got its start in March 2001, during a week when I played host to screenwriter Charly Cantor, who had come to town to collaborate on a shooting script of "Traumatic Descent."

During his visit, Charly grew fascinated with Pittsburgh, taking delight in the hillside neighborhoods and treacherously steep streets that meander through them, and the sidewalks that often turn into stairways when their angles exceeded 20 percent. We visited abandoned industrial sites and derelict bridges, some of them little more than I-beams atop stone abutments, and on his last day in town we rode the Duquesne Incline up the sheer face of Mt. Washington to look out over the V-shaped city, pressed to a point between the Allegheny and Monongahela Rivers.

In the end, I'm not sure which of us was more inspired.

I had been travelling extensively before Charly's visit—spending time in Italy, Paris, England, Ireland, Finland, Russia—exploring interesting locales when all the dramatic real estate I could ever need was right in my backyard.

I recall sitting with Charly in the terminal of Pittsburgh International, poring over maps of the city while he waited to board his plane. (Remember, this was March 2001, half a year before Homeland Security and the TSA made departure terminals off limits to people without boarding passes.) He wanted to be sure he knew the names of the neighborhoods we had visited, all the streets and landmarks, and when he took off, I went to work on a novelette set in downtown Pittsburgh.

The writing took time. It always does. The story required additional research and location scouting—not to mention hours of pedaling around on a bike, getting a feel for the story's central action. But by August, the manuscript was ready. I shared it with Bob Leman, then sent it off to *F&SF* and made arrangements to meet with editor Gordon Van Gelder at Worldcon that September to discuss possible revisions.

The meeting took place on September 3, and it was there that Gordon suggested a few points of revision, which I felt I could take care of within a week after returning home.

The convention ended on September 5, and the new version was ready the following Monday. I put it in an envelope, ready to drop it in the mail the next morning, September 11, 2001.

I didn't mail the manuscript.

It seemed to me that the last thing people needed after that day was a story about the convergence of third-world forces on a US city. Indeed, I almost discarded the manuscript completely. Why save it? It certainly wasn't salable. The world had passed it by.

Or had it?

That evening, the manuscript still in my briefcase, I went out to my back-yard to stand beneath the silent sky. It was getting dark. The first stars were out, unencumbered by contrails or the blinking lights of passing jets. It seemed as if the whole world were holding its breath, waiting for the long darkness.

A week went by.

I heard poet laureate and *Inferno* translator Robert Pinsky talking to Terry Gross on *Fresh Air*. "I have not felt like writing," he said, and I felt as if he were speaking for me.

"I would love to be the kind of person who responds immediately with eloquence and penetration," he went on. "I'm not. I tend to write about things after they've happened by quite a long time."

At first I felt soothed that he too did not feel like writing, but then I thought about the rest of his comment, about not being able to write about things until long after they had happened. That sent me back to the story, and when I reread it I was surprised at how prescient some of it seemed, with its reference to suicide bombers and ground-zero blasts.

I modified some references, added lines about Homeland Security and out-of-work flight attendants, and tried giving the characters and narrator an awareness of things that had happened in the world beyond their story.

The revision finally went in the mail in late October. Then, in November, two things arrived that convinced me I'd done the right thing.

One was an issue of *F&SF* containing a post 9-11 editorial calling on writers to reflect on the changing world. Gordon Van Gelder concluded that editorial by saying, "I'd love to see our genre come forth in this difficult time and build some bridges, foster some cultural understanding, make sense of the tragedy."

The other thing that arrived that month was a check and contract for the revised version of "Decanting Oblivion."

The novelette appeared in March 2003. It was well reviewed and generated some enthusiastic reader responses. A few months later it was included in Audible.com's *The Best of The Magazine of Fantasy and Science Fiction*.

One reviewer suggested that Nix would make a good series character, and she still might. One of these days, I hope to give it a try.

About the time that the March 2003 *F&SF* hit the stands, Robert Morrish contacted me from *Cemetery Dance*, asking if I'd be interested in submitting to the magazine. The request sent me back to my roots, and soon I was working on a story that incorporated the wayward kids of "Mrs. Halfbooger's Basement" and the canine horror of "Moon and the Devil."

Within a month, I sent him "Things."

THINGS

ONE: The Old Man Thing

Small, wiry, bespectacled—Zander wasn't the sort to put a person on guard. He knocked on the door and stood where the old man would see him. The porch light winked on. Zander squinted at the peephole and raised his hands, showing the blood. "I got hit!" His voice trembled, edging toward tears. "I was riding my bike. The car didn't stop. Please help!"

A bolt disengaged. The door jerked inward—stopping at the end of a chain. The old man peeked out. "You were riding your bike?"

"Yeah."

"Where is it?"

"Huh?"

"Your bike."

That's when Jake lunged from the shrubs and rammed the door. The safety chain snapped. The man screamed—no words, just spit and wind. He went down, striking his head as Jake leaped on top of him. Duct tape rasped. Jake tore a piece, slapped it over the man's mouth.

Why? the man said, speaking with his eyes. *Why are you doing this?*

Jake didn't see the voice. He was too busy taping the man's wrists. But Zander saw it, and for a second he just stood there, watching the old man's silent pleas until CJ shoved him from behind.

"Get moving, retard!" CJ was Jake's friend, Zander's enemy. "Move it!"

Zander nearly kicked the man's head before catching his balance.

"And give me those!" CJ grabbed the horn rims. "Don't want you losing these." He shoved the glasses into his pocket, then turned and closed the door.

Zander didn't need glasses. His eyes were good. Better than good. He was always seeing things that other people couldn't. But the glasses were for *looking*, not *seeing*: they made Zander *look* harmless, like a person you could open a door for after dark.

"Now get to work," CJ said.

Zander dashed down the hall.

The house was like many of the others they had invaded—dark, cluttered, smelling of age. A fluorescent light burned in the kitchen. Beneath it, a television sat on the counter, playing the news. On the stove, something simmered, steam escaping from a cocked lid.

Zander passed the kitchen and climbed the stairs. He didn't ransack drawers or closets when he looked for things, and he never broke stuff the way Jake and CJ did. He simply drifted, going through rooms, waiting for hunches to lead him to the hidden treasures that old people usually kept in their cold, dark homes. Sometimes the treasure was jewelry. Other times it was coins. But mostly it was paper money, curled into rolls or lying flat in envelopes. Whatever form it took, if it was in the house, Zander found it.

He came to a bathroom, paused, then slipped inside. The sink was old, two spigots: one for hot, the other cold. He turned them both on and pushed his hands into the flow, swinging them back and forth between the extremes. The cuts didn't look so bad with the blood washed away. But the deeper wounds kept oozing. He dried them on his shirt and looked toward the hall as something crashed downstairs. Jake and CJ were trashing the kitchen.

"Watch this!" CJ said.

Another crash.

Jake laughed.

"The TV," CJ said. "Smash the TV!"

Zander left the bathroom, crossed the hall, and entered a dark room that held a bed, dresser, two nightstands. That's when it came, the wordless voice that told him to get on his knees and reach beneath the bed. A moment later he found a box, pulled it out, flipped the lid. "Hey!" He reached inside. "Hey! Guys!" He removed an envelope, opened the flap. "Got something!" He was still staring at the money when Jake appeared at the bedroom door.

"Give!"

Zander handed over the cash as new sounds erupted from the kitchen, a thud followed by the *phooommf!* of an imploding picture tube.

"CJ's making too much noise," Zander said.

Jake counted the bills. "You want to tell him to be quiet?"

"Uh-uh."

Jake counted again. "There's, like, a couple hundred in here."

"But it's all there is."

"You sure?"

"Uh-huh."

"You're absolutely positive?"

Down in the kitchen, CJ screamed.

Jake and Zander found CJ standing at the foot of the stairs, looking terrified. "There's something out there!" He pointed into the kitchen.

A dog, Zander thought. *He thinks he saw a dog.*

"A dog!" CJ said. "A big freaking *dog*!" CJ hated dogs. "See it?" He pointed toward the back-door window. "On the porch!" There wasn't much to see through the glass, just thick shadows, stacked furniture, plastic sheeting.

"Don't see a dog," Jake said.

"It's there!"

Zander studied the shadows, squinting hard. "Not a dog."

"What?"

"Just a cat."

"Like hell!"

Jake crossed the kitchen, opened the door, snapped the light. A big tom sat on a chaise lounge, eyes glowing. Jake lunged at it.

The cat bolted.

"A cat!" CJ said. "A goddamn *cat*!"

The old man moaned from the front hall.

CJ turned to Jake. "Did we get what we came for?"

"Yeah."

"All right." He didn't look at Zander. He just turned and did his toughguy walk back into the kitchen. "Let's go."

The boys never left the way they came. Back doors were better for getaways, but Zander didn't leave yet. He backtracked to the front hall and knelt beside the man. "Will you be quiet if I take this off?" He fingered the tape. "Will you?" It was a strange request, given the racket Jake and CJ had made, but city people kept to themselves. A crashing TV might be nobody's business. Screams for help were harder to ignore.

The man nodded.

Zander pulled the tape.

CJ called from the porch. "Hey, retard!"

Zander hurried through the kitchen, out the back door, into the night.

TWO: The Dog-Lady Thing

"Down there," CJ said, "That's her." He pointed through the trees that lined the slope between St. Mary's School and Carnegie Drive. There, in the shadows of a gabled row house, an old woman stood staring at the ground.

"What's she looking at?" Jake asked.

"A dog," Zander said. "There's a dog pooping in the weeds."

Jake squinted. "I don't see it."

"It's there. She walks it all the time. Twenty . . . maybe thirty times a day."

Jake frowned. "I don't get it. You want our next *thing* to be a lady with a dog? I thought you hated dogs."

"It's not a *dog* dog. Not a *full-size*."

"Looks like a terrier," Zander said.

Jake snorted, spit a goober. "I still can't see it."

"It's there," CJ said. "It's some kind of midget dog—like the retard said."

Zander hated when CJ called him the retard. It didn't matter that it was true. It was just the way CJ said it, like it was something perverted.

"I think it's like one of those chi-ha-was."

"Chihuahua," Zander said.

"Not talking to you!" CJ spit a goober at Zander, then went back to watching the dog lady. "She walks that little dog all the time." He advanced toward the edge of the slope, standing tall in the snow-white Reeboks that he had bought with the last of the old man's money. "They go up and down the street. Then they go back inside. Then they come back out and do it again. It's like she's got OCD or something." He turned to Zander. "That's like a mental disease, in case you didn't know."

Zander let it pass. He was busy watching the little dog.

"The dog," CJ said. "It's named Mungee."

Zander stepped forward, descending the slope until he came to a leaning poplar. Within seconds he shinnied up to the first branch—a perch of golden leaves that gave him a clear view of the lady, her dog, and the line of row houses. The dog finished its business and started walking, sniffing the weeds that grew along the sidewalk, apparently looking for something.

"You should see what he does when she says its name," CJ said. "He goes totally spaz."

Zander laid his head on the branch as a car whooshed by below.

The people inside were strangers, barely visible through the tinted windshield, but he saw them—father and son. The kid was in a child seat, the kind that faced backward. Zander, who had never ridden in such a thing, felt the contours against his back—the tactile impression of a life he had never known, would never know. Then, with a whoosh, the car was gone. He shivered, wondering how he could see and feel such things, wishing he could trade those skills for ordinary ones—like reading words and numbers as well as he could faces and shadows. He wished he could tell the difference between *d*'s and *b*'s, or *S*s and *5*s. Those skills mattered. Without them, everyone treated you like you were mental.

"She lives in the end house," CJ said. "Her next-door neighbor is never home. We can do it, man. It'll be our easiest *thing* yet."

Thing was CJ's word for what they did. He didn't call it home invasion. Each incident was just a *thing*.

"We should ask Zander," Jake said. "See if he thinks there's—"

"Hell with Zander. We'll do this one for the Mungee dog."

"Steal the dog?"

"No . . . not steal it . . . mess with it." CJ's voice went soft and dreamy, like it was rising from some deep, secret place. "I just wanna . . . like . . . put him in the disposal or something. Or maybe the microwave." He paused, savoring the image. "Yeah. That'd be cool."

Zander wished he could muster the courage to look into CJ's eyes when he said those things. Maybe then he would understand why CJ hated dogs so much.

"Hey! Watch this," CJ said. "She's going to make him go spastic."

The lady gripped the leash as Mungee shoved his head into a stand of grass. He shivered. His belly pulsed—in, out, in, out—like he was sniffing at something.

The lady watched. Then, with a smile, she said: "Mungee! Mungee!" Her voice was high, almost bell-like in the evening air. Zander could hear her as clearly as if she were standing beside him. "Mungee! Mungee!"

The dog shot forward and vanished into the weeds, plunging so deep that Zander thought the little thing might nail his pointy nose right into the ground. But a moment later Mungee jerked back, shaking his head, grinding his jaws around a twisting shadow. Then he did a little dance, a head-shaking hop that aligned his prey with his jaws, and it was then that Zander saw what the little thing was eating.

Jake didn't see it. Neither did CJ. All they saw was a spazzing dog.

"See that!" CJ said. "He goes nuts! It's too freaking weird!"

But the too-weird part had nothing to do with little Mungee's dance and everything to do with what he had just eaten. A worm! Not a smooth-bodied nightcrawler, but a big lumpy thing with twitchy legs and shiny head—a millipede that gave a thousand kicks as little Mungee flipped it lengthwise and—*chomp!*—crushed it with a force that, ounce-for-ounce, looked about as nasty as anything Zander had ever seen.

"Listen!" CJ said. "Here's what I'll do. Tell me if this isn't cool."

Mungee shook his head, turned, and pulled the lady back toward the house.

"Here's how this thing's gonna go," CJ said. "We get inside, you tape the lady, and I'll scream that little dog's name. And while he's spazzing, I'll throw him in the toilet." He was talking too loud, the way he always did when he got excited. But it didn't matter. Even though Mungee and the old lady were right across the street, they didn't seem to realize he was talking about them. They just went about their business, climbed the steps to their townhouse, went inside.

"I'll throw him in the toilet! I'll slam the lid and go, 'Mungee! Mungee!'" He gave the name a ragged falsetto—a parody of the old woman's bell-like song. "'Mungee! Mungee!' And I'll flush the toilet. Over and over. 'Mungee! Mungee!' Until I drown the fucker. Then I'll take a dump on his pipe-clogging ass!"

Jake frowned. "You're sick, CJ." But his tone said something else, something like: *CJ—you're a genius!*

"Naw," CJ said. "I'm not sick. Sick is right over there."

Zander sensed a shift in CJ's attention.

"Sick," CJ said, "is your retard brother humping that tree!"

Zander heard CJ advancing, but he didn't try getting away, didn't even brace himself. He couldn't do any of those things because his attention was suddenly fixed on the front window of the woman's home. He squinted, peering into the darkness beyond the parted curtains. Something was there, a danger that was at once big and small, something that made it clear that the dog-lady thing was a bad idea, a terrible idea, the worst idea CJ had ever had!

I have to tell them! Jake and CJ! I have to tell them both. But in that instant CJ grabbed Zander's leg, yanked him out of the tree. WHOMPH! His breath left him, escaping so fast it seemed to turn him inside out.

"C'mon, gimp!" CJ headed up the slope. "We got to get you ready."

Zander looked at Jake. Not that it did any good. Jake just ignored him, following his best friend toward the clearing at the top of the hill, out into the last rays of setting sunlight.

CJ kept walking. "You knock on her door and tell her you're an epileptic. Tell her you had a seizure. You fell on the sidewalk and cut your hands."

Scabs still covered Zander's palms from when CJ had cut them to make it look like he had fallen from his bike. Zander didn't want to be cut again, and he most definitely didn't want to go into the old woman's townhouse—not after seeing what waited inside.

"An epileptic is just like a retard," CJ said. "You won't even have to fake it."

The situation was hopeless.

Zander realized that the best thing was to run away. But where? Down the slope wouldn't work, since the hillside ended at a retaining wall—twelve feet straight down onto the asphalt of Carnegie Drive. The only way out was back up the slope, past CJ, through the wooded lot, and out along the gravel path that led to the oval track behind St. Mary's School. Zander sometimes walked that track late at night when he couldn't sleep. It was a place where he could get away, follow his own footsteps, pretend he was going somewhere . . . pretend he was free. But there would be no pretending with Jake and CJ in hot pursuit, and even if he kept running till he reached home, Jake and CJ would still catch him. With his mom working late, home would be just another dead end—only slightly more promising than the sudden drop toward Carnegie Drive. Still, it was better than what waited inside the old woman's home.

CJ called again from the top of the slope. "C'mon, retread!" *Retread* was a joke—*retard* with jumbled letters. "Hurry up. We got to work on your disguise."

Zander climbed the slope, waiting until the ground leveled off. When it did, he darted to the left, making his break for home.

CJ bolted after him.

In a fair race, Zander might have made it, but his ribs hurt, bruised from his fall. And just as he reached the gravel path that led to the street, CJ rammed him from behind, sent him flying. He landed hard, face slamming gravel. When he stopped moving, spread eagle at the end of a bloody skid, the whole world seemed to be in pain.

"This works!" CJ walked around him. "We can use this." He tugged Zander's arm, turning him over, looking at his face. "This is good. Looks like you had a fit, fell down, bashed yourself up." CJ pulled the horn-rim glasses from his pocket. "You'll need these too."

Jake just stood there. Some big brother he was. He wouldn't even look at Zander. He just snorted and spit a goober, as if his snotty nose were the only thing happening.

That's when Zander realized what he had to do. The idea came all at once, a full-blown plan for getting back at Jake and CJ—a payback so sweet that it almost made him laugh out loud. But he couldn't do that. Laughing would give it away. So he bit his cheeks, sat up, and covered his face so they couldn't see him smiling.

THREE: The Jake-and-CJ Thing

"I fell."

Silence.

The old lady's door remained closed.

"I'm, like, epileptic! I had a seizure!" He looked straight at the peephole, wiping blood from his nose. He knew the lady was in there, looking out while he shivered on her front porch. "Help me, please!" Standing there in the porch light, hidden from the street by overgrown ivy, he realized that he had never spoken with more conviction. "Please, help me!"

Another moment passed, and then, slowly, the lock snicked. The door opened, stopping at the end of a chain. The woman stood within the gap, one hand on the knob, the other cradling Mungee. The little dog looked incredibly small, all eyes and mouth. The eyes stared. The muzzle twitched. Teeth flashed.

"*Epilessia?*" The woman spoke with an accent, and Zander had just enough time to wonder if she had understood any of what he had said when Jake leaped against the door.

WHAM!

The chain broke.

The door flew back, slamming the woman with a bone-cracking thump. She screamed. The dog remained silent, staring wide-eyed as the woman fell. And then Jake leaped forward, preparing to tape the lady's mouth. But he didn't get the chance. As he tore the tape, Mungee reared up and chomped his thumb. Jake reeled, spinning through the room, flinging his hand, trying to make Mungee let go. "CJ!" He slammed the dog against the wall, but the little jaws held on. "*Help!*"

CJ ran inside, leaping past the woman.

"Get him off me, CJ! Get him off!"

The woman scowled at Zander. He was still in the doorway, backing away. "Sorry," he said. "They made me."

She got up, pushed him back, slammed the door. The deadbolt clicked.

Zander had not envisioned it this way. All he had wanted was to see the look on CJ's face when he glimpsed the horror in the old woman's home. But now CJ and Jake were gone, trapped behind the slammed door, locked in by the dog-lady who let her midget terrier eat worms and who spoke a language that didn't even sound like English. And now there was only one thing to do.

Zander ran.

The horn rims flew from his face as he leaped off the porch. He kept going, down the stairs, into the street. A car blared. Tires squealed. Zander leaped, throwing himself against the retaining wall that abutted Carnegie Drive. A car window whirred down. An angry face leaned out. "Goddamnit! What are you—*retarded*?"

Zander gripped the wall stones, digging his fingers into the chinks, climbing straight up to the leafy slope behind the school. And there he stopped, looked back. A light burned behind the woman's parted curtains, casting shadows . . . strange shadows. CJ had been wrong. The woman didn't have a dog named Mungee that she walked over and over twenty times a day. Instead, she walked different dogs—dozens of them—each with the same pointy teeth, killer instinct, and voracious appetite. Now, looking through the window, Zander saw packs of tiny dogs advancing from the corners of the room while Jake and CJ begged the old woman to let them go. But the woman just smiled . . . smiled and licked her lips . . . smiled and spoke the name that Zander now realized was not a name at all. Unable to hear her bell-like voice, able only to read the vowels in the movement of her lips, Zander saw that she was not saying *Mungee! Mungee!* She was saying something different. Not completely different. Just a little. Like the difference between *retard* and *retread*.

She said it twice: "Munga! Munga!"

It wasn't a name. It was a command.

The dogs responded.

Throughout his hapless life, Zander had never delighted in the sight of another person's pain. True, he had done bad things for Jake and CJ. He had hurt people, but only out of fear of being hurt himself. And so, as the dogs leaped into action, Zander realized that he needed to turn away, avert his eyes and cut a quick course home. He would clean his wounds and wait for his mom to get off work. By then he might look almost presentable. Not perfect, but no worse than usual. And when his mom asked what had happened, he would tell her he had fallen from a tree and tripped on gravel. And when she asked about Jake, he would just say that Jake was with CJ.

Tomorrow, life would be a little brighter. Not perfect, but better than it had been with Jake and his bully friend. And there was no point messing up that brighter life with memories of what a pack of attack-mode dogs could do to a pair of trapped boys. The smart thing to do was look away.

The smart thing!

Zander snorted, cleared his throat, spit a goober. Since when did a retard have to do the *smart* thing?

He watched the window.

"Munga! Munga!"

The dogs lunged, scrambling forward, climbing atop one another as CJ and Jake turned and bolted for the closed door. Dogs climbed CJ's legs, grabbed his windbreaker, and swung like acrobats as CJ stumbled out of sight, momentarily hidden as he passed behind the curtain. Then he was back, falling against the window, clawing the glass, staring toward the slope. Zander read the fear in his eyes. *Dogs!* the eyes said. *Fucking dogs!* His terror widened as the dogs scuttled over his shoulders and dropped onto the window ledge. *The house is full of dogs!*

Zander shivered. Not a bad shiver. The good kind. And the shiver deepened as the dogs on the ledge converged on CJ's face—clawing, biting, rending. CJ recoiled, got tangled in the curtain, and toppled. The curtain went with him, snapping at the rod, fluttering like a falling banner to reveal Jake struggling to open the door. A half-dozen dogs had taken hold of his hands. He shook them, looking like a man with heavy gloves—gloves with dog-shaped fingers that broke away one by one: *Snap! Snap! Snap-snap-snap!*—leaving each dog with a worm-sized meal, leaving Jake to fumble at the deadbolt with just his palms.

FOUR: The Zander Thing

Had he seen those things?

Had he been close enough to make out all those details? Or had he imagined them? And if so, did that make the seeing any less real?

There was one way to find out. He could cross the street again, go to the window, cup his hands, look inside. But now a different urge overtook him, a sense that something precious was waiting up the slope and beyond the gravel path. He did not know yet what this new thing was, but it was there. And it was his.

He turned and ran: up the slope, across the path, and onto the cracked sidewalk that led toward home. His arms tingled. He raised his hands, spreading his fingers against the rushing night, catching the wind that blew against his palms. That was it. The thing he felt was the empty night itself—a night where Jake and CJ no longer existed.

He spun in place, stretching his arms to the sky, reaching high to claim his freedom.

DERELICTS

The Sixties are often cited as a decade that challenged conformity. And they did, in some ways. But those years were also marked by spreading homogeneity, evident in the bedroom communities that sprang up around major cities, displacing the family farms that had once dominated the American landscape. But sometimes, after the farms were paved over, the old houses remained.

In 1968, I discovered a derelict house in a tangled valley a quarter mile behind my home. It stood midway down a slope, partly buried in the hillside. A portion of its roof was gone, but its interior remained intact: floors, stairways, empty rooms. My friends and I hung out in it through the fall, abandoned it when winter came, and returned to the site in the spring only to find that it had been bulldozed to make way for a new development.

A few years ago, I found myself thinking about that house while driving the north-south corridor of freeways, highways, and back roads that lead to the school my daughter was attending in North Carolina. Occasionally, the roads cut past abandoned houses, dead-looking things with half-gone roofs and empty windows. But one was different, dark but intact. I began watching for it each time, noting the weeds that overtook its walk in summer and the unmarked snow that surrounded it in winter. Then, one night, passing it late, I thought I saw a light in an upstairs window—a fleeting flicker, there and gone.

That night, with the radio off and cruise control on, I tended the spark that would become "Flames."

FLAMES

Seth dreamed he sat beside a fire, holding his hands to the flames, trying to dispel a deep chill that permeated his soul. *I need to get closer*, he thought, though the flames already curled around his palms, scorching his hands until they bubbled like roasting peppers. He felt no pain, only the cold that wouldn't go away. And it was then, as he realized he was dreaming, that he awoke to find himself lying in the dark backseat of Bobby Tyson's Cobalt, legs folded against the front seat, head pressed against the door.

He sat up, saw snow on the windshield, and Renee Wagner slumped in the front passenger seat, face glowing in the dashboard lights. Beside her, where Bobby should have been, the driver's seat held only muffin crumbs and an old Pepsi stain.

"Hey." Seth touched Renee's shoulder.

She flinched.

"Renee." He shook her. "Where's Bobby?"

She pulled her head from the window. "What?" She blinked, coming awake. "Are we stopped?"

"Looks that way."

She rubbed her temples. "I feel like crap." Her breath smelled of buttered rum. "Remind me of this the next time Bobby packs a thermos."

"Yeah." Rum rarely gave Seth headaches, but this time he had a killer. "So what's going on? Where are we?"

Something moved outside, a shadow rising beyond the headlights, visible through the side windows—a man in a ski mask.

"Jesus!" Renee sat up, startled.

But it was only Bobby, the high beams illuminating his lanky frame as he studied the ground. He was there for a moment. Then he stepped away, out of sight beyond the snow-covered windshield.

"Man!" Renee said. "Don't tell me we're stuck."

Seth fumbled with the window crank, lowered the glass, and leaned into the falling snow. "Hey, Bobby!"

Bobby stepped back into view.

"What're you doing, Bobby?"

"Digging!" He turned his flashlight toward Seth, blinding him with the beam. "Clearing snow from the wheels."

"Where are we?"

"I'll tell you. Get back inside. Stay warm."

Seth slid back into the seat, shutting out the cold while Bobby rounded the car, waving as he passed the windows. Then he slipped and fell against the raised trunk.

"Is he loaded?" Seth asked.

"No. He didn't drink. He's just a goof."

"And you're sure he's not your boyfriend."

"No, Seth. Nothing's changed. He's just my ride home." She leaned sideways, looking between the seats. "I'm glad you're riding along this time." Her voice was warm, hinting at possibilities.

Seth considered saying something clever, but then Bobby slammed the trunk, drawing Renee's attention to the scene beyond the rear window. "Jeez! This sure isn't the interstate."

The view through the rear window was all barren trees, snow-covered road, tire tracks filling with snow.

The door opened and Bobby climbed in. "Cold out there!" He snapped off the flashlight and threw it onto the dash.

"Bobby," Renee said. "Where are we?"

Bobby pulled off his ski mask, tangled hair crackling with static as he put the car in reverse. "Not sure." He hit the gas. Treads spun without catching. "All I know is we're stuck." He shifted to forward, then to reverse again. The car revved, going nowhere.

Seth leaned forward. "Where's the interstate, Bobby?"

Bobby shut off the engine. "Not sure." He shifted in his seat, the dashboard lights hazing in his scraggly beard. He wasn't a bad-looking kid. He just didn't seem to know the first thing about razors and combs. And his interpersonal skills, which made him a hit in Internet chatrooms, were little help in the offline world. "There was a roadblock. I had to take a detour." He didn't look at Renee as he spoke, but he leaned toward her, gesturing with a gloved hand that came close to touching the knee she had resting on the center island. It was clear he wanted to be more than a friend who drove her home each Thanksgiving. He just wasn't sure how to bridge the gulf that stretched between them.

"Traffic was backed up for miles. The radio said it was a jackknifed tanker. I figured we could do a detour. I tried waking you guys, but you were both out cold. Guess it was the rum."

Renee opened her cell phone.

"That won't work," Bobby said. "I already tried mine. There's no signal."

Renee put the phone away and zipped the lightweight windbreaker: warm enough for North Carolina, worthless against the West Virginia cold. "I'm freezing, Bobby. Put the engine back on."

"I really shouldn't. There's not much gas."

"Christ!" Seth zipped his nylon hoodie. He had to take a piss but didn't feel like announcing it—not yet anyway. "This just gets worse, doesn't it?"

"No. Maybe not," Bobby said. "There's a service station five miles back. Me and Renee could stay with the car. You could—"

"No way," Renee said. "He'll freeze."

Bobby untied his scarf. "He can take my coat. The station's one of those all-nighters, like a BP. You can't miss it if you stay on the road."

"I say we just stay here," Renee said. "Stop the next car that drives by, hitch a ride with them."

Seth took another look out the rear window. "Road doesn't seem to get much traffic. I think our best bet is to get out and push."

"I tried that," Bobby said. "We'd be wasting time." He seemed about to give the BP suggestion another try, but instead he frowned and retied his scarf. "All right. Tell you what. Maybe there's another option." He took his hat and flashlight from the dash. "I saw something when I was outside." He snapped on the beam and shined it across the road. "Over there. You can see a house from those trees. We could knock on the door, use the phone, get warm." He glanced at Renee. "What do you think?"

"I think it's late to go knocking on doors," Seth said.

"And I'm not talking to you!"

Renee frowned. "Jesus, Bobby!"

"I'm just saying, unless he walks to the BP, the house is our best option." He took his keys from the ignition. "You'll both want to get out my side. The snow's not so deep here." He clipped the keys to his belt, letting them dangle as he pushed his door open. "Come on." He leaned toward her, extending his hand. "This way."

She held back. "Maybe me and Seth can wait here."

"Seth can do what he wants, but I'm not leaving you to freeze." Wind gusted, blowing snow onto the front seat. "Come on, Renee." His hand trembled.

She looked back at Seth. "Are you coming?"

"Not sure."

She held his gaze a moment longer, speaking with her eyes: *You have to!* And then Bobby grabbed her hand, pulling her out over the cup holders and gear shift in the center island. A moment later she was gone, standing beside Bobby in the gusting wind. Bobby put his arm around her, an awkward move that seemed to catch her off guard. "Got to keep you warm, girl." He pulled her close. "Don't want you freezing on the way down." Then he started walking, leading her away, the two of them making tracks in the unbroken snow.

Although Seth had known Bobby and Renee since high school, he hadn't paid much attention to either of them until they all became freshmen at the University of North Carolina. Then for a short time they were friends of convenience, three strangers sharing a common background until Renee pledged a sorority, Seth joined the swim team, and Bobby transferred to the pharmacy school at Campbell University. After that Bobby was only seen on the UNC campus when he dropped down to pick up Renee at the start of Thanksgiving break.

Seth generally didn't go home at Thanksgiving. With his parents separated and his only brother serving an extended tour in Iraq, it had seemed less complicated to stay on campus. But this year was different. His folks were back together, his brother was home, and hitching a last-minute ride with Bobby had seemed like a good idea.

Now, Seth wasn't so sure.

He watched Bobby and Renee walking away. Then, realizing he had nothing to gain by sitting in the cold, he opened the door and climbed out.

Bobby looked back, grinning across the arm that still gripped Renee's shoulder. "Coming with us after all?"

Seth slammed the door. "Nowhere else to go."

Bobby turned back around. "You'll see it in a sec." He leaned close to Renee, breath misting around her. "It's just past these trees."

Seth looked at the ground, noting the condition of the snow: smooth, unbroken, no footprints other than the ones they were making now. It didn't figure, but he kept walking, rounding the trees as Bobby swung the beam of his flashlight toward the bottom of the trail. The house stood a few hundred feet away, silhouetted in a forest hollow, so dark that Seth wondered how Bobby had noticed it while working on the car.

"Watch where you walk." Bobby kicked the snow. "This trail's overgrown." Another kick. "There's roots and stuff. Don't trip."

Seth pulled alongside Renee as Bobby led her past the remnants of a fence, rotted and leaning beneath knee-high drifts. Beyond it, the house stood silent and cold: covered porch, dormer windows, snow-capped chimneys.

"No smoke," Seth said. He stopped walking and looked around, sensing the emptiness. "There's no one here."

Bobby kept walking, leading Renee across the porch, calling out when he approached the door. "Hey!" Bobby knocked. "Anyone home?"

Seth looked up at the windows, no light or movement in any of them. "It's abandoned," he said.

Bobby tried the knob. "Unlocked." He leaned in. "Anybody home?" He stepped inside, shining his beam onto a wall switch beside a flight of stairs. He walked toward the switch, slapped it: *click!* The hall stayed dark. "No power."

Seth moved inside. Even without heat, the stale air felt warm. "Tell you what." He stepped toward Renee, who had taken a seat on the stairs. "I'll do it. I'll walk to the BP."

Bobby unzipped his coat. "Now you're talking!" He pulled his arms from the sleeves, revealing the cable-knit sweater that he had been wearing in North Carolina. The coat had evidently come from the trunk of the car.

"What about that flashlight," Seth asked, taking the coat. "Do I get that, too?"

"Are you leaving now?"

"No." Seth wrapped the coat around Renee. "Not just yet."

"Then you don't get the flashlight yet." Bobby stepped back into the foyer where he closed the door, shutting out the wind. "Let me look around." He started down the hall. "You guys stay here. I'll be back."

Seth watched him go. *He's too confident.*

The stairs darkened as Bobby retreated down the hall, leaving Seth and Renee sitting in the gray glow of the front-door window.

"Moonlight," Seth said, looking at the glass. "Storm's passing."

"I guess that's good." Renee leaned forward, shaking snow from her hair. "But I still feel like crap." She sat back, folded her arms beneath the coat, then leaned against Seth. "Does this place smell funny to you?"

"Yeah. Sooty."

"If there're fireplaces, we can light a fire. Get warm."

"Yeah. We could do that. If there's wood and kindling. And matches."

Bobby called from down the hall. "I found the kitchen." A cabinet banged open. "There's food. Crackers and chips. And wine."

Renee leaned against the banister. "Bring the crackers."

"Wine?"

"God, no! That swig of your rum drink did me in. Just crackers." She went back to leaning against Seth, snuggling close to get warm. "I'd like a fire." She set her head on his shoulder. "I could go back to sleep if we had a fire."

"Yeah. Something tells me that's the idea." He looked back along the stairs. "See something?"

"No. Just thinking." It was adding up now: the car in the snowdrift, the quiet country road, the abandoned house. *We're not here by accident. It's been planned.* He stood up.

"What's wrong, Seth?"

More noise from the kitchen: a cabinet closing, a drawer clattering open. "Hey!" Bobby called. "There's cheese!"

Seth set a hand on Renee's shoulder. "Stay here. Keep talking to him. I'll be right back." He started up the stairs.

"You want some cheese?" Bobby called.

"No," Renee said. "Just crackers . . . and Tylenol."

Seth reached the second floor hall. Three doors. All closed. He opened one. It was a small room with a single window. *Bathroom.* He leaned inside. The air smelled funny, like paint or spray enamel.

Downstairs, Bobby kept talking. "Don't see any Tylenol, Renee."

"Aspirin?"

"No. I don't think so."

"Something for a headache?"

"No. But maybe you could drink something. You're probably dehydrated."

Seth made out a book of matches lying beside a candle on a shelf. *Convenient.* He struck a match, lit the candle, and looked around at the heavy fixtures—sink, toilet, claw-footed tub. It all looked a little too clean, or at least a little too white, as if someone had touched things up with fresh paint. He crossed to the toilet. There was water in it, but not much, just a small gray disk deep in the bowl. But there was more water beside the tank, a few gallons of it in a rubber bucket. *Too convenient.* He relieved himself, leaving the door open, not caring if Renee heard him. God, it felt good.

Downstairs, Bobby's footsteps clomped through the hall, returning from the kitchen. "No Tylenol or aspirin. But there's plenty of food." He reached the foot of the stairs. "Did Seth leave?"

"No."

Seth zipped up, tried the flush handle. It worked.

"What the hell? He's upstairs? Hey, Seth!"

The bathroom fell silent as soon as the commode drained, no sound of cycling pipes. The tank wouldn't refill on its own. That would need to be done manually, with water from the bucket.

Seth left the bathroom to see Bobby dropping an armload of food at Renee's feet. Crackers, chips, cheese—it looked like it had all just been purchased at a college town Food Lion. Then, more carefully, he set down a bottle of wine and raised the flashlight, shining it up into Seth's eyes.

"Hey, Seth! You can't—"

"What's going on here, Bobby?"

"On here? What do you mean *on here*?" He started up the stairs. "You said you were going to the BP."

Seth backed away, turned, and approached one of the doors farther down the hall.

"Hey, Seth. Come on, man. You should go now." Bobby stepped toward him. "Seriously." He touched Seth's shoulder, but Seth pulled away, pushing on the closed door and stepping into a clean room with a freshly made bed. Bobby tried pulling him back, but Seth held his ground, staying put as Renee came up behind them.

"Jeez!" She pushed past them, stepped inside. "Look at this." She crossed to the bed, set her hand on the comforter. "Jesus! I could wrap up in this right now."

Seth looked at Bobby, their faces close, almost touching. "That's the idea, isn't it, Bobby?"

"And there's a fireplace!" Renee moved to the foot of the bed. "There's wood in it."

"Wonder who put it there," Seth said.

"What do you mean?" She frowned. "Guys? What's going on?"

"It's a set up," Seth said.

Bobby tightened his grip on Seth's collar.

"I bet that car isn't even stuck in the snow, is it, Bobby?"

"Guys? Am I missing something?"

"I think we've both been missing something." Seth knocked Bobby's hand from his collar. "But I'm getting it now."

"Getting what?" Renee asked.

"The big picture." Seth stepped into the center of the room. "A lonely guy who finds an abandoned house. But not tonight. He doesn't find it tonight. He finds it weeks ago."

"You mean Bobby? You're talking about Bobby?"

Bobby stood stone still, arms crossed, flashlight shining up along his face, jaw clenching and unclenching like a guttering flame.

He's burning, Seth thought. *On fire inside . . . ready to explode. I should stop now.* "You fixed it up. Not much, though. You only needed to work on one room . . . a bedroom—"

"Enough!" Renee said, her tone making it clear that she saw where Seth was going. "That's enough!"

"No," Seth said. "Not yet. Because here's the part I'm just now figuring out." He kept staring at Bobby. "You needed Renee to fall asleep."

"You're crazy," Bobby said. "Frigging crazy!"

"Am I? Or is it possible that a pharmacy major would know just the thing to spike a thermos of hot rum."

"You saying he drugged us?"

"Don't listen to him, Renee. He's paranoid."

Seth pushed on. "But the plan wasn't to drug *two* people. You didn't know I was in the equation until you got to Charlotte and I asked to ride along. That put a wrench in things. You had to split the dose, give us each half. Then you needed to get rid of me."

The darkness closed in, pressing on Bobby and his glowing flashlight.

"There's no service station five miles back, is there, Bobby? And that car in the snow drift—" He turned to look at Renee. "Remember how he told us to get out his side. Maybe if we'd gotten out the other we'd have seen we weren't really stuck at all. Maybe all he did was—"

WHAM!

Bobby struck from behind, cracking Seth across the head, knocking him against the fireplace. A moment later Bobby was on top of him, pummeling until Seth kicked him away. The flashlight went flying, spinning past Renee, filling the room with reeling light until it came to rest beside the door.

"Jesus, Bobby!" Renee's voice echoed in the room. The flashlight was behind her now, throwing her long shadow across Seth as he pinned Bobby to the bed. "Jesus! Is that what happened?"

Bobby leaned back, eyes catching the light as he looked at her.

"Is it, Bobby?"

He just glared at her.

"Jesus, Bobby!" She turned in place, apparently on the verge of running from the room. "I think I'm going . . . I think I'm going to be sick."

Seth pulled Bobby to his feet. "Let's get out of here." He grabbed Bobby's keys, ripped them from the belt loop. "This time, I'll drive."

"No!" Bobby tugged free. "I'm not leaving."

Renee retrieved the flashlight, the beam swinging through the room as she turned toward the door. Bobby's face appeared momentarily in the light, red and streaked with tears. Then the room fell dark again, the beam slipping from view as Renee entered the hall. A second later she was on the stairs.

"You think you're so smart," Bobby said. "You think you know everything, but you have no idea!"

The front door opened and slammed. Renee was gone.

"No idea!"

Seth backed toward the door, feeling his way in the dark.

"No fucking idea!" Bobby was sobbing now.

Seth found the hall and kept moving, leaving Bobby alone in the dark.

With Bobby's winter coat draping her shoulders, Renee ran along the trail, the glowing disk of the flashlight beam gliding ahead of her as she returned to the snow-covered road.

Seth caught her at the top of the rise. He grabbed her shoulder. She recoiled, stumbling toward the car. "I know how you must feel," he said.

She paused beside the car. "Give me the keys. I'll drive. You push."

"We can't leave without him, Renee."

"Like hell we can't!" She grabbed the keys and opened the door. "Go on!" She tossed the flashlight onto the passenger seat and slid behind the wheel. "Push!" She slammed the door and started the car. The lights came on. "Son of a bitch!" She stared at the glowing dash. "The tank's half full!" Her voice came muffled through the raised window. "He lied about everything!"

Seth reached the front of the car as Renee hit the wipers. Her face emerged as the snow tumbled away. "Come on, Seth. Push!"

He set his hands against the hood but paused when he noticed the snow drift beside the right wheel. "Hold on!" He dropped to his knees and uncovered something beside the tire.

Renee opened her door, peered over the hood. "What the hell are you doing, Seth?"

"You've got to see this!"

She climbed out, bringing the flashlight as she stumbled around to kneel beside him in the snow. "What?" She steadied the beam. "Holy shit!" She leaned closer. "A jack? He jacked up the car?"

"Yeah. And we fell for it." He pulled himself up on the bumper. "We need a lug wrench to crank it down. It's probably in the trunk. That must have been what he was putting away when—"

"Screw the wrench, Seth!" She threw herself against the hood. The car rocked, toppled from the jack, thumped down inches from Seth's foot.

"Jesus, Renee!" He stepped back.

She walked out of the headlights, back to the open door. "Push the stupid car, Seth." She climbed behind the wheel and slammed the door. "Get us back on the road."

By the time he had his hands against the hood she was already in reverse and giving it gas. The tires caught. She spun away, doing a 180 into the center of the road before skidding to a stop. "Get in!" She cranked down the window. "Let's go!"

"Not yet." He leaned against the door. "We can't leave him."

She glared. "Easy for you. He wasn't going to—" Her voice hitched. She tried again. "You weren't the one he was going to rape." She shivered, turned away, covered her face.

"Wait for me, OK?" He squeezed her shoulder. This time she didn't recoil. "I'll only be a few minutes." He raced away, heading back to the dark house in the valley.

But the place wasn't dark any longer. Light flickered in the upstairs window, as if Bobby were igniting the wood in the fireplace. But then the light changed, growing brighter. A moment later, flames rose behind the glass.

"Bobby!"

A shape appeared at the window, a face wrapped in flame.

"Bobby!" He screamed it this time, his voice echoing through the valley. "*Bobby!*"

The face vanished, swirling back into the room as Seth ran toward the porch. He wasn't thinking now. Adrenalin propelled him inside, up the stairs to where the bedroom door stood closed against the cold. He threw himself against it, falling forward with a blast of inrushing air. Flames swirled before him, recoiling as the draft blew them back into the fireplace, leaving Bobby trembling against the floor, badly burned.

The stink of scorched flesh assaulted Seth as he moved closer. He zipped his hoodie around his nose and tried breathing through the collar. No good. The smell already coated his throat. "Bobby." He set his hands on the floor, drawing back when he felt something warm and sticky.

Bobby flinched. He raised his head, bringing it around until it was just visible in the glow of the grate's dying embers. "Bring her back." He grabbed Seth's wrist, fingers still hot from the fire, wet with weeping burns. "Please."

Downstairs, the door banged open. Renee called from the foyer. "Seth!"

"No!" Seth shouted back. "Don't come up here!"

But she was already on the stairs, footsteps coming closer until the flashlight beam entered the room, shined on Bobby.

Renee shrieked.

Seth pivoted, blocked the light, waved her away. "Go! Get help!"

She didn't need to be told twice. The room darkened again as she returned to the stairs.

Bobby coughed. "Bring her back!"

"She's going for help, Bobby."

"Not Renee." He stared at the fireplace. "Please." He trembled, going into shock. "Bring her back."

Strangely, the fire had burned nothing else in the room. Even the bed remained untouched. Seth grabbed the comforter and wrapped it around Bobby's shoulders, wincing as he felt cooked flesh shifting beneath the weight. "Jesus, Bobby. I don't know what—"

"Fire." He flinched, wiggling free of the comforter. "Make a fire!"

"Can't. There's no more wood." He moved the comforter back into place. "You're going to have to—"

"Out back!" Bobby rasped the words. "In the woodshed." His shivers deepened. "Please, Seth. I'm cold."

Seth leaned against the hearth, considered the request, realized it was probably Bobby's last. "Where out back?"

"Not far. You'll see." He closed his eyes. "Please!"

The weather had changed again, becoming windy, cloaking the backyard in sheets of blowing snow. Seth felt its full force as he rounded the house, facing into the gale to find an A-frame woodshed standing at the far end of the yard. A drop cloth cracked in the wind, rising and falling across a low stack of split pine logs. He headed toward it, running until his feet struck something hard. His knees buckled. He toppled forward, ground rushing toward him. He put out his hands to break his fall, but his palms passed right through the snow, slamming something sharp and gritty. He flopped onto his side, raising his hands to find them coated with ash and cross-hatched with cuts that were already oozing blood.

Snow billowed as he struggled to his feet, each move uncovering layers in the ground beneath him: first snow, then leaves, then ash. The ash rose as he moved, mixing with the snow to form a dark skid that followed him as he slogged back toward solid ground.

Turning in place, he saw that he was in a shallow pit about twelve-feet around. Stones lined its edges, jammed together, impacted beneath the snow.

A fire pit.

He looked back along the skid of leaves, charcoal, and ash. And there was something else, a cold spark amid the blackness at his feet. He picked it up, rolling it into his palm, drawing it close until he made out its amalgam-filled crown, enameled shaft, broken root. . . .

A human tooth!

He dropped it and backed away, noticing other shapes, some rounded at the ends, others curved like shards of pottery.

Bones!

Something popped behind him. He looked back to find that the wind had thrown the shed's drop-cloth door across one side of the A-frame, exposing a line of things that he hadn't noticed from across the yard: shovels and picks for digging, an ax for splitting wood, bundled fabric for kindling, and two five-gallon jerry cans. What did it all mean? What had happened at this place?

He trudged out of the pit, approached the A-frame, and grabbed an armload of split logs and a sheaf of kindling before returning to the house to find that Bobby had crawled out from under the comforter. The kid now lay prostrate on the hearth, hands inside the fireplace, gripping the hot iron grate.

Seth dropped the wood. "Jesus, Bobby." He pulled him away from the hearth, wincing at the sound the hands made when they broke free of the hot iron.

Bobby's eyes rolled. "Cold."

Seth couldn't believe the kid was still alive. "I'll light a fire. But you've got to stay back." He propped Bobby against the bed. "Stay there. I'll get this place warm."

He felt along the floor to retrieve the kindling, strips of cotton and denim tied together with coarse twine.

Shredded clothes.

He ripped a strip free and held it over the embers, blowing gently until the ashes flared and he saw the fabric's flowery print. And there was something else. He noticed it as he was ready to add wood to the flame.

Bloodstains.

He checked the other strips. More blood.

"Going out!" Bobby gasped. "Fire's going out!"

Seth threw on more kindling, letting it ignite before adding the wood. He had never been good at building fires, but this one caught quickly. A minute later, with the fireplace roaring, he turned back to find Bobby staring at the flames.

"We need to talk, Bobby."

Bobby stared past him, watching the fire.

"This house, Bobby. Whose is it? Talk to me, Bobby! Is this your place?"

"Mine?" A blood bubble formed and broke between his lips. He coughed, swallowed. "Not mine." Blood dribbled from his mouth. "I found it."

"And the pit out back—"

"Not mine. I didn't—" His voice hitched. "I didn't even know what it was. When I first saw it, it was covered with leaves."

"But you know about it now?"

"Yes," Bobby said. "It was his."

"Whose?"

"The man who lived here. A lonely man."

"Did you know him?"

Bobby looked at the fire. "No," he whispered.

"So how do you know *about* him? Was he here when you—"

"Gone. Burned. They burned him."

"Who?"

Bobby watched the fire.

"Bobby? Talk to me. Who burned him?"

"They did." The fire played across his face. "She told me." He seemed to gain strength as the wood ignited. "I didn't know anything. I didn't even know why I came here . . . why this place attracted me. I thought maybe I could bring Renee. But I was confused. Like him, lonely and confused. That's what she told me." His voice trailed off. "She told me everything."

"Who, Bobby? Who told you?"

"She did."

The fire swelled. Bobby's face brightened, the striations in his burned flesh standing out in bas-relief as he watch the flames.

"She came to me when you went back to the car." He seemed to be staring at someone beyond Seth's shoulder, a person who cast no shadow but whose movements were evident in the dappled patterns on Bobby's skin.

Seth turned, glancing back through the flickering air. What he saw sent him recoiling against the foot of the bed, struggling to catch his breath.

In the fireplace, a woman sat cross-legged amid the roaring flames.

"I started a fire," Bobby said, continuing his story. "And she came to me."

The woman shimmered, her body dispersing and reforming in the crackling light, her elongated eyes following Seth as he stood and backed away.

"That's right, Seth. You leave. I want you to go."

But the fire had other plans. It brightened, speaking with light and shadow, telling Seth to stay. Then it tilted forward, stretched a flaming foot over the hearth, and eased off of the grate and into the room.

There was a moment, as the form separated from the logs, when it ceased to resemble a woman. First the arms lost definition. Then the face and head guttered out, sputtered and smoked. In that instant, Seth almost dashed for the door. But then the woman reformed, standing erect with hands resting on her shoulders, fingers dancing in the updraft as she stepped sideways across the hearth. Behind her, more shapes emerged, stepping from the grate, entering the room.

By now Bobby had risen to his knees, reaching out with fused fingers as the flaming women gathered around him. Then they changed again, collapsing into raw fire, swirling inward for a final embrace.

WHOOSH!

The air filled with oily smoke, burning Seth's eyes as he fell back against the window, grabbed the handle, and tugged until a ribbon of wind gusted between sill and pane. The fire reacted instantly, recoiled in the draft, gathered its strength, and surged as Seth forced the window all the way up. In that instant he saw something ignite in the distance, red-and-blue flashers strobing beyond the roadside trees.

And then the room exploded.

The force hurled him into the night, flipping him, feet kicked against the sky. Flames spewed from the room. He fell through them, arcing down to strike the porch roof. Shingles cracked. So did bones. Breath flew from his lungs, leaving a pained vacuum as he tumbled over a rusting gutter and down toward an incline of drifting snow.

He dreamed he sat before a fire, a stone-lined pit roaring with gasoline-fueled flames. He reached out. His heart ached, cold and empty. If only he could get warm.

There were faces in the fire. The girls were back, coming for him, reaching with flaming fingers, engulfing him with the heat that each had denied him when he first brought them home.

"Not mine!" Seth tried pulling back as the flames swirled around him. "This isn't my dream!"

But it was now. He had been inside the house, and now the house was inside him.

It must have been that way for Bobby, too. Although the kid hadn't known the truth until the end, he must have felt the house's longing. Its loneliness had resonated within him, fueled his fantasies.

"But I'm not Bobby!" Seth struggled, pulling free of the dream. "I'm not like him." The words came from deep in his throat, gurgling out as he felt things closing around him. Then, from somewhere beyond the dream, a voice: "Seth! Can you hear me, Seth?"

He opened his eyes to a face of red-and-blue flame. It was Renee, cheeks and forehead strobing in the glare of emergency lights.

A man came up behind her, easing her away. "We need to lift him in."

Renee vanished. Seth felt himself moving, first upward and then head-first into the white bay of an ambulance. Other faces looked down, paramedics with cold eyes.

"Bring her back," Seth said.

They extended his arm, put in a line.

"Bring her back!"

A chill moved through him. He felt himself drifting, losing consciousness, and then she was there again, gripping his hand. Was he dreaming? He pulled her close and closed his eyes.

This time there was no fire in his dreams, no sense of cold, only warmth and the secure grip of Renee's hand as the ambulance flashed away along the snow-covered road.

REDISCOVERING HOLMES

Flames" first appeared in *Shades of Darkness*, an Ash-Tree Press anthology that debuted at the 2008 World Fantasy Convention in Calgary, which is where I first met Charles Prepolec and Jeff Campbell, coeditors of *Gaslight Grimoire*, an anthology of new Sherlock Holmes tales that also debuted that weekend.

I've always been intrigued by Holmes, first discovering him as a kid, then rediscovering him around the time that Nicholas Meyer struck gold with *The Seven Percent Solution*. But it wasn't until I heard Ash-Tree Press editor Barbara Roden reading her story "The Things That Shall Come Upon Them" at the *Grimoire* book launch in Calgary that I began realizing how much story potential remained in Conan Doyle's character.

The day after Barbara's reading, I met with Charles over a pint in the convention bar and listened as he spoke of his plans for a second *Gaslight* book, one in which writers would get to push the horror buttons more heavily than in *Grimoire*. The working title of that second book was *Gaslight Grotesque*, and Charles encouraged me to send him something if I was interested.

I agreed to consider it, wondering how many of the original Holmes stories I would have to reread in order to write a convincing narrative. The answer, it turned out, was all of them. But it was pleasant work, becoming reacquainted with the characters, learning the rhythms of their speech, and establishing a working knowledge of the interior of 221B Baker Street, where I had determined that virtually all of the story's action would take place.

"The Death Lantern" appeared in *Gaslight Grotesque: Nightmare Tales of Sherlock Holmes*, which debuted at World Fantasy in San Jose, October 2009. That's where Charles told me that he and Jeff were planning a third book.

Did I want to try my hand at another Holmes story?

This time, I didn't need to think about it. I started the story on the flight home. "The Executioner," my second Holmes story, is now available in *Gaslight Arcanum: Uncanny Tales of Sherlock Holmes*. It launched at World Fantasy in San Diego, October 2011.

I'm already eager to start work on a third.

THE DEATH LANTERN

I walked home from the station. The air felt cool, mild for December in London, and I soon settled into a steady pace—the kind that I have always found conducive to reflection. Soon memories rose, drawn by familiar landmarks: a corner pub recalling times with friends, a lamppost rekindling thoughts of secret rendezvous, a closed door renewing regrets for things that might have been. I savored them all, lost in my reverie until a sudden thickening of the air drew me back to the moment. I say *sudden*, although the change had surely been brewing for some time, settling around me until the night's mist hovered so close that I could no longer ignore it.

I had reached Baker Street, and here I paused beneath a lamp whose light formed a sphere in the fog. A second sphere hovered above an adjacent corner, while a third, considerably dimmer, waited farther off. It was as if the planets had descended to guide me home, but I no longer recognized the street. Indeed, as I pushed on, I became overwhelmed with a sense that I had lost my way.

The impression grew as I continued, and I soon wondered if I had gone too far, if perhaps I had walked past the flat and was now moving north toward Regent's Park. But then, as I turned to retrace my steps, I glimpsed the glowing oblong of the large bay window of 221B. I eased toward it, staring at an incandescent fog behind the glass, an intense yet muted light that gave the impression that the night's haze had permeated the room.

My friend was there, standing within the bay, face angled down, chin in hand. He seemed to be frowning, though there was no way to be sure, since he appeared only in silhouette.

I studied the scene, watching the figure turn and pace back into the room, and it was then that I realized what I was seeing. The bay was masked on the inside with hanging sheets, lit from within by a single source that lacked the hues of conventional light. "Electric illumination," I muttered. "What the devil is Holmes up to this time?"

Had I known, I might have turned around, slipped back into the fog, and returned to the station. As it was, I climbed the stairs and soon entered a sitting room so rearranged that I hardly recognized it. The chairs had all been stacked higgledy-piggledy against Holmes' desk. Only the settee remained in place, and on it sat a rather agitated-looking Scotland Yard inspector. I recognized him as George Lestrade, a man of little imagination but good intellect, who sometimes consulted Holmes on baffling cases.

Behind Lestrade stood a monstrous thing of wood, metal, and glass. I saw in an instant that it was the source of the room's illumination, but its proportions confounded me.

"Watson?" Holmes had looked up to find me standing in the doorway. "Back so soon?"

"It *is* the thirtieth," I said.

He touched a switch on the side of the contraption, dimming the harsh light before turning to raise the flame on one of the wall fixtures. Then he crossed the room to shake my hand. "It's good to see you, old friend."

"Great to be home," I said. "But I seem to be interrupting something."

"Yes." He leaned away. "It's been quite an evening." He turned, leading me toward the contraption. "Ever seen one of these?"

"Can't say I have."

"It's a Calibrigraphe, a moving picture machine designed by the late Great Calibri."

"The magician?"

"The same."

"I saw him perform once," I said. "He caught a bullet in his teeth, spit it onto a plate. We could have used such skills in Afghanistan." I laughed, stopping when neither Holmes nor Lestrade joined in. It was then that I realized I had missed something. "Excuse me. Did you say the *late* Great Calibri?" I glanced at Lestrade, then back at Holmes. "Calibri is dead?"

"No," Lestrade barked.

"Possibly," Holmes said.

Lestrade turned. "You *still* have doubts, Holmes?"

"A few." Holmes looked at me. "It's an intriguing case. Mrs. Calibri has already seen to the burial, but now the magician's creditors are hounding Scotland Yard, demanding that they reopen the case."

"Creditors hounding the Yard?" I asked. "Why not hound the widow?"

"I'm sure they would. After all, bookkeeping was her responsibility. But she's gone missing."

"Not completely." Lestrade stood. "We have it on good authority that she has boarded a transatlantic steamer, accompanied by none other than the Great Calibri—both traveling under assumed identities."

"So Calibri is alive?"

"It's all conjecture," Holmes said. "What we need is evidence, and most of what we have is in this machine."

"A moving-picture machine?"

"Indeed. It's a clever design, entirely portable. Two men can carry it, and it packs its own charge." He gestured to a black rectangle on the floor.

"Electric battery?"

"Yes. Two of Calibri's former shop workers saw to its charging. They were eager to assist, claiming they haven't been paid in weeks." He ran his hand along a pair of wires that connected to a box on the top of the table. "This is the lamphouse. It holds an electric light, powerful enough to project life-size images onto those sheets." He gestured across the room. "It also generates considerable heat, which is the reason for the vent between lamphouse and shutter assembly." He stepped toward the front of the table, where a frame supported two metal wheels, one above a projection lens, the other below. "And this is the film." He took hold of a loose end dangling from the lower wheel.

I bent close. "Smells of vinegar."

"Nitrocellulose."

"Guncotton?"

"The same chemical compound," Holmes said. "In a different form, but nonetheless combustible." He attached the end of the film to the upper wheel. "If it jams while playing, it can be ignited by the heat from the lamphouse."

"Sounds dangerous."

"Not when the machine is operating properly." He threw a switch. The upper wheel spun, collecting the film.

"So you've already watched the picture?" I asked.

"Yes, but I need to play it once more." The machine hummed, the film picking up speed. "The inspector and I have been studying the images. Unfortunately, we don't agree on what we're seeing."

Holmes turned off the power as the film slipped free of the lower wheel. He looked at me, lips drawn, eyes tense. "You must be exhausted. Shall I help you with your bag? See you to your room?"

"Now?"

"I think that would be wise. You can retire, leave the inspector and me to finish what we've started. Tomorrow, once you're rested—"

"I doubt I'll rest!" I exclaimed. "I must see this contraption in operation."

Holmes frowned. "I daresay that you may not rest ever again if you remain in this room." His voice took on a foreboding edge.

"Gentlemen!" Lestrade turned. "Might we proceed?"

I glanced at Lestrade, then back at Holmes. "Please. I have to stay. I'm far too curious."

Holmes resigned himself to my decision. "I can't force you, Watson. But if you insist on viewing the projection, might I suggest you pull up a chair. Some things are best taken sitting down." Then he set to work threading the film, working carefully as I dragged a chair from the back of the room.

"The projector has an automated shutter," Holmes said. "It's Calibri's own design, easy to set up, but temperamental." He leaned back from the machine, inspected his work, then spun the upper wheel to draw up the slack. "In addition to working as a projector, the device functions as a camera and a film processor. Thus, the Great Calibri was able to use it to record and evaluate his performances before presenting them in public."

"So this is a practice film?"

"It seems so." He threw a switch. A clatter rose, ticking like clockwork as Holmes threw a second switch beside the lamphouse.

Across the room, patterns shimmered on the hanging sheets. A chalkboard appeared, standing on an easel before a curtained backdrop. On the board, written in neat, back-slanting script, were the words:

Exploding-Bullet Catch
26 December 1900

"The trick is a variation of the old bullet catch," Holmes said, raising his voice above the clatter. "But it employs a nasty form of artillery, a projectile containing an explosive charge of tetryl and phosphorous."

"A bullet bomb?"

"That's as good a name as any. But whatever it is called, it generates wounds so disfiguring that the St. Petersburg Declaration banned it in 1868. That is to say, banned it for warfare, not for magic tricks."

I studied the chalkboard, and then, in a blink, it vanished, leaving an empty stage.

"What just happened?" I asked. "The chalkboard? Where did it go?"

"Carried offstage."

"Carried by whom? I didn't see—"

"The camera was turned off during filming. If you'd been watching closely, you would have noticed a shifting of the curtains, as if someone had just walked past them. But the slate isn't our concern. Keep watching, and note this man."

A figure appeared from the right, walking with his back to me, pushing a Chinese screen.

"The man positioning that partition is supposedly a discredited illusionist, one Guy Guignol."

"A mystery man!" Lestrade exclaimed. "No one knows who he really is."

The figure kept his back to us as he angled the partition.

Holmes continued: "According to Calibri's notes, Guignol is the trick's originator. Now brace yourself, Watson. This next sight is not for the squeamish."

Guignol turned, revealing a face that barely qualified as human. He had one eye, a flap of skin for a nose, and a lower jaw that ended in a stump near the top of his throat. A leather harness covered part of his face, although I could not tell if it was for structural support or merely to cover the exposed portions of upper jaw.

"According to the notes," Holmes said, "Guignol nearly died during his first performance of the trick."

In the Afghan War, I had seen faces cleaved with swords and shattered by ordnance. I had seen eyes gouged in combat, faces atomized by high-caliber rifles. But never had I seen a living countenance as ruined as the one that now stared at me from those hanging sheets. My breath raced out in fright as I looked at him.

"Hang on, Watson."

Guignol stepped forward, appearing to come right at me, his face growing larger until it blurred and slipped from view.

"The next sight is a bit more pleasing."

A woman entered, wearing a costume better suited for a brothel than a London stage. In one hand she carried a chair. In the other, a wine table. She placed the table behind the chair, then exited and returned with a brass spittoon. It was of ordinary design: flared top, narrow neck, wide bottom. But instead of placing it upright on the floor beside the chair, she set it on its side upon the wine table.

"The woman is Mrs. Calibri, the magician's wife, bookkeeper, and stage assistant."

"She's quite fetching."

"Yes. *Too* fetching, perhaps. Uncommon beauty has a way of causing uncommon trouble."

I expected him to elaborate, but in that instant Guignol reappeared, wheeling a rifle mounted on a heavy stand.

"Now all the pieces are in view," Holmes said. "Rifle, partition, chair, table, spittoon—all we need is the Great Calibri. And here he is!"

The pleated backdrop parted, making way for a tall man in top hat and cloak. He spread his arms, and in an instant Mrs. Calibri was behind him, catching the cloak as it slipped from his shoulders, accepting the hat as he swept it from his head.

"He looks a bit heavier than I remember," I said.

"The fruit of success."

"But you said he was in debt."

"Debt and penury do not always coincide, Watson. We will explore that later."

Calibri bowed and began speaking, gesturing first to the gun, then to the Chinese screen.

"The magician opens by explaining how the rifle will fire through the rice paper, blasting a visible hole to show the bullet's path."

"When I saw the trick, the rifle fired through a sheet of glass, smashing it to pieces."

"And I'm sure it was quite dramatic. But a bullet bomb would explode upon striking glass. Here the barrier must be paper."

Calibri gestured to the chair.

"Now he explains how he will sit on the chair, face the screen, and wait for the gun to fire. In that instant, he will catch the projectile in his teeth."

"Catch a bullet bomb?"

"So he claims."

"One that would explode if it struck a pane of glass?"

"Quite so."

"Then why won't it explode when he stops it with his teeth?"

"He explains that next."

Calibri folded his hands, striking an exotic pose.

"He claims to have studied the Oriental art of rapid motion, techniques that will enable him to move so fast that the bullet will not discharge until he has redirected it into the spittoon."

"Redirected it?"

"Spit!" Lestrade said. "The notes say he spits it out." He raised some papers from the cushion beside him. "The written record was in his studio. Conveniently placed!"

Calibri waved his hands in a large arc, suggesting an explosion.

"When the trick is performed properly," Holmes said, "the spittoon explodes. I'm sure it would be quite a spectacle. Alas, that is not what we are about to see."

Calibri sat in the chair, positioning himself while Guignol locked the gun into place.

"Supposedly, part of the danger of the trick is that Calibri cannot move once the gun is locked down."

Mrs. Calibri crossed in front of her husband, took hold of the screen, and wheeled it forward until both the gun and Guignol became no more than shadows through the rice paper.

"You see, Watson. Shooter and target are now hidden from each other. Guignol cannot adjust his aim, and Calibri dares not change position. More significantly, the magician must be ready to act the moment the gun fires."

Mrs. Calibri made a final adjustment to the spittoon. Then she backed away, moving out of the projection to leave her husband alone with the rice-paper shadows.

"This last part happens quickly." Holmes stepped forward, advancing toward the hanging sheets, his shadow rising beside Calibri.

My mind raced. The image seemed to slow, and when the paper tore I almost saw the bullet itself, spinning as it flew toward Calibri. . . .

Calibri leaned forward, hands on knees, head erect, mouth drawn. As Holmes had said, it would have been a spectacular trick: Calibri turning with lightning speed, deflecting the projectile to explode within the brass spittoon.

But none of that happened.

Instead, Calibri's head ignited into a ball of flame.

I leaped to my feet. "Good God!" I teetered forward, reaching out as Calibri convulsed and fell. He struck the wine table, knocking it over as his wife ran back into the projection. Grey flecks covered her costume, face, and hands. She had been caught in the spray. . . .

I stepped forward, still reaching out as if to stop the madness.

And now the rice paper screen was moving, sliding back to reveal

Guignol's ruined face and emotionless eye. I could make no sense of his expression. The monster simply stared, straight ahead. "The camera," I muttered. "Guignol is looking at the camera!" But the impression was different. The eye seemed to be staring straight at me.

I stumbled, returning to my seat.

And then, suddenly, the staring eye was gone, eclipsed by Mrs. Calibri's spattered face as she turned, leaned forward, and extended a hand. The screen went white.

"Did you see it that time?" Lestrade asked.

"No," Holmes said. "It wasn't there." He stood before the hanging sheets, chin in hand, looking down. "I tell you it wasn't there."

"What wasn't there?" My voice trembled. "Gentlemen, please. Tell me . . . assure me! What we saw was surely an illusion. Wasn't it? Did we not just witness a trick?"

"Yes," they answered together.

"We agree on that much," Holmes said. "But who is tricking whom? That is where we disagree."

"Play it back," Lestrade said. "Just the end, the last few seconds. It must be there!"

Holmes returned to the machine, closed a douser to block the light, and cut the power to the still-clattering projector. Then, hands trembling, he rethreaded the film.

"May I ask what you're looking for?"

"Movement in the curtains," Lestrade said. "A change in the light. Anything to indicate that the camera was stopped and restarted."

Holmes opened the douser as the film ran backward through the machine. The image leaped back onto the sheets with Mrs. Calibri's gore-smeared face jerking as the film momentarily hung up and started moving again.

"So it *is* a trick." I sounded like a man trying to convince himself.

No one responded.

Mrs. Calibri backed away, and once again I found myself staring at the cyclopean eye of Guy Guignol. The orb looked dead, more like the lens of a machine than the window to a soul. And then it was gone, slipping behind the rice-paper screen as the headless body of the Great Calibri leaped from the floor, bringing the wine table with it before resuming its seat on the chair.

"Watch his body," Holmes said. "If the camera shuts off during filming . . . if another figure takes the magician's place . . . we're sure to see movement in his limbs, a shift in his posture."

Viscera flew through the projection, coalescing in a reverse flash of light, reconstituting to become the living head of the Great Calibri.

"It's him," Holmes said. "It's still him. If there had been a switch, we would have seen it."

"But I saw something!" Lestrade said. "I'm sure of it. A jump in the image!"

The jump came again as he spoke.

"There! You see it, Holmes?"

"That's the projector! A momentary jam. The film's breaking down." He stepped away from the projection. "I need to turn it off."

"No!" Lestrade barked. "Play it again. Good God, man! I'll show you. It was there, a split second before impact."

Holmes hit the switch, freezing the image just as Mrs. Calibri made her final adjustment to the wine table. And then the film rolled forward again, clattering inexorably toward the atomization of Calibri's head.

"Stop," I muttered, finally realizing why Holmes had pressed me to leave the room. "Stop it!" But my voice was lost beneath the clattering machine as the magician's head exploded once more.

And then the film jumped again.

"There!" Lestrade cried, rising to his feet, pointing at the image.

The clattering stopped, giving way to a straining hum.

Holmes turned to the projector.

On the sheets, Calibri sat on his chair, leaning backward, head frozen in the moment of disintegration. I stared, trying to comprehend what I was seeing as the image bubbled, curling back to reveal an empty frame of blinding light.

"The film!" Holmes shouted, covering his face as the projector burst into flames. A gust rose past me, nearly lifting me from the chair as the conflagration erupted first into a pillar of fire, then into a fulmination of noxious smoke. The fire collapsed, leaving the room dark, the air unbreathable. . . .

"Window!" Lestrade coughed, stumbling past me in the heavy air. I heard a hiss of fabric, a rattle of curtain rings, and then the click and groan of an opening casement. I saw him then, silhouetted in the lamplight through the open window, centered in the bay as he leaned out into the night.

I joined him.

"Infernal machine!" Lestrade coughed again as Holmes moved alongside him. "Is the film—"

"Gone," Holmes said.

"But I saw the trick!" Lestrade said. "The image jumped while Guignol was still behind the curtain. The exchange happened then."

"Exchange?" I said.

"Guignol for Calibri," Holmes said. "The good inspector has become quite creative in his deduction."

I tried putting it together. "You're saying that Guignol and Calibri changed places? That it was Guignol who took the bullet?"

"That's my theory," Lestrade said.

"But the rice-paper partition slides back at the end," I said. "Guignol looks out. I saw him!"

"You saw a hideously deformed face, one that might well have been a mask."

"That's likely enough," Holmes said. "Guignol was certainly wearing a mask, a bit of theatre to corroborate the fiction of his failed bullet-catching experiment."

I turned to Holmes, his face now visible in the streetlight. Some of the smoke had cleared, but the smell lingered—a terrible stink like burned vinegar, charred wood, scorched metal. "So then it is Guignol's body in Calibri's grave?"

"That's my suggestion," Lestrade said. "Magicians often employ doubles. I propose that Guignol was an actor whose proportions would make his head-less body a perfect substitute for Calibri."

"Ingenious," I said.

"But not credible." Holmes leaned back from the casement. "It raises too many questions."

"You and your questions!" Lestrade said. "I came here for answers."

"Answers will follow, but first let us consider why Guignol would will-ingly exchange places with Calibri."

"No doubt because he was told to," Lestrade said. "He was the assistant, after all."

"I'm confused," I said. "Do you mean that Guignol consented to having his head blown off?"

"Not at all. The bullet-catch is a trick. The gun is not supposed to be loaded."

"This one was!"

"But the assistant would not have known that. He took the seat because he trusted Calibri."

"These are clever suppositions," Holmes said. "But they hinge on a non-existent detail." He straightened up as he spoke, turning toward us in the dim air. "The image on the film did not jump."

"But it did!" Lestrade said. "Right before the fire!"

"That was a jump within the mechanism, a projection error." He studied us gravely. "I fear, gentleman, that our viewing of the film supports only one conclusion: the man who took the bullet-bomb was none other than the Great Calibri."

"But how?" Lestrade asked. "If the whole thing is supposed to be a trick—"

"*Supposed* to be," Holmes said. "But what if his wife and the actor playing Guignol had conspired together? We know that Mrs. Calibri was in charge of the books. What if she had been diverting the receipts, leaving creditors unpaid while she and her lover planned an escape to America."

"But why leave the film and notes behind?" I asked. "Why leave a record of the murder?"

"Because it appears to be the record of an accident," Holmes said. "The lovers wanted to give the impression that Calibri was working out a way to actually deflect an explosive projectile. But this is all supposition. I suggest that you need to take such questions up with Mrs. Calibri." Holmes turned toward Lestrade. "Does Scotland Yard have the name of the ship that the magician's wife was seen boarding?"

"It does."

"Then a telegraph to the port of destination is certainly in order."

"And Guignol?" Lestrade asked.

"Find the widow, and you'll find your man. At this point, I doubt either is inclined to let the other travel alone."

I sat on the windowsill, putting it all together. "So it *was* a trick," I said. "A trick played on the magician himself." I felt my gorge rise. "That means—" I could not finish the statement.

Holmes understood. He turned away, heading back into the room.

Lestrade looked at me. In our previous meetings, he had never impressed me as a sensitive man. Tonight, however, he seemed shaken. "Strange," he said. "I spent so much time looking for the illusion that—" He swallowed, looked away. "We watched him die, Watson."

"A terrible murder."

"Not just once, but over and over."

"Forward and backward."

He looked into the room, toward Holmes who had once again positioned himself beside the ruins of the infernal device. "Thank God the fire took it!" Lestrade said. "I never thought I would say such a thing about evidence, but I'm glad it's gone!"

"No," Holmes said, still looking down, speaking into his hand. "Not gone. Just beginning."

"And how's that?" I asked.

"This machine. It can record anything."

"*Could*," I said. "It *could* record anything, not anymore."

"But there are others. Soon there will be more. Think of it, Watson. Can you imagine a time when such spectacle as we witnessed tonight can be brought into the home for private viewing, played again and again?"

"I hardly think such things are likely."

Holmes looked at me, eyes dark, face unreadable. "I feel a chill, old friend." He gestured toward the street. "Would you be so kind as to close that casement? And draw those sheets together, least the damage to this room be seen from outside."

I did as he said, suddenly alarmed at the thought of our landlady, the irascible Mrs. Hudson, glimpsing the condition of the flat.

Holmes turned up the mantle flame on the fixture behind him, illuminating the damage, which included a good bit of scorching to the settee and ceiling. We had been fortunate the whole place hadn't ignited.

Lestrade frowned at the machine. "I'll tell the servants down at Calibri's shop to pick that thing up in the morning."

Holmes said nothing.

Lestrade reached for his hat.

"Leaving?" I asked.

"I need air."

"I daresay we all do." I turned to my friend. "Holmes?"

"Not for me. You go if you like. When you return, we can work at putting the room back together."

"I'll stay, then. Help you now."

"No," he said. "I need to be alone. You go. I'll be here when you return."

And so I followed Lestrade down to the street, stepping out into the haze of a nearby lamp.

"They tell me," Lestrade said, "that London will be electrified soon."

"Hard to believe."

"It's already the case in Berlin."

"And in a few American cities," I said. "Thanks to Edison and Tesla."

He frowned. "It isn't ours anymore."

"What isn't?"

"The world." He turned and started away, and as he walked I heard something behind me—a soft wailing, like the weeping of an angel.

I looked up, and there he was: Holmes once again projected as a shadow within the window. He had his violin in hand, the bow moving slowly with the sound. It was an original composition, one that had soothed me in the past. But that night, as I listened, I felt a dread for the things that we had let into our home . . . and into our minds forever.

THE BETWEEN BOOKS SECRET

Between Books, one of the most incredible bookstores I've ever visited, sits in an unremarkable strip mall in Claymont, Delaware. The store has a long, narrow interior stacked floor to ceiling with virtually everything relating to sf, fantasy, horror, comics, and games. In an age when bookstores come and go and the industry giants make news filing bankruptcy and predicting doom, it's nice to find a place that's entering its fourth decade of successful bookselling.

I've been doing readings and signings at Between Books for a few years now, and when owner Greg Schauer announced that he would be doing an anthology to coincide with the store's 30th anniversary, I told him to count me in. That collection, *The Stories in Between*, debuted on November 14, 2009, with an afternoon signing at the bookstore and grand-finale celebration later that night that included a three-band concert at a local club. When was the last time your local superstore staged something like that?

The first thing that impressed me when I arrived for the signing was how many writers had showed up for the release: C.J. Henderson, Jonathan Maberry, John Pasarella, Maria V. Snyder—over a dozen contributors in all.

The second thing that hit me was the setup for the event, which had the authors arranged behind a line of tables flanked by a display of books, cantilevered like a huge Tower of Babel, and a cake topped with a reproduction of *The Stories in Between* cover rendered in full-color icing.

But the most impressive thing came when the customers started filing in . . . not just a few at a time, but a steady stream that soon snaked down the aisles, out the door, and into the parking lot.

We signed nonstop for three hours. And then, when the store closed and the last stragglers slipped away, Greg brought out the cartons of books that had been reserved by people who hadn't been able to attend the event.

Yeah, now that's a book signing!

But you know, perhaps the most incredible thing of all is that no one there (other than Greg and me and maybe one or two members of the staff) had any idea of the secret that lay just beneath their feet, under the floor of the bookstore and accessible only by a locked door in a room right behind the signing authors. I call it a secret, but it isn't really that anymore.

The next story gives it all away.

BENEATH BETWEEN

I was traveling through Delaware when the storm returned, blowing in from the northwest, pelting my windows with rain. I had spent the night at the home of an editor, and was heading toward New Jersey to address a writing group before returning to Pittsburgh. I was tired, road-weary, and in no mood for driving in heavy weather. A dwindling patch of red-sky dawn to the east recalled an old saying. How did it go? *Red sky at morning, sailors take warning.*

I needed to make the state line by 6:00 if I planned to be on time for my talk at the Monmouth Library, but when a fishtailing car nearly ran me off the road, I decided to pull over and wait for the worst to pass.

A McDonald's appeared through the haze. I steered toward it, jumped a curb, and angled into a parking space. Rain assaulted me as I opened the door, soaking me before I reached the restaurant's entrance.

A small crowd had already gathered inside. The air smelled of grease, bacon, and wet shoes. I bought a coffee and made my way to a secluded booth, sliding in to discover that someone had left a paperback book on the seat. It was an old edition. I picked it up, turning it over to find that it was the Harbrace edition of Arthur C. Clarke's *The City and the Stars*. I knew the book, and seeing it brought back childhood memories of reading it for the first time in my uncle's cottage. It had been an old edition then. It was even older now.

I broke it open and pressed the pages to my face. The smell was as I remembered. For a moment, I was twelve again, sitting by a cabin window, listening to waves breaking beyond the forest, reading the story of a young man who left a going-nowhere life to find his destiny among the stars.

Lightning flashed.

The restaurant lights flickered.

A woman spoke in the booth behind me. "Not again!"

"You lost power last night, too?" a man said. "Mine was off for an hour."

I closed the book.

There was something odd about the cover. I pulled it closer, looking again at the illustration of a glowing city beneath a field of stars. Those details matched my memory of the book, but I now realized that the title was not *The City and the Stars*. It was, instead, *Against the Fall of Night*. And the name beneath the title was different, too. Not Arthur C. Clarke, but simply Arthur Clarke.

An earlier edition? A variant?

I opened the book to check the copyright, discovering as I did that both the inside front cover and facing page were covered with a dense cursive script that ran both horizontally and vertically across the panels. The next two pages were much the same, although here the handwriting serpentined around a list of titles by Arthur Clarke on the left and the title-page information on the right. The following pages—the title verso, dedication, half title, and fly-leaves—were much the same, covered horizontally and vertically, as if the writer had felt compelled to continue writing after running out of blank or nearly-blank pages.

The first few handwritten sentences inside the cover were easy to read, since the ragged margin of the vertical script did not overwrite the first couple lines. Farther down, the reading became trickier, but by then I was hooked.

I read it through, lost in the story. And when I finished, sitting back to discover that the storm had broken, I felt as if I had awakened from a lucid dream.

I closed the book, looking again at the cover that was at once familiar and strange.

A hoax?

I doubted that. The book looked authentic, as old as the handwriting was fresh.

But it can't be true. It's too fantastic to be true.

I checked my watch. 6:45. My clothes were nearly dry. Beyond the plate-glass windows, my car waited in a pool of sunlight.

Running late. Time to leave.

I slipped the book into my jacket pocket, got a coffee to go, and hit the road.

Five hours later, after a distracted presentation in the Monmouth Library, I asked the librarian to do a database search for a 1956 Harbrace edition of *Against the Fall of Night*.

"I don't see one," she said.

"You're sure?"

"There's a 1953 Gnome Press edition."

"By Arthur Clarke?"

"Arthur C. Clarke." She emphasized the middle initial. "And there's a 1968 Harcourt edition entitled *The Lion of Comarre and Against the Fall of Night*."

"That's not it."

"But it's all I'm seeing."

"How about anything by Arthur Clarke, no middle initial? Any indication that he ever wrote under that name."

She frowned, the screen reflecting in her bifocals. "No. Nothing like that. It's always with a *C*."

I decided to show her the book. "Here." I reached into my jacket. "I have—" The book wasn't there. "Hold on." I checked the other pocket. My wallet was there. No book.

"Something wrong?"

"It was in my pocket."

"A book?"

I looked back toward the parking lot. "Must have fallen out."

"In your car, maybe?"

"Yeah. Maybe. I'll be right back."

But the book wasn't in my car.

I must have dropped it at the restaurant.

I considered driving back to Delaware, but something came over me as I started the engine, a sense that I had already brushed too close to something better left alone. Besides, I was too tired for backtracking. At least, that's what I told myself as I put the car in gear, pulled out of the lot, and steered for home.

But that night, unable to sleep, I set to work transcribing that handwritten story from memory. It is a strange narrative. I cannot vouch for its validity. But I do not doubt its truth.

I must begin . . . write it down while it's fresh. I'll lose it if I don't.

I'm in a McDonald's, off Philadelphia Pike. Soaking wet. It's raining like a bastard outside. But the restaurant has power. The lights are on, though they're flickering. Don't know what I'll do if I find myself in darkness again. A moment ago I leaned back in this booth and saw my reflection in the window. I thought it was someone looking in. Christ! Nearly crapped myself. Not good. Need to calm down, sort things out, write it all down.

It started when I decided to walk home. My former best friend offered to drive me, but I couldn't see spending twenty minutes in the same car with her.

God, I hate her.

It has nothing to do with her selling yet another story to one of those *A* magazines . . . *Asimov's*, *Analog*, *Apex*, whatever! That doesn't matter. What does is how she keeps reminding everyone about her success without ever mentioning it. It's in her every move, in her every gesture, in her every "Well, you know, what the editors really want is . . ." and "Well, the most important thing I've learned about character development is . . ."

I used to enjoy meeting with the writing group. Not any more. And today, after listening to her pontificate for ten minutes straight, I knew I had to split.

I had my manuscripts with me. The same miserable, unfinished, dog-eared, blue-penciled drafts that I have been rewriting and rethinking since college, three stories and the first few chapters of a novel that always seems to self-destruct after about 30 pages. I shoved them all back into their manila envelope and headed for the door. Didn't say anything, just started walking.

Of course, she called after me. "You all right?" she asked.

"Fine."

"Well, you're not acting fine."

"Then I'm sick, OK?"

"Well, then let me drive you."

"No. I'll walk. I need to walk."

And that was it.

Well, *almost* it. She started to get up, but I kept moving, out the door until I reached the street. Then I jogged all the way to Philadelphia Pike. That's when it hit me.

Stupid!

I gripped my envelope and followed the sidewalk, walking against the traffic.

You know what she's doing now, don't you? She's talking about you! Psychoanalyzing!

I could almost see her waving her hand as she spoke, palm up as if cradling some invisible essence of truth: "Well, you know, we're often our own worst critics. . . ."

Funny thing is, she used to be my closest confident, my soul mate. We go way back. In college we talked endlessly about becoming writers. I even let her read one of my stories, which she insisted I finish and submit for publication.

"I'll get around to it," I told her. "One of these days."

"Well, if I were you, I'd do it now."

"But you're not me."

"Right, but if—"

"No time for *ifs*. My life's just too busy right now."

Problem was, my life was always too busy.

After college came work. And soon after that, life really closed in: family life, professional life, the full-but-empty life of raising kids and cultivating careers. Next thing I knew I was pushing forty. That's when I told her (my one-time soul mate . . . my former best friend . . . the one who always told me what she would do if she were me) that we should start a writing group. She liked the idea, so we put out the word: *Calling all wannabe writers!* And the wannabes came. And it was fun for a while, until she began finishing her stories. And then she submitted them. And then they sold. Pretty soon, she was queen of the club. And I was what? The Knave of Procrastination? The Joker?

Don't flatter yourself. You're nothing.

I paused at an intersection, looking back as I waited for the light to change. The sky had darkened. Leaves turned belly up, hissing in the wind. I considered retracing my steps, returning to the meeting, apologizing.

I shivered.

Can't.

I turned again to face the intersection. The light was still red.

I can't go back.

But I didn't want to be alone. I needed to talk to someone, anyone.

The signal changed.

I pushed on, walking faster as lightning flashed behind me. A few seconds later, I heard the boom.

I started jogging again, keeping the pace until a parking lot opened to my left, bordered on two sides by the storefronts of an L-shaped strip mall. There was a bookstore there. I knew the owner, a pleasant guy who seemed to know everything about science fiction, fantasy, and comics. His store, pressed between two nondescript shops at the southeastern end of the mall, always looked much smaller on the outside than it did from within. But even on the inside it seemed far too compact to accommodate the number of books he apparently had in stock.

Years ago, I used to test the size of his collection with impossible requests. The conversations usually went like this:

"I'm looking for the original *Eerie*," I said.

"Which original *Eerie*?"

"The comic. I think it was published by Warren."

"It was. But do you mean the first *commercial* issue or the *prototype*?"

"What prototype?"

He grinned, stroked his beard, and looked down the aisle to the back of his store. But he wasn't so much looking as thinking, accessing that inexhaustible database behind his eyes. "The first commercial *Eerie* was actually issue two," he said. "The actual first issue, the one listed as issue one, was a prototype that Warren produced for a distribution meeting. Two hundred pamphlet-size copies were printed and bound. That's it, just two hundred. As far as I know, they were never distributed."

"You're joking!"

"You can look it up." He closed his eyes, accessing data. "Archie Goodwin tells the story in *Gore Shriek 5*, 1988. I believe the article is called 'The Warren Empire.' "

"You're serious?"

"Always."

"You have a copy of that one?"

"Which one? *Gore Shriek 5* or *Eerie 1*?"

I called his bluff. "Both."

He thought a moment, then nodded. "Yeah." He looked at me. "Want them?"

"If you have them."

"All right." He stepped out from behind the register. "But it'll take a minute to get them. You'll need to stay here, watch the register." He moved down the center aisle, entered a room in the back of the store, and was gone for maybe five minutes. When he returned, he had the magazines, each wrapped in a plastic sleeve.

Naturally, I bought them. I was too impressed and dumbfounded to do otherwise.

Other challenges followed, all producing similar results: the first issue of Charlton Comic's *Reptilicus*, the January 1963 issue of Forry Ackerman's *Spacemen Magazine*, and an immaculate copy of the Ace Double edition of Theodore S. Drachman's *Cry Plague!* I didn't want any of them. I was just trying to stump him, and eventually I had to stop, since I felt compelled to purchase each obscure gem when he produced it from that mysterious back room. After a while, when life got busy, I stopped going to the store, but now here I was, crossing the parking lot, racing against the darkening sky, trying to keep a few steps ahead of the rain. . . .

The first drops fell, shooting down like bullets, exploding on the sidewalk as I stepped inside.

My friend was there, talking on the phone, looking pensive. He glanced toward me, raised his eyebrows. "Actually," he said, still talking on the phone. "Maybe I can. Hold on." He put the phone on the counter and turned toward me. "Haven't seen you in a while."

"Been busy."

"Writing?"

"I wish."

He glanced at the phone. "Listen," he said. "I'm in a jam. Any chance you'd . . ." He frowned, seemed to reconsider.

"What?" I asked. "You need something?" I was eager for friendship, desperate to feel needed. "Name it!"

"I need to run out for a while."

"Want me to watch the register?"

"Do you mind?"

"Don't mind at all. What are friends for, right?"

He went back to the phone, picked it up, pressed it to his beard. "On my way." Then he hung up and showed me how to lock the door. "Just in case," he said. "In case I'm not back by closing. You're sure you don't mind?"

"Got nothing else to do."

A few minutes later I was behind the register, reading a tattered copy of Theodore Sturgeon's *Voyage to the Bottom of the Sea*, listening to the rain hammer the storefront windows.

At one point the lights winked out, plunging me into a few seconds of darkness. When the power returned, something thumped in the back room, the heavy bang of a restarting compressor. What was back there, anyway?

I checked the clock. Five minutes to kill. I got up from the register, walked down the aisle, and peeked inside the back room.

There was some clutter: empty boxes, trash can, bucket and mop . . . no books. I stepped inside and turned in place. Another door led into a small bathroom, but that was it. No mysterious collection. Not even any shelves. I started to leave, and that's when I noticed the trapdoor.

It was small, barely more than a square hatchway. A piece of knotted rope extended from one end, lying like a coiled centipede on the floor. I picked it up, raising the hatch to uncover a jagged break in the foundation. Beneath the break, a vertical ladder extended down into a flickering space. I leaned closer, listening to the crackling hum of fluorescent lights as the space below came into view.

The lights switched on when I opened the hatch.

I noticed a button inside the trapdoor's frame. I pushed it. The lights winked out. The ladder vanished, all but the top few rungs. Everything below that was now hidden in blackness.

I released the button.

The lights came back on.

I leaned forward, glimpsing the edge of a shelf of books.

So that's where he keeps them!

I remained there a moment, listening to the rain on the roof. Then I got up, hurried back to the front of the store, and locked the door. It was close enough to closing time. Unless my friend returned in the next few minutes, he would never know I had closed early.

A moment later, after returning to the back room, I descended the ladder to find myself standing in a long, narrow space that stretched away in both directions. Floor-to-ceiling shelves lined both walls, magazines and periodicals on one side, books on the other. To my left, a succession of hand-lettered signs read 1950, 1951, 1952. . . .

The numbers faded in the distance.

The other direction was much the same, with years descending through the '40s, '30s, and beyond.

I started walking, moving forward through the '50s, the colorful spines of *The Magazine of Fantasy & Science Fiction* scrolling by on a shelf a little below eyelevel. Above them, complete runs of lesser magazines came and went: *Macabre, Jungle Stories, Infinity Science Fiction, Impulse,* and one that I had heard about but never seen before—an ill-fated magazine titled *If.*

Everything appeared sequential, no missing dates or numbers. To my right, each year of books was arranged alphabetically by author: Asimov near the ceiling, Van Vogt near the floor. The C's ran about eyelevel: de Camp, Clarke, Clement. . . .

I ran my fingers along the spines, noting the red-and-blue of Ace Doubles, the yellow of DAW, and the stark black-on-white of the more traditional, less identifiable imprints. Occasionally a spine bore a sliver of a wrap-around illustration. One of these caught my eye, not because of its design or use of color (both were pedestrian), but because the author was Arthur C. Clarke, one of my childhood favorites. The book was volume one of the Harbrace Paperbound Library, *The City and the Stars*. I took it down, studied it through its plastic sleeve, and returned it to the shelf.

This store really does have everything.

I walked on, the books and magazines becoming newer: complete runs of *Omni* and *Twilight Zone* to my right, works of Stephen King, Marion Zimmer Bradley, Peter Straub, and Ann Rice to my left. . . .

The lights flickered, threatening to cut out, reminding me of the storm that still raged above ground. Looking up, I noted fluorescent tubes hanging from a paneled ceiling. I realized that I must now be walking beneath the alley that ran behind the store, or possibly even the stand of trees that lay beyond that alley. In any event, I was certainly no longer beneath the strip mall. Nor was I in any ordinary basement. Indeed, I suspected I was in some sort of guerrilla interior, a space cut surreptitiously beneath the property behind the mall, the sort of excavation that would need to be done carefully to avoid underground pipes and cables.

How did he do it?

The shelf-lined corridor was perhaps 75 feet long and eight feet high, with three feet between the shelves. Quite an undertaking for one man.

Did he hire a contractor? How long had it taken?

The space ended between a pair of shelves labeled "2000." The back wall was bare, paneled over with the same material that formed the ceiling. And yet, the space did not end there. At my feet, trailing a piece of knotted rope similar to the one I had noticed in the back room above, a square hatch lay in the floor.

Another level!

I raised the door. Once again, lights came on below, illuminating a series of vertical rungs that extended deep into a second shelf-lined space.

Curiosity drove me on, down the rungs and into a deeper corridor that ran at a slight diagonal to the one above. The arrangement made sense, since placing the lower space parallel would undermine the upper corridor's floor.

It's all been carefully planned.

I reached the bottom of the second ladder, feeling and hearing a whoosh of moving air that was even more pronounced in this corridor than it had been in the one above. And I heard other sounds: the steady whirr of dehumidifiers competing with the chug of sump pumps. Even so, the space felt damp, hardly ideal for storing books, yet the spines appeared nicely preserved within their plastic sleeves.

The lower space followed the same layout at the one above, the shelves labeled by year, the ladder occupying a gap between 1950 and 1949.

Once again, the spines of *The Magazine of Fantasy and Science Fiction* greeted me a little below eye level, identical to the ones on the upper level. Or were they? I looked closer, reading through the plastic: *The Magazine of Fantasy*.

I took down one of the issues, January 1953. The title on the cover was the same as the spine: *The Magazine of Fantasy*, no mention of *Science Fiction*.

And yet everything else about the issue appeared as it should. The editors were Anthony Boucher and J. Francis McComas, the imprint was Mercury Publications, the featured writers were Fritz Leiber and John Wyndham. No surprises there. But the title! I was familiar with the magazine, and I knew for certain that only the first issue, published in 1949, had ever been called simply *The Magazine of Fantasy*. After that, *and Science Fiction* had been added to broaden the publication's appeal. But here was a complete run bearing the original title, as if they had been published in some parallel universe, a place where the decision to alter the publication's identity had never been made.

What about the books?

I turned, facing the titles and authors I had encountered on the previous level, but here, too, there were differences: odd color schemes, unfamiliar names, altered titles. One in particular stopped me in my tracks: *Against the Fall of Night*, by Arthur Clarke. I took it down, pulled it from its plastic, opened it. The book seemed to be a retitled edition of *The City and the Stars*, complete with the original artwork and cover design. What was going on here?

I turned back to the magazines and started walking, noting other changes. The ill-fated magazine known as *If*, which had failed in the early 1970s, now seemed to have a run that rivaled the top SF magazines. Each issue had the names of its contributors on the spine: Asimov, Bishop, Bova, and then I saw something that stopped me cold.

It was the July 1989 issue.

My last name was on the spine.

It has been my blessing (or possibly curse) to have a rare surname, one that I seldom encounter in the world at large. But there it was, on the spine between Bova and Davidson.

I pulled the issue from the shelf, unwrapped the plastic, opened to the contents page. My full name was there, as was the title of one of my unfinished stories: "Alternate Paths." I noted the page number, found the story, and read the first page.

It was mine.

That is to say, the concept was mine, but the writing was better than anything I had ever produced, more precise, tighter. . . .

The editor's introduction at the top of the page claimed that "Alternate Paths" was my third story for the magazine. The others were "Parallel Lives" in January 1988 and "The Doppel Gang" in March 1987. More significantly, it announced that my novel *Different Lives* was due out in the spring.

I hurried back along the magazines, found the other stories, and then moved along the other side until I found *Different Lives*, which the subtitle identified as book one of a trilogy. I found the other books, then moved forward, searching for my name and finding that I had become incredibly prolific toward the end of the century. By the time I reached the bare wall at the end of the shelves, I had an armload of books and magazines that did not exist in my world. I did not wonder how such a thing was possible, but already a plan was forming. I could carry these books home, transcribe them, submit the manuscripts, sell them!

I leaned back against the bare wall, intoxicated with the plan. The lights flickered, reminding me yet again of the storm raging two levels above me. The ambient hum of the ventilators changed pitch, straining against the changing current. The lights dimmed once more, then came on full.

I have to get out of here.

Hugging my load of books and magazines, I headed back to the ladder, which now looked incredibly far away.

The lights flickered again.

And this time they went out.

Darkness fell. I paused and waited for the power to kick back on.

It didn't.

The air thickened, becoming stagnant, damp.

I blinked, waiting for my eyes to adjust, but I was in total darkness, completely closed in, cut off from any source of light.

What now?

I pushed on, still carrying the books, wondering how I would know when I came to the ladder.

Have to put the books down . . . feel my way.

The plan made sense. I could always come back for the books when the power returned.

Or I can just stand here and wait for the lights to come back on.

But I didn't like that option. Perhaps it was my imagination, but the air seemed to be growing thicker by the second, closing in until I felt as if I were suffocating in darkness.

I put the books down. They thumped around my feet, settling loudly as I moved away. I took a step, then paused, paralyzed with ambivalence. Did I really want to leave them behind?

The darkness shifted. I felt myself turning about, getting dizzy in the stagnant air.

Get out of here now!

I stumbled forward, steadying myself as I moved along the plastic-wrapped spines, feeling for the gap that held the ladder. But it didn't come. Had I walked too far? I paused, considered backtracking, and then—in the darkness behind me—something moved.

At first it was a dull thump, like the sound the books had made when I dropped them on the floor, only now it sounded as if someone was gathering them back together. I heard a groan, and then a shuffling step . . . then another . . . getting louder . . . coming toward me.

I turned and ran, plastic sleeves crackling beneath my hand as I searched for the ladder. Then, at last, the spines fell away. My hand swept into the gap between the shelves. My fingers closed around the ladder. I climbed as the shuffling sound paused beneath me.

My imagination. There's nothing there.

But I kept climbing, up through the square hole and into the middle passageway. I grabbed the hatch and threw it closed. Then, to make sure it stayed closed, I pulled books and magazines from the shelves and piled them over the door, building a paperback cairn as high as my knees, hoping the weight would be enough to keep whatever was down there from coming after me. Then I hurried on, feeling my way to the next ladder. And then I was climbing again—up into the back room where I again slammed the hatch.

Light seeped through from outside the store, coursing through the windows, lighting my way as I hurried from the back room. The buildings at the far end of the strip mall had electricity.

I stepped outside, set the lock, and dashed into the parking lot. It was still raining, but I kept running, down toward the main road where lights burned inside an Arby's restaurant. I hurried toward it, stopping when I caught sight of someone sitting in a corner booth. It was my friend, the owner of the bookstore, evidently catching a late meal while waiting for the power to return to his store. And he wasn't alone. A woman sat with him. She had her back to me, but I could tell by the tilt of her head and the way she gestured with her hands that it was my nemesis—the Queen of the Writing Group.

I kept walking until I came to a McDonald's. I went inside, and it was only then that I realized that I had left more than an armload of books and magazines in the bookstore. I had left my envelope of unfinished stories, too.

The woman at the register looked at me. "Help you?"

"Coffee." I reached into my pocket, looking for my wallet, coming out instead with the Harbrace edition of *Against the Fall of Night*.

My wallet was in the other pocket.

The woman put the coffee on the counter. "That all?"

I flipped open the book, noticing the empty flyleaves. "Got a pen?"

She took one from her pocket.

"Can I borrow it?"

She set it beside the coffee.

I paid and hurried to a secluded booth, flinching when I glimpsed my reflection in the glass, thinking for a moment that it might be the thing from the bookstore.

But it wasn't a thing.

I looked at the reflection.

It was a possibility . . . another self . . . the me *who couldn't bear leaving those books behind.*

I was used to such concepts. Indeed, I had once tried writing stories about such things—stories about not-quite parallel worlds where the roads not taken were taken, endless successions of universes populated by not-quite congruent selves:

The *me* who writes nothing. . . .

The *me* who writes everything. . . .

The *me* who gets trapped. . . .

The *me* who escapes. . . .

On and on . . . endless possibilities.

I pondered my reflection in the glass.

What if I had actually finished those stories in college?

I shivered, knowing the answer. The feel of those books and magazines lingered in my hands.

But now another possibility was eating at me.

What if I hadn't put those books down when the lights went out?

My shivers deepened.

I would have moved slower, stumbling in the dark. But I still would have gotten out. It just would have taken longer. Unless—

I glanced again at my reflection.

Unless someone sealed me in!

I leaned toward the window, looking through my reflection to see that the lights were coming back on in the strip mall parking lot.

I have to go back.

I clicked the pen.

Can't. Can't go back. Don't need to go back. I'm here. There's nothing back there. This is the me that I am . . . the one I have become . . . everything moves forward from here.

I stared at the blank pages inside the front cover of my stolen book.

Against the Fall of Night.

I must begin.

JAMMING WITH SPRINGSTEEN

Another interesting anthology project that I contributed to recently was *Darkness on the Edge: Tales Inspired by the Songs of Bruce Springsteen.* The title says it all. The book is a fusion of fiction and song, which is a concept that brings us back to my earlier points about the links between story and music.

I first heard about the book when it was little more than a concept being shopped around by editor Harrison Howe. He had received a verbal acceptance from a well-regarded publisher, but he had yet to receive a contract. Usually I steer clear of such things, having learned from experience that writing on spec for an anthology without a publisher is generally a losing game, with the book either winding up stillborn or in some kind of royalty-only arrangement with the authors. But the Springsteen concept was too good to pass up.

All I needed to do was settle on a song to serve as the basis for a story.

You wouldn't think I'd have trouble doing that, especially considering all those Springsteen titles that would look right at home in the TOC of a horror anthology: "Something in the Night," "Point Blank," "Adam Raised a Cain," "Devil's Arcade," "Darkness on the Edge of Town." Yeah, I'd buy that book.

And then there's the soundscape itself, brooding melodies ringing like echoes in the darkness. Take, for example, the working-class anthem "Youngstown" from *The Ghost of Tom Joad.* Listen to it once, it'll haunt you forever. It's a song that often filled my headphones while I worked on the early drafts of my novel *Veins,* a book about life and death in post-industrial America.

Picking a song should have been easy, but by the time I'd agreed to write a story, I was pretty sure that the most obvious titles had already been claimed. No matter. The other writers could cover "Thunder Road" and "I'm on Fire." I would delve deeper, select a tune that wasn't part of the American pop scene, something like The Boss's reinterpretation of Woody Guthrie's "Plane Wreck at Los Gatos" from the tribute album *Till We Outnumber 'em*. Now there's a song just waiting to be spun into a twisty southwestern gothic about fireballs and falling ashes. I figured I could set it in 1937, maybe give Guthrie a cameo. I was sure that would work, but when I proposed the idea, Harrison explained that his vision for the book ran in another direction—away from material that had simply been covered or reinterpreted by Springsteen. This book needed to be based on songs The Boss had written on his own.

Fortunately, I had a backup—a fairly obscure outtake of a tune first recorded in 1982 while Springsteen was working on *Born in the USA*. The track didn't make it onto that album, or the next. Instead, it lay in wait for over a decade, finally coming out (ironically) on the retrospective compilation *Greatest Hits* in 1994. The song was "Murder Incorporated," a vintage slab of rock with driving bass and ringing keyboard indicative of the mid-'80s E Street sound. The reverb is a little heavy, as it is on so many tracks of that era, but the song remains a winner—dark, angry, driving.

The lyrics tell of a world where murder is an institution, where violent death passes without investigation, and where people can only feel safe cradling their guns within barricaded apartments. Harrison agreed it was a good choice, and we were off and running. Well, sort of.

It was now the summer of 2006. Other writing projects vied for attention, and since the Springsteen book still didn't have a publisher, I set "Murder Incorporated" aside and concentrated on the elephants in the room.

Darkness on the Edge eventually found a home with Peter Crowther and PS Publishing, who had been making news by releasing some beautiful editions of books by Stephen King and Joe Hill.

I submitted "Die Angle" in the summer of 2007. Acceptance and payment arrived in short order, then the story went off to Springsteen for final approval, which was given in 2009.

Darkness on the Edge: Tales Inspired by the Songs of Bruce Springsteen debuted at World Horror 2010—nearly four years after I'd first caught wind of the project. The wait was long, but Harrison Howe's vision and determination had paid off.

World Horror was in England that year, a long way from Pennsylvania, but my Ash-Tree Press collection *This Way to Egress* was also debuting there, so I had a doubly good reason to cross the pond.

Darkness on the Edge is a real beauty, boasting a jaw-dropping cover by J.K. Potter and a winning list of contributors. There's also a tray case edition, which arrived compliments of PS Publishing after I returned to the States. Harrison Howe had definitely found the right publisher.

So now here's what happens when a horror writer gets to jam with The Boss.

DIE ANGLE

Music reverberated from the club downstairs as Johnny watched the mice inside Nick's terrarium. White with pink ears and tails, they might have looked cute were it not for the blood that stained their faces. They were eating.

"That used to be a mouse," Nick said, referring to a pulpy mass in the center of the terrarium. "And that one there, the little guy, he's the one that took him down." Nick tapped the glass beside the killer, a piebald fluff ball nibbling a string of viscera. "He attacked from behind, grabbed the big guy's neck, held on until the others joined in."

"A community effort?" Johnny said.

"Right. But it takes one mouse to start it. Without that one, everybody starves."

Johnny turned away, toward a multi-paned window that overlooked the bright lights of the Ironforge Galleria, a garish structure of steel, glass, and cinderblock that occupied the former site of the town's hot-iron mill. Twenty-five years ago, Nick had caught mice in the shadows of that sprawling foundry, starving them in cages before setting them against one another. Now he raised his own victims.

"Do my mice bore you, Johnny?"

"I didn't drive 300 miles to watch you torture mice, Nick."

Nick flashed a smile that seemed not to have changed since Johnny had last seen it a quarter century ago. Age might have left its mark on his other features, but that smile remained the same, at once inscrutable and malicious. "You never know," Nick said. "Maybe there's more here than mice." He turned toward a small refrigerator in the corner, knelt down, opened the door. "You were always a watcher, Johnny. Always scoping things out, noticing details." Nick took a Tupperware container from a bottom shelf and closed the door.

"Maybe my mice can teach you something about Ironforge." He opened the terrarium and popped the top on the Tupperware. Some of the mice looked up, whiskers twitching as Nick dropped the bodies of a dozen infant mice onto the terrarium's sawdust floor. "See how it works, Johnny? Now no one starves."

"You make it sound like you're some great benefactor."

"I am." He replaced the terrarium's cover. "I don't kill animals, Johnny. I never did. I let the animals do it themselves."

"But they wouldn't kill if you fed them regularly."

Nick looked amused. "What're you doing, Johnny? Teaching me ethics? If I want that, I'll call a priest, not a hitman." He returned the container to the fridge. "I suppose you want to get down to business, talk about the job?"

"That's why I'm here."

Nick snapped off the light above the terrarium, leaving the mice to feed in semidarkness.

"My uncle said you requested me specifically, Nick."

"Right. Told him it had to be you." Nick crossed to his desk, its glass top reflecting a line of posters, each for a band that had headlined at the club downstairs. The booking agent was a friend of Johnny's uncle, and it was through that association that Johnny now found himself back in Ironforge, the western Pennsylvania town of his youth, a place he had intended to leave forever.

"I thought it best to hire someone familiar," Nick said. "Someone the victim knows."

"*Client.*"

"What's that?"

"I prefer the term *client*, not *victim.*"

"All right. Your client." Nick took a business card from his Rolodex. "You graduated together." He passed the card to Johnny. "He's got a contracting business, specializing in windows."

Johnny looked at the card. "Milo D'Amico."

"Remember him?"

"High school all-star, state champion." He put the card back on the desk. "We moved in different circles."

"As I recall, you were always in a different circle."

"But not you, Nick. Back then, you and Milo were thick as thieves."

"Still are."

"So why do you want him dead?"

"That's complicated."

"What isn't?"

"What matters is that you'll be calling on him tonight, at his office. You'll tell him you're moving back to Ironforge. You're in the market for some quality windows. Tell him I sent you."

"Really?"

"Absolutely. He's got no reason to suspect I want him dead. Not me specifically."

"So I drop your name and he lets me in?" Johnny checked his watch. It was after 9:00. "His card says he closes at five. You sure he's still there?"

"Yes. Tonight he'll be there, in his office, drinking scotch, catching up on paperwork."

"And why am I buying from him and not a national chain?"

"Because this is Ironforge, Johnny. We don't have national chains."

"Plenty within driving distance."

"Not an option. Everyone who lives here buys here. On the retail level, Ironforge money stays in Ironforge."

"And on the wholesale level?"

"That's different. Most of our businesses contract with out-of-town suppliers. I mean, what kind of club would I have if I relied on local talent? Know what I'm saying?"

"So Milo lets me in, and that's where you want me to do it? In his office? With his gun?"

"That's right. It has to be his gun. Your uncle explained the setup?"

"Yeah. It's tricky."

"But you can do it?"

"I think so." He was eager to get started. "We agreed to half up front. The rest on completion."

Nick took an envelope from the desk. "Call me when it's done." He passed the envelope to Johnny. "I need to know the moment he's dead."

"Then I come back here, right? You'll be waiting?"

"That's right." He led Johnny to the door. "I don't leave this office till the job's over."

The terrarium was silent now. The mice, finished with their meal, had settled down to sleep amid the bones.

A soft wind blew from the river as Johnny left the club, its freshness another reminder of how much things had changed. Like the community, the once-polluted Ohio River had come back to life.

Johnny raised his collar and headed east toward the old business district. People passed him. No one looked familiar, and no one gave him a second glance until a voice called from a parking lot two blocks from the club.

"Hey!"

Johnny kept walking.

"Hey, Johnny Yakulis! Johnny Yak!"

Johnny turned to find a tall figure lumbering forward, long hair backlit by a vapor lamp.

"Son of a bitch!" the man said. "It *is* you. Johnny *fucking* Yak! I thought you were dead!"

Johnny studied the face, lined with the scars of misspent youth. "Tony? Tony Tego?"

"Fucking-A!" Tego kept his hands in his pockets. "I saw you walking by. 'The fuck,' I said. 'That's Johnny Yak!' Where the hell you been, man?"

"New York."

"New York? Like Buffalo, New York?"

"No, like Manhattan."

"Yeah?" Tego looked thoughtful. "I've heard of it. So what the fuck? You moving back to Ironforge?"

"No. Passing through."

"Fucking-A! I think you'll like what you see. You might decide to stay." Like the rest of the town, Tego had done well for himself. His sneakers were two-toned Prada, his jacket loose-fitting Versace—casual but top-of-the-line. A slight bulge in his lapel could have been anything: wallet, wad of bills, handgun. "Tell you what, Yak. Let me give you something." He produced a business card. "You decide to move back, you fucking call me. All right?"

The card identified Tego as Anthony Tegolezzo, owner of Riverfront Estates.

"Upscale homes," Tego said. "Hardwood floors. Beamed ceilings. The fucking works. I'll set you up, man."

Tego had always been big on giving orders, and Johnny, who had spent his adolescence at the bottom of the Ironforge food chain, decided to play along. "Thanks, Tego. If I move back, you'll be the first to know."

"It's a deal." Tego extended his hand, not to shake, but to slap Johnny's shoulder before turning away. "Catch you later." He took a few steps, then looked around. "Fucking Johnny Yak!" He grinned. Then he was gone, ambling through traffic as if he owned the street, reminding Johnny yet again that the visit here was strictly business. Nothing else could have brought him back to Ironforge.

* * *

Rain misted as he reached the old center of town: a five-point intersection lined with storefronts. A pillared façade on the corner of Merchant and Fifth still bore the stone-etched logo of the defunct Ironforge Bank. Beneath the portico, Milo D'Amico's name ran in stenciled letters across a door of triple-paned glass.

According to Nick, Milo's bread-and-butter was selling reinforced windows that protected Ironforge residents from out-of-town thieves. Ironforge might have recovered from the collapse of big steel, but surrounding towns hadn't.

Milo's metal detector was right where Nick had said it would be, the panels toned and textured to blend with the building's masonry. A security cam hung above the door. Below it, a plaque:

Protected by
Brian Goodnight Security

That name was another blast from the past. Like Johnny, Brian had never quite fit in. The two had hung out together, parting company only when Brian's skill at picking locks attracted the attention of Tony Tego. By the time Johnny had moved east, Brian and Tego had seemed destined for the county lockup. For Brian's sake, Johnny was glad things had turned out for the better.

Johnny pressed the intercom, waited a moment, then pressed it again.

Milo came on, sounding pissed: "We're closed!"

"Milo. Hey, man! It's Johnny Yakulis."

A light came on above the door. Johnny stepped back, smiled for the cam.

"Damn!" Milo's voice crackled from the speaker. "Johnny Yak? You son of a bitch! The hell you doing in Ironforge?"

"Looking at property, a place by the river. Nick Argenti tells me you can help."

Silence.

"Milo? You there, man?"

Lights came up inside, illuminating a reception area and a line of office doors. One of the doors opened. Milo emerged: overweight, pale, and sporting a comb-over that started an inch above his left ear. "Damn!" Milo's voice came muffled through the glass. "It *is* you, you crazy bastard!" He took a set of keys from his pocket, unlocked the door. "Get in here, man. Jesus! Johnny *fucking* Yak!"

Johnny entered.

Milo pulled the door closed, locked it, put away the keys. "Goddamn Yak!" He smelled of scotch. "Out shopping? Can't wait till morning?"

"I'm only in town tonight."

"A man on the move!" He clapped Johnny's shoulder. "Come on. You like scotch?"

Milo's office occupied the corner of a large space that resembled an art gallery: white walls, track lights, hanging frames. The frames held model windows, some with cutaway portions revealing layers of reinforced metal and glass. All of these hung from one wall. Across from them, a partition of stuccoed cinderblock ran the length of the room. According to Nick, the gun was behind that wall.

A foamcore cubicle framed an office near the showroom's entrance. Milo's desk was inside, framed photos behind it, a cut-glass tumbler and open bottle of Glenlivet resting on its corner.

"I always drink when I work late." He took a fresh glass from a credenza.

Johnny crossed to the desk, studied one of the pictures. "She looks familiar."

"What?"

Johnny leaned on the desk. "I think I used to date her."

Milo came up behind him. "Dream on, Johnny!"

Johnny backed away. The maneuver had worked. Now it was only a matter of time.

Milo took the bottle from his desk, poured Johnny a stiff one, handed him the glass. "Goddamn Johnny Yak!" He took his own glass from the desk. "For your information, that's my daughter."

"No shit!"

"Yes shit."

"She looks like—"

"Bonnie Lasorta," Milo said. "She looks just like Bonnie Lasorta, who firstly you did not date, and who secondly has been my wife for twenty-four goddamn years. End of digression!" He drank. "Johnny Yak-yak-yak!" He stepped away from his desk. "Since you clearly have no attention span, let me cut to the chase." He waved the bottle, directing Johnny toward the showroom. "If it were business hours, I'd take you through here, show you the models, soften you up for the big demo. But since it's late, we'll start with a bang." He continued toward the cinderblock wall, led Johnny around the corner, and there it was: a Glock 9mm imbedded in a steel rack, the barrel pointed at a wall twenty feet downrange. It was exactly as Nick had described it, but Johnny did his best to look surprised.

"Here's the deal," Milo said. "Ironforge might have rebounded, but the communities around us are still on the skids. Our success breeds contempt. Did Nick explain any of this to you?"

"Yeah. But he said it's still a good place to live."

"Can be. Provided you got the right defense." He crossed to a display of steel-framed windows. "This is my top-of-the-line, multilayered glass and polycarb. Some people think they don't need it, but that changes when I show them what it can do." A clamp dangled from an overhead track. Milo reached up, pulled it down, and fitted it over one of the display windows. "Now watch this." Using a handheld control, he switched on a wench that lifted the window out of the case and down along the firing range. The setup was impressive, but Johnny saw it for what it was: an elaborate indulgence like Nick's mice and Tego's designer sneakers, the sort of thing that a have-not child buys when he becomes a gotta-have adult.

Lights came on at the end of the track, illuminating the window, showing off its design.

"Look at the bevel on that glass, Johnny. You'd probably buy that window on looks alone. But it's . . . more than that . . . more than just a window." His words came in short bursts, as if he were having trouble catching his breath. He wasn't slurring yet, but that would come. "Now check this out." He leaned on the gun rack, teetering as he took a set of muffs from the shooting bench. "You need to . . . put these on."

"This is a hell of a demo, Milo."

"Yeah. Theater. But that's sales. Sizzle . . . not the steak." That wasn't the sort of thing Milo would tell a prospective customer. His inhibitions were failing as quickly as his speech. "This is . . . where it gets good, Johnny." He took a loaded magazine from the gun bench, slid it into the Glock, chambered the first round. "You're about to witness . . . you're going to see . . . I'm going to show you—" He slumped against the bench. "Jesus, Johnny." And now, at last, he slurred the words: *Sheeshus, Ssshonny.* He looked at the Glenlivet bottle. "I'm drunk."

"No, Milo. Not drunk." Johnny reached into his pocket. It was time to begin a demonstration of his own. "It's not the drink, Milo. It's this." He raised his hand, revealing a plastic vial cupped in his palm. "I get it from a lab in Brighton Beach. Special formula, fast-acting, tasteless."

Milo tried focusing, giving the vial a *what-the-fuck?* stare.

"It's empty now, but it was full when I got here." Johnny returned the vial to his pocket. "I squeezed it into your glass back in the office."

"You . . . fuck." He lost balance, went down hard, striking his head on the bench before landing unconscious at Johnny's feet.

Now the real work began.

Milo came to as the track moved him into position, arms suspended from a pair of nylon cuffs.

"You never bothered asking what I did for a living." Johnny worked the handheld remote, activating the track that carried Milo into position at the end of the range.

"What the fuck, Johnny!" Milo's voice was nearly lost beneath the whirr of the motor.

"Nick Argenti hired me." Johnny leaned toward the gun. "He wants you dead."

Milo's eyes widened. He looked at Johnny, then at the gun. "So it's Nick? He got my name."

Johnny touched the gun, noting how the polymer frame had been fused to the steel rack. The Glock's other parts could be removed for cleaning, but the frame remained permanently in line with the far wall and whatever target hung in front of it. Tonight, that target was Milo.

"Listen," Milo said. "You have to go back to Nick. Tell him . . . if he's got my name . . . he has to come himself."

Johnny sighted over the top of the gun, confirming that the aim would place a bullet to the right of Milo's sternum. Then he asked, "What do you mean he's got your name?"

Milo tugged against the overhead track, trying to swing himself out of range.

"Milo. What do you mean—"

"Fuck you, Johnny!"

"All right. If you don't feel like talking, I'll just finish—"

"Jesus, Johnny!" He wasn't slurring now. "Didn't Nick tell you . . . why he wants me dead?"

"No. I don't usually care. But now I'm curious. What do you mean he's got your name?"

Milo looked up at his bound wrists, apparently hoping to see a way of breaking free. Then he lifted his feet from the floor, putting his full weight on the track. The ceiling mounts groaned but held.

"You going to talk or struggle?" Johnny asked.

Milo looked at him again, his comb-over sagging across his brow.

"What do you mean, Milo? Nick's got your name? What is that, some kind of lottery."

"Yeah. A fucking lottery. A triad."

"Triad?"

"It's three names," Milo said. "Selected at random." He licked his lips. "Goddamn, Johnny. I can't talk like this."

Johnny fingered the Glock.

"Christ, Johnny!"

"That all you're going to tell me?"

"This isn't right, Johnny. What you're doing. It isn't—"

"Selected at random?" Johnny said. "Who by?"

Milo stopped struggling. "Borough computer. It's all digital. Each person gets emailed a name."

"Just a name."

"Yeah. Just that. We all know the rules."

"So Nick gets your name and hires me to kill you?"

"Yeah, but it's not supposed to be like that! Triad assignments can't be contracted out. Doing that goes against everything. Ironforge money is supposed to stay in Ironforge."

"As I understand it, that's only true in retail."

"That's altogether different, Johnny. Triad duty has nothing to do with sales."

"Triad duty? A computer sends you a person's name, and it's your duty to kill him?"

"The duty is in participating, not in killing. Each person in the triad has options. He can hide out or take action."

"Take action? You mean—"

"What you're doing right now, Johnny. Only it's not supposed to involve outsiders. If Nick Argenti wants his bonus, he's supposed to earn it himself."

"So there's an incentive?"

"Hell, Johnny. There's always incentives. What's commerce without incentives?"

"Let's back up. I've missed something. How does sending three people out to kill each other benefit the community?"

"It's not three people killing each other. The triad dissolves after one member takes action. Then he calls the computer and punches in the code that sends out the all clear. It's the fire whistle over the courthouse. Two longs and three shorts. That's the signal."

"And you can hear that in here?"

"Hell, Johnny. This building's bullet proof, not sound proof."

"And all this benefits the community how?"

Milo stared a moment, apparently stunned that Johnny didn't understand. "You just said it, Johnny."

"Said what?"

"Benefits! It's about benefits. Each resident has Ironforge listed as his primary beneficiary. The community inherits the wealth and makes it available as business loans and mortgages. See, Ironforge is more than a town. It's a corporation. When big steel left, we replaced it with an entity of the people!"

"And everyone in town's a member?"

"No. Not everyone. Police and doctors are exempt. And so are locksmiths. And minors . . . we can't include them. It's all been totally thought through . . . but then you get a guy like Nick who thinks he can bend the rules. Seriously, Johnny. You have to go back, explain it to him. I'll pay you. Name your price."

"No price." Johnny kept his hand on the gun. "But tell me this, what's keeping Nick from just blowing this building up with you inside it?"

Milo looked aghast. "The hell, Johnny. This isn't the Middle *fucking* East! We're not promoting unregulated destruction. There are guidelines. It has to be a gun . . . a pistol. That's why I use a Glock in my demos."

"Yeah?" Johnny said. "And you do pretty well, don't you? If a prospective resident doesn't buy your top-of-the-line product when you tell him about the danger from neighboring communities, he sure as hell buys it when he learns the real threat is from within."

"It's not that ominous, Johnny."

"No? Or maybe you're just so used to spinning it that you don't realize how it sounds to an outsider. Maybe I should try thinking that way. Maybe I should say I'm not killing you. What I'm doing is saving the life of the person named in *your* email. Think about it. If I don't kill *you*, maybe later tonight you'll decide to kill—"

"Tego," Milo blurted.

"Excuse me?"

Milo blinked. "Tego!"

"You got Tego's name?"

But Milo wasn't talking to Johnny. "*Tego!*"

Johnny turned, looking back at a scarred face, Versace jacket, designer sneakers. It was Tego, all right. But now the bulge in the lapel that Johnny had noticed earlier was gone. The gun was out of its harness, in Tego's hand, aimed at Johnny's head.

"Tego!" Milo thrashed like a hooked marlin, struggling against the cuffs. "Shoot him and get me down!"

Johnny kept his hand on the rack-locked pistol, finger on the trigger, barrel fixed on Milo.

"Shoot him, Tego! Fucking shoot him!"

"Milo!" Tego yelled. "Shut the fuck up! This is between me and Johnny Yak."

The shooting range fell silent.

Tego steadied his aim, right at Johnny. "Know where I've been?"

Johnny put it together, remembering how he and Tego had been heading in opposite directions on Mill Street.

"Nick's." Tego said. "I went to Nick's office, and he was like, 'You don't want me. You want Johnny Yak.' And I'm like, 'Johnny *fucking* Yak? I just saw the fucker.' And he's like, 'Fucking-A. I hired him. He's my subcontractor. You need to kill him, not me.'" Tego shook his head. "You believe that shit?" He glanced at Milo. "What about you? You believe that?"

"Yeah," Milo said. "Now shoot Johnny Yak and get me out of here."

Johnny kept his hand on the gun, looked Tego straight on, and said, "How'd you get in here?"

"The fuck?" He grinned. "Nick's not the only one with ideas. I got my own subcontractor. Only difference is, I kept the money in town." His grin broadened, flashing teeth that, like his face, betrayed the traumas of his hard-knock youth. "Just like the old days, eh Johnny? You remember my partner in crime?"

"Brian Goodnight?"

"Fucking-A."

"Tego!" Milo was thrashing again. "Damnit, Tego! We didn't keep locksmiths out of the corporation so you could hire them freelance!"

Tego swung his gun, aiming at Milo. "And I told you to shut your hole!"

"Tego, listen," Johnny said. "You have to go back to Nick. He's your target, not me."

"That's not what Nick said."

"Right, because he didn't want you shooting him."

"Yeah? Too bad for him it didn't work."

"You shot him?"

"Fucking-A."

"Then why didn't we hear the all clear?" Johnny spoke softly, not want-ing to sound confrontational. "If Nick's dead, why—?"

"Because I didn't phone it in. I don't want my bonus delayed on a tech-nicality. Way I figure it, if I kill both you and Nick before I make the call, I'm covered."

"Do it!" Milo roared.

"No," Johnny said. "You don't want to shoot me." His mind raced, thinking, playing one move ahead. "It's one thing to kill an insider, but kill me and you'll face an outside investigation. Something like that could blow your triad scheme wide open." He paused, gauged Tego's reaction, then pushed on: "Best thing to do is phone it in, take the bonus, let me walk. No one needs to know I was here." He took his hand from the rack-mounted gun. "What do you say, Tego?" He stepped away from the shooting bench, out of the point-blank aim of Tego's 9mm. "We got a deal?"

Tego reached for his cell phone, dialed a number, punched in a code.

Outside, the fire whistle blared, the sound coming muted through the showroom walls.

Johnny left the range, passed Milo's office, and stepped into the lobby. A lone figure stood outside, smoking a cigarette beyond the wall of glass and polycarbonate. It was Brian Goodnight, waiting for Tego.

Johnny looked back toward the showroom, listening to Tego and Milo struggling behind the cinderblock partition.

"The fuck!" Tego said. "He's got you tied up good!"

"Cut it!" Milo said. "Rip the track down! Just get me the fuck out of here."

The voices welled louder as Johnny turned, retraced his steps, and re-entered the narrow space to find Tego and Milo still downrange from the rack-mounted Glock.

Milo saw Johnny first. "The fuck you want now?"

Tego turned. "Aw, shit!"

Johnny fired.

Brian Goodnight finished his cigarette as Johnny pushed out through the unlocked door. He grinned, flashing yellow teeth. "Johnny Yak?"

"Hey, Brian." He extended his hand. Brian took it, pulling Johnny forward into a backslapping embrace.

"I hear you're moving back, Johnny."

"That was just a story. I'm out of here tonight." He glanced at the glass storefront. "You hear those shots, Brian?"

"Yeah. I thought maybe it was Tego's gun. He told me you were in there. Told me Nick said—"

"Listen, Brian. I got a question. You know about this triad business?"

"I'm not a member."

"But you know about it . . . know how it works?

"Yeah. More or less."

"Then maybe you can tell me what happens when all three members of a triad go down? What's that do for the town?"

Brian shrugged. "Hell, guess that'd be some kind of windfall."

"So it'd be like a good thing, right? Ironforge collects three times. Nobody gets too bent out of shape?"

"Yeah." Brian nodded. "Guess so. A trifecta!"

Johnny reached into his pocket, took out Nick's envelope, pulled out two fifties. "What say you lock the door, Brian? Reset the alarm. Forget you saw me."

"No. No way." Brian handed the money back to Johnny. "I can't take this. I'm freelance."

"What're you saying, Brian?"

"I'm like you, man." Brian took a set of keys from his belt. "I'm not supposed to be here either." He turned and reset the locks. Before he finished, Johnny was gone.

Johnny headed back through a misty rain, noticing how the lights from the Galleria pushed against the sky like a midnight dawn, and for a moment he was back in time, looking at the hot-metal glow of the Ironforge Mill. His gait lightened. He felt young again, fifteen and believing that life as he knew it would go on forever. But then a breeze rolled in, sweet and clean from the river, and the illusion shattered.

By the time he was back in sight of the Galleria, he was once again feeling the weight of middle age. Another night, another job, and he wanted nothing more than to be heading east, back to the unfulfilling life that had sprung from a place that no longer existed.

SPARE THE ROD, RAISE THE CAIN

Writing is a bit like parenting.

It begins with conception, the story's idyllic phase, a time when the creation exists entirely in the abstract. But then comes the work and, possibly, a period of disenchantment. I speak from experience as a writer and a son, though not as a parent. My daughter's always had it together. Some children, like some stories, exceed expectations. For the moment, let's consider the ones that don't.

Other writers may disagree, but I find that a phase of disappointment is almost inevitable when raising a story—post*artu*m depression, if you will. Some parents know it as the terrible twos, and, fittingly, I generally become aware of it a couple days after completing a first draft. In my younger days, I sometimes succumbed to disenchantment by doing what I now consider unthinkable. Namely, tossing the unruly story in the trash. Talk about bad parenting!

I now accept that ideas are going to go through rebellious phases, times when they need to be reined in, corrected. In any event, trashing isn't an option. Neither is forcing the story to be what it isn't. And neither is holding it back, keeping it from the world.

Writers need to know when to let go. Overprotection is counterproductive, futile, unhealthy. Eventually, every story must fend for itself. And then? Best case scenario, it becomes successful, sends money home, and tells the world how great you were for showing the way. Not-so-best case? It moves back home.

All of which brings us to our next tale.

"Junk'd" went out into the world in the spring of 2009, was accepted for publication, and then returned home two years later when, after a series of delays, the editor's arrangement with the publisher fell through.

Of course, I knew what to do. I'd experienced the same thing with other stories. But this time, rather than sending it packing right away, I decided to hang out with the concepts for a while, get to know them a little better, help the creation become something more than it had been when it first entered the world. The changes were small, but the differences they made were considerable. What had started as a minor bagatelle for a theme anthology now seemed ready to hold its own with the other stories in this new collection.

Interestingly, "Junk'd" is a story about a young man who might be seen as a metaphor for a failed draft, a prodigal son forced to return to a home where, rather than being coached back into interaction with the world, is pretty much ignored by his parents. Not surprisingly (given that it's a horror story) a number of lives get trashed along the way.

Buckle up if you can find a seatbelt.

We're about to go riding with the bad kids.

JUNK'D

ONE

They're hot!" Chuck drained his beer, thumped the bottle on the table, leaned toward Joey. "You wait, man. You'll see."

Joey glanced toward the front of the bar, past the stage where the band was setting up, toward the door where a bouncer lounged beneath a Coors Light sign. He wondered if he'd recognize the girls when they walked in. If they'd be all Chuck said they'd be? If they'd—

"Stop that, Joey!"

"What?"

"Drooling at the freaking door. You look nervous."

"I am nervous."

"What?"

They were both shouting, competing with a full-throttle jukebox.

"I said I *am* nervous."

"Screw that. Don't go there. Nervous makes you look like a punk, like you're not old enough to be here."

"I'm not."

Chuck made a face like he was trying to work out a fart. "Tonight you are. You got ID, right?"

"*Bogus* ID."

"ID is ID. Besides—" Chuck's phone lit up. He took the call. "Yeah?" He pressed a finger to his free ear, cupped the phone closer, expression changing, smiling now. He wasn't good looking: small eyes, sunken cheeks, tangled hair that was a little bit Robert Plant and a whole lot Iggy Pop. But he was fun to be around, and when he smiled he seemed somehow more than human. He leaned on the table, talking to the phone. "You what?" He glanced at Joey, mouthing: *It's them.*

"Yvonne and Rita?"

Chuck got up. "I can't hear. Hang on." He walked away, past the bar, toward the door.

Joey followed, stumbling. *Drunk already!* He'd need to pace himself, resist matching Chuck drink-for-drink. He straightened up as he neared the bouncer, then followed Chuck through the door and into the sweltering twilight. No stars yet, no moon—just slate-gray sky over a gravel lot.

Chuck had his head down, still talking. "You *what*?"

Joey pulled alongside him.

"You want us to *what*?"

"What's she saying?"

"Okay. That's cool. Yeah!"

"What's she saying?"

Chuck turned away, still cupping the phone. "No! Not me. But Joey! He does."

"Joey does what?"

Chuck pressed the phone to his chest. "She wants to know if we got a car."

"Why?"

Chuck put the phone back to his ear, talking again as he neared Joey's Volvo. Then he climbed in, trying not to ding a white convertible that had wedged in tight against the passenger side.

Joey slipped behind the wheel.

"She's texting directions," Chuck said.

"Directions to where?"

"Where do you think? Her house!"

"Why?"

"So we can drive there."

"I mean . . . why do you need directions? I thought she was your girlfriend."

Chuck shrugged, the movement seeming to say: *There's lots you don't know.* And that was true. Joey and Chuck weren't proper friends, just two guys who'd met a few weeks back and who now got together whenever one of them needed a ride (usually Chuck) or excitement (always Joey).

The phone hummed.

Chuck checked the screen. "Sweet!"

"What's sweet?"

"It's close."

"Yvonne's house?"

"Ten minutes, max."

"You didn't know that?"

"Maybe I did, and maybe—" The phone hummed again. "Oh, yeah!" Chuck showed Joey the screen. "Check this out!" It was a photo. Two red-eyed girls with flash-glared nipples.

"Damn!"

Chuck pulled the phone away.

"So that's them?"

"No more questions. Drive!"

Joey figured he'd feel less smashed once he got on the road. He'd driven drunk before. No big deal. Concentration was the key. He could drive drunk just fine if he concentrated.

"Joey?"

"Right." He turned the key. The switch clicked. That was it. No ignition. Nothing. Just: *click!*

"Joey?"

He tried again. Same thing.

Click!

"You've got to be kidding, Joey!"

A bass drum thumped inside the bar, the band settling in, getting ready to play. *FhooOOOM! FhooOOOM! FhooOOOM!*

"Joey!"

"What?"

"Your car, man! Can you fix it?"

"I don't know."

"Son of a bitch!" Chuck unbuckled. "Pop the hood!" He opened his door, ramming it hard into the car beside them. *Thonk!*

Joey winced. The night was turning to shit.

Chuck climbed out, closed the door, then stopped. Then he just stood there, his back to the Volvo's side window.

"Chuck?"

"Get out here, man!" He was staring at the other car, the white convertible. "Get out here *right* now!"

"Did you ding it bad?"

"Ding what?"

"The door."

"Screw the door. Come here!"

The white convertible was parked so close that there was barely room to stand beside it, but Chuck was doing just that, leaning on its side, staring at the dashboard. "The bastard left his keys!"

A power chord rang inside the bar. Bass and drums followed, launching into some big-haired thing from the '80s. And Chuck was grinning. "Keys, Joey. He left his keys!"

"So?"

"We got ourselves a ride."

"What?"

"Ever drive a convertible?"

"What? Me? You mean this car?"

Chuck made a face, wide eyes going like: *Bingo!*

"No, Chuck. No way."

The sky seemed darker now, pulsing with neon arrows from the roadside readerboard:

CAMSHAFT CAFE
80s NIGHT

"Twenty minutes, Joey. We'll get Yvonne and Rita, bring them here. Mr. Convertible driver won't even know—"

"I'm not stealing—"

"Right! Exactly! Not stealing. *Borrowing*!"

Music filled the night, throbbing like a migraine.

"Damnit, Joey. Yvonne and Rita, man. Tits to die for!"

Joey leaned against his Volvo. "Jesus, Chuck!" The words felt dry. "We can't."

Chuck just stood there, face in shadow, hair full of readerboard light. For a moment he didn't move. Then he shrugged *screw it!* and opened the convertible door, slamming Joey's car. *Thonk!*

"No balls, Joey!"

"What?"

"You heard me." Chuck dropped behind the convertible's wheel. "That's what I get for hanging with a punk." He turned the key. The convertible started right up, exhaust blowing from twin pipes. "I'll tell Rita you were just some jagoff, tell her she's not missing anything." He let out the brake. "Good thing I'm man enough for two." He peeled away, leaving Joey in a haze of dust.

Joey watched the tail lights, bright and red, staring like a pair of flash-burned eyes, glowing nipples. "Chuck!" He ran, waving as the convertible slowed, turning toward the exit. "Wait!" The car slowed again as Joey raced up behind it, stopping abruptly as he grabbed the door. He stumbled, went down hard, scraping his hands on the oiled stones.

"Change your mind?"

Joey pulled himself up, opened the door, climbed in.

"Knew it!" Chuck let out the clutch. "Tonight the boy becomes a man!"

Joey reached for a buckle that wasn't there, and Chuck hit the street, burning rubber into the falling night.

They sped past gas stations and strip malls, through two intersections, then right onto a road that wound into a valley on the east of town, a wooded ravine of mobile homes, abandoned farms, illegal landfills. Joey settled in, hair whipping in the wind. He had slicked it back, better to show off his high forehead, just about the only thing about him that looked older than 18. He closed his eyes. Yvonne and Rita were there, blazing behind his lids, bright as flashbulb ghosts. Which one was Rita? He'd know soon enough.

"Joey! Wake up. Help me look."

They were speeding now, taking turns fast and tight, blurring past road-side trees.

"What're we looking for?"

"Road sign."

The center line became dashes, flashing like tracer bullets. A yellow diamond appeared, emblazoned with a silhouetted buck and a graffiti boner.

"There's a sign!" Joey said.

"That's a sign, all right."

"Think it's—"

"Yvonne said to look for a turnoff."

Joey didn't see one of those, just a sloping shoulder, the leaning remnants of a guardrail, and—way off in the distance—a dark house looking like a cutout against the trees.

"You said 20 minutes, Chuck."

"Yeah."

"This is taking too long."

The dotted line turned solid. The road veered, tires squealed, and there it was, another sign, hand-lettered:

HIDDEN DRIVEWAY
ON LEFT

Chuck turned, jumped a berm, and sped onto a narrow straightaway.

"Don't see a house, Chuck."

The road steepened, the car racing faster now. Chuck toed the brake. It was an instinctive move. Nothing worth noticing. But as he did, something thumped beneath the floor, the clank and grind of realigning gears. And then, with Chuck's foot still on the brake, the car surged forward.

"Chuck?"

Chuck stomped his foot, bringing it down harder, pumping the break, but each time the engine revved.

"Chuck!"

Chuck tugged the hand brake. No good. He took his foot from the pedals, feet flat on the floor now. But the car kept accelerating, winding to a high-pitched roar. "Get out, Joey!"

"What?"

"The car's fucked up!"

"What?"

"Get out!" He let go of the wheel. The damn thing was steering on its own now: a little to the left, a little to the right, driving itself. "*JUMP!*"

A car appeared before them, far off in the headlight's glow, facing them at the end of the narrow drive. It was just sitting there. Parked. Lights off. And there was someone inside, waving, screaming, pounding the windshield.

JUMP!

"No way!" Joey said.

But no one heard. Chuck was gone, his seat empty now, the wheel steering itself in the dashboard lights.

Joey screamed, first Chuck's name, then a long shriek as the convertible hurtled toward the parked car, an old station wagon with dented fenders, wood-grain doors. One moment it was centered in the high beams, and then everything went dark. Headlights shattered, metal compacted. The convertible angled upward, trunk bucking, and Joey was suddenly above it all, catapulted toward the forest beyond the drive.

He didn't remember landing. But he must have come down somewhere in the woods because the next thing he knew he was climbing a slope toward a flickering light. He couldn't feel his body, but his legs kept moving, covered with mud and leaves and carrying him to a break in the trees and into view of two smashed and burning cars. No way to tell one from the other, just one big contorted mass . . . except for a piece of wood-paneled door and shattered but intact safety glass. The fire hadn't reached it yet, and there was movement behind it, someone struggling inside, still alive, trying to get out.

Joey moved closer, numbness giving way to pain, deep and hot as if something bad had dislodged in one of his legs. It worsened when he stepped onto the pavement, but it held, carrying him to the burning wreck. He called toward the shattered window. "Hey!" His voice dry and broken. "Someone in there?"

The wind changed. Smoke swirled. He covered his face. The shadow twitched faster.

"You have to get out of there!"

Fractures laced the glass, webby cracks yielding to his touch, collapsing inward as he set a hand against the window. And then he saw. No one alive. No body either. Just pieces of one, stains amid the flickers. His gorge rose. He urged it back. Couldn't. He doubled over and heaved . . . twice . . . feeling weaker than ever when he was done, but strong enough to stand and shout into the night. "Chuck!" His voice struck the trees, echoed: *Chuck!* But that was it. No answer, just himself shouting back. *Chuck! Chuck!* Fading out, giving way to the sound of crackling flames.

He started walking, his shadow stretching before him like a skid mark, fading as he left the fire behind. And it was sometime after that, far enough along the narrow drive to be out of the flickering light, that he saw what looked like a body face down on the side of the road, arms splayed, left leg bent the wrong way. It had to be Chuck.

Don't stop.

He kept walking.

He woke in a hospital, head bandaged, veins needled, leg plastered. His parents were there, so were the cops. They had questions.

"Why was your car at the Camshaft?"

"Were you drinking?"

"Were you alone?"

He didn't remember.

"Did someone hit you?"

He told them again, tears welling. "I don't remember! I don't. I'm sorry."

And for a while, it was the truth.

TWO

The doctors recommended quiet, and no place was more so than home, a stone house in the heights where his parents came and went. Sometimes they visited his room, looked in, asked questions.

"You all right, Joey?"

"How's the head?"

"Get you anything?"

It was all about putting in appearances, their way of letting him know they were around, though they seldom were.

When the fall semester began, he remained at home. Dorm life was out of the question. His bedroom was better, safer . . . quieter.

The cast came off in October, but pain lingered. And the concussion held on, making it difficult to do anything but sit alone, lights off, music low. Sometimes he used the computer, but sparingly. The screen hurt his eyes. Sometimes the indicator light came on beside his built-in webcam. He wasn't using the camera, it just came on, and sometimes even that little bit of concentrated light could give him a headache. The only fix was to put a piece of tape over it, which he did after a while.

At night, with his room completely dark, he would look out the window at the drive that led to a street of lighted walks and perfect lawns. When snows came, he watched the flakes. Sometimes he fell asleep in the chair and woke to searing sunlight.

Then, around Thanksgiving, the dreams started.

At first they were crazy things: readerboard arrows, gravel lots, white cars, a guy named Chuck.

Chuck? Jesus Christ . . . Chuck!

By early December, he had remembered so much of it that when his parents came to the door he couldn't look at them for fear they'd see it in his eyes.

It occurred to him that the dreams were only dreams. But they felt like memories, so much so that he began using his computer to check the local news archives, scrolling through stories of bake sales, football games, school-board meetings, police reports. He read of moving violations, vandalism, assaults. But no stolen convertible. No fiery collision in the valley east of town. No obituary for a long-haired twenty-something named Chuck.

Then, a week before Christmas, he got an email that nearly killed him. The subject read:

Payback's A Bitch!

He opened it, read the message.

Joey: Look at this. Then get ready. I'm coming. Chuck

There was an attachment.

taking-the-bait.jpg (177.4 KB)

He clicked the mouse, opening a picture of two guys, one a wild man with crazy hair, the other a scrawny teen with a high forehead. The man sat in a white convertible. The teen just stood there, looking drunk. Behind them, a lot full of cars stretched toward a neon readerboard with a glowing arrow.

The email was nearly an hour old.

Joey stared, blinked, stared again.

The phone rang.

He jumped.

Another ring.

He grabbed the phone, tried answering. But he couldn't speak, couldn't breathe.

"Joey!"

He swallowed, found his voice. "Chuck?"

"Get my email?"

Another swallow. "What the hell, Chuck? Where—"

"Outside."

Joey looked out the window, past a glowing manger in the front yard, toward taillights and the rusted fender of a white pickup.

"Joey?" The voice crackled in the phone. "Damnit, Joey! You awake?"

"Jesus, Chuck."

"Get out here."

"Christ, Chuck. What's going on?"

"Now, Joey!"

It had been snowing off and on all day. Now it was on, big flakes swirling around the pickup. Chuck sat behind the wheel. He looked thinner, sicker, not altogether there. A scar ran along his temple, slanting toward his face. "Get in, goddamnit!"

"Where're we going?"

"I said, *get the fuck in!*"

Joey hurried around the front of the truck, past a shattered grill. Impact ripples ran along the fender, leaving the door out of plumb, tight within its frame.

"Pull hard!"

Joey yanked it, forced it open, climbed in. The interior smelled foul, like puke under a pine tree. A deodorizer hung from the mirror. Shag carpeting covered the dash. "This your truck?"

"Shut the door."

He tried. It took three slams, the latch finally catching with a tired groan.

"We going somewhere?"

Chuck pulled from the curb.

"Christ, Chuck! What—"

"You know computers?"

"Me?"

Chuck ran a stop sign, heading east.

Joey looked for a seat belt. There wasn't one.

"Talk to me, Joey. You know computers?"

Joey felt numb. "Jesus, Chuck! I thought you were—"

"Answer, Joey! You know computers? Mainframes? Hard drives? Shit like that?"

"A little."

"You told me you took a tech class, computers and shit."

"A blow-off course."

"Whatever. You know enough." He sounded like he was going to say more, but then he just stopped, the cab silent now except for the humming vents and the heavy *clump-thunk-clump-thunk* of snow-caked wipers.

"You saw me that night, didn't you, Joey?"

"Saw you?"

"Lying by the road? Tell me straight, man. You saw me and kept walking."

How could he answer that?

"Am I right?"

Joey swallowed. "I think so."

"Think so?"

"It was dark."

"You didn't try making sure?"

"I thought you were dead."

Chuck seemed to consider that, nodding as he steered. "Yeah." He made a turn, no signal. "Maybe I was. Close enough, anyway." He eased into the left lane, speeding toward the lights of town. "I saw what I looked like. Face down. Leg bent. I saw it all in the playback."

"Playback?"

"You didn't even stop."

"I was scared, Chuck."

"Yeah. You had reason. Goddamn, you had reason!" He was driving faster now, the snow coming at the windshield like *Star Trek* stars.

"Where're we going, man?"

"Don't do that, Joey."

"Do what?"

"Don't make your voice go like that. Trembly like that. Makes you sound like a kid."

"I *am* a kid."

"No. Don't play that innocent card on me. Not tonight!" He took a ramp to the main boulevard, merging into traffic. "You stopped being anything close to innocent when you stole that car."

"I didn't steal it."

"Rode in it! That's accessory—almost the same as doing the deed." He rubbed his scar. It was an ugly thing, like something from a monster show. "You check your email, Joey? See that picture I sent?"

"Yeah, but how? I mean—"

"From a surveillance camera."

"Whose?"

"The bastards." Chuck looked toward Joey, giving a clear view of his face. "The bastards who stitched me up. It was their camera."

"Doctors?"

"Hell no. You think doctors would do me like this?" He looked back at the road. "I'm talking about the bastards that came for me after you were gone. They would've found you too if you'd stayed. They hadn't counted on that, on you just walking away. That was their first mistake. Pulling me out of that ditch was their second." He sped through the business district, past strip malls, service stations, and a boarded building beside a gravel lot. Joey did a double take. Was that the Camshaft? All closed up and abandoned?

"They screwed us, Joey."

"They?"

"Tonight we screw them back."

"Yvonne and Rita?"

"Christ, no! There never was no Yvonne and Rita."

"But wasn't Yvonne your girl—"

"I never met her. She was just an email, a voice on the phone, tits in a photo. Ever get an email about hot chicks, horny housewives? The kind that go like, 'I'm Yvonne. Wanna party?'"

"Those are phishing scams, Chuck."

"Yeah? Well, I took the bait. And so did you."

They took a right on a winding road, accelerating between snow-covered trees.

"I was nearly dead when they found me. When I came too I was in a room, strapped to a bed, tubes in my arms. The IV bags were labeled in Chinese . . . maybe Japanese."

"You were in a hospital?"

"Hell no. I told you. No doctors! And even then, even when I didn't know for sure where I was, I knew for sure I wasn't in no hospital. Every few hours this woman came in. Dark eyes, blond hair, big teeth. She knew something about medicine, but she wasn't no doctor. Sometimes a guy came with her, carrying a camcorder, shooting her working on me. She told me they were making a video, all about two guys who stole a car to get laid."

"Us?"

"Yeah. They've been pulling this shit for years. Performance pieces. Elaborate set ups. I know because they showed me, showed me everything. I guess they figured there wasn't much chance of me running away." He snapped on the interior lights, letting Joey see the pinned-back leg of his jeans. He was working the gas and brake with his left foot. A crutch leaned beside him, wedged between seat and door.

"The woman said the leg was shattered. She cut it off with a wire saw. Did it fast too. *Zip-zip*—no more leg." He snapped off the light. "When it healed, they gave me a crutch and showed me around. That's when I realized I'd been in a trailer the whole time . . . a rusty doublewide in the middle of a junkyard . . . not more than 200 feet from where they found me."

"Where you jumped from the car?"

"Freakin-A." He took another turn, the way looking familiar in spite of the snow. "Anyway, that's where I've been. In a freaking junkyard, biding my time, making plans for a big payback."

"A junkyard?"

"Like I said."

"But I didn't see a junkyard."

"It was hidden, behind all those trees. Their official business is scrap and salvage. And they make sculptures too, make them out of wrecked cars, post them on their website. It's a cottage industry, except the cottage is like this trailer full of hard drives and servers. That's where you're going, man. You're going to steal those hard drives. You're going to clean those bastards out. Videos, pictures, sound recordings—ten years of heavily encrypted pay-per-view snuff, and you're going to take it all." He slowed, steering across the center line, angling the truck's headlights onto a shattered gate, a flimsy thing made of wood and chicken wire lying in splinters on the pavement, as if someone had rammed it, plowed right through, kept driving. "This is it, Joey. Last time we were here it was marked with a sign. Guess I took that out too."

Snowy tracks showed where someone had driven up the drive, plowed through the gate, swerved into the downhill lane. Joey remembered the truck's flattened grill and knew the tracks were Chuck's.

"Getting keys to this pickup wasn't hard. I knew where they kept those. But I wasn't figuring on a gate, though I should have. It's not like they'd want people wandering in here any old time. It makes sense they'd have a gate for when they're not expecting company . . . and when there's someone they're trying to keep locked away."

The truck bounced over the berm, then down onto the drive.

"When I saw the gate, I figured the best I could do was ram my way out. Figured I'd either crash through or wreck the truck. I was betting on the truck being stronger. Guess I was right."

Joey stared into the distance, remembering how the parked station wagon had appeared in the distance. But tonight there was nothing there, only snow and darkness.

Chuck drove to the end, then backed up and cut the wheels, bringing the pickup around until it faced a slope of chewed-up snow. "Those're my tracks. It's only 100 feet or so to the yard, but I barely made it, and I don't want to risk getting stuck now that I'm out." He put the truck in park. "But you can walk it." He slapped the button on the glove box. "There's a flashlight in there. And a multi-tool. You'll need them both."

Joey took them out. The multi-tool had nearly a dozen fold-outs: pliers, screw drivers, wire cutters, and an array of blades—the longest nearly seven-inches.

"Made in China," Chuck said. "Illegal import. Can't have a folding blade like that in the States." Chuck reached over, folded it closed. "Stick to the wire cutters and screw drivers. They'll do the job."

Joey pocketed the multi-tool and snapped on the flashlight. The beam angled through the windshield, reflecting on the falling snow.

"The main trailer's unlocked. Get the hardware, carry it out, load us up. There's a plastic tub in the back of the truck, should make the carrying easier."

"You want me to steal their stuff?" For a moment he felt as if he were standing outside a bar, beside a convertible with keys in the ignition. "You can't be serious."

"There's no one to stop you, Joey. It's Christmastime. Everyone's gone. It took me four months of ass kissing to gain their trust, convince them they could leave me alone . . . and now, like I said, it's payback."

Joey stared at the path between the trees.

"I'd help, but I don't walk so good." He slapped his leg. "It's got to be you, man. Do it!"

The path opened into a mass of snow-covered wrecks, car bodies sitting on blocks, icicles dangling from wheel wells, grills, hoods. Beyond the wrecks, plastic sheeting cracked and snapped in the wind, covering the windows of a doublewide trailer with a satellite dish on its roof. And there was something else, a giant figure amid the wrecks. Joey hit it with the flashlight, catching his breath when he saw a ten-foot man sculpted from the upended remains of a station wagon, the hood hammered to form an elongated head, wood-paneled doors shaped into a robe. And beside it, a second car—a white convertible. Both cars knelt beside a V-8 engine in an iron manger. It was a nativity scene, sculpted from junk. And above the figures, on braided ignition wires, silver bells swayed in the wind. He raised the flashlight, seeing the bells for what they were: dashboard lighters.

Joey turned and headed for the trailer.

The interior was filled with outdated electronics. A bank of cathode-ray monitors lined one wall, glowing between stacks of external hard drives, disk burners, servers.

It took multiple trips, lugging the components in the plastic bin, dumping them into the pickup, then going back for more. His leg ached, but he pushed on, kept working, and when he finished he stood beside the truck, staring at the piles of hardware. Most of it looked like junk, though he didn't doubt it was functional. He had seen the screen-saving patterns on the monitors, heard the hum of the drives, felt the heat of the cases as he'd pulled them from their racks. But what if they had been decoys?

Chuck thought he had won the confidence of his captors, but what if those captors had really been prepping him for a starring role in a grand finale, a climax to a reality show about two stupid punks who didn't know when to quit?

Wind whipped the trees. Joey looked up, his attention drawn by flickers of light, flashes of green hanging on the forest trees. *Christmas lights?* No. They were too small for that. *Diodes?* He squinted, bring them into focus: *Webcam indicator lights!*

"Chuck!" Joey moved along the side of the pickup. "We have to get out of here." He tugged the passenger door, pulling it hard until it opened. "We have to get out of here now, Chuck!" He climbed in, slammed the door until it latched.

The cab was silent, cold.

The driver's seat was empty, nothing there but a stain on the cushion that became a hole when Joey set his hand on it. Below the hole was a hollow space, foam and springs ripped out to form a gap big enough for. . . .

"Oh, fuck."

Joey moved onto the seat, left foot on the floor, right leg working down into the hole so that when he sat down. . . .

"Oh, fuck me!"

He remembered Chuck's pant leg, folded and pinned like there had been nothing below the knee. But the entire leg had been there, tucked inside the seat, ready for walking away when the time was right.

Performance pieces. Elaborate set ups.

"Bastard!" Joey looked up at the hanging webcams, his fear misting on the windshield. "The hell do you want with me?"

The green eyes bobbed in the wind, watching, recording.

Something flashed at the end of the road, headlights spilling against a sign that had not been there when Chuck had pulled in. It was happening again. One car coming down, another parked in the dead end.

Joey grabbed the headlight switch. Nothing. The truck stayed dark. He reached for the ignition, turned the key. The engine didn't crank. Instead—

THUMP! THUMP!

Bolts latched within the doors, sealing them tight.

The oncoming car was on the drive now, accelerating.

Wind gusted. The webcams bobbed. And something else was watching him too, a lens in the dashboard, nearly hidden among the shag carpeting, glowing like the indicator light on his laptop.

"What do you want from me?"

The eye just stared.

He took out the multi-tool, extended the longest blade, rammed it into the cam—hacking and stabbing until the thing popped from its socket and dangled on its fiber-optic nerve. And still the car was coming down the drive, engine whining, picking up speed.

Do something! Get out of here!

He leaned back and kicked the window, pounding with his feet while the oncoming headlights streaked the windshield to a milky smear, hammering with his heels until the glass gave way. He pushed through. Then he fell, hit the pavement, and rolled to the shoulder.

The cars collided, exploded, filling the night with light, thunder, flying metal. . . .

And there was Chuck, watching beneath the trees, appearing in the orange glow, standing strong and tall on two good legs. No scars on his face, just a few strands of latex and spirit gum. "Goddamn, Joey!" He shouted above the roar. "I told them you'd do something crazy . . . something worth seeing!" He stepped forward. Others followed: a big-toothed woman in a fur parka, a man shouldering a camcorder. "You're like a cat, man! Nine freaking lives! We could do a whole series around you!"

The camcorder's lamp flashed against the illegal blade in Joey's hand.

Chuck had been right twice that night. Joey was indeed a long way from innocent. And payback was definitely going to be a bitch.

ONE FOR THE ROAD

Let's consider that old bugbear, the question of what is and isn't horror. It's been under discussion for as long as I've been writing, even though I think Douglas Winter provided a clear definition in *Revelations (1997)* when he wrote that horror is "about our relentless need to confront the unknown, the unknowable, and the emotion we experience when in its thrall."

That's as perfect a summing up as any, and it's one I keep coming back to.

By Winter's definition, the following story is horror, but it crosses boundaries. Genre-sensitive readers will notice elements of science fiction and fantasy as well as some stylistic touches taken from the non-genre genres of mainstream and literary fiction (though I hope without the pretentions of the latter).

The story began as a project for Thomas and Elizabeth Monteleone's *Borderlands* series, which had previously published "Traumatic Descent" and "Circle of Lias" (reprinted in my Ash-Tree Press collection *This Way to Egress*).

Tom and Elizabeth didn't take the story, but they provided some excellent notes and suggestions, particularly regarding the climax, which they felt came across as abrupt and a little too tidy. They were right, but the problem was finding a way to conclude the story's arc within 5,000 words—the recommended length for a *Borderlands* story.

I put the manuscript away, went on to other projects, and eventually came back to it a few years later, when a much-altered version of its first act became the short story "Painkeeper" (*Cemetery Dance 59*, reprinted in *This Way to Egress*).

A few months ago, I decided to give the full story another shot. Finally, everything fell into place.

One of the rewards of working on a retrospective collection like *Voices* is seeing how story elements and plot devices have evolved over time. Now, taking a look at this final and greatly expanded version of "Shrines," I can see how it builds on elements from many of those early stories: emotional displacement from "Traumatic Descent," flesh artists from "Smuggling the Dead," hidden institutions from "Lesions," cyber horror from "Junk'd." In many ways, the first dozen stories in this book seem to anticipate "Shrines," making this new novelette a fitting finale for this collection.

Nevertheless, in spite of those points of intersection, I think you will find that "Shrines" is also a departure. It's darker perhaps, more brooding, and yet I hope it delivers a note of redemptive truth.

It's about a man on the edge, caught in the thrall and questing toward something unknowable.

Is it a horror story? I think so. At least I know this: it is for me.

SHRINES

ONE

Robert wakes in his empty bed, stares at the darkness, listens. The alarm is set for 4:30, but it's earlier than that. Not yet 4:00.

Yet something has roused him.

He pushes against pain, eases his legs over the side of the bed, then sits while rain pelts the window, cold and hard.

Downstairs, the front door closes, softly, barely audible, first the sound of the jamb's rubber seals, then the clicking latch. A moment later, footsteps enter the hall, thump across hardwood, whisper onto the living room carpet. He hears it all. There's nothing wrong with his ears.

The kid's early.

He tries stretching his legs. The good one tingles. The bad one doesn't do much at all. It's numb and heavy, more like wood than flesh and bone. But it takes his weight, keeps him from falling as he works on one slipper, then the other. His robe hangs from a chair. Beside it, the clothes that he has set out for today's journey lie folded on a table. He puts on the robe and leaves the room, limps into the hall, then descends the stairs one at a time. He'd move faster if he could, if his body were whole again.

Wet footprints stretch through the hall, tracking toward the living room where a 20-something kid sits in an armchair, nylon pack strapped to one shoulder. His left eye glows red. The light isn't reflected. It's internal, like fire in the retina. But Robert isn't frightened. Just perturbed. He's seen this before.

"Good morning, Robert."

"Is that what it is?"

"Technically. Morning, anyway. Whether it's good or not is up to you."

Robert reaches the bottom step, steadies himself, then limps into the hall.

"Didn't mean to wake you." The kid slips his pack from his shoulder, careful not to tangle the wires running from a hub at the base of his neck. "I thought I'd sit here, wait for you to get up." He sets the pack on the floor between his boots. "Hope that's all right."

Robert remembers engaging the security chain before heading upstairs. Now it dangles, swinging loose.

"You can go back to bed if you want." The kid sounds hoarse.

Computer virus? Robert finds that thought amusing.

"Something funny, Robert?"

"No."

"You've got a long day ahead of you. It might help to be rested."

"No." Robert crosses to the couch, eases down. "I wasn't sleeping anyway."

"Want breakfast?"

"Not today." Robert glances toward the door, the dangling chain. "Guess I should have gotten a deadbolt."

"Deadbolts are easy." The kid waves a gloved hand. "You want security? Get a dog."

"A dog would have kept you out?"

"No. But it'd make things interesting." He opens a pocket in his shoulder pack.

Robert turns on a lamp beside the couch. "How come you're early? Making sure I don't chicken out?"

"No. Your profile shows you'll follow through. Ninety-eight percent chance."

"You can give something like that a number?"

"Sure. On some levels, it's all numbers." The kid reaches into the pack, brings out a small box. "I wanted to give you this. For the trip."

Robert takes the box, raises the lid. Inside is a medal embossed with the image of an old man in a robe. A baby rides the man's shoulders. In the baby's hand, a globe. "All right. And this is?"

"St. Christopher."

"I see that, but why?"

"So we can track you."

"GPS?"

"Something like that."

Robert studies the embossed image: old man, infant, world. "I used to have a Christopher medal, when I was a kid in Catholic school." He runs his thumb over the picture. "Know the story?"

"What? You in Catholic school? Three years at St. Mary's? Two years in second grade? That story?"

"No. Not that one."

The baby on the medal looks like Josh—round face, wide eyes, tiny fingers. One hand clutches St. Christopher's hair. The other holds the world.

"What story?" the kid asks.

"The St. Christopher story?" Robert turns the medal, looking for a seam. There isn't one. The thing is all one piece. As always, the kid's stuff is state-of-the-art.

"How's it go?"

"You really don't know?"

"Tell it to me."

"All right." Robert holds the medal to the light. "St. Christopher's walking by the river when he sees this kid. The kid wants to get to the other side, so St. Christopher puts him on his shoulders and starts wading across. It ought to be easy, but by midstream it feels like he's got the weight of the world on his back."

"Heavy boy."

"But it's not the boy that's heavy. It's the world. See, the boy's carrying the world—the whole world. But Christopher doesn't notice that until he's waist deep in the river."

"Not very observant."

"That's how it goes."

"So what's the man walking on? I mean, if the baby's carrying the world—"

"It's supposed to be a miracle."

"Really? So the baby's, like, what—Jesus Christ?"

"Something like that. But it's just a story. The nuns at St. Mary's told us it wasn't true. We were expected to believe in virgin birth, but St. Christopher was just a fable."

"So you like it?" the kid asks.

"The fable?"

"The medal."

"Yes," Robert says. "It's a good choice. Believable."

"That's what we thought."

"Christopher's my middle name."

The kid says nothing. He knows Robert's middle name, where he went to school, the companies he's worked for, the family he made and lost. The kid knows everything about him, but Robert still has trouble getting used to that.

"So I'm supposed to wear it?"

"That's the idea."

Robert slips the chain over his head.

"Under your shirt. Keep it hidden. Clothes won't stop the signal."

Robert does as instructed, letting the medal rest against his chest while the kid seems to pick something from the air.

Robert watches him work. "Everything all right?"

"Yeah. Just finishing up. You're good to go."

The kid's gloves only cover three fingers on each hand. The material is gray, skintight, perforated with ventilation holes and trailing wires that slip beneath his cuffs.

"You'll see yourself out?" Robert asks.

"Sure."

And why not? He's shown himself in.

Robert gets up, climbs the stairs, and begins the slow process of dressing. When he comes down again, the kid is gone, the door locked, the chain back in place. *How does he do that?* All that remains as proof that the kid was there are the tracks on the floor and the medal around Robert's neck. Otherwise, the visit might as well have been a dream.

In the garage, Robert's car waits amid boxes of toys and women's clothes. There's a crib there too—dismantled like a flattened cage.

He gets into the car and waits as the light dims back into darkness. The Chevy still smells new. He considers keeping the garage door closed and starting the engine. He's thought about that before, but here he is, still living, still hurting. Perhaps he doesn't really want to lose his pain. It is, after all, something to live for. But today he has another reason for opening the garage and continuing on.

He removes his wallet, sets it on the passenger seat, then presses the remote and watches the rearview as the rain-slicked drive emerges behind him. Brake lights smear the asphalt. He backs into the downpour, headlights panning across a never-used swing set, one more artifact from days when living in the moment had been all about planning for the future.

Not like now.

He puts the car in drive, toes the gas, accelerates into the street. In seconds the house is gone . . . but the heaviness goes with him, bearing down like the weight of the world.

* * *

He steers toward a light that never goes out—a shrine to American commerce. Red letters, white background:

Always®

This is where they have agreed to meet, a place where strangers come and go, where a black van can idle in shadows without being seen or remembered. It is a place where a man can leave his car, step into the rain, cease to exist.

A GMC Savana waits with its engine running. It's right where they said it would be. Robert steers in front of it, giving the people inside time to read his license plate before killing the lights.

The Savana's passenger door opens. A woman steps out, hooded raincoat belted at the waist.

Robert stands to meet her.

"Good morning, Mr. Jones."

The name sounds like an alias, but it's real. He has no secrets. Like the kid who gave him the medal, the woman's organization has known his name from the beginning.

A tone chimes, reminding him to take his keys. He ignores the warning, closes the door. As per the woman's instructions, he leaves the car unlocked, registration in the glove box, wallet on the seat, keys in the ignition. She has told him to bring nothing and be ready for a full-body search. He takes a prescription bottle from his pocket, shows her. "Are these OK?" He shakes the bottle. "For pain."

"Not my call." She helps him toward the van. "That's the driver's department. You can ask him."

Robert remembers her voice from the phone, Southern accent overgrown with Ivy-League vowels. "He'll probably let you keep them."

That's good news. Rain always aggravates the pain.

He leans against her for support. "Nasty weather."

"It's warmer where you're going."

"Warmer sounds good."

"And drier." She opens the cargo area, revealing a seat and an oval table. The floor is carpeted, the cab partitioned behind a cockpit door.

"Need help getting in?"

"No. I can manage." But he lingers, looking back at his car, realizing he'll never see it again. They'll use it to fake his death, torch it somewhere along Route 51, probably place someone's remains inside to satisfy the adjusters. The kid claims they can do such things. After all, cadavers are their stock and trade.

"Mr. Jones? Getting in?"

"Yes. All right." He steps up with his good leg, drags the bad one after it, slips into the seat and buckles up. She closes the cargo door. Once again, he's alone.

He tries getting comfortable. It's no use. The pain is spreading: up his leg, through his hips, along the small of his back. He is opening his bottle of pills when the cockpit door opens. A man enters from the cab: stocky, no neck, buzz cut.

"You're the driver?"

The man frowns at the bottle. "What's that?" His voice is throaty, his accent nothing like the woman's.

"Medicine," Robert says. "Your colleague told me—"

"What kind?" The accent sounds eastern European. Russian? Slovakian? "The pills. What kind?"

The cockpit door remains open behind him, dome light fading in the cab as a shadow moves across the dash. It's the woman, settling down, buckling in. Robert considers calling to her, asking for back up, but instead he simply hands the bottle to the man who pops the lid and looks inside. "Are you going to frisk me?" Robert asks.

"Frisk?"

"You know, search me."

The man closes the bottle, hands it back. "You nervous?"

"Would that surprise you?"

The man leans forward. "Relax, eh?" He goes to work, first the living leg, then the dead one, then the crotch, which (tragically) is still alive. The search continues, working upward, pausing at Robert's chest. "This?"

"A medal."

"Show me."

Robert opens his shirt.

"You religious?"

"I suppose. I mean, wouldn't you be?"

The man lifts the medal but doesn't remove it. He turns it in the light, then lets go and gestures for Robert to button up. A moment later he is gone.

The van eases forward.

* * *

They take back roads to a working-class district along the banks of the Monongahela. Once a melting pot of immigrant families, the place has become a boulevard of coffeehouses, galleries, and artist lofts. The storefronts blur by, mostly dark, some boarded. A few contain gutted interiors—walls stripped to brick, pipes and girders for that bohemian look. With the van stopped at an intersection, Robert glimpses what looks like a freeform sculpture through a loft window: angled beams, taut cables—a web of tension and balance. He wonders if that's where they're taking him, but when the traffic light changes, the van rumbles on.

The oval table in front of him looks as if it belongs in a living room: wood-veneer sides, faux leather top. Only the cup holders suggest it was designed for a van. There's a water bottle in one of the holders. Robert opens it and washes down two pills. Then he sits back.

His mind races.

He closes his eyes.

Kathy and Josh are there, waiting in a dream that is always brighter and darker than his memories—brighter because when the dream begins it's as if he's never lost them; darker because the loss when it comes is always more terrible than he cares to remember.

TWO

Jets roar.

Robert wakes to the shadow of a wing streaking low beyond the van's window. It's there for an instant, then gone—disappearing over a chain-link fence and a sheet-metal sign:

AIR OPERATIONS AREA

The driver steers through a gate and toward a waiting fuselage. A crew-cut man watches beside the gangway.

The woman's voice comes muffled from the cab, a quick exchange with the driver. Robert can't make out the words.

The driver's reply doesn't sound like English. The woman answers in kind, then climbs out. A moment later, she opens the cargo door. She has lowered her hood, revealing a helmet of form-fitting hair. "First stop, Mr. Jones."

A terminal stands behind her: art deco façade, glass doors, bright interior. It's small, more like an upscale mini-mart than a commercial terminal.

"Bathroom break?" he asks, though he doesn't have to go, hasn't had anything all morning but a few sips of water and the pills. "Do I have time?"

"Yes, but not here." She takes his arm, helping him along the tarmac. "You can go on the plane." She leads him around the van, up the gangway, into a wood-paneled galley where she hangs his coat. She does the same with her own, then points the way to a lavatory in the back of the four-seat cabin.

"Do you need help?"

He wonders how much help she has in mind. Help walking? Entering the lavatory? Holding him as he goes? "I can manage." He moves away, walking easier now that the pills have taken hold, nothing left to slow him down but the weight of the world.

The aisle is wider than a commercial jet's, but the washroom is typical—cramped, steel fixtures in a fiberglass shell. He closes the door, leans against it, steadies himself before the bowl.

Maybe I shouldn't do this. Maybe I should turn around, tell the woman I've reconsidered. Have the driver take me home.

But he can't, of course. The home isn't his anymore, hasn't been for days. Papers have been signed, money transferred. He owns nothing. It's just himself and his memories.

"Mr. Jones," the woman calls from the galley. "You all right?"

"One minute."

He does what he has come to do, then buttons up and turns to the sink. A haggard face greets him in the mirror, middle-aged, drawn cheeks, too many scars.

"Mr. Jones?"

He opens the door to find the woman standing in the galley.

"We're ready when you are."

A piece of a man is visible through the cockpit door: white sleeve, pressed cuff, hand against the controls.

"Where do I sit?"

"Wherever you like."

Robert takes the closest spot, buckles in, stretches out. There's plenty of room.

The woman closes the galley, leaving him alone once more as the engines change pitch. Minutes later they are airborne, climbing steeply.

He sleeps again.

Kathy and Josh are there, riding beside him as he drives east on I-80. He steers with one hand, reaches behind the seat with the other. He's feeling along the floor for something important.

"It's there," Kathy tells him. "I saw it fall."

He looks away from the road. "Here it is!" He pulls it from the mat near Josh's unoccupied safety seat. "Got it!" He holds the pacifier by its ring. Dirt clings to the nipple.

Kathy holds Josh, rubbing his gums with benzocaine. They know the baby should be in his seat, but holding him is the only way to keep him quiet. Besides, what's going to happen?

"Hmmm." She frowns at the dirty pacifier. "Looks like it's got seventy-eleven diseases." That's one of her pet expressions: *seventy-eleven*. Robert never heard it before meeting her. Now that she's gone, he hears it all the time in his dreams.

A jolt rouses him. He wakes, gripping the armrest. Trees blur beyond the windows. He's suddenly wide awake, riding the roar of reverse thrusters, tensing to the thump of wheels touching down, braking hard. The plane slows, but still he sees only trees. No terminal, tower, or lights . . . just tarmac beneath the wing. The rest is forest.

The galley door folds back. The woman appears, backlit by morning sun. "Still with us?" She has fluffed her hair, applied makeup. She looks renewed, almost a different person. "We get off here."

He limps into the aisle, pausing to stretch his leg before moving forward.

"Hurting?"

"I'm all right."

Warm air courses through the open hatch.

"You won't need your coat," she says. "You can leave it here."

First his house, then his car and wallet, now his coat. He knows what's next.

A Chevy Blazer waits beside the stairs. Standard interior: vinyl upholstery, plastic armrests, no amenities. A Plexiglas sheet separates cab and cargo. A driver waits at the wheel, broad shoulders, shaved head that doesn't look around as the woman opens the rear door.

"Where are we?" he asks.

"Close."

He is beginning to understand why she keeps placing him behind partitions. It discourages questions.

The backseat smells of pine, but it isn't from the forest. It's disinfectant.

"You'll want to strap in, Mr. Jones. It'll be bumpy at first." She closes the door, then climbs in front.

Robert buckles in and cracks the window. The Blazer lurches and pulls away. Looking back one last time, he gets a final look at the landing strip among the pines. How far south is he? Virginia? The Carolinas? Georgia?

Branches slap the window, leaving needle smears. This is the worst part of the trip, the jolts dredging memories of a day that changed his life forever.

"Looks like it's got seventy-eleven diseases." Kathy rides beside him, holding Josh, squinting in the rising sun.

A blue Nissan cruises a half dozen car lengths ahead. Beyond it, almost lost in the glare, a cargo trailer bounds behind an SUV. The trailer reminds him of his first major move, relocating from New York to Pittsburgh in his mid-twenties, back when the entire contents of his life could fit into a cargo trailer and a four-cylinder Ford.

Josh reaches for the dirty pacifier, groping with a hand too small to be real. It's a magical moment, and in that instant Robert realizes how lucky he is to have found Kathy . . . and how glad he is that he trusted her to quit working and have a child so late in the game. He looks at them both in the golden light. "Hey, Kathy."

"Hey, what?"

"I was thinking." He looks back at the road. "Remember when—"

Something's wrong.

He sees it through the glare. A thousand feet away the cargo trailer has come loose, hitch swinging, safety chain whipping. It spins toward the Nissan. The driver swerves. Too late. The hitch rams it broadside. Robert doesn't hear the impact. His windows are raised, air conditioner on, radio playing a song from the '70s—"You Are the Woman That I've Always Dreamed Of."

The Nissan loses control, careens over the shoulder, off the road. It seems unreal, like a movie, a YouTube video.

Wake up. Make it stop!

But he rides it out, hands on the wheel. The sun shines as before, and Kathy (still looking at him and not at the road) waits for him to answer her question, and Josh (blissfully oblivious) keeps reaching for the dirty pacifier. Only Robert sees the trailer rebound from its impact with the Nissan, but as it begins to roll and spew its contents across the highway, Kathy finally turns to see it. She doesn't scream. People react that way in movies, not in real life. She sees it, sets her hand on the dash. "Whoa!" That's all. Not a shout, barely a whisper. "Whoa!"

And then. . . .

WHAM!

Robert wakes.

The Chevy Blazer crosses a gravel shoulder, steers onto a two-lane road, rounds a bend onto a straightaway. Robert leans toward the Plexiglas partition. There's something on the horizon. Straight lines cloaked in haze. A city! It doesn't look familiar, but then how many skylines does he really know? New York, of course. Pittsburgh, because it's home. A few eastern cities because he's been. But southern cities are mysteries to him.

Hic sunt dracones!

He considers tapping on the Plexiglas, asking where they are. But instead he sits back as the forest gives way to strip malls, parking lots, fast food joints, gas stations, and an array of one-story warehouses that might contain anything—anonymous structures, the kind most people see but don't remember.

The Blazer slows, angles toward one of the buildings: steel walls, flat roof, garage door that rises as they approach. A moment later they are inside, rolling beneath girders, passing parked cars with license plates from Tennessee, Arkansas, Missouri. . . .

The Blazer parks, and Robert waits for the woman to come around to help him. He's hurting again: legs, hips, back. He stumbles as he gets out, falls against her. "Whoa!" she says. Not a shout, barely a whisper. "You all right?"

Whoa!

Is he back in the dream?

"Mr. Jones?"

He returns to the moment. "I'm OK. Just need to walk. Walking helps."

So they walk, through a fire door and into a drop-ceiling hallway, windowless walls, a floor with eight-inch vinyl squares of alternating green and gray. They pass a line of closed offices, coming at last to a door that opens into a rotunda that seems to have nothing to do with the rest of the building. And its size? It's too large. It can't be part of the same low-slung warehouse.

"Do you need a bathroom, Mr. Jones?"

"No."

"There's time."

"I'm fine."

Doors rim the rotunda. The woman has brought him to the center of something, a hub that may well be one of the last places he'll ever see.

"All right, then. This way." She escorts him through a door and into a smaller room. Inside is a table with two place settings: silverware, bone china, crystal tumblers, glass pitcher filled with water. Behind one of the settings hangs a portrait rendered in shades of green, yellow, red, and brown. It depicts a man with intense eyes, aquiline nose. He holds one hand to his chin; the other holds a pen to an open sketchbook. But the eyes are not focused on the page. Instead, they gaze down and to the left, as if looking at something in the room.

"He'll be with you soon," the woman says. "If you're sure you're fine."

Robert detects something new in her voice. Is it sadness? Regret? Apology? He considers telling her not to worry, that being here is his choice, but she is already passing back toward the rotunda, leaving him alone with the painted man who seems to be looking at something to Robert's right, a low pedestal standing a few feet back from the table. Atop the table, a vase holds an arrangement of roses, baby's breath, and violets. He recalls reading something about violets, how their smell temporarily numbs the nose. One sniff is all you get, then you need to rest before having another go. A few framed photographs lean beside the vase, and beside them is a radio that looks like an old portable that he and Kathy used to carry on trips to the beach, back in the days before iPods and earbuds. He snaps it on. A song plays, starting from the beginning—a '70s tune about love and dreams. Listening to it, he feels the weight of all that has happened, the events that have led him to this place, this moment in time. He removes a family photograph from its frame. He wants to get close to it, no glass or gilt coming between his fingers and the colors of the past. He carries it to one of the place settings, sits down, studies the picture, and remembers.

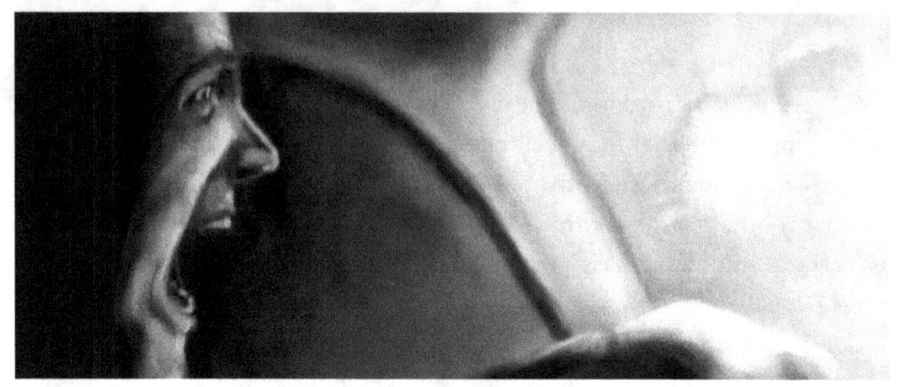

THREE

Kathy rides beside him, morning sun streaming through the windshield, catching in her hair, turning gold against her skin. He starts to tell her that he has been thinking about the early days, when he was young and afraid and not sure he was going to amount to anything. He wants her to know that he is happier now than he has ever been. It isn't that he hasn't said such things before. He simply wants to say them again, but now he can't.

The trailer hurtles toward them.

"Whoa."

That's it, the last thing he remembers before waking to find himself impacted in a mass of steel and sparking wires. The steering wheel is gone from his hands and a line of traffic stretches to his right. Some cars have stopped, others creep along, passing on the shoulder.

Far away, sirens wail.

"It's OK." He turns toward Kathy and Josh, or at least toward the place where they were a moment ago. "We've stopped." Somehow this seems important. If they are stopped, the danger must be over.

But the passenger seat is gone. In its place a twisted chassis hangs above smeared debris. There's blood. And something else. A ragged thing, limp and shapeless. A piece of shoe . . . torn laces so small they seem unreal. But that's all. They're gone now. One second they were beside him. Now he's alone amid the wreckage.

Sirens scream louder, nearer.

The world phases out . . . then back.

Rescue workers hover close, holding cutting tools, pneumatic jaws that bite against the metal, setting him free. He sees what he thinks are his hips, but he can't feel them.

"Stay awake, buddy! We're getting you out!"

The cutting tools keep working, freeing his legs.

People watch. All strangers.

"Come on, buddy. Stay with us."

The world phases out, then in.

IV bags sway on hooks. Tubes dangle. A siren screams, the sound neither approaching nor receding. It moves with him now, keeping pace . . . like the moon through the window of a speeding car.

A voice speaks close to his ear. He can't tell which side of his head it's on, inside or outside. But he hears it. "You're going to be all right." It's Kathy. "You're going to make it. Hold on!" She grips his hand.

He squeezes tight. "Don't let go, Kath."

She doesn't answer.

"Please, Kath. Don't let go." He squeezes harder, but she is already gone.

Healing takes months: first ICU, then the recovery ward, then a rehabilitation hospital 30 miles outside the city. And when it's over, after he's been stitched and stapled and pinned and coached back into something resembling a man, he goes home to a house full of ghosts.

At first he can't bear it. There's too much to process and put away: clothes, toys, photographs, baby food, a voice on the answering machine that he should erase but can't. "Hello! This is Kathy. Rob and I aren't here. Leave a message!"

His sister has honored his request to leave everything in place, but now that he's home she insists on helping him shake the past. When he resists, she pushes back. "You can't live with this stuff, Robert."

But he cannot bear to live without it.

"You have to let go."

"I'll do it my way," he says, making it clear he wants her out of his house. They've never been close. He knows she's here more out of duty than love. "I'll be fine."

He has healed enough to fend for himself. The doctors call it a miracle. But Robert suspects it has to do with Kathy's presence in the ambulance. Her spirit touched him. The touch gave him strength. But inside, things remain broken.

"Please," he tells his sister. "I know what I need. Just leave me alone, all right?"

So she does.

And that evening, he starts working on the shrine.

It begins as a collage of photos, then expands, overrunning a poster board set atop the dining-room table. There is so much to hold on to, organize, arrange.

He buys a digital scanner and studies HTML. The learning curve is slow, but he has time. At first he intends to create a multimedia document for himself, a collection of images, favorite songs, video clips—all stored and accessible forever in incorruptible cyberspace. The project grows quickly. There are so many pieces to include, hyperlinks leading to hyperlinks. When he finishes, he finds he has created something of alarming complexity and beauty, a structure that must be shared.

He considers posting it through existing platforms—Facebook, MySpace, YouTube. But none of those are right for what he has made. The thing requires its own space, its own domain. Naturally, the obvious URLs are taken: memories.com, shrine.com, myfamily.com. Amazed by the profusion of registered URLs, he decides trying something less generic, more personal. He keys it into a search box: seventyeleven.com.

It's available.

He registers it, and four months after the accident he launches the site that reintroduces Kathy and Josh to the world of the living. He does not know who, if anyone, will find it. Having people view the site is less important than making it available, but just in case, he includes his email address, appending it as a link at the bottom of the main page.

The first responses are solicitations from service providers and phishing scams:

Increase Traffic to Your Site!
Enhance Revenues with Click-throughs.
10,000 Real Visitors for $7.95.
You're a Lucky Winner!!!

But within a week, real responses trickled in:

I share your pain.
You are in our prayers.
I also lost a child.

The latter is from a single mother whose daughter died of lupus. The email includes a link to a web shrine featuring photos and text accompanied by a streaming soundtrack of favorite songs and a link to a chat room devoted to discussions of eshrines and memorials. He is astounded. Until now he has assumed that his concept was unique. But it turns out that seventy-eleven.com is one of hundreds, and the number is growing.

Some of the chat-room people offer to link to his page. He reciprocates and soon finds himself part of a growing, grieving community.

And then comes something new, an email with a subject line that nearly stops his heart. He sees it, flinches, looks away, looks again. Does it really say that? He leans forward, bracing on the edge of his desk—staring, reading, rereading:

We can take you to them.

Them can't refer to his family. Can it? And if it does, the email is certainly a scam. He considers deleting it unread, hesitates, then double clicks.

Dear Mr. Jones:

There are few traumas as devastating as the death of a loved one, and you have felt the pangs twice over. Please accept our heartfelt sympathies and assurance that you are not alone. However, since the numerous links on your eshrine indicate that you probably know that already, let us offer something else as well. Something more than a sense of community. Let us offer you this:

We can take you to them.

It is a bold statement, and one that you should not accept without proof.

The link below will provide a preview of the reunion we can deliver, one that begins with you accessing an account that has already been opened in your name.

Your passcode is: 7734

The link is: http://www.fieri-mnemosyne.com
Sincerely,
Fieri Mnemosyne

Robert stares at the name.
Fieri Mnemosyne?
Is it a person, a corporation?
He Googles it, finds nothing, then moves on to dictionary.com where

he finds that *Mnemosyne* is the goddess of memory. But there's nothing for *Fieri*, only a string of close matches: *feirie, fuero, frei, ferie. . . .*

He searches other dictionaries, other languages, finally coming across an online Latin dictionary that defines the word as *to become* or *to be made.* In other words: *To become memory. To be made memory.*

Or maybe it's just someone's name.

He goes back to his email and looks again at the statement in the letter's subject line:

We can take you to them.

If it's a scam, it's an unusually personal one from people familiar with his eshrine. And it's well written, with none of the fractured English of most phishing scams.

Should he try the link? What does he have to lose? He jots the passcode on a sheet of notepaper and double clicks.

The navigation bar vanishes. The screen goes white. Two small frames appear: one contains a blinking cursor.

For his name?

He enters it. The cursor shifts to the second frame.

Passcode?

He keys it in, presses enter. The frames vanish. Text appears.

Dear Robert Christopher Jones:

You are seven steps away from a preview of the reunion we have promised. No doubt you are eager to proceed, but we must ask you to first read and follow the instructions below.

Noncompliance with any step will void the demonstration.

1. The preview must be viewed on a 16:9 monitor, 1080p, 120 hz or greater. We believe you have such a monitor in your home. If not, you must purchase one before proceeding. Size, 40 inches or greater.
2. You must be alone when you begin the demonstration. Do not proceed if there is someone else in the house or if you are expecting visitors.
3. Turn off or disconnect all telephones and automatic devices that might distract you during the demonstration.
4. Position yourself at a distance from your screen equal to 1.5x your monitor's diagonal viewing area.
5. Cover all windows. Place opaque tape over the diodes on your

monitor, hard drive, smoke alarm—any light source that will be visible within your viewing angle.

6. Turn off all room lights and confirm that the only illumination is coming from the monitor.

7. When you have complied with all of the above, click here:

The icon is a wedding ring. He leans closer, making out the inscription along the inner rim. It's *his* ring, the image apparently lifted from seventy-eleven.com. This is not a generic phishing page. This is a page custom made for him, an exclusive demonstration.

He assembles a work area in his game room, positioning a folding table in front of his plasma TV. Connecting the laptop is easy enough, and once it's done he goes upstairs to mute the ringers on the phones. He also checks the front and back doors, making sure both are locked. Not that he is expecting company. His sister has returned to her home in New England, but it doesn't hurt to be sure. He disconnects the bell and engages the chain. Then he takes the slip of paper with the passcode on it and carries it down to the game room where he turns off the lights and takes a seat five feet from the monitor.

The emailed instructions glow back at him.

He palms the mouse and clicks his wedding ring.

His taskbar vanishes. The screen goes black. Power failure? No, the laptop hums. And the TV isn't completely blank. A pattern stirs the darkness. He leans forward, then sits back again, remembering the instructions: 60 inches, no closer.

He straightens his back against the chair, staring, focusing, discerning a rotating cube. He blinks. The movement seems far off, tumbling toward him until the cube pivots, grows larger, breaks apart, then fills his view.

"Whoa."

The desktop speakers are off. The room is silent. He listens with his eyes.

"Rob."

It's Kathy, her voice calling through the expanding angles and lines.

"I'm here, Rob."

He feels her sitting before him, leaning close, alive within the image on the screen.

"Josh is here too."

The image blurs. He blinks, feels a chill on his cheek.

"We love you, Rob."

He wants to reach for her, but he's afraid to move . . . afraid he'll break the spell.

The air quickens with the scent of talc, benzocaine, baby skin.

"We're both here, Rob."

"I can't see you."

He feels pressure on his hand, fingers locking with his. He holds on, squeezing.

"Hold on, Rob."

He doesn't answer.

"Please," she says. "You have to hold on." She squeezes harder.

The screen darkens. White letters appear:

End Preview.
We will contact you with further instructions.

He sits, staring, wondering.

What just happened?

He leans forward, elbows on the table, reading and rereading the second line of text. Who are these people? How will they make contact? And when? And there's another question. A bigger one. That thing, the shape, that arrangement of angles and lines whose ghost even now lingers as a burned-in image on the plasma screen—what was it? What did it do to him? How did it deliver him into the presence of Kathy and Josh?

He closes his eyes.

The shape is there too, haunting his eyes, vague but as undeniable as the ghost in the plasma.

When he looks at the screen again, he finds that his taskbar has returned. He clicks the back arrow, hoping to replay the image, but with the click the current page vanishes, replaced by a black-on-white message clearly not from Fieri Mnemosyne:

404: Page Not Found.

He goes back to his email inbox. Mnemosyne's letter will have the link. He'll use that to replay the demo.

But the email has been removed from his box.

It's as if the demonstration never happened. And yet here he is, in the game room, his computer connected to the TV, everything in compliance with the vanished email.

He sits back, centered in the glow of his giant monitor. The small table, laptop, HDMI cable—everything is where he put it before beginning the demonstration. But the demonstration is gone.

He eases out of the chair, crosses the room, turns on the light. He feels disoriented, as if he has just come out of a long sleep. He does not think he has been down here for more than a few minutes, but somehow the day feels old. And his back is stiff, legs numb. He feels as if he has been sitting for hours.

He climbs the stairs, opens the door, and steps out into the glare of afternoon light through west windows. It was late morning when he closed the door. He checks the kitchen clock. 3:17 PM!

And there's something else. Something stranger. He senses it as he reaches the hall. Someone else is in the house. He's sure of it.

He steadies against the wall, looks toward the living room. He can't see into it, yet he knows someone is in there, waiting.

"Hello?" His voice echoes. He feels stupid, paranoid. Then he sees the door chain hanging limp, swinging.

"I'm in here. In the living room." The voice is thin, young, apparently male.

Robert considers the demonstration's final message, the promise to make contact. Is that what this is? He limps toward the living room to find a seated stranger, a boy in his early 20s: nylon windbreaker, shoulder pack, jeans, gloves, sunglasses, heavy shoes. Robert gives the shoes a double take: platform soles, Frankenstein boots.

"I let myself in. Didn't want to interrupt the demo."

"You're with him, then?"

"Him?"

"Mnemosyne?"

The kid removes his sunglasses, uncovering a mismatched pair of eyes: one bare, the other encased in a patch of molded plastic. There's a diode in the patch's center, glowing like a hot coal. "No. Not with. *Against.*"

Robert wonders if he should get out of the house, escape into the front yard, scream for help. He has heard that attracting attention is the best defense against home invasion. But is that what this is?

"We need to talk, Robert. May I call you *Robert*? Or would you prefer *Mr. Jones*?"

"Who—"

"You should sit down." The kid waves a gloved hand, gesturing to the couch. "Over there, if you like. A safe distance . . . until you're ready to trust me."

Robert remains in the hall, two steps from the door. "What's going on here?"

"I want to talk about the demo."

"What I just saw?"

"Right." The kid taps his diode eye. "I hacked in, watched with you. It was impressive. I've seen them before, other demos, earlier versions. The one you got was more impressive than those. Mnemosyne keeps getting better."

Robert moves to the couch, sits on the far end, close to the door. "You need to tell me—"

"I'll do better than that, Mr. Jones. Better than *tell*. I'll *show*. But first I need you to make a circle. Like this." He brings his hands together, forms a ring with his thumbs and index fingers, then holds the ring to his face.

Robert hesitates.

"Humor me, Robert."

Robert does as the kid asks, or at least tries. His arms don't extend well, but he does his best, makes a circle.

"Now hold it up, look through it. Look at me."

Robert holds his hands as high as he can, lowers his head, peers through the circle.

"OK. Right-eye dominant." The kid removes his shoulder pack, reaches into a pocket, takes out a piece of molded plastic, makes a couple of adjustments. "This goes over your left eye."

Robert frowns at the thing. "What is it?"

"Wireless monocle. Lithium-powered ETD."

"ETD?"

"Eyetop Display. You need to put it on."

"And if I don't?"

"Right. We have backup plans, one of which is to wait for someone who wants our help." The kid gets up, the soles of his boots compressing with his weight. "I'm not one of the bad guys, Robert." He crosses the room, pauses at arm's length, offers the monocle. "Take it."

Robert hesitates.

"My people know all about Mnemosyne—the Internet trawling, email propositions, graphic-induced trances." The kid presses the monocle into

Robert's hand. "I'd like to give you a good look at the thing that you glimpsed in the demonstration, let you see it fully illuminated."

Despite its size, the monocle feels light—no more than a few ounces. There's a hook for the nose, a larger one for the ear. In between hangs a plastic shell, small lens on the outside, not much of anything on the inside.

"Here." The kid helps Robert put it on. The hook for the ear is tight, pinching snuggly. "You'd better sit back for this." The kid eases him against the cushions. "The first time can be disorienting."

Robert is still seeing with both eyes, as if a projector has come on inside the monocle, zapping his retina with an incredibly sharp image. The room looks suddenly brighter, hyper real.

The kid returns to his chair, waves a gloved hand, and places the image of a man in the center of the room. It hovers there, suspended, superimposed over a bare wall, clearly visible until Robert closes the covered eye. Then the man vanishes.

"Keep watching, Robert. Both eyes open. Pay attention."

The man wears a tweed jacket. He looks like a college professor, circa 1950. But there is also a strange precision to his looks: eyebrows so neat they seem to have been painted, hair so straight that it could have been parted with a scalpel.

"Dario Sebastian." The kid says. "See him?"

"I see a man."

"In focus?"

"Yes."

"Take a good look. He's the inspiration behind Fieri Mnemosyne. The image you're seeing is one of the few full-length shots we have. It was taken in Leningrad, 1959, during his Russian period."

"He's Russian?"

"No. American. Son of southern oil. Rich as hell. At least he was. Inherited enough to travel the world studying art and philosophy . . . among other things. In Russia he worked with an underground painter known simply as *Surgeon*." The kid's gloved hand sweeps the air with a clearing motion. The image of Dario Sebastian vanishes, replaced by a grainy shot of a bearded man standing outside a rotting cottage. "Surgeon painted with bone brushes, used body fluids for paint, developed a recipe for human parchment—incredible stuff, delicate, thin as hammered gold."

"Parchment? Made from skin?"

"That's right."

"Human skin?"

"Surgeon was sick, Robert. And Dario Sebastian was his pupil."

New images appear: first a secluded monastery, then three monks dropping sand onto a table, creating a geometrical pattern that quivers as if alive.

"After Leningrad he moved to Napal where he studied *yantras*. Do you know that word?"

"*Yantras?*"

"Trance-inducing symbols, windows for seeing beyond the beyond."

A geometrical pattern appears. Robert tries touching it. His fingers close on empty air. But the kid has cybernetic gloves, able to move the yantra aside and replace it with the image of a saddle-stitched pamphlet: rust-colored ink, tan paper.

"In 1963, Dario self-published *Form and Transformation*, a manifesto on the art of human essence. He made 24 copies, which he circulated among his close circle of students and devotees. My people have procured one of them. The ink is blood, the paper, parchment." The kid fans the air. The pamphlet fades. A brass devil appears. "He also studied the art of demon locks, designs so terrifying that only the owners dared touch them."

The lock is in the shape of a face: eyes rimmed with spikes, the nose a barbed phallus. But the most frightening detail is the mouth, although Robert isn't quite sure why. Something about it repulses him. Is it the angle of the lips? The slant of the teeth? He can't tell.

"Unsettling, isn't it?" The kid fans the air. The demon vanishes.

Robert exhales and realizes he's been holding his breath.

"That last image went right to your nerves. Set off a reflex reaction. If you had continued looking at it, it would have altered your brain chemistry. Dario called that the power of *atavistics*."

Robert tries taking off the monocle.

"No, Robert. Leave it on. We're not finished."

"I don't see where this is going."

"You will. Bear with me." He raises a hand, holds it poised. "Dario also studied psychology in Vienna, anatomy in London. Along the way, he earned a degree in mortuary science. The details seem random until you realize what he was building toward." He taps the air. A warehouse district appears, flat-roof buildings with concrete walls. "In the 1980s, Dario began plying his trade in warehouses scattered throughout the American south." The image fades, replaced by another, then another—a string of anonymous city blocks. "These are some of the places where he set up shop, creating secret studios in right-to-work states. He favored cheap labor but spared no expense when it came to recruiting from the world's best schools. He trained his people well, indoctrinating them to assure absolute loyalty."

"You're talking about brainwashing."

"No. Not *washing*. That's not the word. What he did was more like *casting, reshaping, bossing*—using the power of form and design to put his mark on impressionable minds. But even a loyal workforce is expensive, and a few years ago, after a string of bad investments left him on the verge of bankruptcy, he vanished. No one can account for where he went, what he did. For a year he apparently ceased to exist. Then . . . in late 2010 . . . a new entity emerged. Fieri Mnemosyne. A person's name? An organization? We're not sure. But whatever it is, Mnemosyne's activities seem to have picked up where Sebastian's left off. Early last year, we became aware of *this*!" The kid gestures again. A square appears on his fingertip, balancing, then hovering on its own. "Look familiar?"

The square rotates, becomes a cube, grows.

Robert tenses, gripping the couch, holding on.

"Keep watching."

Robert's nape hairs bristle. A chill moves through him, along his shoulders, down his spine.

"It has a different effect when fully lighted. It's all in how you look at it, the angle of illumination. Point of view changes everything."

Robert considers closing his monocled eye.

"Keep looking, Robert. Know what you're dealing with. Look at the shape of the demon."

The thing fills his view.

"You understand, Robert? Form and content. Physical and spiritual."

And now Robert knows what he is seeing, the fibrous textures, the translucent sheets thin as hammered gold.

"It's made of skin, Robert. And bone. And tendons and viscera. Form and substance. That's the key."

Robert tugs the monocle, pulling it off—or trying to. The hook clings to his ear.

The kid comes toward him, removes the device, puts it away. "That thing . . . the construction you just saw . . . it's made of pieces . . . the pieces of Mnemosyne's victims."

Robert sits back, shaken.

The kid puts his pack over his shoulders, tightens the strap.

"You're leaving?"

"For now. I'll return after they make contact. At that point, they'll ask you to purchase a Skype phone, set up an account. Their calls will be heavily encrypted. Impossible to trace, difficult to intercept."

"What will they want?"

"All you've got."

"As in—"

"Whatever can be liquidated and transferred. That's the first step. After that, they'll send for you. And you'll go with them . . . lured by the promise of rejoining your family, which they will make happen if you let them. Rejoined in death." The kid is whispering now, leaning toward Robert, their faces almost touching. "They'll kill you, Robert. Put you in a wish-fulfilling trance and take you apart . . . deconstruct you . . . use your substance to expand a gigantic yantra that they are building in a warehouse somewhere in the southeast. At least that's their plan. But we can keep that from happening. If you help us, we'll protect you."

"Who's we?"

The kid steps back, takes out his sunglasses, unfolds the stems. "Me and my associates."

"The police?"

"Hardly."

"CIA?"

"We're an intranational concern, Robert."

"International?"

"No, *intra*national. *Between* nations, not *among* them. Our interest in Mnemosyne isn't about justice or protection. We will save you if we can. But our interest is in the yantra."

Robert waits for him to continue.

Instead, the kid heads toward the door.

"But what do I do?"

"Accept Mnemosyne's offer. When they come for you, we'll follow."

"I'm the bait?"

"It might be better if you don't think of it that way." The kid opens the door, adjusts his sunglasses, steps out. The door closes behind him. The simple action is almost startling. And now, standing alone on the edge of his living room, Robert wonders if he has just imagined everything. Perhaps he is still in the game room, entranced in the darkness.

He opens the front door, looks outside, up the street, then down. It's a bedroom community, nearly abandoned during the afternoon, nothing outside but sunlight, trees, and a cloud of starlings fluttering from the branches as he limps onto the walk. A car passes, a vaguely familiar neighbor at the wheel. But that's it. The streets and sidewalks are stone silent.

And the kid is gone.

Robert wanders back downstairs. Everything is as he left it: card table, chair, laptop, cable, plasma monitor. And there's something else, a slip of paper on the floor beside the chair. He picks it up, looks at it. There's something scrawled across it. A single word:

$$\text{HELL}$$

The handwriting is oddly contorted, completely unfamiliar, somehow deranged. But the paper is his, torn from the tablet he keeps on his desk upstairs. But he did not write this.

He sits in the chair. Is he losing his mind? He starts to crumple the sheet, then stops.

Of course!

He looks at it again, then sets the note on the table, rotates it until the word becomes a number, a four-digit passcode:

$$7734$$

The kid's words come back to him.

It's all in how you look at it. Point of view changes everything.

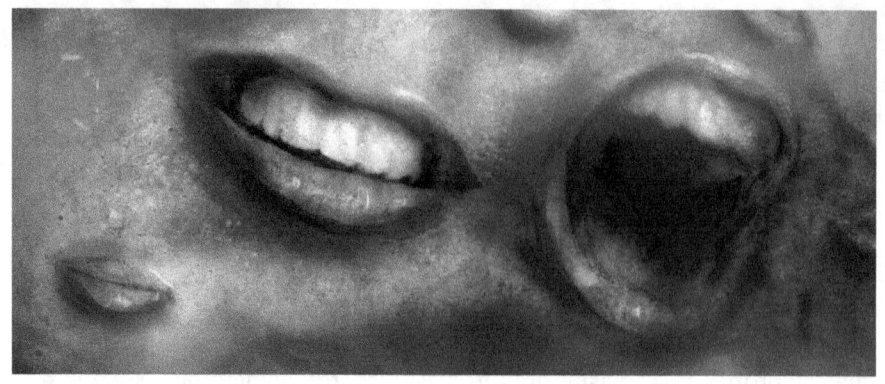

FOUR

The radio is still playing in the small room next to the rotunda in Fieri Mnemosyne's block-long warehouse. The song is yet another one from a life that Robert wishes to reclaim. He's holding a picture of Kathy and Josh, the print from the pedestal in the corner of the room. The paper, though smooth when he took it from the frame, is now smeared and crumpled. He does not want to let it go. He wants to stare at it, slip back into memory, return to the past. But he has been distracted, first by the sound of an opening door, and now by a voice, thin and reedy.

"Hungry, Mr. Jones?"

Robert looks up to find a man standing in an open door beside the hanging portrait. He wears a cable-knit sweater and scrub pants, his face an older version of the one in the painting.

Robert straightens up. *Dario Sebastian?*

Sebastian's eyes are brighter in life than in the portrait, more blue than green. Contacts? That has to be it. A man his age would need corrective lenses. He smiles, teeth perfectly straight, unnaturally white, probably dentures. His hair, too, looks suspect. He snaps off the radio and reverses back through the door, returning with a wheeled cart. "Hungry?" He locks the wheels, lifts a lid. Four tiny birds lie on a tray: legs in the air, wings crimped against glazed breasts. "Quail." Sebastian tongs two onto a plate.

"I'm not hungry."

"I doubt that." Sebastian prepares a plate, arranging the pieces with the care of an artist: redskin potatoes, podded peas, bunched grapes. "Hunger is a distraction, Mr. Jones. Our work will run smoother without it." He places the plate before Robert. "And don't wait for me. Quail cools quickly."

He turns back to the tray, picks up a second plate, repeats the process. "Please, Mr. Jones. Humor me."

Robert picks up his fork, solid silver, heavy but balanced. The knife is the same. He goes to work, cutting into the breast. One slice, he hits bone.

"I prefer using my hands." Sebastian sets his plate across from Robert, unfolds his napkin, presses it flat on the table beside him. Then he grips a quail leg, works it loose, peels the skin. The flesh steams. "Feel free to do likewise."

But Robert already has a piece of meat on his fork. The meat smells sweet and gamey. He tastes it. Lightly seasoned—salt, butter, little else.

"Reaction?"

Robert swallows. "It's good." He cuts some more.

"You're hungrier than you thought."

Robert takes another bite.

"Denial is like that, you know. I learned that in a monastery." Sebastian discards the peeled skin, placing it on the napkin beside his plate. "I lived a year in a stone cell near the Spiti Valley, Tibet—beyond the Kunzum Pass." He licks his fingers, long and sharp, nails filed to points. "It's not a monastery you would know. Not likely, anyway. Quite secluded." He chews as he talks. "The monks did everything by hand . . . no utensils . . . intimate contact only." He places the bone beside the discarded skin, then sets to work on the second leg. "That's the problem, isn't it? The reason you're here. You've tried living without, locked away in a house full of memories, keeping the world away. You thought that was best, but now you know better. One taste, and you knew."

Are they still talking about food? "You mean the demonstration?"

"Yes, partly." Sebastian places more peeled skin on the napkin. "But I'm also talking about breaking bread, conversing—as we're doing." He cleans the second leg and drops its bone at a right angle to the first, its shaft positioned neatly between the pieces of skin.

Robert glances at the emerging design, looks away, then looks again. It's just a couple of bones, right? Bones and skin. But there's something about the points of intersection, something beyond simple geometries.

"How long has it been?" Sebastian asks, working on a wing. "How long since you've shared a hand-cooked meal?"

Robert wonders if he should keep his guard up, but why? He's here now, might as well go with it. "Too long."

"Then it's good you've come." Sebastian places a wing bone on the napkin, then picks up a pea pod and runs a nail along its side. The peas roll into his palm. "I work with symbols." He adds the pod to the bits of skin and bone, then slips the peas into his mouth, helping them along with a sharpened finger. "Like the design I showed you in my demonstration."

Robert can't stop looking at the skin and bones beside Sebastian's plate. The design makes him uneasy, but he can't look away.

"Sorry." Sebastian raises a corner of the napkin, folding it over, covering the scraps. "It's a habit."

But Robert does not think that the design was any less planned than his being here.

"My work is not about structure, Mr. Jones. It's about the spaces between. One does not look *at* my designs . . . but *through* them. Past physicality, toward the spiritual."

Robert takes another bite of quail, eating with his hands now, knife and fork abandoned beside the plate.

"I do not speak metaphorically. You appreciate that, don't you?"

"I think so."

"The demonstration I sent you was successful?"

"It was."

"And you've come for your reunion, to be with your family again."

"Yes." Robert stops eating. "If you can make it happen."

"I can." Sebastian licks his fingers. "I mean . . . I can if I wish it. If it's really the reason you're here. So long as you don't have another agenda."

"What do you mean?"

"You may speak freely."

"What about?"

For a moment, Sebastian just stares, peering deep until Robert looks away.

"Tell me," Sebastian says. "Did they come as one?"

"Who?" On one level, Robert feels he's missed something. On another, he's certain he knows exactly what Sebastian means.

"The people who contacted you, Mr. Jones."

"What makes you think—"

"Please, Mr. Jones. You're in my world now. I know how it works. Did it seem to be one person, a kid suddenly appearing in your home?"

Robert looks away, considers lying. But why? Sebastian obviously knows. "Yes."

"College age? Motion-tracking gloves? Eyetop display?"

"Sounds like you're on to him."

"Not him specifically. There are many such as he. What did they tell you?"

"They?"

"Trust me. He may have appeared to be one man, but his name was Legion."

"Excuse me."

"He did not represent himself, Mr. Jones."

"He told me about that. He spoke of an organization . . . an employer."

"Not that either. They have no hierarchy. What else did they tell you, Mr. Jones?"

Robert looks down at his plate, the twin quail carcasses, a few uneaten vegetables. "OK," he says. "Here's what happened."

And he tells the story, most of it anyway. He does not mention the St. Christopher medal, but what he shares is enough to darken Sebastian's gaze.

"Lies," Sebastian says at last. "Ruthless and cruel." He sits back. "I do not *butcher* my clients. Why would I?"

"For parts."

"Parts of what?"

"The thing you're building."

"And you believed? Did you ask yourself if a sane man would do such a thing?"

Robert hesitates, then speaks his mind. "The kid claims you're insane."

"And still you came?"

"I felt I had nothing to lose."

"You make a compelling case, Mr. Jones. I'm inclined to believe you. But one more question. Maybe two, depending. Will you answer truthfully?"

"I'll try."

"Then tell me. Do you have any reason to suspect you've been followed?"

"Here?"

"Yes."

"By the kid?"

"By his people."

"How would they do that?"

"You tell me."

"How could anyone have followed me?" He stops, caught short by the nervous pitch of his own voice. *Take your time. You're here now. It's almost over.* "Your people take me from a parking lot in the dead of morning, drive me to a private airfield, fly me to the middle of nowhere—"

"You're saying it would be a difficult trail to follow?"

"I'm saying it would be near impossible."

"Unless you wore a tracking device, an electronic marker."

Robert looks away.

"My driver tells me you're wearing something." Sebastian speaks slowly, coldly. "A religious medal. May I see it?"

What now?

"Please, Mr. Jones."

"I'm sorry."

"No need. Just show me."

"I mean . . . I'm sorry. I don't know what you're talking about. I'm not wearing a medal."

"No?" He looks ready to suggest that Robert prove it, but then he pushes back from the table. "Of course, if you are, we will see it soon enough." He directs Robert's attention to the room's four corners. High up, tiny cameras look down.

Sebastian stands. "I have to leave you now. My assistant will be with you shortly. If you try hiding something before she arrives, we will know."

"I have nothing to hide."

Sebastian turns, leaving the cart as he heads for the door. "As it should be." And then he is gone.

Robert looks at the cameras, realizing he would have seen them earlier if so many other things hadn't distracted him: portrait, photographs, food, Sebastian himself.

I'd make a terrible spy.

"Mr. Jones?"

Robert sits up.

"Are you ready, Mr. Jones?"

A woman peers in from the hall. She wears hospital scrubs, hair tucked into a hairnet. She's the same woman who has been with him all along. At least, he thinks she is. "Back this way." She gestures for him to return to the rotunda, and from there they pass through another door and into a white chamber where two orderlies stand beside a wheeled gurney. A hospital gown and plastic bag sit folded atop the sheet.

"Your clothes can go in the bag," she says. "And you, of course, go into the gown. Would you like us to leave while you change?"

He looks up at another set of cameras. This is no time for modesty. Even without the cameras, the woman's going to be seeing quite a bit of his body before long. Besides, as he told Sebastian, he has nothing to hide.

He strips, puts his clothes in the bag, then puts on the gown as the gurney swings behind him.

"One last ride, Mr. Jones." The woman helps him up, then down onto his back.

The orderlies secure his wrists and ankles, working so quickly that he doesn't realize what they have done until he's completely bound.

"For your protection," she says. "Can't have you ambulating during the trance." Her voice is reassuring, matter of fact, just as it was when she first explained the process over the phone, telling him that the procedure would free his spirit and leave all physical weight behind. Naturally, she did not mention what would happen to his body.

The orderlies place a strap across his head. Robert is looking straight at the ceiling now: foam panels in suspended frames. Then something else glides into position, a set of blinders, one on either side of his face, reducing his field of view so that he seems to be lying at the bottom of a well. And suddenly the gurney is moving, gliding into a dim, indeterminate space. Looking straight up, he sees only darkness now. Then the gurney stops. Wheels lock. An armature-mounted mirror swings into view. The woman adjusts it, momentarily catching Robert's reflection, his face blurring overhead like a wide-eyed meteor, streaking past, then gone. She gives the mirror one final nudge, then lets go. It seems to reflect nothing, but he suspects the yantra is there, positioned in a dark corner, waiting to be mirrored into view.

"We're almost there, Mr. Jones. Just one more—"

Something thumps in the distance.

The woman turns from the gurney, mutters a question to someone next to her, then returns. "We're almost there, Mr. Jones." She looks slightly distracted, as if she too is wondering what caused the thump. Robert thinks about the kid and his team of Intranationals and the kind of noise that might herald a forced entry into the warehouse. But the cavalry won't be coming today. Robert took care of that hours ago, before the jet left Pennsylvania.

"The sculpture is right beside us," the woman says. "The lights will come up on it slowly. When they do, just relax and focus. The transition will be different from the demo. You may be aware of the presence of others. Ignore them. Stay focused on the design and wait for contact. When you sense the approach of your loved ones, let your spirit fly."

"And my body?" He hadn't planned on asking this. It just slips out. "What happens to my body?" He isn't concerned. He simply wants to know.

Will her story differ from the kid's? Is it possible that the kid was lying, using fear to secure cooperation.

She bends low. "We'll take care of it."

He senses many people in the room now, moving just out of view, pushing carts and instruments into position.

"Take care of it how?" He really isn't afraid, just curious. "How will you take care of it?"

She squeezes his arm. "Does it matter?" And then she steps back, moving out of view, leaving him alone with the mirror. Something flickers, a star in the dimness. He focuses. The light expands, cutting behind foreground shapes, illuminating angles and beams. And as the light spreads, a structure appears, growing larger, overrunning the mirror, filling his view. He is struck by a sense of scale. The thing is huge, and yet it floats in the air, rotating, reaching out, drawing him in.

He stands on the edge of a dark expanse, watching strange geometries coalesce before him. He can't determine their distance, only that they are impossibly large, immeasurable, infinite.

And they are growing.

And they are alive.

Light rises within them, casting patterns. Things move in the shadows, rising up, advancing, resolving into people who ignore him as they walk by. None are looking at the yantra. They are part of the design, but they ignore it, pushing onward, talking among themselves. He studies their faces, looking for Kathy. Their features twist like masks, distortions in carnival mirrors. He panics, but then the woman's words come back to him.

Stay focused on the design.

He stands in place. The crowd throngs, parting in front, closing behind. He looks over their heads, concentrating on the still-brightening sculpture, staring as light creeps along its angles and curves. The kid told him it was made out of Mnemosyne's victims: viscera, bone, skin, and hair. But what Robert sees is nothing like that. Instead, the design has the elegance of a cathedral, a perfect meld of form and spirit, lifting him, resonating with the pulse of his life, echoing with the cadence of an approaching voice.

"Rob!"

He looks for the source.

"I'm here, Rob."

It comes from the center of the design, from an intersection of shafts and beams that seemed to be simultaneously tilting toward and away from him.

"Josh is here too."

The image blurs. He tries blinking back tears. No good. They stream faster, diffusing the light.

"We love you, Rob."

He reaches out. His arms are straight and strong, no scars.

"We're both here, Rob."

He smells talc and benzocaine, feels a ghostly presence touch his hands, grip his fingers, squeeze.

"Don't let go, Rob."

He feels the stab of something sharp gliding along his sternum, toward his abdomen, a sensation at once distant and immediate, a cutting of flesh that is no longer his own. He flinches. The flaying has begun.

"Rob! They're hurting you."

"It's all right. I've decided to let them."

"No, Rob!"

"It's all right, Kath. It's what I want." He touches his chest. "There was a way out if I had wanted it, a tracking device. But I got rid of it, ditched it in the lavatory of the jet that brought me here." He squeezes her hands tighter. "I'll never let you go, Kath. Never leave you again. Never let anything come between—"

Wham!

He looks around.

The sound is the same one that he heard before entering the trance, but it's closer now, louder.

A voice shouts, but it isn't Kathy's. It's part of a different existence. "Does anyone have any idea what that is?" It's the voice of the woman who brought him to the warehouse. "Call security!"

He tries tuning out the distractions, struggles to concentrate on the yantra, but the thing seems to be quaking, trembling like a mirror suspended on an armature.

"Rob!" It's Kathy again, receding now. "You have to hold on."

He squeezes her hands. At least, he thinks they are her hands. When he looks down, he sees only darkness. "I will. I promise. I'll never let you go."

"But that's not what I'm saying."

He feels another slice of pain, moving laterally this time, shoulder to shoulder.

Josh cries, loud and piercing. No pause for breath, just a shrill wail like an approaching siren.

"Rob! Listen, Rob! I'm not talking about me. It's you. You have a chance to start over. You need to take it. Hang on to it. Hold on to what's left!"

Another crash, this time accompanied by a blast of light, and suddenly he's strapped to a gurney, looking up at a trembling mirror. He hears people running, but he can't see them. He sees only the mirror and the monstrosity reflected in it, brightly lit, terrible beyond belief. And then suddenly it's gone. The gurney is moving. People run with it. Robert sees their panicked faces. One of them is the woman.

"Stop her!" The voice shouts from across the room. "Now! Get her! And get the gurney!"

The air crackles, a report like the discharge of an electronic gun. The woman's face flies out of view, and Robert feels himself falling as the gurney careens onto its side. The cart-mounted armature comes lose. The mirror swings past him, explodes against the floor. The woman falls beside it, one of her eyes gone, hollowed out, socket steaming as if run through with a bolt of lightning. The other eye is intact but dead. And behind her, still bathed in glare, the yantra crouches like a skinned demon.

"Don't look at it!" The voice isn't talking to Robert. It's barking orders at people running toward him, their thick-soled boots compressing against the floor. "Get that man out of here. Don't look at the sculpture!"

Bones angle like girders, held in place by meaty ropes, guts, and tendons. Shriveled organs hang from braided hair. Skulls run like crenels along parchment walls. And everywhere, arranged like portals, lips open and close, some twitching in silent screams, others speaking voices he can no longer hear. . . .

"Get him up! Now!"

People grab the gurney, setting it back onto its wheels. Gloved hands knock away the blinders and take the strap from his head. He no longer wears the hospital gown. Ink marks cover his skin, a map of incisions waiting to be made. And running along his chest, two hair-thin cuts oozing blood.

"Cauterize those wounds!"

The person barking orders is a small man, curly hair, thready beard. He wears a glowing diode over one eye, carries a nylon pack. He is one of maybe a dozen, not one of whom appears to be over thirty. Robert looks for the kid, can't find him. They're all kids.

A face looks down, mismatched eyes, nose ring, pierced ear. "This is going to sting." A hand comes into view. It holds a kind of probe, at least that's what Robert thinks it is until it touches his skin. The tip crackles. The incision smokes. Robert screams, but it's over in seconds, and then the gurney is rolling again, this time past a line of nurses and technicians who moments ago had been preparing to peel his skin and harvest his parts. A woman with a diode eye stands before the prisoners, brandishing something that might be a gun. Robert sees it for a second, then loses sight of it as his handlers hurry him into an adjoining room where an old man sits zip tied to a chair. He looks frightened. One of his eyebrows has been smeared by a blow to the face. The other is perfectly formed, apparently painted on. Disheveled bangs fall into his eyes, but from the side the hair appears neatly combed, parted with surgical precision.

"Sebastian!"

The man turns, then looks away. Then he is gone.

The gurney keeps moving.

FIVE

A car races east behind a cargo trailer. Robert sits in the passenger seat, riding beside the kid.

"We figured you'd do that, you know?" the kid says. "That medal-in-the-toilet trick? Eighty-three percent chance."

Robert wonders if the kid is putting him on. "I didn't plan that. How can you predict impulse?"

"It's easy when you have the algorithms. At any rate, we made the thing waterproof. It functioned throughout the flight, got us close enough to make some educated guesses. You got lucky."

"More algorithms?"

"Something like that."

"And now you've got what you wanted."

"Yeah. We got it."

The cargo trailer sways in front of them. Even with the gate closed and locked, Robert senses the presence of the thing inside.

"What now?" Robert asks. "What do you do with it now that you've got it?"

"Can't tell you that."

Robert considers the potential of such a thing, its implication in an age of streaming video. The possibilities are vast and frightening, but they don't matter. He has more immediate things on his mind. "How about me? What are you going to do with me?"

"Nothing."

"Meaning?"

"Meaning we drive you to the airport, put you on a plane. That's it. We're done."

"Just like that?"

"Pretty much." A nylon pack rides on the island between the seats. The kid reaches into a pocket, pulls out a wallet, hands it to Robert. "Open it."

Robert does, checking the cards: American Express Gold, Visa Slate, Blue Cross, Social Security, driver's license. There's also an ATM card for Central Illinois Bank. The person's name is the same on all the cards, but it isn't his name. He takes out the bankcard.

"There's plenty of money in that account," the kid says. "Consider it payment for services rendered."

Robert runs a finger over the raised letters, reads the name. "Eric Joseph Thorn?"

"That's you," the kid says. "Most of you, anyway. It's almost an anagram for Christopher Jones."

"What about Robert?"

"He had to go. But the anagram is still your name, right? It's all in how you look at it."

Robert closes the wallet.

"Fieri Mnemosyne will be looking for Robert Christopher Jones. The way we see it, the best thing for you is to stop being him."

"How?"

"By taking that wallet. There's a ticket in your new name waiting at the Delta counter. The plane will land within twenty miles of the address on that driver's license. It's a one-bedroom, but it's a nice one, and it's a start."

Robert checks the billfold. There's a door key in there, along with a couple hundred in tens and twenties. "What about my *life*?"

"You've got that."

"But all my things."

"What? The heavy stuff? All that clutter?" The kid shrugs. "Sometimes it's best to just start over, take everything down to ones and zeros."

Robert turns to the window beside him, looks out at the racing night.

"When you think of it," the kid says, "a man can carry everything that matters inside himself. You can augment it with interfaces, but the mind's the key. You know what I'm saying?"

The cargo trailer continues north while the kid takes an off ramp.

Robert leans back, closes his eyes. But this time, the accident isn't there. It's just the three of them riding east on open highway. Josh sleeps. Kathy holds Robert's hand. And for a little while that's all there is, just moving forward and holding on.

THE HAUNTED ATTIC: 2011

These days I live in a house with an attic much larger than the one where TC staged his five-cent ambush. It's cold in winter, stifling in summer, always dark, ceiling beams framing a triangular space that runs the length of the house. A few summers ago it was home to nesting bats that I left alone until the young were old enough to fly. Then I sealed the crack in the eaves that had been their front door and began using the space to warehouse old notes and manuscripts. That's my world. Lots of paper. Efficient or not, one thing's for sure, when the apocalypse comes and computers go down, when the cities fall and the zombies are at the door, I'll still be able to edit my stories.

Or burn them for heat.

Writers like to talk about their muses. Dante presents his as a goddess in Canto II of *The Inferno*. Stephen King describes his as a guy who sits in the basement, smokes cigars, and offers grunts of inspiration. For me, the muse is a punk kid just like my old buddy TC. He's hiding behind the house with both hands on the garden hose while I'm out front trying to water a garden. Sometimes TC lets the water flow just fine, but other times he pinches the hose, cuts the flow, and waits for me to look down the nozzle to see if it's clogged. Then he lets me have it, soaking me through. But most of the time TC keeps things half pinched, sending through just enough to keep me from storming around the side of the house for a showdown. Not that fighting ever solves anything. Duking it out with the muse is always counterproductive, especially when he's backed up by his brother Bill.

Usually, I'm content with the trickle.

But other times, to avoid fighting, I climb the stairs to that attic above my office and look through the old stuff.

A film actor once spoke of growing old on camera, of watching himself age by watching his films. But writers have something more sublime, the detailed record of past thoughts and impressions. That, at least, is the way it is for me. In this attic, pressed between angled beams and plywood sheets, I hear the voices of the people I have been, characters and narrators speaking from the past, sometimes half forgotten, always audible, calling through the years, compelling me to listen.

"Can you hear us?" they say. "Are we coming through? We're separated by time, but not by space. Turn the pages. Stay awhile. Consider who we were . . . and what you have become."

ALIUNDE

Much has happened since the first print edition of this book appeared in the final days of 2011. Within a few weeks, it became a finalist for the Bram Stoker Award®, losing to Joyce Carole Oates's *The Corn Maiden and Other Nightmares*. (No shame there.) After that, editor Benoît Domis translated "Mrs. Halfbooger's Basement" for appearance in the well-regarded French anthology *Ténèbres*, "Things" was selected to appear in the forthcoming *Best of Cemetery Dance 2*, and "Prime Time!" (from the *Voices* companion collection, *Visions*) was optioned for film. But perhaps the most interesting development occurred when David Slade called with news that Mick Garris was assembling a team to work on a new anthology film to be titled *Nightmare Cinema*. David's question: Was I interested in cowriting a new script based on "Traumatic Descent" for the film?

Some things you don't need to think twice about.

As I write this, *Nightmare Cinema* is set to premiere at the Fantasia Film Festival in Montreal, with an anticipated theatrical release later in the year. It's a terrific conclusion to the story that I cover briefly in this book (see "Music, Dreams, and Trauma" and "Revision") and recount at length in *This Way to Egress* (Ash-Tree Press 2010).

To help celebrate the film's premiere, Fantasist Enterprises is releasing *Voices* for the first time in ebook. And to help launch the ebook, I will be appearing (again, as I write this) at the Fantastic Fiction Reading Series at New York's fabled KGB Bar in the East Village. It will be my third appearance there, but I won't be reading. I never do. Instead, much like the ancient scops that I write about in this book's introduction to "Traumatic Descent," I'll be presenting from memory.

All of this brings us to this book's bonus story, a version of a longer piece that originally appeared in the anthology *Fear the Abyss* (Post-Mortem Press, 2013) under the title "Human Caverns."

The story changed as I revisited it for presentation. Not in elaborate ways, but enough for me to begin thinking of it as a separate piece. The result is the version of the story that appears here, retitled and included as a bonus text for this edition.

Now pack your energy bars, strap on your backpack, and let's go see what strange things lie waiting for us in the American wilderness.

SIREN

Kevin stopped by a frozen creek to check his GPS. He was in deep, far from the road, surrounded by old-growth pines. It was getting late, but there was something about the stillness of the frozen valley, the soft shadows of the trees, the shimmer of light on glazed rocks that made him want to stay a little longer. He took some pictures and kept exploring.

The creek valley was steep, contoured by centuries of flowing water. He climbed out, rested beside a leaning spruce, roots exposed along the brink. He took a long piss against its trunk, then turned and headed south to a deeper valley where he came upon the remnants of a farmhouse, scorched posts standing upright amid drifting snow and ash. It had been recently burned, the smell of char still fresh in the air. He snapped some more pictures, then headed along a flood plain, coming out into sight of a deformed hillside: right angles, stunted trees, tangled weeds. He knew the signs. Years ago, the slope had been strip-mined.

He climbed the bench cuts and came at last to the brink of another valley, and there, a hundred yards distant, lay the remains of a mining town—dark, silent, abandoned.

The sky above it was deep blue, almost purple. Behind him it was turning black. Time to return to the car. He took a wide-angle shot of the town, marked its location on the digital map, and began retracing his steps, making good time until his sense of solitude was broken by five men approaching through the trees on his left. There were more to his right, and one of them carried a shotgun.

They spread out, surrounded him.

He reached for his phone.

"Hold on!" The shotgun man stepped closer. "Hold it right there." He wore a patchwork of Appalachian hides, fur turned inward for warmth. His hat was a hollowed-out raccoon, head facing front, jaws molded into a dead snarl. But the man's accent didn't sound local.

"You with the government?" the man said.

"Me? No."

"Who then?"

"No one . . . I'm a blogger. I write about ghost towns, abandoned buildings, things like that."

"People pay you?"

"No. It's just a hobby."

"Got a name?"

"Kevin."

"Where you from, Kevin?"

"Pittsburgh."

"How'd you get here?"

"Car."

"Who drove?"

"No one."

"Car drove itself?"

"No. I drove. It's just me."

"Where's the car?"

Kevin pointed. "County road. I'm heading back now."

"What's in the pack?"

"What? My backpack? Not much. Just some food, water—"

"And that?" He pointed to Kevin's hand.

"It's my phone. I use it to—"

"All right, Kevin. I know what phones do. Now here's what I want you to do. I want you to take everything you're wearing and carrying and put it into that pack of yours. Understand?"

"Why?"

"You're going to mash it in real tight, as much as you can fit. Everything else I want you to just fold up and put on the ground."

"I don't understand."

"It's not complicated, Kevin."

"I'm calling 911."

"And tell them what? Come get you? Even if you can get a signal, how long do you think it'll take them to get here? This isn't the city, Kevin." The gun's barrels became 12-gauge holes as they took aim at Kevin's face.

"Now, Kevin. In the pack. Phone, clothes, everything."

"I'll freeze."

"Not if you hurry."

Kevin felt something break inside him. He pulled off his gloves, felt the chill against his skin, then put the gloves into the pack and unzipped his coat.

The other men watched. They weren't armed, not with guns anyway. Some carried shovels, one a pickaxe.

Shotgun Man turned toward Pickaxe Man. "All right. Do it."

Pickaxe Man looked young, wispy beard, rash of acne. Barely college age. He approached Kevin, raised his pick, and swung it hard against the frozen ground. Dirt flew. The impact echoed from the trees.

"What's he doing?"

"Digging."

"Why?"

"We're waiting, Kevin. And you're wasting time."

Kevin took off his coat and tried shoving it into the pack. It wouldn't fit. He set it on the ground, unbuttoned his shirt.

By now Pickaxe Man had cut a two-foot trench and was stepping back as the shovel men approached. They set about clearing the trench as Kevin removed the rest of his clothes. The cold bit hard. He stuffed what he could into the pack then tried zipping it closed. The seams popped, but the zipper held. Only his coat and boots remained outside.

The shovel men piled the loose dirt into a berm beside the trench. The thing looked like a miniature grave. Too small for a man, unless that man were hacked apart with a pickaxe.

"It'll do." Shotgun man turned to one of the diggers. "Trevor. Finish it."

Trevor stepped toward Kevin, looked him in the eye. "Hey, man. For what it's worth . . . this isn't personal." Trevor's accent had little in common with Shotgun Man's, except that it too was foreign to these hills. "It's not against you, per se." Then Trevor swung his shovel, brought it down hard against the side of Kevin's pack, knocked it into the trench. A few more swings took care of the coat and boots. Then Trevor and the other shovel men set to work putting the dirt back in the hole.

"You got anything else, Kevin? Things I can't see? Hearing aid? Contact lenses?"

"No." He was freezing.

"Implants?"

"What're you going to do?"

One of the men threw a sack at Kevin. It landed at his feet, rolled like a giant head.

"Clothes," Shotgun man said. "Shoes too. Put them on before you freeze."

The sack had loop handles knotted together to secure the things inside. Kevin fumbled with the knot, opened the sack to find a wool sweater, flannel shirt, vintage jeans, rawhide belt, leather boots. No underclothes. The pants were wide and long. He cinched them tight at his waist and rolled the legs to his ankles. The boots were straight-cut, no curves to differentiate right from left. The innersoles bore the imprints of another man's toes.

"The sack too, Kevin. Put it on. Over your head, cover your face."

"You going to . . . shoot me?"

"Not unless I have to."

"So why do I need a mask?"

"To keep you from seeing."

By now the shovel men had finished putting the dirt back into the hole, covering Kevin's things with a mound of earth. If they killed him now and carted the body away, there'd be nothing above ground to prove he'd ever been there.

"The sack, Kevin. Over your head. Cover your face."

Kevin put on the sack.

Trevor came up behind him, tugged the handles, knotted them tight behind his head. Then he took Kevin's arm. "Walk with us, now. Slow and steady."

They hiked for a quarter of an hour. Then Trevor tugged Kevin's arm. "There's a stoop here."

Kevin's next step thumped on wood. The wind fell away. He felt warmer. His footsteps echoed from close-set walls. A left turn. Then a right. Then pressure on his shoulder, easing him down. "Sit here."

Kevin sat.

Trevor removed the boots and clicked something hard and cold into place around Kevin's ankle. "Like I said, nothing personal."

Footsteps receded. When Trevor spoke again, it was from a dozen feet away: "You can take the sack off now, Kevin."

Kevin removed the sack to see Trevor exiting down a dim hallway, leaving him alone in a near-empty room with one high plastic-covered window.

He was sitting on a makeshift bed—plywood pallet on cinder-block legs. No mattress or pillow, just two handmade quilts one atop the other. On the floor, two buckets, dented and empty. In the corner, a cast-iron stove spread a feeble glow against the walls. He got up, walked toward it. A chain dragged behind him, went taut after three steps.

He returned to the bed, stood atop it, tried seeing out the window. The translucent plastic snapped in the wind. Outside, something banged, lonely and intermittent.

"No. You can't do that!" A girl entered from the hall. "You can't see out that window. It's plastic, not glass." Here at last was someone who sounded as if she could be local to the hills. She carried a tray, set it on the floor, stepped back. "They found your car. It was where you said. That's why they say you can eat. Go on. It's honest food." The tray held a covered bowl, wooden spoon, mealy biscuit, mug of tea. He uncovered the bowl. Steam rose.

"Mother made it," the girl said. "She won't visit till you eat. And she can't let you go till she visits."

"She'll let me go?"

"If you want. She don't care to harm you. Just wants to talk." The girl gestured to the bowl. "Go on. She made it special."

It was stew, vegetables mostly, some meat—slow-boiled pieces that came apart beneath his spoon. He tasted it. It was surprisingly good.

"That's it. You eat. I'll tell her." The girl hurried away.

He finished it quickly, then set the tray aside, called out to let them know he was done.

His voice echoed.

No one came.

He returned to the bed, sat on it, waited. A bitter taste clung to his throat. It was probably from the tea. He felt suddenly tired, exhausted.

He had no intention of sleeping. But for a while . . . he did.

Pain woke him.

He lunged for one of the buckets, hugged it, vomited hard. Then he collapsed on the floor as pain forced him to drop his pants and straddle the second bucket. Then he hitched up the pants and collapsed again, exhausted, shivering.

In the corner the cast-iron stove glowed bright red, almost molten, but he was chilled to the core. He climbed back under the quilts. It didn't help.

The cold was inside him. He rolled into a ball, plunged into icy sleep, and woke when he realized someone new was sitting beside him—a woman with a three-string dulcimer. The floor had been cleaned. A tray of fresh food lay where the buckets had been.

"You had a rough night," the woman said. "Breakfast will fix that." She had eyes like stones, cold and blind. Her hair was gray, pulled back, braided like ropes. Behind her, morning sun glowed through the plastic window.

"They call me Mother. It's not what I am, just what they call me now that I've led them off grid. You can call me that too if you like. If it feels right." She reached for the tray. Didn't grope for it but grabbed it as surely as if she could see it. "Take this. Fill your terrible hollows."

He sat up. Both legs moved freely beneath the quilt. The manacle was gone. He stared at the tray. Sliced fruit, steamed milk. "No. Don't want it."

"You're suspicious." She returned the tray to the floor. "But there was nothing in that stew to make you ill. The illness was already there. The honest food merely purged that, cleansed you of the terrible things you'd brought with you. We can't be around them. We've come too far to let them back into our world."

"What're you talking about?"

"Your system was corrupted, contaminated with additives from processed foods, micro-components that lodged in your gut and assembled over time. Why, if we hadn't got those out of you, their signals would have led the agents right to us."

"Agents?"

"The ones who are looking for us. They think they ought to be able to find us in these hills, but there's more land here than you'd think by looking at a map. Take a few acres of mountains and valleys, flatten them out, and you've got miles of country. And there are always places to live, houses and towns abandoned by folks wanting to live closer to the grid. We move in, take up residence, stay for a while, then move on. We burn our tracks behind us—always one step ahead." She seemed to look at the tray of food. "Are you sure you won't eat? It's just food. Filling food. Just what a hollow man needs. We'll teach you to eat right if you stay. Not that you have to. We're not about kidnapping."

"So it's true. I can go?"

She opened her mouth as if to laugh, but only sighed. "You don't see it, do you, Kevin? What brought you here wasn't a desire to take pictures of some old mining town. You might have thought that was it, but there was more. You're a hollow searcher. I knew it the moment I saw you." She tapped her temple as if to indicate a vision behind her eyes. "I saw it, and I knew. And something else. I knew even then that you'd decide not to stay. Not right away. The pull of the hollow world is too strong. The hollow world of hollow people, all drained from years of living on the grid. That's what we fear, Kevin. That hollowness. And although you don't know it yet, it's that same fear that led you to us—the fear of the human abyss, the immeasurable cavern that once held your soul." She moved her hands, slid one into position on the dulcimer's neck, the other to rest on the bridge, perched like a claw.

"You've lost your soul, Kevin. That's the sorry truth of it. The on-grid world has put its codes in you, altered your system, degraded you with unnatural needs and desires. But there are other codes—simpler, older." She plucked a chord. "We can make you whole again, give you the things to set you right. It won't be easy . . . won't happen all at once . . . best I can do today is plant the seed."

She sat back and began to play.

He woke in his car, sat up, thoughts spinning. Beyond the hood, footprints stretched through the trees, filling with snow, vanishing. He remembered taking pictures of an abandoned town before starting back to the car. It had been getting dark then, just like now. But everything else was blank.

His coat was filthy, smeared with clay. Perhaps he'd fallen, knocked himself out, returned to the car in a daze. But there were no lumps or abrasions on his head, only a strange, hollow ache that suggested something more serious—a stroke perhaps.

His backpack lay beside him, stitching strained and ripped as if the zipper had been forced closed around an excessive load. He didn't remember it being that way before, and the pack did not seem overly full now. He unzipped it and took out his phone. The display showed 21 photos, all saved between late afternoon and early evening. The most recent had been taken at 4:21 PM. He opened the image to find a wide-angle shot of a derelict town, the one he had snapped while standing on the ridge of the deformed hillside. He enlarged it, zoomed in on a building with gray windows. Plastic sheeting? Hands trembling, he panned along the building until he came to a rusted door hanging from broken hinges. He could almost hear it swinging in the breeze—lonely and intermittent.

And someone stood in the doorway.

He enlarged again, zoomed in on the blurred figure of a woman—features vague, little more than pixilated shadow, suggestions of braided hair, a narrow face, stone-cold eyes that seemed to stare at the camera. It came back to him. He remembered sitting on a bed, listening as she sang a song so achingly beautiful that it unmanned him.

He closed the picture, noticed the current date on the main screen, and realized the photo had been taken the day before.

He was out of the car now, armed with flashlight and GPS, retracing his trail through the forest. It was all coming back to him—how she looked as she sang, thin as a tendril of mist, clothed in a dress that wrapped her like an encroaching shadow. Her head rocked as she sang, rolled with the music. He remembered those things as he climbed the bench-cut stair of the scarred hillside. But most of all he remembered what he told her when she stopped singing. "I've changed my mind. I don't want to leave. I want to stay."

And he remembered her reaction, how she studied him with eyes that weren't as blind as they seemed, touched his brow with probing hands, and spoke with a voice like whispering wind. "No. Your mind hasn't changed. Not yet. It's just moved beyond you for a moment. The real change will take time. Days maybe. Maybe longer. When it does, if you still want to join us, you'll find your way."

He crossed the top of the ridge, approached the brink, and stopped when he saw what lay below.

The town was gone; in its place, a smear of glowing ash and charred beams. Mother and her followers had moved on, burned their tracks behind them.

A tree clung to the brink, a young poplar with bare limbs and frosted bark. He leaned on it, braced against the chill, considered the long walk back to his car and the longer drive out of the hills and back to a world of strip malls and parking lots, power lines and high rises, surveillance drones and facial-recognition cameras. He would use his eye to unlock his apartment, his thumb print to access his blog, his fingers to transform the wild adventure of the past 24 hours to a screed of bytes and pixels. And maybe in time he would again feel at home within the grid. But for now he stood and stared into the darkness beyond the glowing valley, wondered at the fears that had first brought him to this wilderness, and shivered at the promise of the song that now echoed within him.

AVAILABLE NOW

Fleeing from what should have been a perfect crime, four crooks in a black Mustang race into the Pennsylvania highlands. On the backseat, a briefcase full of cash. On their tail, a tattooed madman who wants them dead.

The driver calls himself Axle. A local boy, he knows the landscape, the coal-hauling roads and steep trails that lead to the perfect hideout: the crater of an abandoned mine. But Axle fears the crater. Terrible things happened there. Things that he has spent years trying to forget.

Enter Kwetis, the nightflyer, a specter from Axle's ancestral past. Part memory, part nightmare, Kwetis has planned a heist of his own. And soon Axle, his partners in crime, and their pursuer will learn that their arrival at the mine was foretold long ago . . . and that each of them is a piece of a plan devised by the spirits of the Earth.

A finalist for the 2009 Eric Hoffer Award.

Nominated for the 2nd Annual Black Quill Award for Best Small-Press Chill.

Appeared on the Preliminary Ballot for the 2008 Bram Stoker Award for Superior Achievement in a First Novel.

Trade Paperback • 260 Pages • 8 Illustrations • $16.00
ISBN 13: 978-1-934571-00-2 • ISBN 10: 1-934571-00-8

www.VeinsTheNovel.com | www.FantasistEnt.com

Fasten your seatbelts and prepare to take your reading experience to a whole new level. With *Veins: The Soundtrack*, author and musician Lawrence C. Connolly provides a series of instrumental soundscapes inspired by themes and scenes from his critically acclaimed supernatural thriller *Veins*. Performing with his band, Connolly delivers a mix of trance, rock, and  ambient compositions designed to complement the novel.

The CD also includes two music and spoken-word bonus tracks, each showcasing a complete story from *Visions*, "Aberrations" and "Echoes."

Packaged with Star E. Olson's distinctive cover art and including a synopsis and full production credits, *Veins: The Soundtrack* is a must for every dark fantasy reader.

Read the book. Hear the soundtrack. Enter a world where fantasy lives.

6 Tracks & 2 Bonus Tracks • Total Run Time: 38:13 • $10.00
UPC: 700261267371 • ID#: FE-934571-00-2

AVAILABLE NOW

Axle and Bird are back from the dead. No longer merely human, they must now work to further the oohaate—the spirit path. Whether they will like what they find at the journey's end remains to be seen, but for now, there's no turning back.

An explosion at Windslow Mine has set things in motion. The forest is crawling with snakes, driven from their nests by underground fires.

And the snakes are not alone.

Other forces are emerging, rising from the earth's molten veins, preparing to reclaim a smoldering world. By daybreak, the residents of Windslow, Pennsylvania, will know that the world is burning beneath them.

By daybreak, the nightmare begins.

"Lawrence C. Connolly has the rare ability to completely transport the reader."
    —**Alice Henderson, author of** *Voracious*

Trade Paperback • 276 Pages • 16 Illustrations • $17.00
ISBN 13: 978-1-934571-03-3 • ISBN 10: 1-934571-03-2

www.FEBooks.net

Twenty classic and two all new stories explore three realms, in one visionary collection!

For three decades, Lawrence C. Connolly has defied category, writing across genre to create stories where dreams are reality, the future is now, and a lone madman may be the sanest person in the room.

Presented here with all new introductions that discuss the origins of the stories and featuring a retrospective essay about the road to publication and beyond, *Visions: Fantasy & SF* is a must for lovers of dark fantasy, science fiction, and heroic adventure.

PRAISE FOR THE STORIES

GREAT HEART RISING: ". . . gritty believability."—*Tangent Online*
DAUGHTERS OF PRIME: ". . . a tantalizing enigma."—*Locus*
FLASHBACK: ". . . a great psychological tale of deception."—*DreadCentral.com*
PRIME TIME!: "Clever stuff."—*The Fix*

Trade Paperback • 264 Pages
22 Stories • Lightly Illustrated • $16.00
ISBN 13: 978-1-934571-01-9 • ISBN 10: 1-934571-01-6

www.ingramcontent.com/pod-product-compliance
Lightning Source LLC
Chambersburg PA
CBHW070926260626
47162CB00007B/2808